2065
nw

"A uniquely rewarding read ... Amber Dawn keeps the proceedings at a darkly whimsical remove from the real hurts of the world. She knows we know that pain is real, that women are made chattels, that masters are cruel. She's after a larger vision that raises questions about the entire emotionally fraught edifice of our received beliefs about sex, men and women, roles and rights and abuses." —*The Globe and Mail*

"Amber Dawn's story is a sinister fairy tale, as intoxicating as any of the Glories [characters] but also an allegory for the emotional hazards of sex work." —*Bust*

"Channeling Evelyn Lau's realism, Thomas Hardy at his most macabre, and the Brothers Grimm, Dawn's style—part documentary and part magic realism —makes *Sub Rosa* totally enthralling." —*NOW Magazine*

"Amber Dawn takes us to a dark and magical place in her debut novel ... *Sub Rosa* is an enormous satisfaction, an immersion in gritty magical realism." —*Xtra*

"Both whimsical and profound, the kind of book that could acquire a cult status." —*Gay & Lesbian Review*

Amber Dawn

ARSENAL PULP PRESS

Vancouver

ARSENAL PULP PRESS
#202-211 East Georgia St.
Vancouver, BC
Canada V6A 1Z6
arsenalpulp.com

The publisher gratefully acknowledges the support of the Canada Council for the Arts
and the British Columbia Arts Council for its publishing program, and the Government of Canada through the Book Publishing Industry Development Program and the
Government of British Columbia through the Book Publishing Tax Credit Program
for its publishing activities.

This is a work of fiction. Any resemblance of characters to persons either living or
deceased is purely coincidental.

Book design by Shyla Seller
Editing by Susan Safyan
Cover art by Amy Alice Thompson

Printed and bound in Canada on 100% PCW recycled paper

Library and Archives Canada Cataloguing in Publication:

Dawn, Amber, 1974-
          Sub Rosa / Amber Dawn.

ISBN 978-1-55152-361-3

          I. Title.

PS8607.A9598S92 2010   C813'.6   C2010-900741-7

Acknowledgments

Wholehearted thanks to:

The hard-working and gutsy team at Arsenal Pulp Press—
Brian Lam, Robert Ballantyne, Susan Safyan, Shyla Seller,
and Janice Beley

My mentors at the Creative Writing Department at the University of
British Columbia—Rhea Tregebov, Meryn Cadell, Annabel Lyon, and
Maureen Medved

The many genius friends and colleagues who offered support—Elizabeth
Bachinsky, Michelle Tea, Hiromi Goto, Zena Sharman, Michael V. Smith,
Amanda Lamarche, Matt Rader, Zoya Harris, Rob Weston, Catharine
Chen, Chris Labonte, Bethanne Grabham, Pat Rose, Carmen Dodds, and
C.J. Rowe

The cover artist, Amy Alice Thompson

And Rika Moorhouse, to whom this book is dedicated

I

A horseshoe-shaped fountain spills its luck in the city centre.

The first seat of the Number 9 bus is perpetually occupied by an old lady, who watches her days pass through a moving window.

Each April there's an infant twister of cherry blossoms—if I'm picturing it right—on the corner of 2nd and Main. Commuters are greeted by the pink swirl as they ascend the subway stairs.

If I concentrate long enough, I can see streets worked over all day by traffic. But whenever there's a lull, those streets turn into corridors for the view: a beach I should have gone to more often. I can picture the so-called dodgy blocks with connect-the-dot trails of bloodstains and happy-coloured "revitalize the neighbourhood" campaign banners hanging from streetlamps. Lately, I can picture them pretty darn well.

And maybe, just maybe, I can see a house where I once lived. Not a storybook house; no glowing windows in the winter night, no doves nesting on the roof. It's a stucco bungalow. Red paint has given up on the front steps and is peeling into flakes. Moss dots the old shingles. The narrow yard is crowded with vegetables—tomatoes grow in chicken-wire cages, green beans climb a chainlink fence.

I used to think these places had nothing to do with me. They were unsolicited scenery, the backdrop to other people's lives. Now I would give anything just to stand on those faded front steps and look through the tattered screen door at who or what is inside. I *am* about to give everything for it.

Everything is a place called Sub Rosa. I don't have a perfect word to describe it, so I'll call this place a street. No other street intersects it. No map will lead you there. No one has directions committed to memory. Sub Rosa is above memory. Or rather, below it. It's amnesic. Visitors aren't exactly sure how they find their way there. They are guided only by the belief that they are entitled to a little fulfillment. They leave knowing only that they are somehow better than when they arrived. Most visitors are men—what we on Sub Rosa call "live ones." They drive off in their well-kept cars with glazed grins on their faces. I'm jealous—not of their money to spend, but jealous that, for them, going home is a simple matter of turning down the correct lane.

I've been on Sub Rosa so long I can't remember where home is anymore. How long is long? I can't remember that, either. There's nothing wrong with me, so I've been told. The past is a burden Sub Rosa won't bear. Its energy is spent on being Neverland. A fairytale place with a steady rotation of happy endings.

Sub Rosa has been described in so many ways, I won't bother trying to sum it up. No testimony of mine could capture it. If you've ever overheard someone dreamily sermoning about true happiness, they were probably talking about Sub Rosa. A Sub Rosa sunrise is never spoiled by smog or storm. Wind won't blow strong enough to ruin a hairdo. The air gently conveys itself along the street; always clean, always warm. Water for drinking is sweet; water for bathing, soft.

On Sub Rosa we eat diner fineness—gravy-soaked and heavily salted meals—as much and as often as we want. There are no stomach aches on Sub Rosa. Nobody is ever sick or injured or ugly or unloved. Sub Rosa wants you. It wants anyone, no matter how back-broken and bitter you are when you arrive.

It's turned me into a true beauty, the kind that's crafted, laboured over, a beauty that city folk endlessly fantasize about.

My trips to the city are rare and always chaperoned. City ills are kept out of Sub Rosa. Hardship is our myth, our campfire story; it's a ghost that quietly haunts us but rarely materializes. There is a long-standing ban on television and radio. A newspaper is like a virus on Sub Rosa, its tales of trauma are venom. Yes, I'm afraid of the city. Even though the city is largely fuzzy memory, I fear it. All the forgotten details have been filled in with horror stories. And some of the parts I do remember aren't always picturesque.

The last memory I have of the city is the Legion Pub. I was a girl about to fall—reckless on a slew of free drinks, beer and bourbon mostly, and dancing on a table at the back of the room.

My sugar daddy du jour was Nino, though there wasn't much sugar to him. Not much sugar could be found in his shag-carpeted, lino-leum-floored apartment, either. But I was used to sofa hopping and beer for breakfast back then.

Every night we'd come to the Legion; Nino through the front door and me hopping over the back patio fence, rust rubbing its colour onto my jeans as I'd scramble over. Nino once said that I wouldn't have to jump the fence anymore, that he'd get me fake ID and then we'd hit all the uptown clubs. He told me we wouldn't wait in line-ups, or pay cover, and bartenders would make all our drinks doubles just because *he* was Nino. He said all this around day two of me staying with him, back when I was his petite sidekick, the strange runaway he'd discovered, like an unknown species, near the Steelworkers' Memorial Bridge. For a stretch, he used to show me off to the regulars, get them all laughing at the "cute fucking" way I screamed or swore, spilled beer, and started fights with the pinball machine. "Where do you come from, girl?" Nino would shout so that everyone in the bar heard his question. "I found her under a goddamn bridge like a stinking old mattress or a sack of drowned kittens." He always summed up the story with, "And I took her home and cleaned her up, and now look at her."

But after I'd been with him for eighteen straight days he stopped asking me where I'd come from. He stopped asking me anything at all. I was not much more to him than a stain on his shirt, something that was already there, which he carelessly continued to wear.

I started seeking new sponsorship at the Legion. You'd think there I'd have easily secured a new man, a lonely type whose standards had slipped down to the unwashed floor. I was low rent, which is exactly what they could afford. No one made me any offers. If those losers could see me now—the angel I've become—they'd line up just for a look.

No one noticed sweet fuck-all around there, anyway. There was a constant bar fight, a cycle of sucker-punch champs and men down, a woman always crying to the unoccupied chair next to her. These, and any other actions, were absorbed into the Legion's slow motion. The air in there was a murmuring haze. The carpet was sticky because it didn't want you to move too fast or too far.

I figured I'd be better off trying to keep my place as Nino's sidekick. It was old hat, as far as I can remember, for me to hang on until the end got worse than ugly. And I thought Nino needed me, or at least he needed someone around. Couldn't stand being alone, Nino. He knew half the people at the Legion like family. After last call he'd gather anyone who'd come with him. "Come, barflies and hooches, come," he'd call. We'd cram into a taxi to Nino's for a game of poker and the bottomless bottle of J.D. always kept under the kitchen sink.

I had assumed my customary role of drink nurse, circling behind the scenes with a bottle, topping up. I learned that some men have poker faces, but no one has a poker back. Hairs can stand shifty on the nape of a neck. Spines lean a little to the left or the right. Nino's shoulder blades nearly touched, gathering the fabric of his T-shirt, when he was bluffing. It didn't matter to me who won, as long as Nino was too drunk at the end of the night to kick up a fuss. If he went on a tilt I'd hit his glass every few minutes.

The waitress from the Legion kept offering to teach me how to play, but I refused to sit at the table. "A woman should be able to hold her own at cards," she said, holding her hand up for me to see, tapping black diamonds with her lopsided French-manicured fingernails. I'd only splash her glass when I poured her another.

I'm not sure why this mean little scene made me as happy as I believe it did. I liked when there were four or five players hunched around the dented pine table and the ante remained sane: fives and tens; twenties were whistled at. Mainly, Nino took the pot in those games, especially when the waitress dealt. She had a false shuffle and was sweet for him. No one caught on to this except me. The waitress was slick; she juggled the cards like a vaudeville act, too quickly for most drunkards to see. Plus this crew was too macho to suspect a woman of being better than they were.

When the table was packed with men, the waitress lay low. When six or seven or ten players sat in, things of value went missing: watches were tossed into the pile, a ring was twisted from an index finger. On day fourteen of my stay, my second Saturday at chez Nino, he lost his thirty-inch television. It used to be the only object on the north wall; its staccato blue light overtook the whole room. A big man named Short Stack pulled a belly buster straight in the last game of the evening. I remember his lip curled from the weight of the TV as he carried it to the elevator. I expected the room to look empty afterwards. Instead, there was this rectangular space, highlighted by lack of carpet stain or yellowed wall, which took up as much room as the TV itself did. When I saw that spot, I thought, *Good, Nino will need me around for company more than ever.*

I couldn't have been more wrong. The TV was our liaison, our mutual friend, without whom we had nothing in common. Our daytimes were spent sitting and conversing with the TV. All of our inside jokes and personalized buddy-buddy expressions were nothing but commentary on talk shows and televised sports.

Maybe it was the loss of his TV that had made Nino give in to the waitress. They stumbled into his bedroom after cards, and I listened from the living room sofa to her sounding like a whole pack of hunting dogs through the thin walls. After, she wandered naked until she found the washroom and peed with the door open. I watched her through half-opened eyes, pretending to be asleep. I couldn't help peeking; I was awestruck by how she moved through the apartment just like normal, like she didn't notice she had no clothes on. Even the dimpled flesh on her thighs trembled at the brazenly heavy steps she took. I knew this thundering drunken nude was a threat to my tenancy. There was only one thing to do:

It was two p.m.—a decent hour, I thought, for a barfly to wake. I came at him without a shirt. I couldn't make myself remove any more clothes than that; the only time I used to pull my pants down was when I peed. Nino squinted at me as I located his penis under the sheets and coaxed it into an erection. "You ever wonder what this would be like?" I said, taking his half-chub in my mouth. His hands, like a freak storm, were suddenly all over. Luckily my trusty unicorn belt buckle gave him some trouble and he settled for the tangle of my bra, digging at my nipples like they were coins fallen in the cracks of a sofa. I wasn't doing much better with the blowjob, gagging and drooling as I worked. I gave up too soon and simply held my mouth open to let Nino pump himself in and out until he finished. The best I could do was keep my lips curled over my teeth to avoid scratching him. I spit his semen on his stomach with a retch.

No post-coital affections. We went straight into our routine: staring at the space where the TV once was, him making phone calls that sounded like the same sound bite looped: "Is that fucking right? When did this happen? Not if I have something to say about it." I grabbed the bottle of Windex and sprayed anything inanimate. I remember wiping behind the toilet bowl and feeling like I was earning my keep. We didn't say much to each other. He didn't even look at me except for when he asked me, "How long have you been staying here?" I'd seen that look before. It would only be a day or two before he showed me the door.

My last night at the Legion, otherwise known as the night I was saved, I took my first drink to relax, my second for courage, and on my third I shot my mouth off. I pronounced myself a virgin for all the lowlifes to hear. Sure, I had sung (and swallowed) for my supper, but my pussy had remained unspoiled. *That explains the shitty blowjob*, I imagined Nino thinking as his crooked grin widened, then, *Not for long*. A booze-chugging virgin would be just the thing to perk him up; maybe it perked him up too much. He stopped flashing smiles at the waitress and small-talking the men lined up at the bar. Suddenly, I had all his attention. I slipped between pool players or fit myself among the bar stools for a breather, and Nino was there with another drink. He kept pulling me back to our seats, sandwiching me between himself and his pretty friend with the missing front teeth, his hand rooting around under the table for the fly of my jeans. "I wanna dance sexy for you," I slurred and wriggled away from them, climbing onto a table.

I was now far enough from Nino for him not to usher me into a cab or a bathroom stall. Him and Teeth had lined up another round for me. I saw the tall slender glass of whatever-the-piss was on tap and a tumbler of Jim Beam squatting next to it on the table; beer because it was cheap and bourbon because I'd been putting on a good show flinching when I swallowed it. I got my ratings up again, no denying that. Nino and Teeth leaned into each other, mirroring my drinks-in-waiting: Teeth the tall glass, golden, a smooth swallow, and Nino short, thick, and mean. The triangular scar along the bridge of his nose was a mate to the chip in the whiskey glass. They probably discussed the precise dimensions of my virgin pussy.

In between them and me was a gathering of half-interested onlookers, a few men pounding their fists on tabletops. Most stood around muttering at each other. Their eyes were glassy, like I was a TV set they were watching, and not even a ball game but a crappy re-run. I called out "Whoop whoop," but got only a couple of weak parrot-calls in reply. I wanted a bar brawl over me—that was my exit plan. I was a prisoner inciting a riot so that I might escape Alcatraz. Why didn't I just walk out the front door? It never occurred to me.

I swung my hips around like I unscrewed at the waist. There was a guy with a Trans-Am baseball cap and a red flannel shirt who I hoped would make a move for me, but he walked over to Nino and gave him a congratulatory punch on the arm. Then the pair at the pool table turned in creepy unison and gave Nino the thumbs up. Someone shouted, "Nino's got a ripe cherry." Apparently, Nino had made his claim on my virginity bar-wide news. I wouldn't have put it past him to have had wagers going with a handful of the other barflies; *Ten bucks says I pop her tonight; twenty I take it right here in the bar.* Any notion I might have had to give in to him was long gone. I wasn't going to be thrown down on some table like a mismatched hand of clubs and hearts. But how to get out of the game?

I closed my eyes and listened to the music. I could always tell when a song was older than me because it felt as if I was the only one outside of an inside joke, laughing along when I didn't get what was funny. It made no difference that I had learned the words to "Help" or "Stairway to Heaven" or "Hotel California"; I was still outside. I wouldn't be able to dance for much longer to those songs, getting soberer as I did. But if I climbed down from the table, it would only be to hear the jingle of loose change in Nino's pants pocket, to taste metallic reflux in my mouth as he sat me back down in his lap. The worst part was, I suspected if I gave it up to him, it would only earn me another four days at best. In a month's time, or less, no one at the Legion, including Nino, would even remember my name.

"Somebody?" I said out loud. "Somebody see me."

And a man did appear. He pushed through the front door and slowly made his way around the room. Judging by his deliberate walk as he wove through the crowd without watching where he was going, he did seem to be coming for me. Wide shoulders. Square jaw. A bit of gold flashed on his left hand, another glint in one earlobe. Handsome, even with my dizzy vision. I lifted my shirt a little to reel him in. This stirred the onlookers. A half dozen more men stood up and gave half-hearted shouts. As soon as my stranger was beside me I collapsed into his arms. "Let's go," he said. "Now."

I heard a name being called several times before I realized it was mine. Nino reached his arm out in front of him and grabbed at air; the table I had been dancing on was lying overturned on the floor. When I replay this memory, I always imagine looking back and knowing that it was the last time I'd see inside of the Legion, or any other hole-in-the-wall pub, that my world was about to change completely. But I truly had no idea what was going to happen next.

The stranger carried me through the front door; it bounced against the doorframe a few times before closing. My shirt remained hiked up as we drove down Park Street. He drove a shiny black Italian car that smelled of leather and perfume. I reclined my seat as far back as it would go and watched the street lamps streak by. "My bra has daisies on it," I said a bit too loud. He glanced back at me as I reached beneath my unicorn belt. "My panties do, too," I told him. "Daisies."

II

I woke up smothered under a black bedspread. Only my arm had discovered the way out. I studied it dangling off the bed like it was a dismembered limb not my own, an alien object that had fallen through a tear in the sky. My hangover head was still falling. I began to untwist myself from the blanket and found that I was neither naked nor wearing my own clothes. A large white T-shirt stuck to my skin like I'd been sweating all night. My nipples showed through the fabric, and I covered myself again with the heavy spread. Across the room, on top of a long black lacquer dresser, my clothes were folded in a pile: jeans on the bottom, striped T-shirt, daisy print bra and underwear, and my belt rolled into a coil with the unicorn belt buckle facing me. "Where are we?" I asked it.

I always wore the unicorn. I slept in it. Sometimes I'd lay awake and press that belt buckle into me until it hurt, then I'd undo my pants to see little unicorn imprints left on my belly. I believe this was my home remedy for the teenage blues.

But I wasn't blue in the stranger's bed. Only my stomach was alarmed at the unfamiliar surroundings. It rumbled in a way that said *no sudden movements.* The bed I was in was enormous, with enough room for me to sweat, then inch over onto dry sheet and sweat again. I wondered if the sheets and pillowcases were silk, and I felt a bit guilty. There was nothing on the walls but a framed print of Muhammad Ali submerged in a pool of water. Ali stood upright like the bottom of the pool was any old corner of a gym. His gloves raised, boxing the water all around him. I couldn't tell if the water was real or superimposed.

Morning came in through the blinds, cutting everything into ribbons. I made a couple of attempts to get up and failed, managing only to get one leg dangling ineffectually off the bed. The stranger's voice was in the next room. All I could recall were his eyes, not his name, how we got here, or what we did. I wanted to call out to him, but how do you call a nameless pair of eyes? And besides, my voice was a whisper.

When he did appear his eyes were as brown as I remembered, pupils flecked with gold like beach pebbles. He offered me watered-down apple juice, raising his eyebrow at the meek sips I took from the glass. He laid the back of his hand on my forehead and sucked his teeth. "You've got a fever," he said. "You're too young yet to be all that drink sick. A day's rest will set you right again." I feigned a cough. Sank deeper into the bed. "You got someplace to be?" he asked. "Where's home?" I shrugged my shoulders and he nodded back at me. "You're not on the back of a milk carton? No search parties dragging Moore Park Ravine for you?"

"Yeah right," I said.

"Arsen," he told me. "Not a pseudonym *de flava*, my birth name." He burned for nine months in his mamma's womb; she swore she was pregnant with a dragon. As a child he would break into the boarded-up, abandoned steel mill near his home and shout just to see if he could make flames shoot out of his mouth.

He toured me around his spacious one-bedroom apartment: the view of the city from the balcony; the marble tile on the kitchen floor; the Jacuzzi jets in the tub. Toro, his French bulldog, kept his big paw draped over his food bowl. There was a soapstone wolf howling on the coffee table, a leather three-piece sofa suite with very few scratch marks. And a bookshelf covered in framed photographs of aunties holding flowers in front of a church, wearing impossible hairdos at spring dances, and gathered around Arsen's pregnant mother, rows of hands on her huge belly. Pictures of what must have been young cousins wearing home-sewn dresses on the porch steps of old brownstones. My favourite was of six-year-old Arsen—the closest somebody to a man in any of the photos—looking down at his birthday cake, his mouth puckered and ready to blow out the candles. There was only one book on the shelves, the Bible on the bottom shelf. As a boy, he told me, he sang in a gospel choir. "What do you think of the place?" he asked.

It was the best apartment I had ever seen. I wouldn't last very long in a place like this, was what I thought of it. Arsen didn't seem to mind me not answering him. He turned back to his photos, looking at them in a way I didn't want to interrupt. I fixated on him the same as he did on his photos. I focused so intently he nearly disappeared, just breath and flesh beside me. I hoped that I would fall in love with him.

On our second morning, it was me who woke up first. He had insisted, again, on giving me the bed and was sleeping on the sofa. I snuck across the living room carpet on my hands and knees. Each time he stirred, I froze low to the carpet and held my breath. It must have taken me twenty minutes to get close to him; the whole time I was scolding myself for being such a little creep. It couldn't be helped; I'd already convinced myself that he was everything. I curled up quietly beside the sofa and listened to the sound of his breath against the leather. His knee bent over the edge of the sofa, and I was so grateful to have just that small, naked part of him in clear view. I didn't take my eyes off it until he woke and said, "Come closer, little one." He reached for me with his eyes still closed. When I offered my hand he tucked it under him like a stuffed toy, close to his face, and fell back asleep. I knelt on the floor beside him as the pins-and-needles numbed my hand. *I can take it,* I thought. *I'll give all four limbs if he wants them.*

We shared the breakfast he made: finger-like strips of toast rolled in cinnamon sugar, poached eggs, and ham steak. I'd only seen men cook on talk shows. I let each bite sit in my mouth, reciting a full "m-i-s-s-i-s-s-i-p-p-i" before I chewed, making the meal last. When he asked, "Food's going down alright today?" I slumped over in the chair and held my gut, even though the nausea had stopped a full twenty-four hours before.

He drew me a bath, with bubbles. What he was doing with bubble bath I did not care. He posed in front of the medicine cabinet mirror and sang to me as I bathed, "Nobody knows the trouble I've seen ..." Gospel music was beyond me, but somehow he chose the one song I knew. "... The trou-ah-ah-ble I've seen, but the Lord." He reached through the shower curtain, and I prepared for his touch, shifting so that his fingers would connect with my cheek first. But he was only passing me a razor. A fresh, pink plastic razor. And he didn't even peek through the shower curtain as he passed it to me. "I have shaving cream too, cocoa butter, anything you want." I leaned my head against the tiles and decided that was the moment I fell in love.

"Telephone is right there," he told me several times, pointing out a cordless phone that seemed to follow me from room to room. It appeared on the coffee table, then on the dresser in the bedroom. It even made an appearance on the balcony. I never used it.

And when I lay in his bed he said, "You can stop pretending to be drink sick and just stay because I want you to." He pulled the cover up to my chin, clicked off the light as he left, and I swear I felt each and every pore on my body open up like the mouths of baby birds, hungry. That, for real now, was the moment I fell in love.

On day three we did it all again; he cooked, he sang, he said sweet things to me. What he did not do was take me out, not even when he walked the dog. From the balcony I spied on him leading Toro along the thin strip of manicured grass in between the sidewalk and the road. Nino had taken me out; he made me a fixture in his day-to-day. That's why I hung on so long with him; I didn't conflict with his bartrolling schedule. During my stay at Arsen's, on the other hand, Arsen barely used the phone or left the apartment for any reason (apart from Toro's walks). He must have had something or someone he was keeping me hidden from, I was sure of it. I gave the stint with him a realistic six-day maximum. I prayed for more.

"Who was that calling your name at the bar?" he asked from the other side of the bathroom door as I was changing into the dress he'd somehow procured for me during his dog walk. It was pretty if I pretended it wasn't me wearing it. I only wore jeans then, boy-cut jeans. This dress was merely a slip with tricky lace straps that tied at the shoulders. It smelled slightly of someone else, the incense smell of girl skin, but I wasn't about to mention it to Arsen. It was better than my own clothes that still stunk of the Legion. And it almost fit. Dresses loosely hung off me as if they were refusing to commit to my body.

"Nobody," I said, delaying opening the bathroom door for him to see me.

"Is he your man?"

"He wishes he was," I said, attempting to sass-talk.

Arsen cracked the bathroom door, tapped the doorframe a few times as if counting down the seconds before he entered. We were crowded in his bathroom, which I should have enjoyed except there was this strange look to him. "He wishes he was," Arsen repeated my words one by one, each word sounding graver than the last. I tried to backtrack, but I couldn't come up with a sure fix. If I told him Nino was nothing special, I might make myself seem like slut. If I told him I was using Nino for a place to stay, I'd seem like a freeloader. It was too late to say we were only friends. So I stammered without an explanation. Arsen took this worse than anything I could have said. "If you two still have business together ..." he told me, "then I'll take you to him."

He didn't ask me to take my clothes with me as he pointed me to the door; they were left in their tidy pile on his dresser. I took that as an indication that it wasn't the last time I'd see his apartment. But with my clothes left behind, I'd have to face Nino wearing a little black dress. I folded my arms tight across my chest as we rode toward the old section of town. I didn't bother lying about Nino's address. There wasn't time to lie; Arsen's questions were so rapid-fire:

"How long have you lived with him?"

"You got belongings moved into his place?"

"Are there other men you're stringing along?"

"You sleeping with them?"

He must have pulled every pathetic detail out of me. I doubt I had considered my life pathetic before. Spontaneous, sure. Wayward— well, probably. But hearing myself stumble through it all while sitting in the deep leather passenger seat of his car, I felt very small. As if I was being drained of my stories. The Nino part wasn't nearly as bad as the string of second-rate Ninos: the small-time pot pushers; the crash pads; the buildings I'd used as squats then abandoned because of fire or rats. Yes, I told him about dumpster diving behind the Nabisco factory for breakfast. Yes, I told him about letting men feel me up behind the liquor store for spare change. Yes, I told him—promised him, in fact—that despite all the scrounging, I was still a virgin. A diamond in coal is how I liked to think of it.

"Why?" was his next question. "Why put yourself through all that?" This is where I fell silent. I didn't put myself anywhere. It just was there—life was—long before I had anything to do with it.

"Stuff just happens to me," I shrugged.

I leaned my head out the car window; hair blew around my face in damp yarns. In the passenger side mirror I looked almost invisible:

black hair cocoon, black dress against the black upholstery. There was no asking why.

"You look pretty, by the way," he said just as a lace strap fell down my shoulder. I caught the dress before it fell down past my left breast.

He made me list the things I had at Nino's: a second pair of jeans; a Hello Kitty sweatshirt from Chinatown; a glitter lip gloss; a skin-tight, floor length, neon-green velvet dress given to me by a stripper at Nino's cousin Johnny-V's stag party (this dress had made Nino laugh until he choked because it was long enough to make me look like I'd grown a mermaid tail); a toothbrush; a few pairs of dirty underwear; and a pocket-sized stuffed bunny with a tuft of real rabbit fur on its head that found its way into my pocket again and again. None of which I cared too much about, but Arsen said he wanted every last trace of me out of Nino's place. I was either to make a clean break or not bother coming back to down to the car.

I buzzed #210 at the front door with Arsen watching from his near-by parking spot. "Don't be home," I said through clenched teeth. It wasn't late enough for the bar, but if I was lucky he would have started early that day. Nino answered, his voice a scratch over the intercom. Next I wished for the waitress to be with him as I climbed the stairs to his floor, stirring up dust bunnies on each step. He opened the door before I knocked. Nino paused, like I knew he would, to take in my dress before he asked, "What the hell happened to you?"

"You won't believe the shit I've been through. This guy just dragged me out of the bar. I've been trying to get back here ever since," I lied.

Nino stood aside to let me in. He was alone. He was never alone, except on that day. My duffle bag was in the same place I'd left it, half tucked under the sofa. Everything, including my toothbrush, was in there. I never left any of my stuff out, for fear that it would infringe on Nino's space, remind him that he was aiming to get rid of me soon.

"Who was that freakin' guy?"

"Arsen," I said, then immediately regretted it.

"Arsen? What kind of a freakin' name is that? He looks like some kind of uptown faggot or something." Nino raked his hand through his messy curled hair. I wanted to tell him he was full of shit. I only blinked my eyes at him as if he'd said something in a different language. "Teeth and I went driving around looking for you."

"You did?"

"Yeah, you could have at least called." He paced the length of the apartment a couple times, and then sat backwards on a kitchen chair. "Whatcha standing there for?" Nino kicked out a second chair for me. I didn't expect that. I was ready for indifference. I stared piteously at the rawboned wooden chair he offered.

"I'm not staying, Nino."

"Fuck off. Sit your tiny ass down."

I yanked at my duffle bag wedged firmly beneath the sofa. I felt the dress riding up in the back as I bent over to wrestle with the bag. He was looking, he had to be. When I pulled it out, I flung it over my shoulder and marched, heavy-footed, back to the door. "Thanks for taking me in, Nino," I said in a voice so deadpan even I couldn't tell if I was sincere or sarcastic.

"Ah, come on. Don't say you're going with that guy," he said. So I didn't say it. This time Nino didn't call after me. The only sound was the swish of the dress as I went back down the stairs.

"That was quick," Arsen said.

"I didn't want to make you wait," I told him. "Besides, we had nothing to say to each other." *We had nothing to say to each other* was what I reminded myself of, if ever I got sentimental about Nino. Which wasn't often. The guy was no dreamboat. I suppose I remember him like Alice might remember the gilded frame before she fell through the looking glass. Angel Gabriel remembering the specific handle on the pearly gates. Nino was the last regular person I remembered before leaving the city. And at the time, there was nothing significant about that final scene at Nino's. I was preoccupied; leaving Nino made me draw even closer to Arsen.

Arsen wanted to celebrate my "break-up," so he ordered Chinese delivery: deep-fried prawns, sweet-and-sour chicken balls, cashew green beans. He put on his favourite album by a singer I didn't recognize, although it turned out I knew the words to her songs. All of them stories about being in love with a man who wasn't worth it. Later I would learn she was Billie Holiday. Later I would also wonder if the dinner and music were band-aids for Arsen's guilt, not a celebration at all. Why should he feel guilty? He was about to change my life. I'm not talking about the kind of change that makes you decide to go to college or quit smoking. Big change. Another-world change. For the good or for the bad is beside the point; with each tender word he spoke he was changing it.

"Your scrounging days are over. You're too good for that," he told me. "You're looking much better. Your skin's got colour again. You're a pretty girl, you know that?"

I kept my eyes on my plate as he spoke. The way he stared at me, I thought I might unravel. I could feel the black dress sliding off me, my hair loosening from the ponytail I had tied it into. I was relieved when he picked up his fork.

I wanted to lick the last bit of saucy glaze to prolong the meal, and not just because the Chinese was tasty. I knew what would happen after dinner was cleared. I fingered the bowl and licked my fingertip. I'd been told this was sexy.

"I had my run-around days, too. I used to sleep with a lot of women," he said—it seemed more to himself than to me—as he stared up at the wall behind us. "I was raised to be better than that; you know what I'm saying."

He turned to face his bookshelf of framed photographs. "Do you want family, Little?" he asked. I shrugged and kept my eyes on the empty bowl in front of me. He repeated the question, word for word, and was about to repeat it a third time.

"I don't know." My voice sounded whinier than I wanted it to.

I followed his pointed gaze to the collection of photos. "I guess it's hard to know with family, isn't it?" he shrugged.

I pushed my chair out from the table and made my way to him very slowly. My bare toes touched his leather shoe and I leaned into him so I could feel the stiff cotton of his jeans against my leg. He put his arm around my waist and squeezed. "You can't go through life being alone, you know?"

I squirmed a bit in his arms. Splashes of glistening pink plum sauce lined the rim of Arsen's dinner plate. I wriggled an arm free of his embrace to place a paper napkin overtop the mess. I suspected Arsen wouldn't like a dirty table.

"Three nights ago I was walking back to my car on Front Street, and I stopped in front of a bar. I stopped because I felt something. Something reached out and grabbed me. And as soon as I stepped into the place and saw you, I knew you were what gave me that feeling. I was meant to find you there. Do you believe me, little one?"

I believed him because believing made what was about to happen right. I followed him into his bedroom. We stood together at the foot of the bed for a long time. I watched his chest move with his breath. His height and size overwhelmed me then, and the longer we stood wordlessly together the bigger he became. I lurched my hand to his groin. I needed us to begin before what little confidence I had diminished altogether. When he removed my hand from his zipper, I snapped, "Are we doing this, or what?" My tone was more brat than seductress, like a toddler about to throw a tantrum.

"Relax," he said. "Just lie down." I lowered onto his bed; he remained standing. He reached for my foot, pulling me to the edge of the mattress. The dress slid up to my waist. He took up my other foot, propped both against his chest and inched closer. My legs started trembling against his torso, toes curled into his warm skin. He mouthed "shhh" without the sound: a mute comfort. Without actually touching me, his hands travelled down my legs. The heat from his palms tingled as he grabbed hold of my underwear, the daisy print underwear I'd been washing in the sink with hand soap, then wearing again. He stared at me, holding my underwear in his big hand. "Pretty girl," he said as he tightened his grip around my feet, holding them apart. For a second I felt like a baby laid out on a change table. I had to fight the urge to cover myself with my hands. "So tiny and pretty." Reaching down, he touched me between my legs and then my insides did unravel. I had touched myself before, not many times, but enough to know the drowsy flesh there. I opened my legs so slightly, hoping he wouldn't notice. I bit the inside of mouth to keep in the noises I might have made.

"I'm not like other guys you've been with. I don't mess around," he said. "How do I know you're not going to run off on me, like you did to the last guy?"

"I would never do that," I said, tilting my hips up toward him. The truth is I did not run off on Nino; if it weren't for Arsen, I wouldn't have left. And I would never leave Arsen, I thought, because I couldn't conceive of anyone better than him ever coming along. I was sure he was aware of this as he nodded to himself and unbuttoned his pants. They dropped to his ankles. He shoved his briefs down after them. I made fists with both my hands.

"We have to both want this," he told me.

I believed I wanted him, but *this* I wasn't sure about. I saw his erection bobbing between my knees and I knew it was too late for second-guessing. He took me by the ankles, holding my feet to his shoulder's height, and hoisted me onto his dick. I remember the immediate pang that made my legs spasm, an expected pain that I had been warned of for years. My ass and lower back floated above the mattress. The dress fell around my breasts. I didn't know if I was supposed to take it off so I just left it bunched up around me.

Everything about him was still. Barely a pelvic thrust or strained facial expression. Only his arms were flexed and moving as he pulled me up and down the length of him by my ankles. "You want a home?" he asked, abruptly. "I could give you a home."

My reply came out like a gust of wind; I must have been holding my breath.

"You want a family?" he asked. The sure and even syllables of his speech copied his body's movements. There was a second round of pain in my gut as I panicked, too late, over the forgotten condom. The photo of his pregnant mother flashed in my head. What had I gotten myself into? I told him "yes," anyway, and he continued asking me these questions, offering me things I'd never been offered before, and I repeated "yes" and "yes" until he dropped my ankles and walked out of the bedroom. "You're such a pretty girl," he called from the bathroom. I heard the faucet running from where I still lay on the bed.

When he returned he was wringing water from his hands, his jeans done up, shirt tucked in. I hadn't moved. He sat beside me on the bed. Some of my hair got trapped beneath him, forcing my head to turn toward him. "I have to go out for a little bit. Got some errands to take care of," he said. I considered it a bad sign that he barely touched me during sex. I *knew* it was a bad sign that he was leaving. I wanted to pick a fight with him, so he would stay, but I couldn't come up with an opening jab. "This is the first time we've been apart in days. I'm trusting you here. Don't run. Give me your word on that."

"Where would I go?" I said.

I didn't move until the lock clicked shut. Suddenly, I regretted not walking him to the door, not smiling or saying something sweet like *I had a nice time* or *I think I love you* or whatever it was that should be said. I stood on wobbly legs. My left thigh was wet. Blood mixed with a thick glistening fluid, like the film on a newly opened jar of jam. The same glint of goo was beaded on the bed, where my ass would have been had I not been held up in the air the whole time. It stained Arsen's silk sheets a darker shade of black.

III

"Open your eyes."

I was having one of those dreams where your dream self begs you to stay. Where the alarm clock or the cat meowing becomes part of the dream rather than waking you from it. In the dream, there was a statuesque woman holding a piece of red string between her thumb and pointer finger; her middle, ring, and pinkie were outstretched in an okay gesture. Behind her a tornado of red wool raged. Yarn twisted into massive red towers, unravelled into red pools at her feet, a world created and undone, again and again.

"Wake up, you little gutternip!"

I sat upright with a start. A woman sat at the corner of the bed, sweeping her arms in wide, dramatic motions as she worked a comb through her hair. She was monstrous. As if someone had taken an average-sized woman and inflated her. The skin around her neck looked like it was straining to keep her body and head together; it clung to the underside of her jaw like damp cloth. Her breasts floated in front of her like balloons stuck to the wall by static electricity. Black cherry hair looped in large loose curls around her huge face. And her lips, already full, were drawn in even fuller by bronze lip-liner and filled in with shiny gold gloss. "Your eyes!" she blurted out. "They're bloodshot awful. After a night with Arsen they shouldn't be red like that."

"Where …?" I started to say, but in Arsen's bed, naked, I was in no position to question her. I quietly prepared for the worst.

"Arsen's not here," she answered the question I was too scared to ask. "He brought me 'round and dropped me off here, same as you." Her big head rolled from side to side, her curls bouncing around her shoulders, as she looked around the room. "I keep tellin' him to do something—anything—with this city apartment. What colour would you say these walls is?" Reaching over my head she rapped her knuckles against the wall above me. I could smell her then: incense, like the faint fragrance left on my black dress. I took little comfort knowing the dress was far too small to actually be hers. She had touched it, though, my nose told me that much. "What colour?" she asked again.

I could barely whisper the word "beige."

"Arsen calls it sandstone. Him and his namin' things," she laughed at this, and then eyeballed me when she noticed I wasn't laughing along with her. "You scared? Of me? Don't upset yourself, girl, I'm not here to toss you out. We gonna get along, right?" She smiled big for me; her lips parted to show a row of square white teeth.

"Right," I was quick to repeat.

"Good. Now, my name is Della O'Kande. Now you think, what kinda name is that?" she said, though that was not what I was thinking at all. I was thinking about how it was the very first morning I'd woken up naked, ever, and I was doomed. "It means the first girl child. Or was it the last girl child born after many boys?" She thought about this for a half second, taking up the comb again. Her hair unwound under the comb's teeth, reaching well past her waist, then snapped back into its original coil. "Anyway, my whole life I been surrounded by nothin' but men. Men and boys, boys and men, and me. I do get lonesome for girlfriends. But only the right kind of girl, if you know what I mean. Arsen, he thinks you may be the right kind. So what's your name?"

The question caught me off guard; there was an awkward pause before I answered.

"Pretty name," she remarked. "Might be Spanish, or Irish, or from the Far East. Might even be African. A name like that make everybody feel at home." She looked at me like a man might, like she was trying to see my body through the covers. "You haven't grown much, have you? You look like someone slapped a pair of melons on a nine-year-old child. God gave you melons and few bad memories to boot, eh?" She pinched the bedspread around my chest and peeked in at me. I froze. "This *is* a nice little chat we're havin'. Like friends, tellin' each other our birth names. Course, names aren't much more than a pair of shoes. Somethin' to wear. Most people call me Candy. And you'll be callin' me First." She threw her meaty hand at me and I too eagerly retrieved my own from under the covers to shake hers. "Do you know who I am, now?"

"No. I'm sorry." I could hear the fear in my voice. I'm sure she could too. I wished I was wearing at least some underwear.

"I'm Arsen's first wife." She lifted her hand again, streaking it in front of my face. A trail of gold went by before I flinched. There was a ring on her finger.

"I didn't know," I whispered.

"Oh. You're just a lamb, you are," she sighed. "Well, I can see we need to have a real big talk. I'll put on the tea. You get dressed and come to breakfast." She left the door open as she left the room.

I spent some time pondering the eight-storey drop from the window. There wasn't even a patch of grass outside the bedroom window to land on, just parking lot. Arsen's empty parking spot taunted me in a way I never knew asphalt could.

In front of the smoky-glass, full-length mirror, I got dressed in my unwashed clothes and smoothed the tangles from my hair with my fingers. I went, defeated, into the kitchen to meet her. "Oh, hi there," she greeted me again as if it was our first time seeing each other. On the table sat a plate of apple slices smeared with peanut butter for my breakfast. She had the expression of someone who'd prepared a monologue, as if she were reciting words in her head, waiting for the right moment.

"Here it is," she began. "We need our man back. He's been on holiday with you for long enough. So it's time for you to make your decision. Arsen likes you. There are plenty of girls who'd wanna turn out with Arsen. He wants you. He only has two Wifeys, me and Second, and he don't care too much for Second, you know. Hasn't touched her forever. I shouldn't run my mouth like this, but the truth is you are *worth* more than Second. You oughta consider that, right?" Across the room the kettle hollered on the stove. She knew exactly where the mugs were, and the spoons and the honey. She banged down a large mug in front of me. The teabag bled chai into the steaming water. "Drink," she commanded, and I lifted the too-hot tea to my lips. "I'll spell it out for you. You can stick with us, and I promise you'll have the best house and all the clothes and gifts you want. It's a queen's life, really. We take care of each other, like family. Some girls ain't cut out for it. It don't start out easy. I have this hunch you won't have too hard a time. You gotta earn your keep. But soon enough you'll figure it out and be as happy as me, and that is happy. Arsen is a good man, he don't run his girls on smack or none of that kinda city business, he don't work us around the clock, he don't starve us. I mean, take a look at me." First grabbed a handful of her hefty flesh. "I know your story, girl. You got nowhere to be, do you?"

"Not really," I shrugged.

"You been sick? Your skin is a hint … beige."

"Yeah, that's the colour of my skin. That way I blend in with the walls," I said, mustering up a shred of sarcasm. But I was fidgeting so much I had to tuck my hands behind my back.

"Well then, eat your breakfast, beige girl," she told me. She didn't take her eyes off me until I ate all four apple slices. The sound of my chewing filled the small space between us. She handed me a napkin when I was finished. "You been runnin' yourself on drink and city men and whatever scraps you can get?"

She knew the answer already, like she knew the answer to her last couple questions. Without a doubt, she and Arsen were in on this together. He had told her everything about me. I suspected the only reason she was asking questions at all was so I would be further humiliated by answering them. There was no pride in figuring her out, no advantage. She was still bigger. She was still Arsen's wife. I was still in a shitty spot.

"You're free to go back to that life," she said. "'Course, I have to beat you before you go loose. Seein' as you fucked my man and all." She moved her chair closer to me, it squeaked against the marble tile. My instinct was to move away, widen the gap between us again, but I held my ground. "It's not my rule says I have to beat you. This is a mean city. I'd rather we stay friends, you treat me like family. Can you do that?"

"If I wanted to," I had the guts to say. There was a tear in the corner of my eye that I was willing not to fall.

"You think you gonna fall in love with Arsen? 'Cause it's easier if you got a man to love. And trust me, he's the best." She leaned toward me. Her tongue pushed out a tiny spit bubble between her lips. "Oh, you think you already are," she said; the bubble popped. "Well that suits me just fine."

"It's none of your business." I managed to look her square in the face, but as soon as I did the tear rolled down my cheek. I bowed my head, letting my hair hide me.

"You're right, what do I know about your business? You could very well be a smart one. You got yourself here somehow. I doubt you landed here just to have me crack your teeth."

First noticed my foot tapping. She pressed her own big foot on top of mine to keep it still, and I thought of Arsen's hands on my ankles the night before—the memory sent a shiver up my body. She came in even closer; her breath smelled of spiced tea. Across the table a gold lip print was stamped on the rim of her mug. She wrapped both her arms around me and started to rock back and forth. "I don't wanna hurt you, little one. It just how things work in the ugly city. You already been through enough trouble, I can tell. Poor Little, all alone. You think I don't know. I know. I know very well 'cause I came from nothin', just like you. I can fix that, if you only let me. I can see you never alone and hurtin' again." She spoke low and sweetly, and I began to cry. She took my arm and looped it around her neck; my arm was unexpectedly willing to hug her. The skin beneath her hair was cool; it was like putting my hand in a cave. "I got you," she whispered. "You cry now, I got you."

IV

When the towering flesh spectacle who had me calling her First let go of my hand to unlock the double dead-bolt on Arsen's apartment door, my equilibrium fell out-of-kilter. As if, after spending only a few hours with her, I had forgotten how to stand on my own. Her touch was ever-present. From the moment she wiped her fleshy thumb over my tear-streaked cheeks, she had her hands on me. Rough at first, like I was a hostage being led from Arsen's apartment to the street. Her body overflowed into my seat as we rode the subway, smothering me. Each and every man we passed stared at her, and at me. Her beauty was an eyesore. They probably would have stared at her sheer size anyway, but her hand clamped to the back of my neck didn't help us be less noticeable.

She used this force so that she could take me shopping; it seemed absurd as she hauled me from one ladies' boutique to another. I would have willingly gone with anyone offering me free stuff. When we were crammed into cheap lingerie store fitting rooms, her touch went gentle as she helped me in and out of the clothes. Each time she lifted a dress over my head, she tidied my hair. "You are a tiny thing," she said, shaking her head at how low-cut necklines simply fell off me. "Soon you'll have everythin' tailored for you, but for now these city threads will have to do." No matter how many outfits I tried, she never tired of touching me. I got used to her more quickly than I would have liked. A couple of times I caught myself turning around so she could zip me up.

It wasn't until we were done shopping and back on the subway that I figured out she was nervous. She squeezed my hand until it was throbbing. "It sure is stuffy in here," she said. "It sure is noisy." She complained about me too: "Uncross your arms," and "Don't slouch," and "Quit hidin' your pretty face behind that hair."

Several other passengers—men, of course—started up conversations with her, and only then did she leave me be. She fanned her neck and cleavage with a subway map as they spoke. "I'm goin' to the end of the line. You ever pass by No's Smoke Shoppe? Cuban cigars," she whispered. "I live near there. Me and a handful of my girlfriends. We just love visitors, if you're ever nearby."

Others watched us like we were on exhibition. A couple of times I tried staring them down, but their eyes would not budge. There was an old man with an indigo ship on his forearm, maybe a navy tattoo, who planted himself beside First and just gawked. When we finally got off the subway she told me he was one of her customers. I didn't understand how this could be true. He ogled her as if she were from a different world altogether, an alien beauty. There wasn't a scrap of recognition in his stare. "He don't know he seen me," she explained. "Poor dear, to him I'm some sweet dream, dissolvin' into morning."

I wondered what kind of a fierce bender the old man must have been on for her to dissolve. After one day, she was part of my balance. I had to lean up against the hallway wall while she wrestled with the sticky lock on Arsen's door. Her threat to beat me was nowhere near as serious as her vow to take me in. I knew getting away from her wouldn't be easy.

I was disappointed when Arsen still wasn't home, then, giving it another thought, thankful. Surely he would have turned to her first, smiled for her first. Maybe he wouldn't have had any greeting for me at all. I jumped when I heard banging in the bathroom.

"Nah, don't worry. That's just Second. Arsen figures you ought to meet the whole family." First pounded on the back of the door. "What in the Lord's name are you doin' in there?"

A tall willowy girl emerged, blonde and pale. She did a good job of not looking at me.

"This is the one Arsen is takin' as Third," First slowly explained to Second, like she was bearing bad news.

"I already told you I don't care," said Second. She backed into the bathroom again. The sink counter was covered with cosmetics. Second twirled a blush brush in a pot of powder. I caught her gaze in the medicine cabinet before she squeezed her eyes shut, dragging the blush brush across her face, masked in a white powder cloud.

"Don't think you're the only one needin' the bathroom," First warned her. "This little one has to pretty herself up too, you know."

When Arsen arrived to pick us up, it was as bad as I had predicted. He held the car door open for First while I crawled in the back beside Second. First sat sideways in the passenger seat, bent forward toward Arsen to talk in his ear as he drove. Her voice, loud as a bass line pouring out a bar door, was lowered to a coo. I still heard every word.

"Smells clean in the city. No piss. No smoke. Nothin'."

"Night's young," Arsen said, rolling his window down. He took an abnormally long route, looping around a block twice or more, stopping curbside every so often to idle a minute or two. I thought it was because he didn't really want to drop me on some corner, but was going to.

Doom struck me as we circled the skids and as I spotted the threadbare women, the lacklustre women, working there. "We don't work 'longside them hoodrats," said First. "Wait 'til you see the Glories." She turned around to face me—wide-eyed and with a toothy smile, but Arsen nudged her shoulder and she quickly turned back around again.

After we pulled off the main road and wove through a few more streets I was completely lost. I hated going to unfamiliar neighbour-hoods; in this one I couldn't see a bus stop or a gas station or even a street sign. Until that moment, I'd been mentally mapping my escape route. I even noted where some doughnut shops were situated so I could wash off some of the makeup First put on my face before making my way back toward downtown. I didn't look forward to riding the bus looking like a hooker, but that was better than actually being a hooker.

But as Arsen's car inched down the unknown streets, my map and my plan had deteriorated. I was lost. What's worse is I could barely keep track of familiar landmarks we'd past before getting lost. *Was that a Donut Diner or a Waffle House a few blocks back?* The last of summer's sandflies swarmed the flickering streetlamps. I watched a sheet of stray white paper blow past the car and hug the curb. Most of the buildings around us were abandoned: boarded up with ply-wood or left without glass in their empty windows. Only one busi-ness remained. A neon sign in front of us read EAT CIGARETTES 24 HOURS. It was No's Smoke Shoppe, the place First had talked about on the subway. Arsen half-waved to a boy sweeping the front stoop. We parked out front awhile. Arsen kept his left turn signal blinking. To our left was a blind alley, the kind of alley victims in crime movies find themselves in. It was pot-holed and seemed too narrow for any car to fit through it. Arsen turned down it anyway. I braced, expect-ing to hear the scrap of metal against brick. To my surprise the alley widened—like some sort of enchanted red sea or something—to let us through. Someone had written in red spray paint on the side of the Smoke Shoppe; the words bled through the darkness, *I left my heart in Sub Rosa*. Arsen lurched the car forward. I couldn't see where we were going. Again, I thought we were going to hit a wall, head-on this time. The tires squealed and suddenly light rolled across the hood of the car; it was pink and patterned like a little girl's nightlight. First's cherry hair seemed to switch on like a red lantern in this new light.

Arsen's gold twinkled on his fingers like jewellery does in television commercials. What I thought was a loading zone or a dead end turned out to be the entrance to an entire street. Second rolled her window all the way down and let her arm drape out of the car. I caught a whiff of spring leaves, but there wasn't a single tree in sight. There were girls decorating the corners. Soft, like watercolour paintings, as if they were carefully cut from a coffee table book and pasted onto the street. While I'd been relieved to drive past the skids hos, I couldn't look away from these women. At a glance, I understood that everything about them was right. They stood as if the sidewalk was laid out just for them. The late-afternoon sun arranged itself beautifully across their shoulders. One of them smiled and pointed as we passed, and I realized I was dressed almost the same as her and I was suddenly pleased with my outfit. The lamplights turned my white dress and boots a pale pinkish hue, like I too had been washed in colour. First had chosen the outfit for me: ankle boots and a stretch lace dress with an empire waist, scalloped sleeves, and little plastic rhinestones glued on in no particular pattern. Basically, I wore an oversized christening dress, cut off several inches above the knee.

"Where you gonna put Little?" asked First.

"She has to do her Dark Days, same as everyone else."

"I was thinking." First usually trailed her "g"s. She was always "thinkin'" or "havin'" or "pleasin'." I wasn't sure yet, but I suspected First's "gs" were reserved for serious discussions.

"Maybe Little should shadow me from the get-go. I can break her in better than the Dark can. You know how I been waiting for a baby girl I could train up for myself. You see, Second doesn't listen to a thing I say anymore."

I turned to Second sitting beside me in the back seat. We'd been ignoring each other the entire ride. She mouthed "bitch" at me again and again until I looked away. Out of the corner of my eye, her white frosted lips continued to lip-sync curses at me. I knew better than to steal a third look. Besides, the scene on the street—the glowing shop windows, the cobblestone sidewalk, the girls—was too captivating to bother with Second's insults.

"Just the other night," First went on, "I asks her to come up an' entertain a couple of live ones, and the minute I turn my back she's walkin' off like she has some other thing to be doin'."

The car swerved slightly as Arsen turned around. "You mind your First," he told Second. First snapped her head from side to side as he spoke.

"I'm sayin', what kinda Glory turns down a live one? Little wouldn't. Would you, Little?" She nodded her head in my direction as if I had already said *yes* to this. "So, if it is okay by you, I could use her right away."

"She won't be of any use if she jinxes you. She has to do her Dark Days. That's the way it is. I'd change it if I could, Mommy."

"There are ways around it. It's not like we don't got money," grumbled First.

"Dark Days can't be bought out," said Arsen.

"With a little bit of smarts they could be. I'd think up something," said First. I had no clue what her argument was, but I was inclined to agree with her. We were leaving the beauties behind us.

"You know where she'll wind up if she don't do her Days," said Arsen, cryptically. First only sighed at this. She had no further debate. Straight ahead more darkness was about to meet our path. Sickness stirred up in my stomach as I began to disappear. All the lamplights at this end of the street were out; some were burnt-out globes at the end of rusted metal poles, others had been smashed and left jagged and broken. Even Second's heavy layer of frosty makeup vanished in the night. She whispered, "You ain't worth light." I inched away from her, pressing up against the car door.

"How much you have her at?" First asked.

"Five."

"Fuck off. Five," Second blurted out. Arsen jerked the car to a halt. I slipped half way off the seat, vinyl squeaking under my thighs.

"Five," Second repeated. "Why does she only have to do five? You had me at a grand."

"Little comes to us pure. I hand-picked her myself. You came from low track," said Arsen.

"Beggin' to get into the Rosa, as I recall," said First. "And I can't wait and wait forever for her, like I had to wait for you."

"Like you even remember how long it took me to get out of the Dark?"

"Twenty-seven nights," First chirped.

"What did you do, write it down in your fucking diary? I don't need to write it down to remember, twenty-seven fucking nights of this place." Second trembled in anger. I couldn't see her. I only felt the back seat vibrating. My dress, barely covering me already, rode up with the vibration. Upholstery stuck to my skin. I reached under me and pulled my g-string underwear from out of my ass crack. What the hell, no one could see me.

"Don't be mad at *us*, Second, honey, if you took your time gettin' out," said First. Her fingernails started tapping the window glass.

"And this little one can do better?" Second asked. "You know what happens to darlings in the Dark? You think she's such a virgin prize. She's virgin stupid, hasn't learned how to fight her way out of a wet paper bag. I bet she gives up before morning, just like the last loser did."

I heard First's nails scrape up the glass with a high-pitched squeak and run across the car ceiling, followed by a yelp from Second. "That mouth will only bring bad luck on yourself," said First. "Or I could square up your fortune right now with the back of my hand if you don't quit. We ain't on the Rosa, so there ain't much to stop me."

"I hear you," grumbled Second. "I hear," she said again. "Let go of my hair."

Arsen opened his door a crack and the inside light flickered on. First was leaning over the back seat, inches away from Second. One of Second's long blonde hairs hung from a prong of First's diamond ring. There was a fist-sized hole in Second's teased hair.

"Are we finished this nonsense?" asked Arsen. First lowered herself back into her seat. Second rifled through her purse for a hair pick and wordlessly fluffed her hair back in place. Arsen surveyed me with his head cocked to one side. A queasiness gripped me, and I wished Second would pick another fight. The arguing might have bought me a few more minutes before I was dumped out of the car.

"We'll see you in the mornin', won't we, Little?"

"Sure." I was revamping my plan: as soon as I was out of the car, I planned on getting far enough away to never see any of them again. For some reason I still stalled, though. Why did it have to be so dark out there?

"This is your stop, Little," said Arsen. "You being a smart girl, I suppose you've already caught on to how this works."

"Dark Days," I said, staring him straight in the face.

"Good girl. It's only 'til you make five bills."

"How do you suppose I do that?" I asked. First chewed her bottom lip; neither she nor Arsen said a thing. "I mean, who's going to come out here? It's completely deserted."

"There won't be many live ones, but there's no competition either. You're the only darling out here," Second said, her voice thin, probably straining with the effort of being slightly kind.

"Get whatever you can, any way you can. There are no rules out here, not like the rest of Sub Rosa." First reached her hand behind her seat and poked my knee with a plump finger.

"You know you can't give her advice." Arsen grabbed First by the elbow and turned her forward in her seat again. "You're on your own, Little."

"We've all had to do it," First reassured.

"Yeah, some of us for twenty-seven damn days."

Arsen faced the vacant windshield in front of him and told me again to get out of the car. I grabbed the little white purse First had bought for me in the city and stepped out into the black. I had barely shut the car door behind me before he pulled away.

The taillights trailed until they were two distant red eyes that winked shut. "Fuck me," I whispered, then immediately felt as if someone had heard me, something was listening. The darkness was so dark it breathed, an ongoing loop of asthmatic gasp and cough. There was the sound of rainwater emptying into a sewer and of winter wind blowing through metal pipes. But there was no rain and no wind.

I discovered the weight of the Dark after taking my first step. It bore down on top of my head and shoulders. I strained to walk, as if I had to drag the darkness behind me. Slowly and instinctually, I moved toward the direction we drove in from, toward the beauty. I figured that course would take me back to where I had come from. Every dozen or so steps I felt the curb brush up against my foot, even though I thought I was walking a perfectly straight line. I righted myself again and again. I started counting my steps (if they could be called steps, since my feet barely lifted from the pavement) but the numbers kept switching around on me: eighty-four became forty-eight. I never reached one hundred.

I still don't know how much of the night I spent just learning how to walk through the Dark. Eventually, I could take on what felt like twenty yards at a time before losing my balance or my breath. Then I got so I could sprint short distances, twisting my ankles each time I ran in my heeled boots. No matter how much ground I covered the darkness didn't let up.

When delirium offered to lead the way, I was too exhausted to decline. I teetered and tripped along and quickly found myself, nose to an unseen wall, swearing and laughing hysterically. The laughter felt like it was being sucked out of me. The night was a finger in my throat, gagging out more and more laughter. My cheeks grew hot, my tongue dried up. I didn't think I'd be able to stop. I slapped myself in the face and it only made me laugh harder. I had to wrestle my possessed head, one arm braced under my chin, the other yanking my hair downward, in order to force my mouth shut. And still there was my laugh, puffing my cheeks out, slipping through my clamped teeth.

When it was done I was slumped against a wall; it was cold and hard like corrugated metal. Around a corner, there was a weak bluish light, the only light. I made my way, quietly and deliberately, toward it. The closer I got the more my eyes adjusted, and I could make out the barn-like building I had walked beside, ghosts of steam rising out of high windows, rust patches on the steel. I got closer still, and the sidewalk glittered under the blue light. I was encouraged by this until I realized that I was walking on tiny shards of broken glass. The blue light was a halogen bulb in a wire frame cage, plastered with dingy feathers and dead flies, and hung in an alcove that had been used as a urinal more than once. I stared into the light for a good while, until I could make out the delicate opalescent wings stuck to the bulb. I wasn't so bad off. At least I wasn't one of the fried black flies that flew too close to the light.

That light was enough to see myself—my pretty boots and dress. What I needed was a man in a plush car to carry me out of there. I looked good enough for a stretch limousine. I would have given anything for a ride and a bit of money. I imagined crisp bills between my fingers. The scent of leather upholstery, like in Arsen's car.

Like Arsen's scent. He smelled a bit like leather. Leather and toasted vanilla pipe tobacco, smoking, not in the canister. And maybe of black pepper, and maybe grapefruit. I never considered his scent until he was naked; even then I'm not sure I had noticed. I remembered it when I couldn't see worth shit and all I could smell was piss. It was his scent that kept filling my nose. I wished he had touched me more so that his scent was left on my skin. I wondered if he'd come after me. If he'd feel a pinprick or hear a buzz in his ear as I stepped into the car that would take me away.

Except there were no polished Lincolns, no sports coupes, no cars cruising the street. On both sides of my peripheral vision, small unknowns darted and crept. For comfort, I counted them like sheep. I forced myself to be happy whenever I could keep my numbers in order. Simple victories. I reached a whopping 174 before admitting to myself that I was really counting how many times I felt afraid. I wanted a drink. A sip of whisky to relax my breathing and warm me up. I had never been cold in August before. I squeezed my hands under my armpits to keep them warm.

Nothing changed for hours. The only tangible measure of time passing was how tired my feet grew inside my high-heeled ankle boots. I stood on one foot to give the other a break, then switched. Each raised foot tingled as I wiggled my toes. I squatted for a while, tucking my knees into the stretch-lace of my dress, rocking from heel to toe. I remembered doing that when I was little; squatting down into a tiny ball and pulling my T-shirts over my legs. I used to pretend my kneecaps were breasts. I used to also stuff rolled socks, or Tupperware bowls, or anything round that would fit up my shirt. I couldn't wait to be a woman. What did I know?

I walked in circles so many times I was surprised the sidewalk didn't form a whirlpool. I would have paced, but I didn't want to wander out of the blue light. The pain in my feet gradually did outweigh the fear. It climbed up my legs and nested in the small of my back. I could not continue standing, but I refused to sit on the urine-soaked concrete, so I stepped out of the blue light a little to search the ground for a cardboard box or newspaper, anything to sit on and rest. Eyes straining, I imaged things that weren't really there. A crushed pop can became a baby's shoe; a mound of dirt, a fetal puppy dog, lifeless. At last, I found a strip of clear plastic that was somewhat wet, but not with urine, which was good enough for me. I laid it down under the light. The pavement was chilly through the layer of plastic. Still, it was a relief from standing. I propped my little purse under me like a cushion, leaned back onto my tailbone and gazed up at the splinter of a moon. A waxing moon.

After so many nights outside I had learned to identify the moon's different faces. By the size of it I guessed there'd be at least ten or eleven days before it was full. I remember telling myself I had better be out of the Dark before the moon was full. It was as subtle as that—I looked up at the moon and my plan shifted from running off at the first available chance to earning that $500. I wanted back into Arsen's big bed, or even in the back seat of his car. I let myself daydream about him, my legs relaxing toward the ground as I imagined his silk bedding when he tucked me in. And I visualized the money I was supposed to be making too; five brown bills with prime ministers' faces etched in raised pixels and Canadian geese trapped, mid-air.

I suppose I should have hated him. Hate, however, would have done nothing to improve my situation. In the Dark you take whatever comforts there are. Even though it was him that stuck me there, I still wanted him. I was comforted by want. The lack of light and city sounds made for vivid musing. When I wasn't chock-full of fear, the Dark became a void for my thoughts to empty into. It was simply easier to desire. I imagined the home that I had been promised, plotting out elaborate floor plans and expensive furniture. I made lists of the gifts First said I would receive—chandelier earrings and cut flowers, maybe my own TV. Glimpses of places I'd been appeared in my imagination;

I'd return to them wearing a fancy dress in my daydreams. Always Arsen would arrive to carry me off. I could almost feel the warmth of his hands through the sheer cloth of my make-believe dress. Would he sling me over his shoulder or hook his arm under my knees? Sex was part of my imagination for the first time, although I still didn't have enough experience then to conjure specific pictures or words. Instead, sex entered me as a series of undeveloped sensations. It crept up my spine in shivers. It warmed me so I could forget about the cold concrete permeating through the makeshift plastic seat where I sat.

When I opened my eyes there was a man lumbering down the street toward me. He zigzagged up the sidewalk, slipped off of the curb, and, with deliberate effort, lifted his leg with two hands and put himself right again. I smelled the beer before I could distinguish any other feature about him.

"Looks like you're having a rough night," I spoke up, though he was only several paces away. Drunks need to be spoken to slowly and loudly.

"Nah," he bellowed back. "It's a good night. Every night is a good night."

"Yeah. Betcha I can make your night even better." He was not the gentleman I was waiting for. He was the only person I'd seen in hours. Isolation had greatly lowered my prospects.

"That's why I'm here." He held his hand out. I watched it wobble mid-air for a short while before I shook it. He smiled at me with the same smile all piss-drunks have. A watery smile, as if his face had turned to liquid and the corners of his mouth were treading water. I knew this routine, I reminded myself. I knew the languid passions of alcoholics. This one embodied all the characteristics: his eyes, unfocused, fell off me, then struggled back to me again; his legs trembled as if negotiating with gravity; he smelled worse than other drunks, more like a corpse.

We didn't leave the blue-light building. I made him give me the money there so I could count the meagre forty dollars in the dim light. All fives. The chilly air nipped at my already cold hands as I handled the blue money. I leaned him up against the steel wall and lowered myself. The ground was sharp with broken glass, so I knelt on his shoes. Pressing my body tight to his legs, I wrapped my arms behind his knees, the vice-grip of blowjobs. He was easy. Banged his head on the steel wall a couple times, hard enough to have a lump in the morning, and then his body went slack. I released him back into the night. I couldn't help feeling a little proud at how quickly I turned him over.

Another two lurked around me; maybe they had picked up a scent. Like the one before, they came trembling along the sidewalk on foot. Their eyes stumbled the same way, loose in their sockets. There was no introductory greeting, no bartering or flirting. Drunk, each of them. Soiled fingers, stubble-soiled faces. Each reached into his button-down shirt to retrieve crumpled money in small bills. They had the distinct death stink of the first guy. The hardest part was swallowing my gag reflex.

One more arrived, or maybe he was the first one coming back for another go. It was hard to tell them apart in that light. I barely made out a few more standing in the darkness, the same hunched stance. One by one I latched onto them as they tripped into my boudoir of blue light.

And they kept coming. Circling closer. "One at a time," I said just before two of them were on me.

I was soon buried in limp-bodied men. I felt my little purse squished beneath my left shoulder as I struggled, and was simultaneously relieved and terrified that it wasn't my money they were after.

My face was forced to the ground in such alcoholic slow motion that I could distinguish each nick and callous on the hands that held me down. Careless fingers pushed into my mouth to block my screaming. A thumb in my eye.

My legs were pulled open no matter how wildly I kicked. The fight was useless, but I struggled until exhausted anyway, until the only thing I was able to move was the wheezing breath inside my chest. More than two pairs of hands worked over me. What sounded like a small crowd of feet scratched at the sidewalk.

I waited to be raped.

I had always expected that this would happen to me. I had spent so much time secretly scared of rape that in that moment I was hardly even afraid anymore. Or rather I had moved on to my next fear—what happens when it's over? Would I be left there, alone? Injured? Or worse?

A set of knuckles clunked against my thighs, over and over. A set of teeth bit my breast through my dress, failing to find my nipple. A man dry-humped my face; his belt buckle caught my hair in clumps. They couldn't seem to connect, failed to enter me, grunting and cursing at my body.

I heard one say, "I'm gonna rip. I'm gonna rip ..." My skin raked and pounded on. "I'm gonna rip," I heard again, and, in my mind, I filled in *rip into you, rip you in half, rip your heart out*. But the speaker never finished his sentence; maybe he didn't know who, or what, he was tearing at. I could have been anything at the bottom of their heap.

The drunk latched onto my head released me to undo his pants. He let out a series of yips like he was the first man to discover his penis. A second man stood up to do the same, then a third. I saw them grab themselves as their pants slid around their knees. I squirmed toward the opening this made in the fence of hands. I managed to flip over to my stomach, kicking and shouting, making sounds I'd never heard myself make before. Loud and deep sounds that seemed to erupt from the centre of the earth. Another man let go of my arm to grapple for my face and silence me. I bit down hard on his finger and he reeled back, lifting me upright as he jerked away. I found my feet beneath me and ran, almost tripping on the first step as I discovered my right boot had been removed. I went on running, desperately clacking the pavement with every other stride.

That was when I spotted it in the distance: a light that appeared to have no source, like a reflection bouncing off water or a mirror. The light was encouraging enough, but then the glints and sparks fused together and took the form of a girl. I didn't bother thinking this was an impossibility. I decided this shining girl was there for the sole purpose of saving me. She would save me from the drove of men. I ran toward her and she shone even brighter. I followed her around the corner, then another corner. Her beacon illuminated a break in a chainlink fence, and I eagerly went through it. Her light ricocheted off twisted iron and rusted metal drums. She led me through some sort of scrap yard to a row of jumbo tractor tires leaned against one another.

"Hide here," she whispered in a low vibrato. The junk metal around her chimed as she spoke. I climbed inside the tractor tires, crawled to the third one in and curled up, fetal. I soon heard the men's voices, the chainlink fence rattling; one man vomited close enough that I got a whiff of beer-turned-rot.

Long after the noises stopped completely, and early morning started to usher in small scraps of pale purple, I peeked outside for my glowing angel. Bits of muted dawn littered the scrap yard; there was not one inch of smooth sheet metal or unbroken glass. Everything was covered with rust and jagged rifts. As Second had said, there was nothing around worth being lit. I eased back into the tractor tire. I tasted blood, tonguing the cuts inside my mouth. There was a slice inside my lower lip where my own teeth must have cut through the flesh. My fingertips looked ink-stained. My sock was completely black. I tore it off to find the skin underneath black too. "Foot, where are you?" I asked out loud. My voice sounded so unfamiliar then. I peeked outside the tires again to see if someone was out there. Empty.

Fishing through the purse First packed for me, I retrieved a wet-nap. Frantically, I rubbed from toe to heel with the damp cloth until it broke down into shreds. My skin was still masked in black. I pulled my foot up to my chest and held it like a baby. No one heard me sing a little lullaby; I'm not even sure how I knew the words to the song, but they fell unconscious out of my mouth. I was tired enough to fall asleep in my rubber cradle.

When I next looked out, it was the same—purple and just as dark. The clouds were thin inky wisps waiting for the sun to get itself up. I heard First calling my name. My plan to run off was an official failure. There was no rich trick, no getaway car. I had less than when I came, a missing boot, a torn dress. I didn't move. *Let her worry that I'm dead*, I decided stubbornly. Arsen chimed in with his choirboy voice. There wasn't a hint of distress or anger as he called; only a steady baritone note echoing, "Little, Little, Little." His voice reminded me that I was hungry and sore, and I certainly didn't want to stay where I was. I tumbled out of the tires toward the street and slipped through the same hole in the chainlinks. The frayed fence caught my lace dress. Arsen found me cursing and tugging my sleeve from a snare of curled metal.

"Baby girl," he said, scooping me up in his arms. I heard fabric tear as he lifted me. "Another minute and I woulda been worried." He was *almost* worried. His hands almost touched my bare skin as he lifted me. First rushed in, pressing herself into us for a group hug.

"Dear Lord, what happened to you, Little?" she asked and squished me firmly. "We've been lookin' and lookin'." I imagined she was being melodramatic. But they truly had been looking for me all day. It was two in the afternoon when they found me. Daytime never reaches the

Dark. After such a long search it was little wonder First was so flustered. She squeezed and cooed at me. She rocked me in her arms. Just when I was about to give in to her comforts and relax a little, her face twisted up and she eased away. I slid down from between Arsen and First to the ground. They both took a step back. First held my hand in hers, tightly. The two of them stared hard at my blackened fingertips.

"Let's get you home," said First. She turned and marched, dragging me behind her. Arsen walked, without a word, beside us.

First put me in the front seat of Arsen's car. A pink cardboard and cellophane box filled with tiny powdered doughnuts was sitting on the dash. Arsen smiled weakly as he offered me the box. I tore into them, white icing sugar dusting my dark fingertips.

"What's with darling in the front?" Second asked as First squashed herself into the back beside her. "Is she half dead or something?"

"What the fuck do you care," I said with a mouth full of doughnut. Arsen smiled a real smile at this, that quasi-embarrassed grin that appeared each time I swore. He laid his palm, face up, on my knee and I was quick to put my hand in his. He rubbed at my fingertips. A tickle of pins-and-needles spread through my hand.

"Yeah," First said, long after the moment had already passed. "What the fuck do you care?" Outside, the scenery was less threatening then I imagined it would be. Rows of brick and rusted metal and grimy glass, buildings so sad it was no wonder the sun skipped over the place.

"I bet she didn't even break, eh, darling?" Second started in again. First cleared her throat to cue me. She kicked at the back of my seat. Second laughed an artificial laugh, then quit and still no one said anything. "You dumb bitch, *break* means did you make money? Meaning, last night I broke four times, I had four tricks, I got paid four times," Second finally said, sounding exasperated.

"You broke five times," First corrected her.

"Nah, ah. Four. And I broke for a bill a go. Didn't even have to drop my drawers."

"Oh my, what big money, and no pussy," First faux-exclaimed. "I'm still sure I seen you follow that Eddie Junior through the back door of No's Smoke Shoppe. By my calculation that's five."

"Shut up, Candy."

"Oh, that's right; he don't pay you, do he? You just love that boy so much, you give it away."

"It ain't like that," Second said, raising her raspy voice.

"Eddie from the Smoke Shoppe. You sure, Candy?" Arsen pulled the car to the curb, left the motor running like a drum roll.

"Oh, they been goin' on for a while, as far as I can tell."

"Ed was warning me about the cops. They were parked down the street from the shop. I was gonna tell you later when there weren't no little ears listening," said Second.

"Cops around Sub Rosa," First balked. "Haven't you figured out yet you're not in the skids no more? Do you even know where you are?" Arsen continued scouring my fingertips with his. I watched the black wear away, my fingers underneath turned red from the friction.

"Ed seen them. You can ask him."

"First is right." Arsen turned around to face Second. "Glories never have to worry about police. And Eddie can come to me if he thinks he sees something."

"You keep away from him," added First.

"We was only talking."

"You have me to talk to, Second, honey. You don't need nobody else." In the rear view mirror I saw First's hand on Second's shoulder like a C-clamp.

"Tell me something good, Little," Arsen said, changing the subject. "You make any money last night?"

"Arsen, please, it's her first night," said First.

I opened my mouth to tell him no. Before I said anything a series of images funnelled out of my head: a stiff jean zipper, coarse stubble on a chin, then nothing but the blank underside of pavement. I palmed my forehead as a migraine shot up between my eyes.

"We don't expect you to break yet," First said quietly.

"Two hundred and ten," I said. I wasn't sure where that figure came from, but when I opened my purse, dug around for the filthy money, and counted it, the total was two hundred and ten, exactly. I was ecstatic. I wanted to toss it in the air like a Hollywood actress.

Second expelled an "f", like she was about to curse, then sighed instead.

"Girls always blank their first few Dark Days," First told me.

"Everyone blanks," said Second.

"Everyone but my Little," said Arsen. "My little hero."

Arsen took up my hand again, gave it one last squeeze, and plucked the money from me. I knew it would be like that. That I would simply pass over the money. What would I have done with $210, anyway? Get a room at a rooming house for a week? Find a new bar that served buck-a-beer? I would have felt ashamed to go back to drinking and moving around from place to place. I bet I would have forever heard Arsen's voice asking, "Why put yourself through this?" Even though it was Arsen who sent me into that darkness, I still wanted to impress him. It was almost worth it to have him call me his little hero. I crumpled the empty, sugar-lined doughnut box.

I fell asleep in lukewarm dirty bath water. First woke me by reaching into the tub and pulling the plug. Water emptied with a gurgle.

"Arsen says you can come in the bed with us." She laid a towel on the bathtub rim. "Or you can sleep on the sofa if you like." Arsen had dropped Second off at their apartment; First claimed she was too worried about me to go with her. I wasn't sure if she wanted to take care of me or if she just didn't want Arsen to.

"You two don't have to share the bed with me," I said.

"Yes, of course we'll share, Little. There's plenty of room. Arsen don't stay in bed long, anyway." The last of the water drained from the tub. I gave First a polite smile, but she didn't leave the room. I held the towel in front of me like a screen as I stood, then wrapped it fully around my body as I patted myself dry.

"There's no reason to be shy with Mommy," she said, reaching around me to dry my back. I was motionless as she wrung the water from my hair. "You're going to have some good bruises when you wake up. Your back is one big scratch. Not deep, thank God. Whatever got at you didn't go deep." She took the towel and ran it up and down my legs, making me dizzy. I don't know many hours it had been since I'd slept.

Out of habit, I folded my arms in front of my chest; the scratched skin on my back itched with the simple movement. I'd been punctured. There were holes in me that weren't there before. My memory was just the same—scratched and full of holes. An image or two raced through my head. But they were only fragments of the night, uncertain as the things I'd imagined darting around my peripheral vision in the Dark. "I can't remember what got me," I said, sleepily.

First wrapped me in her arms, suddenly. The towel had dropped to the tile floor. I was stiff and naked as she hugged me. "It's all over now. Even your foot's fine now, see?" She jerked my foot out from under me to show me. "You're fine. Just fine," she repeated.

In bed, First situated herself in between Arsen and me. I curled into a ball at the edge of the bed, but she rolled me into her and tucked me under her arm. Unable to fight sleep, I dozed off in the warm barricade of her body. If her torso had been hollow I could have crawled into it like a tractor tire and slept there.

V

"Leave her be," Arsen said. First was one step into the room; her silhouette crowded the doorframe.

"She's awake," she called back, even though my eyelids were closed tight in mock-sleep.

"Leave her," he repeated, and First backed away on her tiptoes.

Later he escorted her to the door; their murmuring dragged on before I heard her high heels down the hall and him draw the chain lock into the metal slot. Toro whined for a while after she left.

Later he bent me over the back of his living room sofa and begged me not to leave him. There was a particular desperation in his voice that had me willing to agree. I reached behind me to touch him as he fucked me, but only grazed his moving hips with my fingers. He was impossibly far away for being inside me. I frantically kicked the back of the sofa, buried my face into its buttery leather, opened my mouth to taste its stale skin as stand-in for Arsen's absent tastes and textures. Noise. That time, at least, he made noise. His moans were like a vocal warm-up, notes ascending a scale.

And later we were in his car, and I wondered how the day was already spent. He took the rich route: the shopping district, restaurant row, the boulevard lined with big-windowed houses. He had the city mapped by capital, by desirability. Even while we were in the skids he could locate each and every heritage building. He toured me past the first Buddhist temple, a neo-Gothic Catholic church, recited mini-histories of the Steelworkers' Memorial and the fabric stores in Little India. This excess of facts glazed over me like icing. "It's important to remember these things," he said. "That way, if a live one—a customer—talks about them, you'll have something to say. You'll be working on Sub Rosa in no time."

How I would sop up those city sites now, waterlog myself in them, but they meant very little to me at the time.

Only one story really sunk in: *the story of us*. We did not go past the Legion where he and I met; Arsen said Front Street would ruin the drive. But he put on his bedtime-story voice as he told me that above the Legion pub there was a great hall where live bands used to play while married couples danced the polka. Except for the rare Polish seniors' folk dance or Ukrainian Orthodox church bazaar, the hall now remained empty. Arsen said he'd seen the can lights hung despondently from the rafters, their cellophane gels of red and blue covered in dust. He spoke about it with such preciousness that I felt slightly ashamed for the nights I'd spent in a crowd of drunks, all of us oblivious to the bigger and better place right above our heads. That vacant hall is where Arsen imagined our first meeting, or so he claimed. His telling never explained what force or intuition led him past the Legion that night. He was there to find me, period. "Why bother with explanations," he often said, accusing my questions of ruining the moment. "It just happened." I didn't argue. I didn't argue over his image of me standing in a solitary shaft of white light, laid out on the oak dance floor like sleeping beauty, though that's not what he found. The lights were dusty and unused. The dance floor scuffed. And while he searched the hall, I was below, a mess with my shirt half off—the antithesis of fairytale beautiful. He doesn't tell that part. In Arsen's version of *the story of us* his call was still echoing through the empty hall, forever seeking me out. His desire could increase the value of just about anything.

Like the night before, the city I knew fell away and we drove the strip I'd learned is called Sub Rosa. The blind alley bedside No's snuck up on me, though once we were through it, I wasn't surprised. It felt normal, easy. Girls marked each corner like statues, triumphant and ideal. Again, I wished Arsen would have driven slower so I could have gotten a better look. "The Glories," he said under his breath. Superstitious: Arsen firmly believed leaking any information about Sub Rosa would further jinx my chances in the Dark. There was no way the Glories could be concealed, however. To see them is to know you're in a different place. Elsewhere.

First was the most beautiful. Her garish size suited Sub Rosa. She stood like a vamp monument—a slab of red satin and leather—in front of a warehouse-sized pawnshop. Neon lights that read GOLD and DIAMONDS bounced off the metal panel doors, giving First a backdrop of flashing pink. Poised a few paces away from her was Second, a brush stroke of blonde. We just about passed them, then Arsen halted the car. He stuck his head out the driver's side window and First met him with a kiss on the lips. Her hand wrapped around his face as they stole a quick moment to cluck at each other. My own hand balled into fist, a vein in my wrist rose up blue.

She stretched her arm into the car, rapped her knuckles on the dash a few times to get my attention and dropped a pair of white stretch gloves. "So you stay warm tonight, Little. It's gonna be cold." I suspected they were also to prevent my fingertips from turning black again. I shoved the gloves into my purse with the condoms and wet-naps. I also had new shoes and long white socks that covered the scrapes on my knees. I wore the same lace dress, bloodstains on the back scrubbed to a vague pink, a little rip above my left breast.

"The record for making it out of the Dark is five days," Arsen told me as we pulled away.

"You think I can beat that?"

"You'd be a celebrity if you did." I was greedy to hear more about it.

Arsen didn't indulge me. "You're already my hero. I've never met a girl like you before, Little. I think you can do this, if you want it."

A streetlamp blipped. Then we passed the sad row of burnt out lamps. Then the only the light was on Arsen's dashboard. I sat there gawking like a dummy at the darkness. I had somehow forgotten how frightening it was.

"Dark Days," I mumbled. Arsen had nothing more to say, so I pushed open the door, savouring the overhead light for a moment before I stepped out. "Don't go," I said out loud after he had pulled away. The brake lights flashed and I hoped I had some sort of special power. "Come back," I tried, but Arsen's car slipped from sight.

The air hummed a continuous "L", as if it might have said my name. Far off, there was clinking, like a glass wind chime. I headed for a glowing blue light.

I'll stay right here, I decided, situating myself under the dim spotlight. Lying on the sidewalk was a single plastic rhinestone, out-sparkling the grains of broken glass. I bent to pick it up and shivered. I became abruptly aware of how raw my throat was from screaming the night before. A lump of hard glue marked the spot on my dress where the rhinestone had come from. The blue light pretended it knew nothing about what happened to me here; it sat in its cage innocently. "I'm not hanging out with you again, asshole," I told it. I left my fallen rhinestone where it was. It was jinxed, as Arsen would say. That whole spot was jinxed.

But a hundred paces into the Dark I was overcome by the hum and heaviness of the night and I turned again toward the blue light. Maybe it wasn't such a bad thing. From a distance, it was merely a dingy light doing the best it could to struggle against the pitch-black. I felt a strange sympathy for it, but as I approached again a black moth flew in from the Dark and flung itself against the hot bulb. The moth squealed, or rather its body squealed as it soldered to the light, and I suddenly remembered the chorus of zombie men with too much detail. *No,* I definitely would not go back there.

I inched along, shutting my eyes for several steps, then opening them in hopes that the dark would be less so. Now and then I caught a glimpse of near-white. Each time, this startled me, and each time I discovered it was my reflection as I passed a cracked factory window. I heard footsteps and convinced myself it must be unseen litter blowing in the nonexistent breeze. Being alone in the dark was terrifying; the idea that someone was nearby was worse.

"I got a pair," a voice hissed, close to me. I jumped backwards, fists swinging. My left hand swiped the night, hit no one. My right collided with a rocklike surface; there wasn't the thud that comes when punching a wall, just the faint whimper of my own bones cracking. I retracted my fist, felt my knuckles for splits or trickling blood. "I can't hurt you … much," the voice said. A strange radiance bled through the darkness. A glimmering silhouette: slender arms and legs, a long neck, no face, no clothes, no visible features. Then gone. A pitter-patter on the sidewalk, invisible feet.

"You're my angel?" I reached for the free space where the girl/ the thing/the angel who saved me had been. A cold current wrapped around my wrist and solidified, like cement being poured.

"Live ones. I got two." Its voice had softened to a woman's tongue, a kind warble. She tugged my arm. "Don't be scared," she said even more softly. "Little new, I show you to the ride." For a single second there was a glint of luminosity again before she turned blacker than the night.

I was led by a hole, a tear in the sky. Against her blackness the surroundings seemed weak. I didn't try to pull away. I didn't ask again if she was my angel. I already knew I'd have no luck with either.

A truck appeared a few feet down the street. I wondered how long it had been there and why I hadn't noticed it before. Radio leaked out the open windows. Not music; the static-scratched nasal voice of a ballgame announcer. A chorus of cheers crackled at us as we approached the driver's side; somewhere a game had been won. Two men hooted and waved, overlooking us altogether. I caught the glow of a wristwatch; the wearer beat his hand on the truck's ceiling.

"Let's have a look," one said finally, pushing the door open. The overhead light clicked on; two heads peeked out at us, mumbling to each other as they squinted to inspect us. I barely looked back at them. Instead, I scanned the dark face, the almost-absent beauty beside me. She had huge eyes and sparkling dewdrops on her curled eyelashes. That was all I could recognize in the short time before the man on the passenger side stepped out of the truck and ushered me up the tall chrome running board. "Stick with this ride," the strange girl whispered as I climbed into the seat. The overhead light went out and the passenger slammed the door shut behind me.

"Welcome aboard," said the driver. Tiny red and green lights along the dash were enough for me to see him wriggle out of his pants.

"What about the other girl?" I asked, panicked, like a kid who'd lost her mommy at the shopping mall.

"I won't have that hocus-pocus in the truck," he said. "I only come down here for my buddy. Keep him out of trouble." Out the front window, I saw a long shadow crawl onto the hood. The passenger stood before the truck and bowed his head down, burying it in what must have been the oil spill of her hair.

"You look new. Brand new?" the driver asked me.

"Yup."

"I wasn't going to see a girl, not here. But you look normal. Really small, but I guess you're just young, still." He sat, wide-legged, with his pants balled on the floor. I started to lift my dress up, then unsure if I should, I paused holding my dress up stupidly around my waist. "It's a fluke I have money on me," the driver continued. He grabbed a hundred-dollar bill from off the dash. "This is for you."

"Thanks," I forced myself to say as I took his money. The bill was crisp. I remembered it was a Friday, probably this man's payday. I spread myself over his legs, teased the tip of his cock with my tongue for a second before my blitzkrieg blowjob.

"Slow." He pushed me off him after a minute. "Let's slow down." He tugged at my dress like a boy in a playground. I just stared at him, my eyes growing accustomed to the darkness at the most inopportune time. He had thick eyebrows that curled at the ends, a wide forehead. "Okay, I'll let you do it," he said, retracting his hands and holding them up, arrested. "Please, I only want to see your tits." My chest tightened as I slipped out of the scalloped sleeves and let my dress fall around my waist. The man reached for one of my nipples, caught it between his thumb and forefinger and guided it to his open mouth. I knelt in front of him as he sucked my left breast up and spit it back out. I could have kneed him in the balls and darted away. He wouldn't have chased me with his pants off. Or maybe he would have; no one could see him. He fumbled under my dress for my panties, taking them down. I almost tipped over as he tried to get them past my knees.

Outside, the other man was fucking emptiness. Half his body was lost in her. She sat up, wrapped her arms and legs around him, swallowing him up. I could see the whites of his eyes through the darkness. His mouth was open in a mimed scream. They were almost silent. Even the hood of the car bobbed noiselessly. The man below me wasn't loud either; like a small dog dreaming, he only made little whimpers and growls. I was as far away from him as I could be; my head grazed the ceiling as he lifted his body up to me. It occurred to me I should have touched this man. At least run my fingers through his hair. I kept my hands firmly pressed against the driver's side window. The sensation of his legs brushing up against mine nauseated me and I spread my legs apart until my right foot was hooked on the steering wheel. The horn squeaked out a half-beep as I shifted into place. The man squeaked too;

he latched onto my waist and lowered me to meet him. I felt the coarse curled hair on his legs brush against my thighs.

The passenger was gone. I leaned into the windshield to relocate him.

"You're watching her, eh. Scariest thing you'll ever see," the man beneath me said. I couldn't tell if he was finished or not.

"Your friend is gone," I said.

The man gaped into the darkness. "Jake," he yelled out the window. "Buddy?" I couldn't see my angel anymore, either. Not even a spark. "Shit. I told him not to fucking go off with that freaky bitch."

"I know where she is," I lied and patted his shoulder, the only touch I'd offered him. My purse and underwear were on the passenger seat floor beside his pants. His wallet was there too, poking out of his back pocket. *Idiot*, I thought. If we drove around searching we would surely have found our way back to the city again. It wasn't his first visit to the Dark: he must have known the way. That was my wish, wasn't it? A ride and bit of money. All I needed to do was stay in the passenger seat.

Instead, I hopped down from the running boards, fixing my dress as I put some distance between the truck and me. "Jake," I called for effect. The man was scrambling back into his pants. "I bet they're over here. She likes this alley," I said without turning back. I raced behind the zigzag of building, tracing my hand along the rough plaster and metal exteriors. As I wove through narrow alleys and tight spaces between fences, I heard a dog barking or a man yelling, I didn't know which, but I picked up the pace. After I rounded several corners and raced across a couple streets, I found my scrap yard.

From inside the rubber safety of the tractor tires, I frantically swabbed off the man-residue from my legs, stomach, and chest. My nipples buzzed like his fingers were still on them. But I had his wallet. I fingered the soft leather in the dark, took out what felt like all the money, and tossed the rest far back into the tunnel of tires. I didn't want his licence or any photo ID near me when the dim morning light came. In no time at all, I'd already forgotten what he looked like. When I re-emerged from the tires, the whole experience had faded to a few glimpses of chrome and skin. The only thing for certain was I was getting used to the Dark. I had run through it. I had found my way.

The rest of the night followed this pattern. I moved through the Dark with increasing ease and absence of details. Almost audible words. Scarce sightings of men skulking, pacing. The cherry glow of a cigarette. The smell of gasoline. The arm wrapped around my waist— never really there. Each time I re-counted my money I seemed to re-member less and less how I got it. The blue bills I tucked deep in my purse. I hated to think of what I had done for as little as five dollars. The other money, the green and red, I balled up in my fist to keep my hand warm.

My angel slunk up beside me as I was unconsciously picking more rhinestones off my dress. The collection of plastic gems sparkled in my hand as she lit up beside me. I got the feeling she had been beside me for a while. "Why are you still here?" Her voice was a strange croon: an old record that hadn't been played since forever ago.

"Yeah, what a long night," I said to her, as though she had a regular face, as though I could talk to her like a regular girl. "I hope my ride picks me up soon."

"You missed your ride," she said. "You missed it."

"I don't know where he is," I said slowly, so she'd understand. "I'm still waiting for my ride to take me home. Well, not home, but out of here."

"Where's home?" she asked. "Forgotten already?" I imagined I would go home with Arsen like I had the night before. There was sad-ness or maybe disdain in her voice. Maybe she wanted to come with me? It had to be lonely for her; she couldn't possibly exist in daylight, walk or eat or sleep side by side with other people. The thin spaghetti straps of her dress looked like scars along her shoulders; her parted lips were red like lava waiting in a crack in the earth. She had saved my life. She helped me find a man with money. She showed me the one safe place in this Darkness. And I was ready to ditch her the minute Arsen arrived to pick me up.

"Do you have any place to go?" I asked her, although I really didn't want to know the answer. Her home must have been more awful than I could imagine.

"Do you have a place?" she said. "I can take you."

"Look, I could come find you. Maybe I could come back and find you, later on or something." I reached out to pat what I hoped was her shoulder.

"Cold," she said.

"Oh, you're cold." I scrambled through my purse for the white gloves. "Here put these on." Her hands were warm; they turned almost hot as I held them. I realized that she wasn't cold at all, it was my touch that felt cold to her, but I helped her into the gloves anyway, not knowing what else to do.

Her glow went out as she left. Only a pair of white hands floated away and disappeared. I didn't shout a farewell into the Dark. I was still too scared to draw attention to myself. So I stood silently replaying our conversation in my head until our words seemed even more diluted and dim.

Arsen arrived well before the sky changed to navy blue, long before it turned purple. I recognized the particular hum of his motor before I spotted his car. Two warm muffins and a tiny glass bottle of chocolate milk sat in the passenger seat.

"You got a split in your lip," he said as I ate.

I found the cut he was talking about with my tongue. I put down the muffin; crumbs rolled down my leg to the seat. "I wonder when I did that?"

"How much did you make?"

"I can't even remember splitting my lip." My thumb sunk into the muffin, more crumbs rolled off my leg.

"That's good. It must not hurt if you didn't notice."

"But I don't think anything hit my face," I said, distressed. "I *can't* remember."

"I hear you, Little." Arsen was calm. "Start counting the money. Don't worry about your lip for a moment." I couldn't have cared less about the money, so I unzipped my purse, dramatically dumping a pile of money and condoms over my lap. I expected Arsen to lose his temper at this. "Don't you eat that muffin now that you got dirty money on it," he said. "It's too bad. I bought them at that fancy café near my house that you like."

"Where?"

"Café Amici."

"What? I don't know that place," I said. Arsen thrummed the steering wheel with his thumbs, abandoning the dead-end café conversation as he eyed the bills in my lap. "There's over three hundred there."

I piled the money on my left knee. Before I gave him the report I peeled off the outer layer of muffin and took another bite. "Three hundred and sixty," I confirmed, mouth full.

"Dark Day girls never make that kind of money," he said, slowing the car, but not parking it. "You did stay in the Dark the whole time, right?"

"No, I took a quick trip to Disneyland. Sorry I forgot to buy you a Mickey Mouse hat."

"No need for lip. Just answer my question."

"Believe me, I would have left if I could."

"You are a very special girl, Little. The best." As soon as he said this

I recalled the wallet I'd thrown deep in the tractor tires. I hadn't forgotten everything after all. But I wasn't about to tell Arsen I had stolen. "You'll be a Sub Rosa legend," he was telling me.

"I'm not going back there, then?"

Arsen pulled the car over. Turned the engine off completely. "Your dowry is paid. You never have to go back. You're my third wife now." He said a short list of vows: how he would care for me and keep me always—mostly recycled material he'd already used during sex, but I listened all the same until I was nodding in happy agreement. Hearing such sentiments was new to me; I was eager to hear them repeated. He stroked the cleft under my nose with his pinkie. Traced the outline of my lips. My jaw, clenched from the weight of the Dark, went slack and I parted my lips a little and tasted the salt of his fingers, resting my cheek on his wrist. He gathered up my hair, twirling coils of it around his fingers.

"Damn," he said, and suddenly forced my head against the seat. "Sorry, sorry, Little. You got another spot of black behind your ear."

Beneath my ear, where my jawbone begins, I felt a patch of a heat rash, prickly and hot. "What's wrong with me?"

"It washed off your foot. Your head will be fine too," he said with assurance, although when he removed his hand from my head he held it the air, as if it were soiled. I caught him wiping it on the underside of his seat before he returned it to the wheel. He turned the engine on again. "We'll get you cleaned up before First comes home."

"What is it? I want to know what's wrong with me."

"It's nothing I haven't seen before."

"Good for you. I still don't know what the hell it is."

"I told you already, fresh girls like you are jinxed. The Dark can charm you in many ways. Some girls lose their voices or go blind for a short while. Most get Dark amnesia, like you got. I picked Second up one morning wearing nothing but a sheet of bubble wrap, she had no idea, walked right up to me smiling, 'I made $150,' she tells me. Wasn't until we were in the elevator back home that she figures out she's got no clothes on."

"I saw a girl who is completely black," I chimed in, happy to have my own Dark Days tale to tell.

"Jellyfish?" Arsen muttered.

"Who's Jellyfish? Was that the name of my angel?"

Again Arsen ignored my question for a while, jingling his keys. "Where do you want to go to celebrate?"

"You know her?"

"Know who? Ah, Little, you've got Dark amnesia for sure," he said. "Now don't let your imagination go filling in the blanks. Besides, that was the hard part; now that it's over I can show you your fancy new home."

"But this girl helped me, Arsen. If you know her, then we should go find her. She wanted to come home with me, I'm pretty sure," I poked the hot spot behind my ear, bent to look at the black smear there in the passenger's side mirror. I wondered if my angel was as dark as the mark I had. Or darker. "I'll show you. Let's go back and find her."

"Little, the Dark isn't anything to trouble yourself over. Forget about anything you saw there. All we have to do now is celebrate."

"I know what I saw in the Dark," I said under my breath. "You only drive by in your car."

Arsen took up my hair once more, leashed it tight in his fist. The skin on the left side of my face stretched with force of it. "Never question what I've seen. Never, ever question what I know." He held me there until he was sure I had fully absorbed what he'd said before loosening his grip. He collected the pile of money from my lap. "Now we're going home, and you get yourself straight into the shower and wash the black from your head. And after you calm down and this nonsense is behind you, then we'll all have the night off to celebrate our honey-moon."

For the rest of the drive we said nothing. Although the gravel shoulder we passed was hypnotizing as I stared out the window at it, and although I wondered how much it might hurt if I flung myself from the car and landed there, I stayed where I was. I didn't want to scuff my new shoes. And inside the car there was chocolate milk and Arsen was smoothing my hair gently behind my ear and the car stereo was playing a song I liked.

VI

Arsen let me choose what we'd do to celebrate our honeymoon. I chose the carnival. First dropped hints about going to a high-priced, exclusive restaurant; crowds made her anxious. She had a firm hold of my hand the second we stepped on to the fairgrounds. First wore heels. Not the shiny red pair she wore to work, but heels all the same. She said pain shoots up her calves if she wears flat shoes. "My legs are used to 'em. Heels been bracin' me for many years. How old do you think I am?" she asked me, pausing only long enough for me to half-shrug. "Let's just say I been wearin' heels before you was even born."

No one could guess how old she was. A wrinkle or a grey hair would be consumed by the rest of her expansive self; like a drop of white paint into a gallon of red. Who could guess her height or weight, except to say she was big. Her shoes were anvils of patent leather. An entire day could perch on her hips. I swear her hair could ensnare a shark and pull it ashore. I started to imagine her with her men, her live ones. I didn't want to, but I couldn't help wondering what it must be like to be able to swallow a man with your body. I pictured men folded inside her, lost but for an occasional arm reaching skyward. Spit out after a short while, dizzy as leaves rolled under truck tires, dancing in the autumn streets. Maybe once she was small like me, but stuffed herself with remnants of men left behind over the years. An overflowing lost-and-found box.

It was men's attention that eased her nerves at the carnival. "We never talk 'bout Sub Rosa when we're in the city," First warned. "But we can drop clues. It's good for business." As she had on the subway, she mentioned No's Smoke Shoppe to strangers, winking and biting her thick bottom lip as she flirted. Arsen just let her do it; I didn't mind either because while she was flirting with strangers he was winning me stuffed animals and buying me funnel cakes, candy floss, whatever I wanted.

He was not the only one either. In the middle of the midway's smash pile of screams and beeps and blinking lights, people turned and stared at me. "Uncross your arms," First told me, but only once. I was already flaunting, just a little, like she did, embellishing the swing of my hips as I walked.

"Are you good luck?" a man at the duck shoot asked me. I blew him a kiss, and it earned me a fist full of Mardi Gras beads and a glow-in-the-dark lei. The man would have won me a blinking-light tiara, too, but First moved us along.

A group of teenaged boys asked me to pose with them on top of a statue of a circus lion. All five offered their arms to help me up the slippery fibreglass king of beasts. I smirked as they took turns with their arms around me; their friend with the camera gestured for us to move closer together.

"Good work, Little," Arsen said after the boys awkwardly shuffled away. "Those boys are the type to share photos with all their friends. You're on your way to becoming a beautiful mystery girl with hundreds of young city guys."

Second had a following of interested strangers too, but Arsen didn't offer her any praise. Instead he and First kept close watch on her. "Don't wander too far," warned First.

I sat on First's lap and let Arsen hand feed us cotton candy. I already felt famous. And attention wasn't all that I was aware of. I sensed money, smelled money. The odour was everywhere and overwhelming.

It wafted by, stuck to passing strangers. Men in the beer tent reeked of it. "I bet I could make my dowry all over again," I whispered to First, but she warned me that Sub Rosa business was best left on Sub Rosa.

Sub Rosa was with me, though. Whenever I passed one of the fair's many funhouse mirrors I saw an imposter. My cheeks were rouged. My bare legs looked as if I had borrowed them from a catalogue lady. My hair bounced like it was in a commercial.

My feet had definitely changed. My heels were blistered from wearing high heels; my pinkie toes were rubbed raw. First said they'd heal quickly once I got started on Sub Rosa, same with the scuffed knees and scratched back. She told me Sub Rosa could cure anything from a cold to a callous. In the meantime, she had painted my toenails fuchsia pink, which made my feet look even less like my own. Maybe they weren't that different. Maybe I had never contemplated my feet much before. But I stared hard at them as I rode the swings at the fair. And as they dangled high in the air, I was pretty sure they'd changed into something different from my own.

When I boarded those swings, the carnie operating the ride approached me. A little flirting is what I thought he was after. No different from the rest. Then he said my name. I was hysterical on sugar and fanfare, and this boy was holding the safety chain at my waist in his handsome hand, and for a moment I didn't register the name was mine. It tripped out of his mouth a second time as a question. I looked over my shoulder at Arsen on the other side of the guardrail, busy juggling the herd of stuffed animals he'd won for First, Second, and me.

"Yeah," I said. My voice overcautiously lowered.

"You remember me?"

A whistle sounded. He jingled the safety chain between my legs and the swings rose up.

This boy—his name came to me after several seconds—was Eli. His name mixed with mine caused a reaction. The swings turned and turned up the past. Involuntarily, I found myself remembering the Kingsgate Street house where I lived for a short while, perhaps a year before I stayed with Nino. It was a juvenile crash pad, a refuge for teen angst. It didn't matter how the suburban runaways occupied that house, how their dog-eared postcards of Bettie Page and the Royal Canadian Mounted Police stuck to the refrigerator, their collection of stray cats pissed in and scratched up every corner. It didn't matter that they stormed from room to room in their ratty underwear, kicking holes in the drywall with their steel-toed boots, sleeping four to a room, then six, until the house was crammed full of them—it still didn't seem like *their* house.

I used to sleep in-between the tea-stain-coloured drapes and the bay window, where I couldn't be seen. That was my miniscule squat. I'd lie awake looking up at the dying ivy plant that clung to the curtain rod and wait for one of those dry leaves to snap off and land on my face. Sometimes when I woke there would be leaves, curled like brown withered Valentine's hearts around me. But no matter how much I wanted to, I never got to witness their last moments. I imagined something magical would happen, like a tiny light would spark just before the leaf fell. I began to crash there more and more just to watch that plant. The runaways told me I was crazy and needed "professional help." Most of them even called me by the name *Crazy*. At first, they'd lure me out from behind the curtain with Baby Duck wine and paper bags of modelling glue. A few boys brought me to their nests of stolen gym mats and Salvation Army blankets. All of them slept with their limbs fallen carelessly over me, pinning me down, their dreaming fingers twitching on my back as they slept. I was a blip in their erratic-romantic lives. Even the worst speed-acned tit-fumblers quickly traded me in for another. They never forewarned me; I'd just find their bedrolls occupied by other girls, amateur outlaws in fishnet stockings probably picked up from a nearby high school parking lot.

Eli was almost different. I almost got to know him. He occupied the upstairs hall closet. He had a string of blue Christmas tree lights, a clock radio tuned to the university station, and enough Star Wars, Snoopy and the Peanuts gang, and hockey-motif sleeping bags for us to get lost in. When we kissed he kept his lazy left eye open, and I'd take peeks at him staring off at the wall. He talked a lot about how he was going to return home one day and kill his old man. I listened to his detailed scenarios, most involving claw hammers or fire, until his face inevitably crinkled and he cried. Late at night, when he thought I was sleeping, he'd whisper that he loved me. I would lie there, pissed that he was too chickenshit to say it when I was awake, but also thankful. I guess I was thankful that anyone said it to me at all.

We lasted the better part of an August, hot-boxed in his closet, sweaty and sliding over each other. He tried to fuck me once, only once, and when he did his dick turned soft the moment before he entered me. This too made him cry. Afterward, I saw him brush my long dark hairs off his pillow before he turned away from me and pulled out the string lights. I forced myself to stay awake that night, pinched my arms under the sleeping bags. I was waiting to hear him whisper, "I love you," but he never did.

I stole his copy of Kurt Vonnegut's *Slaughterhouse-Five*—a mean retaliation on my part since he treasured that book—and returned to my place under the doomed plant. For a couple of nights, he'd sit on the other side of the curtains and plead for me to come back to his room. Others piped in. "Come on, Crazy. Don't be such a bitch," they'd say. Eventually Eli said it too: *crazy bitch.*

After Eli gave up, no one else spoke to me. The offers of cheap drugstore-concocted highs stopped; none of the boys tried to grope me in the night. I don't know why I kept going back, but I did. At around two or three a.m., I'd slip in through the living room window to lie down unseen and sleep. If I was lucky, all of them would be out cold at the same time, and I could tiptoe around to brush my teeth or drink a glass of water. I had a collection of fallen leaves lined up along the windowsill, and Vonnegut's Billy Pilgrim still hadn't found anyone who believed in time travel or the planet Tralfamadore. I believed in Tralfamadore, not that it made any difference to Billy Pilgrim; real people couldn't care less what I thought, never mind fictional people. I never understood why Billy Pilgrim didn't try to break out of the zoo. That was the one question that might have got me talking to Eli again, to ask him why Billy Pilgrim was so content with imprisonment. But Eli himself lived in a closet. I guessed that men didn't mind tight quarters if there was a desirable girl around.

I found the curtains yanked down, rod and all, one morning as I was trying to sneak in. I stood and stared in at the pile of dirt and dead ivy on the carpet. *Fuck you,* someone had written on the window in red marker, except it wasn't the words *fuck you,* it was an illustration of a hand with the middle finger extended, clearly meant for me. I stared, but only for a moment, at the half-dozen runaways looking back at me blankly. They didn't shout or curse, they didn't acknowledge me in any way. Their stoic expressions confirmed that, to them, I no longer existed.

I bet I could have peeked in the very same window years earlier and the real people, the ones who were supposed to live in that house, would have been there. The kind of family that might hang framed photographs of themselves wearing monochromatic colours and practised smiles. The kind of people who let their youngest dance and sing on the coffee table while they vacuumed to Billy Joel. People who sleep in beds at night. Then, without much time passing at all, there were new people, with sleeping bags and cigarette-burned skin. Ivy-killing people. Who was I to judge? I never once watered that plant.

Most of this was absent from my mind. I didn't spend my days grieving a dead plant. I wasn't keeping tabs of how my feet, or other extremities, had changed. If someone had asked me, *Has anyone ever told you they loved you?* I'd say, *No.* The whole memory would have struck me as make-believe if Eli hadn't been below me, working the swings at the fair. He knew I was up there and that the ride would stop and I'd have to talk to him. He asked me to remember him, and I had no choice but to remember. Like this carnival ride, once the memory started it spun right to the end, and further. *What now?* it asked, and *What if?* I wondered if I'd lost my virginity to Eli, would I now be in a closet-sized room somewhere with unpainted toenails, reading Beat novels, waiting for him to come home? Would I have been working several feet away at the snow-cone stand?

I saw Arsen on one side of the guardrail and Eli on the other side. And there was me spinning through the air with newfangled fuchsia pink toenails. Only the safety chain fastened me to my surroundings.

When the swings lowered back down I stayed in my seat, vaguely engaged with my reflection in the ride's mirrored tiles. I pretended I was trying to score a second ride, but really I was waiting.

"I guess you survived," Eli said. Kids filed off around us, their feet clacking against the steel flooring.

"It's only a ride." I fidgeted with the rusted clip of the safety chain.

"Not the swings," said Eli. "The world … life. The last thing I heard about you was you were sleeping in Rat Park and spare-changing subway stations. I guess that was a bunch of bull; look at you." I unclipped myself from the seat, knowing what was coming next. "I mean, you look really good."

I didn't return the compliment. I could have. His once round, perpetually blush-stained cheeks had given way to strong lines and five o'clock shadow. His lazy eye was much less lazy, which made me think either he was crying less or drinking less cheap wine.

"You getting home-cooked meals and proper bed times or something?"

The question confused me. "What time is proper?" Eli shrugged his shoulders. He stepped back to let me off, then forward again like he was unsure about what he was about to say.

"We should hang out sometime. Swap fond memories about that house."

"I was never part of that house," I told him. A new batch of children ran for the empty swings. A blonde girl wearing glittery alien antennae on her head took my place.

"Can't blame a guy for trying," said Eli, as I slid past him. Maybe he called out, "Have a nice life," and "Nice knowing ya," but it was muffled by the sounds of rattling chains and squealing children.

"Who's that boy yellin' after you?" First asked as I walked back to them. She used her rebuking voice, the same tone she spoke to Second in.

"Just someone I used to know."

"Someone you don't know anymore," said Arsen, taking up my hand, a stuffed tiger and two white lambs balanced precariously in his other arm. I hoped Eli wasn't watching us. Suddenly, I was embarrassed of First's blown-up body, the gold rings on Arsen's fingers, my short dress. It was obvious what we were. I was eager to get back to Arsen's car.

"That's what I'm saying," I said. "Someone I used to know. No one I know anymore."

After the fair, Arsen dropped First and Second off behind the Smoke Shoppe. Second wordlessly climbed out of the car, her arms so crowded with stuffed animals that her face was buried. She hogged all the prizes. I was annoyed at first, but actually she'd been using them to hide behind. All night she was hidden behind something: line-ups, puffs of cotton candy, her own hair blown across her face. I saw her nuzzle into one of the new lambs, and I might have almost liked her then if she wasn't so mean to me. First remained planted in the car, recapping the night as if we hadn't been there ourselves. "It was so humid out tonight the caramel on my candy apple melted right off," and "Little loves her rides. Didn't even scream on that roller coaster." She was stalling Arsen, I could tell. I pushed at First with my mind; her foot dangled outside the car door for a good while before she followed Second to their home.

By the time Arsen and I were alone together my body was limp and tired and needed peace. The jazz station had slipped out of tune and filled his apartment with static and detached guitar riffs. His phone was ringing. Toro was barking at the balcony window. We didn't go to the bedroom. We didn't fully make it inside at all. He held me up against the wall in the front hallway, hastily kicking the row of his shoes out from beneath us. I reached for his silver belt buckle. He kissed me, same way he kissed First, as I pried at his heavy leather belt. I wrestled his pants down with my feet. The hall closet doors rattled furiously as we fucked. Everything fell away, like loose change being shaken from my pockets.

VII

For once there was evidence: an egg-white shimmer beside my breast marked where his mouth had breathed against me all night. His mark felt alive, I can't explain it any better. As if everywhere else on my body was simply dumb skin, but where he had marked me was electric. I stayed in bed for as long as possible, cocooned myself up in his silk sheets.

When I finally got up Arsen said I would be going to my new home. His first words of the day: "You ready to go to your new home?" Why even bother posing the question? It was clear I was going, ready or not. He promised it was much better than his own apartment. In the shower, I worked the soap roughly over my skin. Why should my body have to bear any part of him? He certainly wasn't clinging to me.

I heard his car keys jingling as he paced from room to room. I spent extra time on everything: drank my juice with baby sips, got dressed in slow motion. I brushed my hair for so long it animated, twitching at the ends with static. I petted Toro until wisps of his fur came off in my hands. Arsen's patience faded. "Hey, pretty girl, we need to get going," he said, half sugar, half sharp.

"I'd rather stay here with you." I felt pathetic and turned my back to him as if I hadn't said it.

"I'll bring you here all the time." He tied his shoes, eyes on his laces, not on me. I figured he'd be a better liar. Maybe I should have been flattered that he was bad at lying to me. He had straightened his shoes back into a perfect row of six pairs. My duffle bag sat beside them, packed to go.

It was an August city day that Arsen moved me out of his apartment and into Sub Rosa. His car, baked in the sun all morning, was a sauna. Sweat pooled on the leather upholstery under my thighs; I worried about the squeaking sound I made each time I moved. When we pulled into the alley on the right side of No's Smoke Shoppe, a breeze rushed in the window to relieve us of the heat. Even in the daytime, the alley looked, at a glance, like a dead-end. "Advent Alley, this is called," said Arsen. "We've passed through it before. It's the only way into Sub Rosa." He took it slow so I could see the bouquets of flowers resting against the brick, as if marking the site of a death, or a saint. I noticed new graffiti: *Blessed Is She,* in streaky white paint. A payphone receiver swung in the breeze from a phone booth near the back of the building; Arsen stuck his hand out the window to put the receiver back in its cradle. "Check this out." He pointed to a tiny red rose someone had stuck in the phone's coin slot, still as red and fresh as it would be on the bush. "Check that." His pointing finger swung to the windshield. Little blushing lights floated in the air outside. One flew in and landed on my lap. I swear there was a tiny spark as it touched down upon my bare thigh and I saw what it was. A cherry blossom.

There aren't any trees on Sub Rosa. If there were, they wouldn't have been in bloom that late in the summer. I raised a dumbfounded finger to point at them too.

"Just enjoy it," he said, shrugging off my disbelief. But these petals were more than springtime beauties. They acted organized; their sparse airborne trail seemed to be leading us to the Pawn Shop, where First was waiting in her customary spot, noontime light haloing her hair and shoulders. Beside her stood the source of the petals. A woman, stunning just like First, with an impossibly slender waist, held a bouquet of cut cherry blossom branches, waving them like a victory flag.

"Little, this is Ling," First introduced her as Arsen and I stepped out of the car.

"Welcome to Sub Rosa." When Ling smiled half her face gave way to gleaming teeth. She handed me the bouquet. More petals loosened from the branches and leapt for her. I hardly blamed them.

"How...?" I asked. Several more petals fluttered from the branch toward her. I watched them fall down her bare legs to the sidewalk.

"I think she likes you," First laughed to Ling. I was open-mouth dim, my words full-halt on my tongue.

"If you can make it out of the Dark in two days, Little one," said Ling, "then I think I can find you cherry blossoms in August."

Arsen had to nudge me before I said, "Thank you."

"How'd she do that?" I asked as Ling left us. Stray cherry blossoms pursued her as she crossed the street.

"This," said First, picking off a petal that stuck her lip. "It's just her thing that she do."

Every Glory has a thing that they do, First explained. When Ling wasn't hypnotizing flowers, she had foil-wrapped bonbons rolling across the candy counter toward her; decanters of wine loosened their lids when Ling walked into a room. Ling was the first wife in the House of Klime. Unlike Arsen, Klime was a scarcely seen Daddy, making cameos at Sub Rosa functions or slipping in for midnight rendezvous with his girls. "Ling's no crybaby. You never catch her saying boo about her man," First said. "She just goes about her house business, happy-like." It is said that in Klime's absence Ling has had a lot of time to perfect her charms.

From house to house, the talents of First Wives are grander than Seconds or Thirds. Fauxnique, the first from the House of Man, our next-door-neighbour, can twist and shape her body into impossible configurations. When a live one pulls up in his car, she bends backwards through his window to say hello. One-Tonne Beauty, Miss Alps, and Goddesszilla are but a few of the pet names the live ones have for First. Her size has made House of Arsen renowned.

"Other Glories' gifts aren't so clear," Arsen mumbled and looked up at the apartment window where Second stood with her hand against the glass. He grabbed my duffle bag out of his car.

"Whatcha' doin' with that?" First rushed toward him. Arsen swept back her thick red spread of hair to whisper in her ear. First tapped her foot as she listened. I shuffled mine awkwardly, unable to hear a single word. "Arsen gonna put your things away," she said finally, wrapping her arm around me as if she was delivering bad news. Arsen and duffle bag quickly disappeared through an apartment door marked with a 9.

First stopped me as I followed behind. "Let him go up without us, Little, honey," she said. "He'll put your stuff away. And the truth is, Second's in a bit of a fuss about you movin' in, but Arsen will put her right.

"Besides, we got trainin' to do. Listen now, it starts right here. Here at your front door." First pointed at the door with the polished bronze number just beside the Pawnshop window. "There are three rules for caring for our home and our livelihood. You want to live comfortable, don't ya? So number one—we bless where we dwell. Keep charms. Pray before bed. You can pray other times too, if you wanna. And most important, is makin' offerings at our track patch. Now, we're standin' on our track patch right now, here in front of the Pawnshop. We meet all our live ones here. And we want lots of live ones, so whenever we out here we make an offerin' to the offerin' tar." She tapped her toe in a metre-long spot on the sidewalk where the cobblestones had been pulled up. The tar was soft and squishy under the pointed toe of her shoe. I spotted a pair of dangly silver earrings stuck in the gunk. From her pocket First drew a tube of lipstick for me to offer. I felt silly pushing it into the tar, but I carefully worked the lipstick deliberately into the ground with both hands anyway. "It's all about givin' back to the place that be providin' for us."

The second rule was to buy Sub Rosa whenever possible. "Everythin' you want is here." First pointed out the six businesses that accommodated all of Sub Rosa's needs: No's Smoke Shoppe at the end of the street; Babycakes Bakery and Sweets to our right; our home base—the Pawnshop; Spa Rosa to our left; across the street, the Mayflower Diner and banquet room; and Launderlove, where we had our first appointment that day.

"Launderlove, the biggest laundromat you'll ever see. I'll show you." First genuflected slightly as she stepped off our track patch.

"Whose house is that?" At the end of the street there was an old Victorian mansion that First had overlooked entirely. It spanned a good half-block. The mansion and its surrounding grounds were a homogeneous clay colour, every surface cracked and thirsty. The windows were walled over with heavy black drapes, except for one. In an upstairs room a curtain billowed out from an open window like an escapee ghost. I noticed a single wisteria flower hung on a struggling vine. "That poor house," I said.

"That's the house of the Diamond Dowager," First said briskly, "mother of all Sub Rosa! She don't need your sympathy." She tugged at my arm to get me to follow her.

Hot steam welcomed us as we entered Launderlove. It certainly was big. Rows upon rows of dryers tumbled clothes, but no one waited for their laundry. The only person there was a woman sewing furiously at the back. The seamstress peeked at us from behind a sturdy metal sewing machine. "Candy, what do you need today?" she asked as she noisily finished a seam.

"Well, June, this girl here needs some work clothes. She's been wearing city clothes." The seamstress wrinkled her nose at that. First imitated her, the two of them sneering at my T-shirt and jeans. "It ain't you, baby girl. Most city things just aren't as good as what we got here on Sub Rosa. Apart from gifts from live ones, which we accept outta politeness, we has a ban on city things. No phones. No newspapers. No television."

"But there's a TV right there," I pointed up at the set mounted above the washing machines.

"DVD," said the seamstress. "I have every episode of *Cheers*. Ask me anything about *Cheers*, anything. I'll tell you."

"Tell me you got whites," said First, putting us back on track.

The seamstress pushed herself up from the table with some effort. Her lip curled as she looked me over, revealing a gold eyetooth. "Whites? This is your newest one?"

"That's right. Came out of the Dark yesterday."

"So … two days," said the seamstress. A measuring tape sprang from her sleeve and circled my waist.

"See, Little, even June knows you. Now introduce yourself."

The seamstress might have known me, but she didn't talk to me. She ignored my offer to shake her hand. "How many whites?" she asked First as she slid the measuring tape under my breasts. I lifted my arms for her.

"Well, she's barely broken in. Then again, she is so quick at every darn thing I bet she'll debut sooner than most. And she's going to the Pawnshop soon for her ring. " First tapped her nails on the folding counter. "How many whites you got in her size?" The seamstress folded back a paper screen behind her workspace, revealing half a dozen racks packed tight with clothes. She produced a small sailor suit: white shorty-shorts and a cropped middy blouse. This seemed to appease First, who started to lift my dress off right there. The seamstress unclipped the shorts from the hanger and held them out for me. "Step in," she commanded. "Shoes off," she barked again as I lifted my foot. I was a human kewpie doll with embroidered anchors on my ass cheeks. First was fucking thrilled.

"And I have this one." The seamstress opened a zip-lock baggie and poured a swatch of cloth into First's hand.

"This barely covers my head." First showed me what looked like a figure skating dress made of white mesh. "Would you wear this?"

"Maybe with some new tall boots," I said, spying the rack of shoes. Why not milk the situation for all it was worth?

First sighed. "What else?"

"Today, I have only the two outfits. I didn't expect her so soon," said the seamstress. "You can order more."

"Order more! We need them now." First puffed up and began to complain that she couldn't have me starting work with just two outfits. I was a Dark Days champion, and do champions wear the same outfit over and over? No, they don't. That made June scramble through her rack of clothes, grabbing anything white that was smaller than a size six. Most of these dresses were the same: strapless and stretchy, nothing more than tiny tubes of cloth chosen because they were easy to take in. She fit me in a pearly white tube, a white tube with a star print up the sides, and a pleather tube. I froze as she lined the pins up along my body. First crossed her arms in front of her chest. "They're all so skimpy."

I smiled at myself in the full-length mirror. "Tighter," I told the seamstress, and sucked my stomach in as she pinned.

I left Launderlove swinging my shopping bags beside me. "Don't think you gonna wear that pleather on your first night," said First. She'd been clicking her tongue since she paid the seamstress. "We never even got started on your debut dress." She shook her head, fatigued from it all.

"When is her debut? We all have to plan our outfits, you know!"

A man came racing up behind us; his shiny black shoes sounded like a show pony's hooves clacking against the cobblestones. This can't be one of the live ones that First told me about, I thought. He was more perfect than Arsen: glossy black hair with a flawless side part, crisp white shirt, four or five buttons undone; a red silk scarf tied around his long neck; heavy eyelashes, and a gift-box bow of a mouth.

First clicked her tongue one last time before introducing him. "This is Second Man, our neighbour from the House of Man." He held his hand out to me, horizontally, as if I should have kissed it. I laughed, thinking it was a joke. When he didn't retract, I gave it my best friendly squeeze; his skin was velvety in my hand. "And there is no debut date, not yet," First told him. "She's only startin' work tonight. I'll let you know when to start polishin' your dancin' shoes." She put her hand on my back, signalling that we should move on. I was already getting good at translating her language of touch.

"Two days. Brava," Second Man said as we started to go. I lowered my head and shrugged, only pretending to be embarrassed at the compliment. He pursed his pretty pink lips at me. "You cost me a whole night's work," he said. I didn't understand and looked to First to answer this. She gave Second Man an icy stare, the three of us caught in a triangle of fixed eyes. "I can't blame Arsen now, can I? He predicted you'd be out in two days before the bets were taken, but my girlish pride got the better of me." Second Man ran his hand, not through, but slightly above his glossy hair as he said "girlish pride." My cheeks grew hot and prickly as I caught on. Arsen had wagered on my speedy return. That was why he wanted me out so quickly—for money. All the talk about me being a hero, *his* hero, was probably all just to help secure his winnings. I was sure Second Man thought I was blushing over his tongue-in-cheek compliment. He let a dramatic pause pass before he said to First, "What? You're telling me she does not know who I am?"

"Before you, Second Man had the title for Dark Days," First explained flatly.

"Five days." He held up hand so I might count his five digits; his fingers were bent slightly like a cat's claw. "Just tell me how you did it," he said, dropping all airs. "Some say you found a second Advent Alley in the Dark. You danced the line, didn't you? You lured live ones in somehow?"

"Leave it to you to think up sucha scheme. Nothin' says you can't go back in there, with your bright ideas, and set a new record, hmm? Make for the Dark now and we'll see you, with five bills, in time for supper."

"Maybe I'll do that," Second Man shouted as First led me briskly away, cursing under her breath.

"Don't worry none, Little. He won't go for the Dark title. Dark Days is bad enough for us fresh from the city. But once ya been a Glory, the very thought of goin' back to the Dark is enough to make you crazy. Imagine Second Man prancin' around in the Dark? The fool."

"How much money did Arsen make off of my Dark Days title?" First frowned at this question. Frowned and tapped her index finger on her chin without answering. "Arsen's winning is paying for all this, right?" It was the one question I really wanted answered. I rattled my shopping bags to prompt First to tell me.

"Sure. Sure he's payin'," she said, "for some. But I got money tucked away, and I don't mind spendin' it on you. It's better this way. That gamblin' money is not fit for a hero like you. We're spendin' Sub Rosa money on Sub Rosa gifts. The best of the best." First certainly was spending money, lots of money, on me. "I got more surprises for you," she said, and I decided to shut up and enjoy it.

Our next stop was the Spa Rosa, a remodelled dirty-picture theatre with an ostentatious marquee, each light bulb a tiny blinking red rose.

The signboard out front read, THIS WEEK'S SPECIAL, PARAFFIN WAX PEDICURES, ASTROLOGY READINGS.

Through the chrome-handled double doors there was still a recognizable theatre lobby. The concession stand had been turned into a cosmetics counter, the ticket booth housed a stand-up tanning bed. But the red paisley carpet was original, or so First told me. Everything past the lobby was less like a theatre and more like a futuristic factory. Along the left wall was a row of manicure tables; large metal arms with lamps and magnifying glasses, drills and files and other attachments shot up from the corner of each table. More metal arms grew along a second row of dentist chairs. Even the sinks and hair styling stations were crowded with surgical-looking instruments that I'd never seen before.

The same instruments danced across a huge screen—all that was left of the dirty-picture show. But instead of pornography, a softly lit infomercial demonstrated beauty and cosmetic procedures. I watched a woman onscreen having her eyebrows surgically arched higher. I hadn't even tweezed my own eyebrows before. Is this what all women do? I wondered. Or was this house of sci-fi beauty particular to Sub Rosa?

"You'll love this place," said First, as she eased herself into one of the dentist chairs. "Their manicures last for months. And their facials … fountain of youth, I tell you."

"Hello, Candy." A woman with an apron and what sounded like a put-on Slavic accent approached. "You've come for pedicure?"

"Yes, Astrid. And she has a full-set appointment with Eartha."

Eartha, who could have been Astrid's twin sister with her identical child-bearing hips and strong shoulders, brought me over to a manicure desk. She flinched as she took my hand. "She's had the mark! I can still see it in her fingers."

"There is nothing to see," First told her firmly. "Her fingers are perfect. I cleaned them myself." I agreed with First, I couldn't see a trace of black left on my fingers. I had just about forgot about the black marks completely.

Eartha switched on an electric file and dragged it slowly over my nails until they were hot with friction. Her touch was forceful despite my wincing and I found myself appreciating First for her gentle fleshy hands. Heavy blonde bangs covered Eartha's eyes as she inspected her work under the magnifying glass.

"Give her something cute, like round tips with a coral polish," First instructed her. Unlike me, she was perfectly comfortable; her feet propped in metal stirrups as she leaned back in the chair looking at a picture book on tropical birds. Astrid raked First's foot with what looked like a cheese grater. Flakes of calloused skin flew through the air.

"No," said Eartha. "Coral will not look good with her ring."

"You seen her ring!" First wriggled to an upright position, Astrid latched onto her left foot.

"Don't ask me to tell you. You'll ruin the surprise for the little girl here." Eartha blew up at her hair and her bangs parted just enough for me to see her wink. "Astrid, can you picture what I picture?"

"Silver polish," said Astrid, her eyes in a trance-like roll toward the ceiling.

"That's a mistake," snapped First, kicking a bit in her stirrups. The cheese grating paused and resumed again. "Little gonna get better than a silver ring. You'll see."

"Did I say silver? Are you paying for nails or for fortune today?" Eartha snapped back. She picked up a pair of miniature scissors and began to trim my cuticles. Blood peeked out of the base of my thumb-nail. She had trimmed too deep. "Christ," she said, pressing a tissue to the cut. "I thought you had thicker skin."

When she was finished my nails were as long and metallic as the instruments used to make them. "You think they're pretty?" First asked.

This was another personality trait of hers I had already cracked: when she asked if I liked something, it meant that she didn't. I hid my newly manicured hands behind my back. "Oh! Oh! Doncha worry. You could have tree bark for fingernails and still be pretty," she said and hugged me, like I knew she would.

I thought I had her good. Had her spending money, time, and affection on me. Any small wound I made up, I could count on her to kiss it better. I would never be hurting or alone with First around. She might hesitate for a second or two, think it was odd that I'd have anything ailing me on Sub Rosa, but she seemed to like rushing in with her embellished comforts. If I crumpled my brow, she'd stop talking and massage my forehead. If I smacked my lips, she'd retrieve a cinnamon candy from her purse.

I complained that my feet hurt and she offered to carry me home.

VIII

"Arsen calls it the Wifey Wing." It might have been a wing of some mansion—not like I'd been to any mansions (the first one I'd seen up close was the tragic monstrosity across the street from us), but I knew that they were big and overwhelming and had lots of stuff you're not supposed to touch. So did the Wifey Wing.

Like Arsen, First was fond of her photographs. Framed pictures covered the gold chrysanthemum-pattern wallpaper from the ceiling to the baseboards. Some were pictures of saints, others were of old men posing with alligators or men on mountain expeditions or in diving suits about to jump into the water. There were bugs and butterflies in floating frames and fossils hanging in glass boxes. Out of the dozens of photos, only one showed First's family. The photo of her and her mama hung in a gilded frame, the nicest frame—yet it was tucked close to the baseboard at the far end of the sofa. The photo was overexposed. Still, there was First's undeniably toothy smile and bulky curls. The biggest teeth and hair a toddler could have without falling over top-heavy. As for her Mama, or what I guessed to be her Mama, she was only legs—legs and a pair of hands reaching down to balance her daughter. After a minute of letting me look at the photo, First started showing off her bric-a-brac. "See my collection of seashells," she said, and, "Aren't the people who make this blown glass skilled?" Each object was from some exotic place: indigo-dyed pillows from the Ivory Coast; a jagged chunk of amethyst from Brazil; even the feather duster she used to clean with was made from Arabian ostrich feathers. She stressed which were gifts and which she had purchased herself. "I always buy my collectables from the Sub Rosa Pawnshop." She reminded me of rule number two, but then lowered her voice to tell me: "If they don't have what I want, I ask the live ones to bring it to me. Then I sleep with it under my pillow to get the city off." She polished the round back of a brass swan paperweight as she spoke. I noticed it had a hundred-dollar bill tucked under its wing. I spotted more money lining the bottom of a crystal candy dish, buried in saltwater taffy.

Next, she slid open a door to a hallway. I had been under the impression that the sitting room was the whole apartment. The "workin'" room was double the size of the sitting room, or maybe it just seemed that way because the walls and ceiling were mirrored, and because our heels echoed on the tiled floor as she toured me around the round novelty beds and kidney-bean-shaped chaise longues. Nowhere did I spot a dust bunny or fingerprint or scuff mark. Everything was white. Not white like a sheet of paper is white, more like the look (or feel) of crisp winter air when the morning sun is shining directly in your eyes. When I stood in the corner, my reflection reproduced itself uncountable times in the mirrored surfaces.

There was also a library, a ladies' bathroom, and a live ones' bathroom, "'cause we can't be sharin' our private business with the live ones." The dressing room brought us to the end of First's tour. Arsen was nowhere in sight. He'd left without so much as a goodbye note. I predicted right, that my stay at his place wouldn't last a week. I'd had longer stints in abandoned houses.

I would last in the Wifey Wing, I vowed, where the vanity table and dressers were strewn with perfume decanters and jewellery boxes. "This ..." First squealed, as she presented a black lacquer armoire on the far side of the room, "... is my gift to you." I felt like I was being shown the entrance to heaven. The thing was massive. Enamel-painted birds and flowers crowded every inch of its shiny surface. I could see my reflection in the spaces between the gold and green brush strokes; the black lacquer finish was glassy smooth. First lifted the brass latch in the centre, and the double doors swung open with a swish.

Inside, I spotted my old duffle bag cowering in the corner. First pushed it further back in the armoire and began to hang up my new dresses. The clothing bar was so high, I knew I would need a stool to get them down again. Or maybe First would always retrieve and put my clothes away for me; she didn't seem to mind. She finished arranging my new clothes with a satisfied clap of her hands, then reached into her bra and found a set of keys.

"The keys to Wifey Wing."

"Really?" I hesitated to take them.

"Yes, really, this is your home now. We share everything."

"Not me." Second's voice came out of nowhere. "Stay away from my bed. Stay away from my hairbrush. And stay away from my clothes." First went to the window, which wasn't a window at all, but a partition of lace.

"Our bedroom," she said, drawing the curtains back. The room was in a cloud of lacy layers. Two beds hid in the chantilly and the tatting: one king with crisp white sheets, the other a twin covered in plush toys. This was when I noticed Second, her slender arm jutting out from beneath the fuzzy animal heap. It was late for her to be in bed, and I wondered if she and Arsen had had sex while First and I were out shopping. Who cared about a worthless hairbrush? I didn't want to share *him*, especially not with Second.

"She don't want your skanky clothes," First said to her. "She's got clothes of her own. Come to think of it, that pleather dress you had on hold, I think the seamstress must have taken that in—sewn it up real small—and sold it to Little."

Second shook the stuffed animals off her in every direction and came storming toward us. "You bought that, turn out? That was my fucking dress."

"How was I supposed to know?" I tried to explain. Neither of them listened.

"Don't worry," said First. "She couldn't possibly look more like a hooker than you."

"Fuck you, Candy. Fuck you and your bullshit gowns and bullshit opera gloves. You said you was dressing her like your dolly. That you were so pleased to have a baby to play dress-up with."

"Little can wear whatever she wants."

"Oh, Little can do whatever she wants, is that right?" Second lunged toward me, swung a false fist. I flinched as it sailed beside my head. "What's your name, darling?" she asked. I felt my heart beat in my throat. "You stupid or something? Don't know your name? First name or last?"

"Quit your racket, Second." First positioned herself between us, her hands firmly at her hips. "She got things to do and besides, she's not interested in your hysteria. You should know better than to act crazy over a dress."

"I'm not the one who's crazy." Second didn't quit. "Have the fucking dress. You should wear it, Candy. Wear your whites like a clueless turn-out. You and your darling doll. I don't want nothing from you. Nothing." Second shouted the last word in First's face, and I expected fists to fly.

"You may not want it," First said sweetly. "But you'll keep gettin' it. I will keep givin' to you because, remember, I love you." Hearing this made my heart pound harder: Second got an "I love you" for being an asshole. For some reason it made Second madder too. She bolted around First to the dresser, grabbed one of my new dresses, and threw it at First's face. The thin fabric didn't travel well through air and missed First by a foot, falling dejectedly into her effortless catch like a poorly folded paper plane. When I saw Second's impotent throw, I figured I could take her.

"Stay away from my things!" I screamed. She paused, shocked that I had a voice, then took a hard step toward me, fist up. This time I was ready to do more than flinch. I wound up and kicked her in the shin. I wished I had my new boots on. She fell, taking me with her, and the two of us rolled on the floor, grabbing the meagre flesh on each other's bodies. I got a few good punches in; Second's nose crunched under my fist. But, like everyone else, she was bigger than me, and once she had me pinned I was stuck. Each time she let go of my wrists to take a smack at me, I'd grab for her hair, jerking her head until it cracked against the carpet. We repeated this a few times, getting more and more tired until all we could do is stare each other down. First didn't come to my rescue; she busied herself picking up the stuffed animals Second had scattered around the bedroom. Periodically, she yelled for us to stop. We spent a while longer in a body lock before rolling apart, both of us panting where we lay.

"You two are supposed to be sisters," said First. "Get up now, Second. You've caused enough grief today." With one arm, First yanked Second to her feet. "Little can't be wound up her first night." Second gave me a final kick before heading out the door.

"You broke rule number three," First said after Second left. I was seeing spots, confused. "You ain't hurt," she said, yanking me up like she did Second, except I practically sailed through the air and landed on the big bed. Her strength winded me, but she was right, I wasn't hurt. Not a scratch or bruise on me. I wondered what Second's damages were.

"What's rule number three?" I asked as soon as my head cleared.

First smacked herself on her cheek. "I forgot to tell you! Rule number three is the most important of all. Without it Sub Rosa would be just another city stroll, and us Glories, lord forbid, would be common hos." First straightened the stuffed animals on the twin bed, lining them up so they faced her as she sat down to tell me. "We don't allow nasty city behaviour," she said firmly. As a Glory I was forbidden to fight other Glories or Daddies or live ones. Punching, hair-pulling, scratching, kicking, elbow-jabbing, biting, strangling, clubbing, cutting, poisoning, raping, killing—these did not exist on Sub Rosa. Furthermore, I could never steal wallets or watches or anything while working; stealing from Sub Rosa businesses was unthinkable. Glories were not runaways. They didn't abandon their new families and homes. Rule number three would be the easiest one to keep. Why anyone would want to be thieving or violent in a place as wonderful as Sub Rosa was beyond First.

"Second breaks this rule from time to time. But don't you mind her," she warned. "You can't learn a thing from a girl like her. Can't teach her, neither. Arsen had me to train her like a new vine, slow and deliberate. Showed her how to recite a pickup like a poem. How to unbow her legs and walk like an angel. How to put some pedigree into her routine. Yes, she lands the dates, but a live one never sees her twice. You know why?"

"Because she's an asshole?"

"Because she insists on being hateful and dumb. Just like she was when Arsen brought her from the skids. She hates me, after everythin' I done. She hates the men. She even hates herself." First picked a plush ladybug out of the line and started to knead its soft body with both hands. "What troubles me is you two are alike in some ways. Seeing you scrap so worries me. I suppose you got reasons to be hot-tempered, we all do, but them reasons are done with now. The city is one place, and we are in another. You can't go around acting like that no more, especially with the live ones. You don't hate men, do you?" I shook my head no without really considering it.

"That's a relief. Sometimes the way you cross your arms so tight in front of you I wonder. Don't be fooled by men; they may be bangin' their fists on countertops, buyin' the next round, molestin' under-aged girls, or buyin' magazines about molestin' under-aged girls. I haven't been here so long I totally forgot what the city does to men. No doubt a man thinkin' one thing when he look at you. Probably got the episode in his mind, the one where he lays into your girlish places. You're not dumb; you know what goes on in his head, so now you're imaginin' it too; him takin' you out, hard. It stirs you up, right? The man, well, he's not dumb neither. He can feel you gettin' disturbed, and does it turn him off? No, it don't.

"Men got no problem sexin' a girl who hates 'em, then tossin' her away after. Plenty of men visit the skids and do just that. But a Glory ... a Glory can turn these devils good again. We get right inside them and pull out their deepest wants. We become more than sex, we nurse their deepest insides, the parts that aren't covered in city filth. We make them good again." First was still working the ladybug over with her chubby fingers. "And since we do this, we never have to be ill-treated no more. We get everythin' we want. Sub Rosa never dries up. Its wealth is endless, and it's all for us. Glories rule Sub Rosa, you'll see, Little. Soon you'll have everythin' you ever wanted."

Second appeared in the doorway with a snort. She'd been standing there long enough to catch the tail end of First's speech. She had a rip in her blouse and maybe a fat lip, or maybe she was just wearing too much makeup again. I hoped it was the former.

"You two should bring an offering to the tar to undo the bad luck you probably caused with your fightin'," First told us.

I looked into the armoire at the clothes I hadn't even had a chance to wear yet and tried to act indifferent. The hangers chattered and chimed as I ran an aloof hand across the dresses. I didn't want to sacrifice any of them. I reached for my lump of a duffle bag, stuck my hand in and stirred the contents as if I were bobbing blindly through a whole pile of goods. I pulled out my old stuffed rabbit. Second eyed it. "Why'd you buy that ratty thing?" she asked. I shrugged, and she crossed her eyes at me like I was some sort of idiot.

"I didn't buy it," I said. "It was a gift that I've kept since I was a kid. And it wasn't always this ratty."

"Are you serious?" Second rushed toward me and I raised my fists at her again. She held her hand low, palm up. "Can I hold it?" I figured she'd draw her hand away, like we were playing a game of slaps. She cupped the rabbit in two hands, rubbing its matted fur with her thumb. "What is it?" she asked.

"Rabbit paw, for good luck," I said slowly. I suspected she was tricking me with her stupid question.

"You can't offer this. You'll never get it back again. Don't let First make you do it." I turned toward First, puzzled. She too peeked over at the rabbit with the corners of her mouth turned down.

"Offer that pleather dress. Both of you together. It got you fighting in the first place." I didn't want to offer it. I had just earned it. I would rather have given up the bunny.

"How about this?" I found the green velvet stripper's dress from Johnny-V's stag. The dress was too long for me, anyway.

"It would fit me!" Second snatched it from my hands.

"It's a city dress." First ripped it away from Second. She balled the dress up and tucked it under her arm. "You'll offer the city dress," she said. "It won't fit none of us right."

First wore an uneasy expression as we pushed the dress into the tar. "Filthy thing," she mumbled. Good thing she didn't know I got it from a stripper, a drunk stripper, if I remembered right. When the last bit of neon green was sunk, First stopped tsking, cocked her round hip to one side, and before very long had cars lined up waiting to see her.

The other Glories were busy enough. I watched Ling down the

street guiding plenty of men in and out of the Mayflower Diner. Next door to us, I saw Second Man go for several car rides with live ones, taking his Third, a baby-faced Glory named Dearest, with him. And in front of the old Victorian house, a row of black lace appeared, Glories dressed like paper dolls, hand in hand. First called them the orphan children. One by one, they took live ones into their sad-looking mansion. Even Second had a live one come for her, with a teddy bear and a bunch of yellow roses. But First had the most.

"Do you do duos?" a live one called from his car.

"Honey, I am a duo," First said, turning around for the live one to look her over. "I'm practically a threesome all on my own." And at that he followed her up to our apartment.

"I like a firm touch," another one said to First when she'd returned to the track patch. First showed him her hands, big enough to strangle an ox. I watched her push that live one up the steps as they went.

Later, another said, "I like a gentle touch," and I saw, with my own eyes, First's hands soften until her fingers were like the plumes of her ostrich feather duster. It was then that I realized First gets what she wants. If she'd really wanted that pleather dress gone, it would now be sunk down into the tar patch.

She had me shadow her so I could learn more about being a Glory. I sat in the corner of the working room trying, at first, not to stare. The wall-to-wall mirrors didn't provide any privacy. First sounded nothing like the yelping waitress in Nino's bedroom. She did not fumble like I did when twisted inside sleeping bags with drunken runaways. She had her live ones spinning like a lumps of wet clay on a potter's wheel.

One man said, "Bury me alive." He lay on the bed with his arms dead-man crossed over his chest. First knelt at his feet and dropped her body down, little by little. I imagined it felt like heavy clods of sod covering him from the ankles up. She unhooked her bra, and her breasts fell over his face. I heard his gasps, his muffled "yes"; I watched her hold her breath and her body grow even bigger so that not a hint of him was left.

"Do you want to revive our dear departed man here?" First signalled me over as she rolled off of him. His eyes were closed, his skin purple. A smear of semen on his thigh. I blew into his mouth.

"Come toward the light." What else could I have said as I propped his head on my lap? First nodded in encouragement. "Come to the light," I repeated in what I hoped was an ethereal voice.

"I'm a new man," he cried as the colour returned to his skin. I bit down on my disbelieving smirk as he pressed a hundred-dollar bill into my hand. The money seemed alive, like I was holding a baby bird; it pulsed.

Unlike Arsen, First let me pocket the money if I promised not to tell. "Stash it somewhere private," she advised.

IX

If we can claim the air around Sub Rosa has a calming effect in the day, it can only be described as intoxicating at night. At eight o'clock the street turns into a corridor of light. The sun makes a special appearance on Sub Rosa before setting, blazing in windows on either side of the road, blanching the cobblestones, cleansing them in its white heat. Glories become overexposed silhouettes in the glow. My favourite thing was watching the lamps go on—the neon, the strobes, the hanging paper lanterns. Sub Rosa streetlamps are masters at their jobs. They know not to flood us; they never leave any corner darkened. They don't pull our shadows into unsightly forms. After midnight, the street gets a second wind: The sidewalk warms. The air sweetens. Our most valued live ones visit then.

This was the hour I paid my first visit to the Pawnshop. Six minutes past twelve o'clock; I was a bit late because of First. "I'm not done with you yet." First motioned for me to hold still under her gold powder makeup brush. She kept re-doing my makeup, saying my appointment with Mr Saragosa, the Pawnshop owner, was the most important date I'd ever have. I could tell by the way she wielded the hair spray over my head that she was serious. I really had become more beautiful. Nothing of my sallow fly-speck self was left. That girl seemed to have lived a lifetime ago. I couldn't even think of a single ugly trait I used to have. I just knew I once was ugly. And now the ring would complete me—that's what First said.

She'd put on her finest too. Even though it was a warm late-summer night, she was wearing embroidered calfskin gloves as she shook hands with the barrel-chested man waiting outside the Pawnshop. Even Second was wearing a silk shawl; she sang, "Good evening, Mr Saragosa," and pulled the shawl across her chest modestly.

"So, this is the two-day miracle?" he asked First, lowering white panel doors down over the Pawnshop windows with a turn crank. It felt strange and outdated to be called a two-day miracle. The Dark already felt so far away. I stood and puzzled as to whether it had been a week ago, or two.

"Yes, sir. She has been a wonder child. And she's got a real knack with the live ones already. Arsen wants to show her off. He wanted me to remind you that a Tiffany setting is still the most popular kinda ring in the city." First nudged me toward the man.

Mr Saragosa held the shop door open for me while the girls said farewell, First in her elegant gloves and Second waving the corner of her shawl like a handkerchief. Barely in the door, I heard a half dozen locks twist into place behind us. The Pawnshop owner had reason to be cautious. I had to squint at the brightness of the sight before me: gold. Long glass display cases snaked around the room like a labyrinth. "I've had my business here since I was a young man. 'Course, I didn't know then what I know now, that Sub Rosa would be a haven for such fine ladies and fine jewellery." By the hunch of his shoulder and the drag of his gait I guessed the shop had been open for a very long time.

"There is a trick to buying and selling jewellery. Sure, you've got to know your green amber from your peridot, yes, yes, yes. You mustn't confuse glass for crystal." He was already waist deep in the jewellery maze. I hurried behind him, but the glimmering collection of necklaces and bracelets made me slow on my feet. After a few steps my nose was pressed against the jewellery counter. The display was almost as tall as me and the glass warm and spotless. "The trick is to understand the life of each piece. This eternity band, for example—" Mr Saragosa leaned over the countertop with a ring of square-cut sapphires in his outstretched hand. "This simple classic began its life on the tiny, tear-shaped island of Sri Lanka. Some fine miner, a braver man than I, sank twenty, maybe thirty feet into the earth—rice farmers working the land over his head, his feet wet and cold from ancient underground rivers—to find these little cornflower-blue sapphires." He took my hand. No surprise, the ring was loose on my slender finger. He moved it to my thumb. "A divorcée brought it to me in January. Her husband left her one night and never spoke to her again except through his lawyers. She never saw it coming. Nice lady. Mad as hell.

"Filigree," he told me, as he next worked a band of curled gold leaves and red garnets imitating fruit onto my index finger. "It must be four times your age. Women were smaller then, like you, my dear. I spent hours cleaning the soot off of this one. House fire." He made the sign of the cross and quickly moved on to an Irish wedding ring. Softly, he tapped my middle knuckle and the ring slid on effortlessly. "Married in sin," he said, crossing himself a second time. "Doomed to fail, the poor dears."

An emerald ring found my pinkie. "The girl grew up and didn't want her father's gifts anymore. She left quite a few items with me—tennis bracelet, gold locket, and the jewellery box they all came in, if I remember right."

Mr Saragosa paced around the display, returning to the same spot again and again, before he reached into the glass. He was after a diamond solitaire. His fingers trembled as he hovered over it for several seconds, then scooped it up. The stone was blue and deep, a prism of infinite angles and shapes. "A person can get lost in it." His breath was misty against my cheek as he put it on. A zap shot through my finger. I didn't care what unhappy story was attached to it, it was tremendous. I didn't care that he unzipped his trousers. We wordlessly watched the ebb and flow of my jewel-bedecked hand. His cock a minor detail, obscured by the diamond's firefly trial. For the shortest second I worried that the rings might have rubbed him too hard. His teeth clacked like he was cold. He slowed me down, showed me how to run my knuckles across the head of his penis, rings bumping the tiny slippery opening there. After a few seconds of this, he slumped against the display. I stood quietly with a handful of precious stones and his sticky ooze.

He only needed a moment to recompose himself and return to the rings. I balled my hand in protest as he attempted to take them off. "These are not for you. As I was saying earlier, the trick to buying and selling is in the life of the jewellery. All of these rings have been sitting in my shop for far too long. I've had customers ask for an Irish wedding ring; I show this, at a bargain price, and they won't buy. An imprint of pain is stamped on each one of these things. However! What I have discovered is a new Glory, like you, my dear, newly unburdened from the woes of the life you've left behind ..." He slid off the Irish wedding ring. "You have the power to restore my rings. Depending on the girl, the rings might even go up in value." I handed him the filigree and the emerald. He inspected them with one eye.

"I'd like to wash my hands now, Mr Saragosa," I said, backing away with the diamond still on my finger. There was no way I'd get away with stealing it, but maybe if I wore it for awhile, he'd see how well it suited me.

"Only the Dowager wears a diamond," he said with a firm hand on my shoulder. I stared at him incredulously as he stripped me of the solitaire.

"First has a diamond," I argued, picturing her monstrous gem jutting out from the long-pronged setting.

"Candy, your First, wears a fancy yellow sapphire. It's an expensive stone, mind you. The very best in sapphire. Yellow Indian gold band. Expensive, but not a diamond. Look closely at it when you get the chance; you'll notice it doesn't have that same fire as a diamond." He brought the solitaire before me again, tilting it in the light. Rainbows lived inside that stone. My index finger ached for it. "A Glory hasn't worn one of these since the Diamond Dowager was wed."

"Why does only she get one?"

"Sit here and let me explain something to you." He attempted, with some trouble, to boost me onto the countertop. I scrambled up most of the way myself, thanking him anyway. I still hadn't been offered a ring, and unless I wanted to walk out of there with a cubic zirconia I knew to be on my best behaviour. "If it weren't for Diamond and her late husband, Royal, none of you girls would be here. I might not even be here myself. You young Glories, gifted as you are, have a bad habit of overlooking history. Good thing we old folks still remember some truths about this place. Now, I remember Royal. I shook his hand on many occasions. Do not go thinking that Royal was just a man.

"Royal was no man. He was an angel. A benevolent angel from heaven. But he was restless. Rather than residing in heaven, Royal watched over the downtrodden and mistreated people on earth. He would disguise himself as a human to test the decency of us humans. I suppose nothing gave him more pleasure than rewarding those in need, the good and honest ones, that is, with happiness and wealth.

"Once he dressed himself like an old alcoholic widower and set off—in a run-down Ford is what they say—for the skids, searching for any woman who might accept his patronage at a fair price and offer kind service.

"He began his search on the main streets where there were supper clubs and ballrooms. Quite similar then to how it is now. Rows of young women wearing their finery smiled at him as he circled. He stopped for several of these women, but when he named his price they demanded more money. 'I'm sorry, I don't mean to insult you. The price is fixed; you see, I am only a poor man,' he told them. And one by one they waved him away, yelling rude words and insulting his weathered skin and gin breath as he went.

"Royal decided he should try another, more destitute neighbourhood, where perhaps the women would better understand hardship and sympathize with him. He drove the industrial streets where the girls wore ill-fitting clothes and had vacant stares. It didn't take long for Royal to find a taker on his offer. He took the woman to a shabby apartment, which he pretended was his. Together they lay in bed and the woman draped an arm over Royal, but after only a few minutes she excused herself to powder her nose. Royal heard her dash down the hall and out the door. Not only had she taken the money he paid her, she had stolen his wallet from the nightstand.

"Any other man might have thrown in the towel. Royal was no man, I say, and so he kept searching. He must have driven every street from here to the Number 4 Highway and back again. This is when he found Diamond. She was sitting on a bench on a secluded street, an unlikely spot for a prostitute to attract any customers. Royal wasn't sure if she was working, so in the politest manner he approached her. To his surprise, Diamond accepted his offer.

"No one can say for sure what took place that night. Some say they made passionate love. Others say Royal, being the kind soul he was, only asked Diamond to lie next to him. Some believe that they stayed up late into the night discussing the troubles of the world, human suffering and such. I bet Arsen's stocked your library with a several books on these kinds of matters. As I was saying, whatever happened that night, so long ago, Royal vowed to forever protect and care for Diamond. He blessed the street, this very street, where he found her and, in a little time, it became the haven for the Glories and live ones that you see today. Men who are searching for good, as Royal was, even if they don't know what good they seek, they'll find it here at Sub Rosa."

Mr Saragosa touched my nose with his finger, playfully, like a grandparent might touch their grandchild. I wasn't sure how to respond to his remarkable story, and so I just shifted uncomfortably. The display case was hot against my thighs. "After watching over Diamond for many years as an angel," he continued, rapping his wrinkle-skinned knuckles on the glass beside me, "Royal fell in love with her. The love a husband has for his wife. He sacrificed his place among the angels and took human form so that they could be wed. This is when Diamond received her ring. Understand? She was the first Glory to wear a ring.

"Tragically, Royal's mortal body could only live so long, even on Sub Rosa. He passed away long before your time." He patted my back, as though I was personally grieved by Royal's death.

"Royal knew he couldn't stay forever and so he bought Diamond the biggest diamond ring in the shop, because diamonds are forever, as the saying goes. Since then, no Glory has received a diamond. You must respect this, just as you must respect Royal's spirit, which still remains and protects Sub Rosa today.

"Well, now, you have your own story. And what a little legend it is! Two days in the Dark. When I heard the news, I put this aside for you. It's as dark and captivating as the sun-forsaken streets you so quickly mastered." This was the moment I'd been waiting for. I held my breath, and he held up a ring. It was an eclipse. It punctured the Pawnshop's hot white light. I wanted something girlish and pretty—it was neither. Mr Saragosa had to pull up my hand and reel it into the ring. "You have no idea what this is worth," he said, struggling to put the ring on my finger. "Platinum band and a South Seas black pearl. Lucky girl," he told me. I looked down at it, and the ring stared hard back at me. A heavy band of metal, almost as thick as the bulbous pearl sandwiched precariously in the centre. A hint of green luminosity gleamed in the pearl. I guessed that was something. And it fit. It fit my unusually tiny finger so, of course, ugly or not, it had to be mine. I left the Pawnshop.

"Show it, baby girl," said Arsen. He was posed a few feet shy of our track patch—probably a pose he'd practised for ages, body arched forward in a way that made his handlebar hipbones knob under his pants. A pose that drew all my attention to his groin; there may as well have been arrows pointing at his zipper. He had come to see my ring. I stalled for a moment, arms folded behind me, embarrassed at the band of gloom on my finger. Second crowded me, circling behind my back. First wrung her hands in anticipation, and so I reluctantly lifted the ring above my head to their eye level. "Black pearl," First announced.

Arsen's face crumpled. Play by play: his mouth dropped, a brief—very brief—trembling of the chin; the chin then stiffened, tongue peeked out to wet his lips; and he forged a smile to cover his brief unravelling. "I can't take my eyes off it," First said. "It's haunting. I think I've dreamed 'bout this ring before."

As First admired my ring, Arsen clapped his hand over mine to hide it. I waited for First to say something; she could get an answer out of him faster than I ever could. Before she could say a word, however, Arsen directed her attention toward someone else altogether. He raised his finger to his lips, then pointed behind him. "The Dowager?" First whispered. No one moved from our tight huddle. I squatted down an inch or two; from between Arsen's legs I saw a wall of black lace moving in.

"Diamond, Sadie, and company. To what do we owe this visit?" said Arsen, turning to face the funereal gaggle. The black-lace clad orphan dollies, six of them, formed a perfect line in front of us. I noticed each wore a cameo ring, blue or pink coral backgrounds with a ghostly lady's face carved in the centre. All of them resembled the portraits in their rings; their hair twisted into complicated buns and braids, their mouths painted pale. In unison, they stopped, and the Diamond Dowager stepped forward. It could only be her, the legend I'd just learned about. There was the telltale flash of fire on her finger, and then the

Diamond Dowager's hand was at my cheek. She was nowhere near as rare and extraordinary looking as First. Oddly human for a Glory; her eyes had crow's feet. But behind her, a wind gathered that made her undone hair flutter around her shoulders. Her long black dress twirled up and then hugged her legs again, as if it was breathing. No one else was affected by this wind; the dollies' layered crinolines were absolutely still. First folded her arms around me. Her heartbeat knocked on the back of my head.

"There was a time when a new Glory went door to door to introduce herself. My girls certainly take the time to call upon our neighbours," said the Dowager. Her voice was like that of an actress in a play, polished and, without being raised, loud enough to hear from a hundred yards away. "Since all manners have been traded for the almighty desire to start earning profits, I took it upon myself to make whatever brief introduction you can afford to receive."

First's palm grew warm against my shoulder. I felt fighting words rattling up toward her lips and wondered under what condition rule number three could be broken. "Nothin' wrong with lettin' her settle in with her kin and find her feet before she goes paradin' around the Rosa. 'Course, most anything can seem rude if you lookin' for a quarrel."

The Diamond Dowager waved her hand to dismiss First's oncoming argument. "Oh, she is still getting acquainted. Is that right, tiny Glory?"

"Little," I introduced myself and offered my hand to shake. Our rings clanged together. First gathered me in even closer. I looked up to see the mandible muscles on the underside of her jaw tighten on her otherwise stone-calm face.

"It would seem that you're quick to adjust to your surroundings. You see, I've come to congratulate you, though I am also curious. Very curious about how you got out of the Dark so quickly, Little."

"That is the question on everyone's mind," laughed Arsen, his voice sounding too casual, too slapdash. He was nervous and so was I. As the Dowager turned my hand over to inspect my ring, a cool current ran from my fingertips up my arm to my shoulder, where First pressed her protective weight on me.

"Strange," said the Dowager. "Jellyfish had a black pearl, too." The line of black dollies began to retreat as if that was their cue. First's hand grew slack for a second.

"Jellyfish?" I asked. "Isn't that the name of the girl I saw in the Dark?"

"What's this you're saying?" The Dowager's question sent ripples of wind across my dress.

"She's saying nothing," Arsen told her. "She got a typical case of Dark delusion, that's all. They all see things in the Dark, as you know. Especially the more triumphant Glories. Their visions help guide them. This one saw a girl. She hallucinated a girl, that is."

"You mean to tell me that Little, now wearing a black pearl, imagined up Jellyfish as a symptom of the Dark? Tell me, little one," the Dowager said, turning to me. "What was this vision you saw?"

"The dark girl, you mean?" I shrugged. There was a pause in which I waited for someone to fill in the blanks about my mysterious angel.

"Don't encourage her Dark madness. She's on the mend still and don't need to be thinkin' about Dark creeps," First said loudly.

The Diamond Dowager came at First with such cruelty on her face it made me nuzzle into First's tummy rolls. "Creeps! Show some respect," the Dowager boomed. "Real or imagined, she still was your First!"

Arsen jumped in between the two just before they collided. There was a scuffle of heeled shoes against the pavement. First tried to get in a low swing before she got a hold of herself. She reigned in her rough fist with a sigh, and returned it to its place on my shoulder. For a moment the thrill of the near-fight stirred me. I got the urge to topple the line of orphan girls. I bet my sucker punch would have been mean with my new bulbous ring on. My hand twitched with the thought of it. I stared hard at the line of orphans and one of them did stumble. Her footing faltered as if an imaginary hand had pushed her. No one seemed to notice except me and the orphan, who recovered with a hasty step back into line with the others. "This scene has become disagreeable, my children. Let's leave House of Arsen to their own quarrel," said Diamond.

After the Diamond Dowager and her orphans were well across the street, First loosened her grip on me. I eased away, straightening my clothes and hair. On her stretch velvet dress was the outline of my head. She rubbed at it unconsciously as she started to cry. Not tears. But dry sobs that trembled on her lip. Arsen was so taken aback that it took him a minute before he thought to hug her and shush her.

Second slipped up beside me. She'd been tucked behind a streetlamp this whole time. "Nice work," she said in my ear. "No one ever cries on Sub Rosa."

X

I was sure my ring was jinxed. It cast a mood as dark as its oversized pearl. Thankfully, it did not jinx our track patch. We saw back-to-back live ones right until sunrise. But First's dim spirits never broke. She never really perked up as we worked. She'd be jumbled up with a live one, going through her usual motions of bouncing and clucking, and her breath would catch. Maybe to a live one it came across as passion's hiccups, but I was the one who'd been studying her night and day—I knew she was gulping down some kind of worry. I blamed the black pearl. When my right hand wasn't busy, I cupped it over my left, concealing my ring guiltily.

Second did nothing to spice up the working room. Her lousy performance could only be indifference. I had her figured out, too. Her signature positions, which she'd crafted to appear as though she was overcome by pleasure, really were nothing more than her putting distance between her and the live ones. To me it was obvious that her screams into the pillow were not of ecstasy; she just didn't want to look at the men. Seeing her made me think of how I would intentionally tangle my legs up in sleeping bags as I rolled around with city boys so that half of me could be spared their adolescent probing. I felt sorry for Second; she was still clowning around sex even though she'd been a Glory much longer than I had. And for some reason, maybe the funk was contagious, I started feeling sorry for myself too. Not my self as a Glory, but for that girl with the unicorn belt. And I wondered if Second was thinking about some former incarnation of herself, and why, after all this time, she would still want to. Myself, I couldn't wait for those city memories to fade away. They made me sluggish and unable to keep up with the work in front of me.

What was worse was that Arsen paced the sitting room like an expectant father the whole night. Waiting for a better mood to be birthed, I suppose. He mumbled something about trading in my ring when it wasn't so busy. But the live ones were lined up along our stairs. I'd run in between them to give Arsen an update. "We're fine," I kept telling him. "We're busy." I wanted to tell him to go home, but each time I passed him I ended up firing off some chipper reassurance before I ushered in the next in line.

I realized it was up to me to keep morale up. I had to be the cheer-leader-seductress-vixen-goddess-baby-doll-centrepiece. I changed my flavour with every new live one and their assortment of tastes. I don't know how I managed to keep my "yes, sirs" and "bad boys" from getting confused. It was like dreaming, the kind of dream where you figure out you can fly just before falling to your death, or you've dropped into the ocean only to realize you can breathe under water. I was delirious, blowing kisses in the air to the last couple of live ones to leave our track patch. The work it took, pleasing all those men, made me appreciate First and her skills more than ever.

I was unsure of just how much money I had made until we had closed our doors and I began to pull dollars out of my bra. Hundred-dollar bills stuck to my feet as I took my boots off. There were fifties tangled in my hair. The work bed I had used that night was sheeted in money. My palms grew hot as I counted it.

I showed First my earnings, hoping she'd gush over me. I had certainly outdone myself; I was sure I'd outdone most Glories, new or old. I even wondered if attracting money was my Glory power. I wanted it to be. If Ling could enchant flower petals, why couldn't I attract money? That would be the best Glory power ever. I hinted around at it: "Cash and I have this symbiotic relationship, eh, First?" I was vaguely remembering a nature program I'd seen where tiny oxpecker birds flocked to the backs of zebras and fed on the ticks that live on the zebras' skin. First didn't explore the metaphor with me at all. She was so tired, a flat, "I'll tuck some cash away for us," was all she said before Arsen put her to bed. He sat in our room with us, rubbing First's feet until she fell asleep. I snuck my foot over to him too, touched him with my big toe under the covers, but he shifted over an inch or so, and I knew not to expect any attention for myself.

Second smiled smugly at me from under her pile of stuffed animals. This whole situation was probably fantastic as far as she was concerned: First was miserable and I was being ignored. I could hardly sleep under her stare.

Then, once I did, I couldn't stay asleep. I woke up to what must have been Arsen finally pulling away in his car. The sound of his car made me want attention all over again. I squirmed in bed, my thoughts involuntarily concentrated on a sensory collage made up of his leather upholstery, the gold stud in his perfect earlobe, the lazy curl of his fingers on the steering wheel. The wanting baffled me. I wasn't living in his house; I had my own. He no longer cooked for me, or sang, or found me in the Dark. Yet I still wanted. I was too wound up from the night, was my excuse. My body didn't know to stop Glorying for the night. I would have settled for another roll with a live one; after the relay race of their pleasure my body felt deserted. I turned to First, but didn't dare disturb her for fear that she'd wake up just as glum as she'd fallen asleep. For a long while, I lay very still and waited for the urges to pass. When they refused to, I quietly reached under my scalloped-cotton nightie with my own hand. I rubbed myself as wet and spent as I could without making noise, but my hand refused to slow down. I grew frustrated. I had relived a procession of live ones, but I couldn't satisfy myself. The black pearl felt cold between my legs. For the first time I wasn't repelled by my ring. Instead, it was like a reset button; each time it butted up against my flesh, I began again. Nothing was a turn-off. Hearing First breathing, the cotton pillow sham against my cheek—ordinary things—kept me up and stirring. Even the air was needling me.

I looked at Second's slender wrist, her fingers twitching with dreams, with irrational desire. It made me hate her more. She didn't deserve to have me watch her as she slept. I should have been sleeping peacefully, while she tossed and turned and wanted.

As soon as I thought this, Second did start tossing in her bed. I quit moving my hands and held my breath. My vision was starry and exhausted, and the room was very dark. Still, I was sure I saw something. Something hovered over top of Second. I covered my mouth, my uncontrollable masturbating finally over. It was a hand that I saw, faint as a watermark emblem, but definitely there, inches above Second's face. It dipped down and poked Second's forehead. I gaped and cupped my hands tighter to my mouth. The phantom hand froze, as if it realized it suddenly had an audience, fingers stiffly pointed up. It wore a ghostly pearl.

A horrible feeling seized me. I wore a haunted ring, I was sure of it. It was worse than any jinx—it was possessed. I tried to wrench it from my finger, but my hands were clumsy with fear and still slippery from masturbating. Desperate, I hid my ring finger inside my mouth. My finger tasted like salt: the ring, like blood. An electric shock ran across my front teeth as I attempted to bite it loose. No ring was small enough to get stuck on my finger, no ring but this black pearl. The phantom hand left Second and hung near my own face. I pushed my finger deeper in my mouth, gagging a little. The phantom hand's ring finger was missing. It twitched beside me; its middle finger searched the space where the ring finger should have been. I was choking as I slid my ring finger out of my mouth. The ring finger on phantom hand rematerialized. I repeated this twice, watching the phantom finger vanish and reappear as I stuck my ring finger in my mouth and pulled it out. I balled my hand into a fist. Phantom hand copied me. I pointed at the ceiling and so did phantom hand. I lay my hand palm up in a gesture of offering. Phantom hand did the same.

XI

Many widowers visit Sub Rosa, but only one is called the Widower. His title wasn't earned because his grief was any greater than the others; he paid more, much more, and he visited often. He bought himself the name.

"He's no one's regular," First told me. "He don't wanna be gettin' close to any of us. Most times he picks one of the Dowager's orphan children. Probably he can't tell them apart. None of them got a drop of personality."

The Widower was the first live one to take me off Sub Rosa.

I wasn't even on our track patch when he picked me up. First had brought me to the Mayflower for soda floats and to introduce me to a few of the Glories. I suspected that the Dowager's visit the night before had something to do with First suddenly wanting me to make friends.

A wooden ship's figurehead of a windswept woman hung above the Mayflower's door to make it look like the prow of great ship. "Is that bust supposed to be you, First?" I asked, pointing above our heads. First took my hand and pulled me through the entrance, saying hurriedly, "She's whoever you want her to be. If folks say she resembles me, I don't tell them different."

Inside the Mayflower Diner smelled of orange-oil wood polish and pan-fried meats. It was difficult to clearly see who anyone was in its oak and stained-glass lit interior. The floors were thick and soft, like railroad tie wood. As I stepped in after First, the floorboards seemed to sink slightly around my feet. The booth seats were old church pews, each strewn with handmade pillows. The tables were topped with such a thick coat of shellac, I made a palm print while leaning against one. What wasn't wood was glass. Glass bottles, to be specific. The walls were covered with ships in bottles, little sailboats in Coca-Cola bottles, and large war vessels in glass jugs. Each protruded out of the wall on precarious wooden arms. First and I sat under a large pirate ship, sharing onion rings and drinking from frosted glasses that were brought to us (without her having to take our order) by a slouching waitress. We waved at Ling as she sat down with a live one for a dinner date, but besides her, First didn't greet anyone. After a minute or two of silence she started talking about Glorying again; briefing me on all the Sub Rosa regulars and their various tastes and wants.

Fauxnique was the first to visit our booth. Her hair was the same colour as the cream soda she drank. She sat with a casual leg draped over the corner of our table as she spoke. Like her Second, Second Man, she complimented me on my quick time in and out of the Dark, a hint of contempt in her flattery. I didn't care; the Dark was old news to me.

"If you could only see her earnin's from the last few nights. She was made for Glorydom, I swear," beamed First.

Fauxnique twisted her lip, then flattened it into a wide smile. "My Dearest is filling our vault with riches too. These young things, huh, Candy. I spend so much time in the city entertaining at parties and nightclubs, then the live ones turn around and come for Dearest." The two of them nodded at each other vacantly. I had earlier peeked at Dearest, the Third from next door, as she was watering the potted plants outside their track patch with a pink plastic watering can. She was as small as me but with no hips or tits. I didn't like being compared to a child.

Only one of the younger Glories had gained my admiration. Well, three actually—the triplets. Ling's Thirds, identical blondes, could always be found sitting in a booth by the front window of the diner. I bet First was hoping that they'd come to us, like Fauxnique, and say "hi." But after picking at onion ring crumbs a few times over, First took me by the hand and led me to the triplets' booth. Embroidery hoops and glass beads, old *Vogue* magazines and crime novels were strewn across the table. The window was plastered with cut-out pictures of pop stars. The triplets themselves, glossy and airbrushed, resembled pop stars. I imagined a ton of effort had gone into making them look identical; matching shades of blonde hair and blue eyes and beach-tanned skin. Their breasts were D-cup peas in a pod. The story goes that they weren't always alike. One was once white as bone china. The other two came from northern towns, had slow-paced intonation, heavy eyebrows, and working folk's ruddy cheeks. It was on Sub Rosa that they morphed into teen queens, holding court at the front of the Mayflower. They couldn't be bothered standing out on their track patch. Live ones would seek them out. They'd tread softly up to Ling and whisper when they asked after the triplets, as if the girls were a threesome of unicorns that they didn't want to scare away. Lady live ones were the triplets' specialty; after a visit with the triplets, live ones would leave looking more beautiful. It was said they could take the weary, the bowed-down, the bookish and turn them *Cosmo*, or at least *Cosmo* for a day. Likka, Portia, and Myra were their names. First had to introduce them to me, for all they could seem to do was stare at me with their heads tilted atop their swan necks. She said their names slowly, probably to avoid making a mistake over who was who.

"I like your black hair," Likka finally said.

"I like your black ring. It's, like, so mysterious," said Myra. My awkward thank you was followed by a more awkward pause. Making conversation with them was about as easy as trying to make friends with the popular girls at high school. This would have been a great time for First to jump in with an anecdote about how wonderful I was. She was distracted by something outside the window. Beyond the collage of glossy paper pop stars, a black town car made its way down the street.

"The Widower. Why bother?" said Likka, rolling her eyes at me. I rolled mine back, eager to show I knew who she was talking about, even if my knowledge was only from First's lectures.

"He's probably headed straight for the Dowager's house," I said.

"Too bad he wasn't coming for Candy. Then we could hang out," Portia said under her breath. She moved over so I might sit beside her, but First turned to me with a rushed set of hasty instructions as to how to woo the Widower. "Go!" She shooed me out of the restaurant and the second I hit the pavement the Widower's car reversed and stopped for me.

As First had instructed, I didn't greet him as I opened the passenger door. "Have I seen you before?" he asked, though he hadn't taken as much as a quick peek at me. I didn't look at him either, only out of the side of my eye, only enough to see the sad sag of skin at his jaw. I could, however, see the triplets pointing as we passed by the Mayflower. I was sure that First was bragging then.

"No," I told him, monotone. "I haven't seen you." Not "No, sir" or "I would certainly remember you, honey."

"On the dash is $500 for you." I took the plain letter envelope without opening it to spare us both the sound of money being counted. Five hundred was also the amount First had quoted. "Fastest five bills you'll make," she'd said. I figured there was no reason to question that it would add up to anything but that amount. He left the radio off and kept to the side streets as we drove. I forgot how humid city summer nights were. I wanted to open the windows more than the crack he had them at, but I knew better than to touch the power windows. I also noticed he kept the automatic doors locked. This made me nervous, but I sat perfectly still and quiet. First said the Widower lived in the Lakeshore Properties about twenty minutes away from Sub Rosa; I was grateful she'd told me or else I'd have grown hot and anxious on those meandering roads. Why do rich people need such wide and winding streets? It was so quiet. We only passed two, maybe three, other cars. I caught myself making my breath shallower, making myself as silent as possible.

His house was perched on top of a hill. The driveway was steep and lined with tufts of decorative grass. The Widower walked like he drove—on autopilot—to his front door. The house was smaller than I expected, but still way too big for one person to live in alone. He held the door open, eyes cast down, as I entered. We stood uncomfortably together in a large foyer with a giant painting of grey with strokes of darker grey bleeding through. I tried to see a storm in it or a slab of granite. It resembled nothing.

"Please, use this washroom to undress." He limply pointed to a slate grey sliding door, then to a room down the hall. "In the living room, I've placed a blanket in front of the TV. You can go there and lie face down and wait for me. Quietly, please," he added as he left me.

I was naked and wondering where to put my clothes and purse. There was nowhere to put them in his undecorated bathroom except in a bundle on the floor under the pedestal sink. I stood on the toilet to check myself in the undersized circular mirror, only seeing a segment at a time; my face, my breasts, my hips.

Salt and pepper static filled the TV screen. As I waited for him on the blanket, I stared at the TV and thought I saw a woman's face behind the static. Like me, the Widower came to the room naked, and I sank my head into the pillow he'd laid out for me. He touched me in cautious strokes before his hands moved to their position on the blanket above my head. I was relieved when the sound on the TV came on, as it drowned out the squish of his body on top of mine. Soon I realized he was watching a recording of himself having sex with some other woman. I figured this out listening to him grunt and moan in time with the TV, like an old movie that he'd memorized line for line.

I should have been proud of how still I kept. I was so still I felt traces of my makeup ooze into the pillowcase. I considered all the phrases and strokes First had taught me; it hardly seemed fair to waste all that training. I had hoped to never again end up face to the floor. This date was not so different from my rank in the city—a vague stand-in for something better.

The Widower's "something better" was his wife. "Happy anniversary," she repeated, hiccupped and low. He slowed after this; his dead weight pressed into me until I could hardly breathe. First forgot to mention that sex outside of Sub Rosa was heavy and dull. I inhaled deeply, my back expanded with the breath and pushed against his body. I wanted my exhalation to inflate him, make him somehow more buoyant, but my deep breathing only relaxed him more. I was smothered by him and his replayed memories. Just when I thought I couldn't bear it a second longer, the TV flicked off.

"Susan," the Widower called what must have been his wife's name. The room was almost black, but I could see the phantom hand floating near the bottom of the TV. "Susan," the Widower said again and began to tremble. I wasn't sure if it was a strangely timed orgasm or grief, but his trembles became a quake, so hard that I shook too. My hands, which had been tucked beneath me so long that they'd lost circulation, quivered and danced on top of the blanket. I felt pins and needles through my fingertips; my arms had gone numb, and I couldn't have held my hands still if I wanted to. The Widower grabbed my wrists. By the way he squeezed I guessed he was angry. I almost fought against him. I had a strong impulse to bite his arm. Then I saw phantom hand fingering the buttons on the DVD player. I took another deep breath.

"Susan," I whispered. "If you are here, give us a sign." The Widower gasped at me as I spoke, and gasped again as the DVD player ejected the disc, which shone in its mechanical tray like a full moon. Even though it was, in part, my own doing—this trick—I stared, wide-mouthed and in awe. There *was* a presence in the room. I sensed something beside our two bare bodies. Phantom hand lifted my chin slightly, tenderly. My ring finger surged, electric. The Widower fidgeted and choked a little, but he stayed on top of me as if his passion was paused in time. When movement returned to us it was animated enough that a flicker of air rushed between us, then his chilly skin slid over my own. I did lift my hips, despite what I'd been instructed, and I made the faintest "mmm." And, just before he got up to leave, I laced my fingers through his and squeezed.

"Please let yourself out. A taxi is waiting," he said before I returned to the washroom to retrieve my clothes. I expected more; hadn't I just made his wife contact us from the dead?

I wobbled down the Widower's steep driveway with stiff legs to get to the cab. Without asking where I wanted to go, the driver took the freeway back to Sub Rosa.

"Take exit 130," I told him, unsure how far off route it would take us. "I'd rather go down West Way." My visit to the Widower's had left me wistful. I wanted to drive past my old haunts. The streets there were narrower than on the lake shore, and the traffic comforted me. People crowded the sidewalks; some shot out into traffic, too impatient or too reckless to wait for the light to change. I saw women in their miniskirts and big bauble-jewellery and figured I had beaten them at their game. *I'm beautiful*, I told myself. *I'm a miracle.* I considered stopping somewhere for a drink and to flaunt myself. A couple of times I asked the driver to pull over. But when I opened my door the city seemed so noisy. It was nearly the end of summer, and droves of frat boys on bar crawls infested the streets, girls following with drunken whines. I hated this time of year. From the curb I craned my neck to see through bar windows, imagining them filled with seasonal work-ers drinking down their almost-last paycheques, fathers unwinding from family barbecues, everyone going full tilt to nowhere. I smelled pub food scraps rotting in the dumpsters, urine in the lanes. I heard a hazy guitar solo playing on a patio, and I couldn't think of one thing I liked about the city. I get paid for my time here now, I reminded myself, reaching into my purse to tear into the Widower's envelope.

I counted the money four times before we reached Sub Rosa, shredding the envelope. The driver rushed through Advent Alley, old bouquets crunching under his wheels. I tried to see if Arsen's little rose was still stuck in the phone booth coin slot, but we passed by too fast. "Since I'm here, I may as well stay," said the driver. By the way he smiled stupidly at me I thought he wanted my company. He parked in front of the Mayflower and rushed in to one of Ling's girls instead.

"The cabbie always takes dates with my Second," said Ling when she saw me let myself out of the empty taxi, dejected. She had peacock feathers woven into her straight black hair. They seemed to stir, life-like, as she spoke. "But I see you already have your own regular." The Widower's car sat in front of our track patch, again. How did he get back here so fast? He must have left right after I did. I wished I could have pretended I never saw it. I wasn't up for another hour of playing a mute. First was waving me over.

"Little, what did you do to him?" she asked as she quickly fixed my eye makeup with a spittle-covered finger, guiding me toward his car as she rubbed and dabbed. "He never visits twice in a night."

Everything looped again, but worse. The lake shore road was darker now, his instructions shorter, the word "please" missing from his vocabulary altogether, the TV smudged with fingerprints. I saw an imprint of my mascara on the pillow before I pushed my face into it.

Before the same DVD came on he said, "I don't know how you did it, but this time we're doing it right." This time he was late delivering his grunting lines. My part was off too; I refused to keep still. If he was going to accuse me of mischief, then mischief I'd give him. I moved as though it was him making me move, sneaky-like. I let my legs spread further and further as he thrust. I exhaled in short rhythmic "ah, ah, ahs." I inched forward, toward his firmly rooted hands, until my hair touched his fingers, then my forehead, my eyelid. I felt the cold gold of a wedding band graze my cheek. He played right along, adjusting his once rooted hands so they, by pseudo-coincidence, became wrapped up in my hair. Letting his face lower down until it rested on the back of my head.

During the part when the wife says, "Happy anniversary," I concentrated on pausing the DVD. Phantom hand messed this up at first, pressing the search button and speeding up the movie. "Happy anniversary" ended up sounding warped and non-human. Then the pause shocked the room. I tried to imagine the frozen picture. Rashly, I lifted my head to see. Susan took up most of the screen with her soft folds of flesh. She had short hair that flipped up at the ends; I couldn't make out her face because his hand cupped her cheek. His thumb covered her mouth—he must have been tracing her lips with it. At that paused moment, however, Susan looked mouthless and strangled, and I regretted what I had done. Why couldn't I have stopped the DVD while she was smiling? Behind Susan was our reflection on the screen. "Why," he whimpered. He looked like a soul rising out from my body in his slow attempt to get up.

"Please," I said. I don't why that word. Maybe I said it because earlier he refused to. More likely I said it because of Susan. I watched his reflection lower back down: a soul returning to the body.

He walked me to the door, coldly, no afterglow grins or winks. His tension poked my back as I stepped outside. He did say, "I'd like to hire you again," before slamming the door.

The cabbie flashed his high beams at me from the bottom of the driveway. I walked down, squinting in the light.

XII

What I did, pretty much all I did for days on end, was practise my phantom hand. Who knew what it was capable of? I'd lower it outside the Wifey Wing window, calling it back just before it touched down upon our track patch. I switched lights on and off. Pushed doors shut. I often poked at Second while she slept. She developed a bad case of the jitters; I had her jumping at the slightest sound.

At Babycakes Bakery I discovered I could taste whatever phantom hand touched if I stuck my ring finger in my mouth. I scooped a bit of meringue from a pie. I plunged phantom hand into a vat of bubbling fudge and sucked the warm chocolate from my finger. And one night at the Mayflower, I dipped it into Dearest's vanilla milkshake and stole a taste. Like everyone else, she was oblivious; that moonstruck smile didn't leave her face. From a distance, I developed a low-burning hatred for her smile. It was too juvenile and hasty, as if her mouth was a tattoo she'd gotten when she was too young or too drunk to know any better.

Phantom hand wasn't always naughty. When First and I would eat our corned beef hash at the diner in the morning, I would dust the ships in bottles. I wanted to spare the old waitress, and her osteoporosis-bent back, from climbing on the tabletops with her dust cloth. She did this every morning out of habit more than cleanliness. Phantom hand wasn't actually helping her; she still routinely reached and stretched to get to her bottles. But I tried. Sometimes an older, even more bent woman would emerge from the kitchen to polish the booths with orange oil. For her, I'd flick large crumbs and crumbled napkins to the floor, clearing a path for her oncoming sponge. I felt sorry for these women. I figured they had been through some bad sort of trouble to be looking so elderly even though they lived on Sub Rosa. If they lived in the city, they'd probably be dead by now.

The live ones benefited from phantom hand, that was certain. I tickled earlobes and traced spines with both my hands busy. I used it the most with the Widower. He came for me so many times that I grew used to the desolate drive out to his house. I started noticing things along the lake shore: a tree fort built in a low-slung willow, geese sleeping in someone's front yard. I started talking too, mostly to Susan. "Susan, are you with us tonight?" and, "Susan, your husband says he misses you." I was soon familiar with every second of that DVD. I paused and rewound to capture a breathy bit of dialogue, a "yes" or an "I love you." I suppose he would have paid me solely for my psychic ability, but I had just gotten good at sex, and I couldn't image myself anywhere other than on the Widower's neatly laid blanket.

I didn't tell anyone about phantom hand. If I had, then Second would have figured out who was playing tricks on her while she slept. Plus, I couldn't risk one of the Glories sneaking a message to the Widower or my other regulars about it. We weren't supposed to act out of jealousy, we Glories, but—let's be honest—I attracted a mess of rival sideways stares each time I rode off in the Widower's passenger seat. Phantom hand was more powerful as a secret. And it was powerful; I figured it was the best Glory magic I'd seen on Sub Rosa. I came close to confessing once when I overheard Arsen and First planning my debut party.

They'd locked themselves in the ladies' bathroom, not knowing, I guess, that every sound from the bathroom leaked into the library— where I sat with my ear against the vent.

First, always in my corner, wanted the party right away. "She's earned it," she said. "And we should have it before her fame dies down." I agreed. I didn't understand what exactly a debut party involved, but I was certain I had earned it.

"She doesn't have a specialty yet. She lacks that Glory magic. And city men expect more these days," Arsen argued. Even through the metal vent, I clearly heard frustration in his voice, and my chest began to pound in defence. First told him I was lucky, that I was a goldmine, that she had never seen a Glory as good as me. "She has no magic," Arsen countered each of First's praises. "She's the Dark Days title holder; people want to see a warrior. She still acts so young." He said it so many times I couldn't lie there and listen any longer. I paced the library with my hands cupped over my ears. I threw a few books on to the floor—big books, like *The Best Poems of the English Language* and *Gray's Anatomy*—so that they might hear me in the next room and quit their conversation. I marched out of the library, through the living room, and knocked on the ladies' room door.

"Little, we were just talkin' 'bout you," said First as she came out. "We decided to throw your debut a week from Saturday." Behind her Arsen was slumped on the bathtub's rim, his foot tapping against the tiles.

We started party planning the next morning. First woke us up before noon with a long list of to-dos. Second was bleary-eyed from lack of sleep. On our way out, she took a satisfying spill on the last step, thumping into the back of the door. She complained of wanting to go back up to bed. "This party reflects our whole family, and so we're plannin' it as a family," First told her.

We did the same rounds as on my first day on Sub Rosa, except this time I knew exactly where we were going and exactly what I wanted to buy. "What's your favourite colour?" asked First as the seamstress showed us samples. I chose green, like the sheen of my pearl ring or, it just so happens, the colour of Arsen's eyes, but that was incidental. First adjusted my choice slightly to turquoise, and ordered us each a silk strapless dress and crepe scarves.

We dropped a fabric swatch with Eartha and Astrid for them to arrange matching nail polish and hair accessories. Eartha held the swatch up to her forehead and murmured, trance-like. "Some party," she said, waving the fabric at me.

"Just make sure we have the place to ourselves. We'll be needin' all of Astrid and your attention for ourselves," First said. She booked our appointments and shuffled us out of there in a hurry.

Another swatch was brought to Babycakes, so that even the cake would complement our dresses. Maria, the baker, made cakes that could wake the dead. Second livened up after tasting half a dozen samples. She refused to offer her opinion, though judging by the speed with which she swallowed up the Black Forest, I'd say she has a taste for cherries. I ordered a Hungarian dobosh torte before I even knew what it tasted like. Maria said the words "hazelnut" and "caramel," and it was decided. My ring finger sunk under my tongue; phantom hand slipping between cake layers. "This is serious, Little!" warned First, waving a fork full of cake at me. "You will taste all the cakes, then decide."

"I can decorate it with candy almonds, if you like, Little," said Maria. "Turquoise candy almonds to match your dress."

Arsen turned up around dinnertime with invitations already printed on scallop-trimmed paper. "Little" was embossed on the front in glossy letters, white on white, mirage-like, in Gothic lettering. It reminded me of how I saw phantom hand, an apparition floating around in the tangible world. "Simple and tasteful. Subtly feminine. This style is the stationery shop's best seller," Arsen boasted. He opened the card and read from the metallic silver writing. "The House of Arsen is pleased to introduce Little," he said, giving my hand a squeeze as he said my name. I couldn't help but giggle. "Join us Saturday for her debut party in the Mayflower Ballroom." He finished reading before I noticed that all of us were huddled together, inspecting the invitation. First's idea had come to fruition; we were practically acting like a family. She was so pleased with this glimpse of amity that she sent Second and me to deliver the invitations together.

"Give twenty to every business, and make sure they put a few up in the window. Put two through each apartment letter slot. And most important—listen careful—go to No's, and throw a few handfuls into Advent Alley so live ones will find them around." Arsen winced, though he didn't object to her instructions.

"Can we please stop at the Mayflower for something to eat?" asked Second. Arsen double winced. First patted him on the cheek as he gave us permission.

"Be back by sundown," he shouted after us.

"Yeah, like you have any say around here," Second mumbled after we were out the door.

I expected Second would suggest we split up, or at least that she would argue about which side of the street we should start with. To my surprise, we agreed: the Diamond Dowager's would be our worst stop, so we should start there.

The air around the Dowager's house smelled like the old bouquets in Advent Alley. "Why doesn't the Dowager fix up her house?" I asked, but Second just widened her eyes and shushed me. We crept up the dirt path, the invitations already in my hand, my eyes fixed on the letter slot. "Watch she doesn't sic Royal's ghost on you," Second said, slowing down so that I'd have to cross the veranda alone to get to the front door. The floorboards groaned a predictable groan. The letter slot squeaked when I pushed the invitation in. Someone inside was singing. I pressed my ear to the door and listened. There were no lyrics that

I could hear, just a whole song of "ah," like sex noises put to a melody. Second stamped her foot, urging me to leave, but I wanted another moment of this enchanting wordless song. I could have told you I'd get caught crouched there, that the song was a lure, and I was trapped well before the black curtain in the bay window was flung open. I could have told you the Diamond Dowager would be standing there with her fierce eyes fixed on me, the curtains billowing behind her like living fury. What was I supposed to do but run? I scooped up Second's hand as I hit the path and the two of us ran together like schoolgirls. I would have taken anyone's hand then.

"She's going to hate me," I said as we hid across the street in the beauty shop lobby.

"Us," said Second. "She'll hate us." And she started describing the many horrible things the Dowager might do to avenge herself; leeching and strangling and slaps, oh my! We didn't know whether we should laugh or convulse with fear. Second stuck out her tongue and rolled her eyes back in mock death, then collapsed on the paisley carpet. "If I die," she said, her eyes still half closed, "I want you to know that my real name is Jill."

"Jill? That's your Glory name?" I asked without thinking. For once, I didn't mean to judge Second. It was just that all of us had special names, like Little.

"No," Second spat out. "Don't you notice anything around here? Apart from the live ones, everyone around here calls us Seconds by rank, by a fucking number. Like prisoners, right?" I nodded slightly, and screwed up my mouth with scepticism at the same time. She had a point; I had learned Second Man's name was Emanuel, the same name as his Daddy, though no one ever called him that. I had never heard Ling's Second's name, she was only referred to as "Ling's Second." The Seconds in all three families seemed to suffer from a kind of middle-child syndrome; they were place markers for the Glories before or after them. "Jill might be a dumb name," Second went on. "Nothing fancy like Della O'Kande, but it's mine. Mine. I came into the world with it. And don't you forget it."

Though she spoke in her usual abrasive manner, there was a low note of vitality in her voice that I had never heard. She closed her eyes completely and turned her head away from me. I promised I would remember her name, always.

Jill, I repeated in my head as we continued to deliver the invitations. I let my arm brush against Second a few times as we walked. Unlike First, she didn't take my hand. And when we reached the Mayflower, she stiffened up as Ling greeted us out front.

I trailed behind her to a booth where Ling's Second slouched across the table. I'd been on Sub Rosa long enough that I should have known everyone, but I still had yet to say a word to this red-haired Glory. I hovered around them for a while, waiting for an introduction. Neither of them acknowledged me. Second's face resumed its normal snobbery. She was probably trying to outwait me with her silence, until I got discouraged and left. "You're Ling's Second, right?" I finally asked.

"She has a name," Second hissed, "remember."

"I'm sorry," I started to say, then thought better than to let Second give me attitude. "Well, are you going to fucking introduce me?"

Second put her arm around me. "Listen, if you just leave us alone for a while, then maybe I won't kick your teeth in."

"You can hang out with the triplets," offered Ling's Second, sounding more exhausted than mean. I turned to see the triplets in their regular booth, all drinking coffee and knitting. "They keep asking about you. Little this and Little that."

"Oh my god, you guys, look who's finally coming over here," I heard the triplets say as I shyly approached them. Their clicking knitting needles froze in mid-air. Myra patted the seat beside her. "Spill it," she said as I squeezed in, trying not to crowd her.

"Spill what?"

"Duh, everything. You're so overdue." Likka and Portia tapped a drum roll with their fingernails on the table. They were different than when I met them with First, more animated and human.

"Let's review, shall we?" said Portia. "Two Dark Days, girlfriend. Then you land the Widower as a regular—you've got the Dowager pissed at that."

"We've been waiting for you. Any longer and the gossip would have been yesterday's news," Likka said, sinking her knitting needles into a ball of yarn.

"You can't expect to be the 'it' girl if you don't mingle with your public."

"We had to bite our loose lips, didn't we, when you came over with Candy. You know how she hates gossip."

"But now we've got you alone, girl. I hear the rules are pretty strict at House of Arsen. How'd you weasel away from your First, anyway?"

I was too stunned to answer for a second or two. I'd never given much thought to First being strict; if anything, she spoiled me. Then again, it was the first time I'd left her side. I slid the party invitation across the table, speechless. The triplets scooped up the invite and began to comment on the font: it was too delicate, too fine; and the paper: too virgin white. "Arsen kept it really simple, eh?" Likka said as she stuck the invitation to the window next to their fashion-magazine collage. The three of them exchanged glances that I couldn't interpret. "He doesn't get you ... yet. But we do. We see what you're up to. We expect great things from you."

"Now this ring, this ring is you." Likka pulled my finger so hard it felt as if it would pop off. "Gorgeous," she said as she held my ring finger under her nose.

"Gorgeous," Myra and Portia agreed, looking from their rings to mine. "It's like, kinda unusual. Like weird pretty."

"Mr Saragosa said it captures the spirit of the Dark," I said with a shrug. The triplets gasped and barraged me with questions:

"How much of the Dark did you cover?"

"Or does it go on forever?"

"Did you run into any wild dogs?"

"And those flying bugs?"

But I was unable to answer any of their rapid-fire questions. The only thing that went through my mind was the Jellyfish, and every time I had mentioned her someone got upset. "I got the amnesia," I confessed, and the triplets let out a disappointed sigh.

"It's okay," Myra patted my shoulder. "We probably would have got it too, but we had each other to help us remember."

"We did our Dark Days together," Likka lifted her hand for a high five. "Power of three!"

"You remember it being cold?" Portia probed on. Myra tried to shush her without me seeing.

"Listen, we're not twisted or anything. We just like to figure stuff out about the Dark. Like a mystery novel, you know?" said Likka.

"Yeah, we're not obsessed with it. We just think it's neat, in a scary way."

"Right. So do you remember being cold?" Portia started chanting "cold, cold, cold," her hands on either side of my head to draw the memory out through my temples. Sure enough, a funny chill came over me. "Well, maybe. I remember First bought me these cheap white gloves to keep warm."

"Cold, check," said Myra, making an invisible check-mark in the air with her finger.

"Chronic humming?" Portia asked. I concentrated again and then nodded my head.

"Zombie men?"

"Zombie men? Wait ... Eww, yeah," I said, my voice high and excited like theirs. "I wish I could forget them."

"Glories always think they got amnesia, but it's more like we just don't bother to ask questions," said Portia.

"Don't be so weird, Portia," Myra told her, then turned to me with an apologetic face. "You know who those men are?" she said. "The zombie men? They're all the Dowager's bad dates, from back in the day when she was a prostitute. After she became a Glory, she banished them to the Dark."

"No, they're not. They're live ones who refused to leave Sub Rosa. They'd rather stay captive in the Dark than go back to the city."

"They're not live ones! They're pure evil, you know? Everything that lives in the Dark is bad. The Dark is, like, evil things' natural habitat."

"Unless ..." Likka leaned in, her voice low. "They've escaped through the 'other Advent Alley' and they're loose on the city streets terrorizing women and children right now." She let out a horror-film laugh and the triplets shrieked and wriggled in their seats.

"That can't happen, can it?" I asked. "I have friends in the city."

"Eww, city people are so depressing. No one in their right mind would want to live there."

"I don't know," said Portia. "Some Glories—not me—but some Glories love their trips to the city. They can't be totally wrong about it." Myra scolded her for saying it. The three looked over at Second's table and flashed knowing glances at one another.

Just then, the waitress, in her pink gingham apron, plunked a burger platter in front of me. "On the house, Little." The fries were arranged like a smile on the plate, the halves of the burger laid out like eyes, with a tiny paper cup of ketchup for a nose.

"Shirley owns the place," Myra said as the waitress went back to the kitchen. "She's a 101 years old."

"Maggie and Shirley and Al are siblings. They all own it."

"No, Maggie and Al are husband and wife and Shirley is Maggie's live-in lesbian lover."

The triplets' conversation moved too quickly for me. After they debated the relationship status of the Mayflower staff, they debated the merits of gloss versus matte lipstick, the best brand of embroidery thread, and how soon their most recent order of platform Mary Jane shoes would arrive. Each new topic brought squeals and shouting, as if the fate of the world were at stake. "When was the last time you three left Sub Rosa?" I interrupted. The triplets tilted their heads at me, confused by my question.

"Ling always says you can't leave heaven, but who would want to?" Likka told me firmly. She wiped a bit of spilled coffee to make a clean spot for her to rest her elbows on the table and then got serious about gossiping once more. "We don't like to go to live one's homes. We'd rather stay here. But our Second has a city boyfriend—an old flame found her here on Sub Rosa. Now look at her. She's so mopey, can you imagine?"

"I'd be depressed too, if my city ex showed up. I don't even know his name anymore, but I never want to see him again," said Myra.

"I never want to see the city again. It stinks. I bet ya that's what we used to look like all the time. Depressed." Likka motioned to her Second. She had a fork stuck into her pastry, but wasn't taking a bite. She chewed on a strand of her red hair instead. "Those two are always together, bitching and scheming. We call them two squared because they are so square and boring sometimes."

"Nah, nah. That's yesterday's nickname. We call them two plus two equals five because their logic doesn't add up." The triplets giggled. Myra elbowed me in the side.

"What doesn't add up?" I asked.

"All of it." Myra lowered her voice to a whisper. "Like we said, our

Second has contact with her city ex-boyfriend. We're, like, ninety-nine percent sure of it. Come on, what Glory does that?"

"And *your* Second fools around with the boy who works at the Smoke Shoppe. For free!" added Likka. The triplets sat back in their seats, sipping their coffee and making faces at the Seconds. I put the two halves—the eyes—of my burger together and ate. The sun was killing time near the Smoke Shoppe rooftop, nearly ready to make its final rounds down Sub Rosa.

Second came to get me so we could finish delivering the invitations. Her face was somewhere in-between bitchy and impish. I meet her gaze with a smile so crooked it was practically a frown. "Wait," said Likka to her Second. "You're not going?" The redhead was skulking behind us.

"I'm not going to smoke cigarettes. It's been forever since I had one and you know it," she said. The triplets exchanged more knowing looks. Ling's Second scooted out without waiting for what they might say next.

Second pounded on the metal door behind No's Smoke Shoppe until Eddie Junior, the younger shopkeeper, peeked his head out. He brightened at seeing her, opening the door wide for her to step in. "Not you," she said, her arm stretched across the entrance. "There's beer in here and you wouldn't wanna fall off the wagon." The door slammed shut as I was telling her what a cunt she was being. I banged, but no one answered. There was no latch or doorknob. Exit only.

I wouldn't have guessed that the metal door was part of the same building as the sign that read EAT CIGARETTES 24 HOURS in neon. From the back, all it looked like was a brick wall oddly plunked down at the end of Sub Rosa. Actually, it was Sub Rosa that was misplaced. What ought to be behind that building was a parking lot or a loading zone, not a street as beautiful as Sub Rosa. Straight down the street, past the shops and track patches, was another wall—the Dark. It claimed Sub

Rosa well before the vanishing point. I noticed that if I stared at it too long it would play tricks, closing in on me. Sub Rosa seemed so big whenever I was facing away from the Dark. But looking at it straight on made me feel suffocated, stir-crazy.

I heard a car idle in Advent Alley and perked up. I imagined the driver entering Sub Rosa for, perhaps, the first time. I could almost feel his uncertainty. Where will this grimy, narrow alley lead me, he would wonder. By all appearances, a place like Advent Alley should be avoided. The driver entered it out of blind faith that something crucial lay ahead, as if the Alley had spoken his name, pulled him in. When he saw the first glint of Sub Rosa light, all his doubts would be washed away. I wanted to see his face the moment he saw that light. The car's windows rattled as it pulled onto Sub Rosa. A warm arid whoosh of early autumn air tailgated the car for a moment. City heat; I pictured cars baking on hot tarmac during Indian summer, heat-warped air haloing their hoods and front windows. The driver was wiping his brow with a handkerchief. He stopped in front of the House of Man track patch. Dearest popped out of the bakery and went to the car. She didn't go to the passenger door. Instead, the driver picked her up as if she'd been an infant left on the side of the road. They drove back through the alley again with Dearest sitting in his lap.

Sub Rosa can't be seen from the threshold of Advent Alley, but from behind No's, I was able to catch the tiniest peek at the city. All I saw was the abandoned building across from the Smoke Shoppe. I kicked a pebble down the alley; it stopped rolling well before it made it to the other side. Just as I was about kick a second stone, the pay phone started ringing. Arsen's mini-rose was long gone, and the slot for change was filled in with chewing gum. The numbers were scratched off of the buttons. "Hello," I said, breathy, as if my secret lover was calling.

"Treasure? My treasure?" a man said.

"Hello," I said again. Sure I was a treasure, I played along.

"Tell me you can see me."

I thought maybe he wanted to play the guess-what-I'm-wearing game. I should have been paid for a game like that, but I was bored. "Oh, I can see you," I said.

"I waited for you for the last two nights and you never showed. I can't handle it much longer, treasure. Swear to me that you'll see me."

"I swear." I guess I was already used to telling the live ones whatever they wanted to hear.

"I'm taking you with me this time. I'm going to take you away."

"Oh, take me," I said with a giggle.

"Saturday. Just like we planned before. Our time. Our place." The man hung up. I didn't even get to describe my panties. I let the phone receiver hang. It looked as restless as I was, swinging at the end of its cord. I decided to go inside; Second could screw herself.

Advent Alley grew hotter and stuffier the closer I got to the city side. I noticed a couple of my invitations spinning a whirlwind on the street. After only two steps out of the alley, I was caught up in that same current. It was fiercer than the dancing invitations made it look. The wind was dirty; it made my eyes water immediately. Through the blur I saw dozens of invitations blown flat against the front of No's; several more blew at me as I stumbled toward the entrance. I crossed my arms in front of my face to protect my eyes from the maddened invitations. I felt my skirt blow up around my waist. For a moment, I swear my feet almost lifted off the ground. I stumbled up the front stoop to No's and reached for the door handle. The door opened inward, luckily for me, and I flung myself inside, stumbling across the rubber welcome mat. A doorbell rang wildly above my head. Paper cuts stung my cheeks. The young store clerk struggled to close the door; as soon as it clicked, everything was dead quiet.

The girls and Eddie Junior didn't offer any help as I straightened my clothes. I dabbed the speck of blood from my cheek with my sleeve;

it looked like maraschino cherry syrup. "What are you doing?" Second asked.

"What am *I* doing? What are *you* doing? I've been waiting forever." She looked scared. They all looked scared. I wondered if the sight of blood unnerved them, but what was more likely is that they'd been up to something. I gave the place a once-over: a wall of cigarette cartons behind the counter; cigars in a locked display; pipe tobacco in glass decanters on the counter top; Boston baked beans and licorice and lollipops in the candy aisle. Nothing out of the ordinary. Ling's Second was tucked behind a magazine rack. I rushed over, determined to find what they were hiding. She was gluing my invitations to the covers of automotive and porn mags, a glue stick in her pale, freckled hand. I lifted a girly magazine out of the rack. An invitation was stuck over the model's face. "That's a good idea," I said..

"I've done the whole rack," she told me weakly.

"You just walked through Advent Alley?" Second, unlike Ling's Second, was terrible at hiding the evidence. Her voice was trembling, and I saw the clerk had lipstick smeared in the corner of his mouth— the same colour that Second wore. That was what she was worked up about? I couldn't have cared less about her pathetic romance. The triplets had already spilled her secret.

"I can go anywhere I want," I told her.

"Go out that door, then," Second challenged.

"You go," I told her. Second shook her head, but slowly went to the door anyway. She made a big production of rooting her feet on the welcome mat, running her finger along the seam of the door, touching the knob. It wouldn't open for her. At first, I thought it was because she was pushing, the idiot, when she should have been pulling. But she was pulling, yanking more like it, and getting herself all worked up doing so. When she gave up, the scrawny Eddie Junior put a tentative hand on her back.

"Glories aren't supposed to leave," she said. "Unless a live one or a Daddy takes them."

"I could take you," said Eddy Junior. Second swatted his arm away.

"Glories aren't allowed through the alley, either, not alone," Ling's Second added quietly from behind the magazine rack.

"We're prisoners here," said Second.

"I guess I'm not actually standing here, then. Except I am standing here, so I guess that means you're making shit up."

"Don't cuss," said Eddie Junior, only to have Second and I shush him in unison.

"What was it like out there?" Second asked. "How far did you go? Did you see the downtown skyline? Did you see any city people?" Second's voice was grave again, like it was in the Spa lobby when she told me her name. I wasn't about to soften up with her again.

"Oh, Second, quit your tricks. I'm not stupid," I snapped. I suspected I was the butt of one of her jokes; her friends were in on it, too. I headed for the door. Second stepped back to let me through. They were going to lock me out as soon as I was out the door, I bet. I didn't care. It was almost time to go to work, and besides there wasn't anything so great about the Smoke Shoppe. The clerk and Ling's Second watched me pull the knob.

"Wind's gone," I said, stepping only halfway outside. "It smells like some guy took a piss nearby. You should come get a whiff, Second." I kept a firm grip on the doorknob, letting the city smells in. There were sticky spots on the pavement outside where a soda must have been spilled; there were bug nests up in the Smoke Shoppe awning. A black convertible was pulling up out front. I hiked my skirt up an inch and the convertible stopped right beside me, his front wheel practically drove up onto the store's front stoop. "You know where the Mayflower ballroom is?" the driver asked me. One of my invitations sat on his dashboard. I got into his car, leaving Second to her nonsense. I turned my attention to the driver; he was saying something worth hearing. "To be honest, this invitation flew into my car. I don't even know who Little is. But I have this gut feeling I'm supposed to go to her party on Saturday. I must be out of my mind."

"I'm Little," I said. "You've come to the right place." He clapped his hand to his heart as if I was the queen of somewhere good. "Why don't you come for a visit right now; then, by Saturday, you'll know me very well. I just live through this alley."

XIII

"You danced the line!" First gasped. "You lured a live one from outside of Sub Rosa!"

Second swore it wasn't her, but how else would First have found out I had met the black convertible man out front of the Smoke Shoppe? I didn't see any cause for alarm; the convertible man was a good live one, paid well enough, and he said he'd come back for my party. First gave me quite the lecture on not doing what she called "dancing the line" or trolling around the city side of Advent Alley looking for live ones. Abduction and being arrested were the serious consequences she described at length. She went on to include having my photo taken, my shoes stolen, and having teen hoodlums throw raw eggs at me.

"She could escape," Second added. First slapped her forehead for saying it, then she gave one to me for causing the trouble in the first place. First can't punch. I doubt she would punch us though, even if she wanted to; she couldn't on account of her fingernails being too long to make a proper fist. Her slaps didn't hurt much, but Second and I were both left with red foreheads, the mark of First's frustration. I hated having the same mark as Second. I lowered my head and waited for First's hand to fall gently upon my crown, or the back of my neck, for a pat. How did Second do it, I wondered, how did she go through her days with so little love? She didn't have my sympathy. I was just pissed that she had smeared me with her sour luck. I was pissed at

First, too. If she didn't want me to dance the damn line, she should have told me when she trained me. "No's Smoke Shoppe is a landmark for finding Advent Alley. It's not a display window. We don't go advertising our wares at No's, do you understand?" First only huffed as I nodded in agreement. "Arsen is coming to get you. He'll deal with you," she said with her arms folded tight behind her.

Arsen dealt with me by putting his hand up my skirt as he drove me to his place. "Don't touch me," he said when I reached for his pant leg.

His game still thrilled me, though I played it like I was bored. I held a grudge against him for gambling on my Dark Days, for thinking I didn't have any magic, and for making my party invitation cards so girlish and plain. The chance for a quick brush against his chest or brief bump with his lips hadn't lost its appeal, however. I could brew all I wanted to, my body still twitched at his touch. I wanted to be big like First and smother him. I wanted my limbs to bend like Fauxnique's; I would have wrapped my arms around him and squeezed like a snake. I wanted to force my finger into his mouth—the mouth he rarely kissed me with—past the closed gate of his faultless teeth, down his tongue's easy runway, and retch the fleshy hole of his throat. I mulled this fantasy over for so long that I got a sympathetic gag reflex. I turned to the passenger window so Arsen wouldn't see, choking a bit. "All right there, Little?" he asked.

"City smog," I lied. There was a strange and queasy lump in my throat. I thought about cock. Not live one cock, the kind that that I'd lovingly milked for money. No, this was tangled-up-in-polyester-sheets cock, drunk-in-the-backseat-of-a-moving-car cock, can-I-please-sleep-on-your-couch-tonight-mister cock. City cock. Or, more accurately, city me, fumbling my way around the crude wants of city men. I tried to spit up the memory. I didn't want it associated with Arsen. I guess it served me right. I should never have thought violent thoughts about him. Glories should never want to force another. We're above it.

My guts were still punishing me when we got to his place. I skipped petting Toro and lingering around his photos and CD collection. I took off my own panties and let him arrange me on the kitchen table. It went down routinely, our fuck. He hitched my legs in the air, my arms were tangled in the dress that never fully made it over my head. A coffee cup danced across the tabletop, splashing a creamy brown trail behind it until it fell. Neither of us cared if it was broken or not. He said, "Never worry me like that again. I don't want to lose you." I promised him and promised him and promised.

And I meant it. I meant to do almost everything he told me. Then he had to start chattering about magic. Still hard inside me, he says, "Let me hear you say, 'I can take away your pain.'"

"Why?"

"Plan B. I'm going to bill you as a healer. Live ones want healers; city life is more painful than ever. I have it all planned out. You'll be a hit as a healer. But you'll need to practise to be convincing."

"Now?"

"Right now." I felt him pulse inside me like a second heartbeat and it made me dizzy. His idea of a healer was characterized by divine touch and long sermons full of lulls and crescendos, by intuitive buzz words like "energy" and "transformative" and dumb faith.

We rehearsed his lines together, shouting them in our leg-locked position. I couldn't get his voice to rise quite like that during sex ever before. His passions were marching orders, instructions for the body:

"Who here wants to be free from pain?"

"Who is ready to say goodbye to misery?"

"Let me hear you say it."

"Louder now!"

"Little," said Arsen. "You have to believe what you say. You have to *move* your audience. I don't feel moved yet."

I'll show him, I thought. Phantom hand followed the coffee trail off the table to the tile floor. I could feel everything it could: the difference between the smooth marble tiles and the grout that filled the gaps between them. I felt Arsen's body heat as phantom hand dragged up his leg, the fine mist of sweat behind his knees. Arsen stopped to scratch at his thigh; I cried out a line from his healer's address and he gave me a sideways smile and grabbed my ankles tighter. First might have forgot to warn me about dancing the line, but she'd told me everything about how men work. I knew just where to wriggle a finger, where to push. Phantom hand seized Arsen's testicles like a throat. I'd learned this would make him last longer. I lay back and let him tire himself out on me. His throat dried out while I spoke on and on about redemption.

Years ago, long before I arrived on Sub Rosa, a leather-bound copy of the Holy Bible had been bought for the Wifey Wing library. It was shelved beside Mary Shelley's *Frankenstein*. In it, there were many mentions of both hands and ghosts. Almighty hands always reached through a hole in the sky, lifting hearts up to heaven, striking down the Egyptians, and so on. After a career of placing his hands on lepers and sinners, a dying Christ cried, "Father, into your hands I entrust my spirit."

To prepare for the party, Arsen had me read this Bible, or at least the New Testament, and practise saying Christ's lines. "You could read the paperbacks by Shirley MacLaine, too, if you like. But Jesus will always be more 'in' than any New Age babble," he instructed.

I flipped through the Bible like the triplets flipped through their magazines, looking for images to add to their collage. From it, I daydreamed an explanation for phantom hand. Like the Holy Ghost, phantom hand was a part of a greater entity. Me. As Arsen instructed, I imitated Christ. I pretended phantom hand was the Holy Ghost. Sub Rosa was heaven. The Glories were angels. (Second was the fallen one.) Live ones were sinners come to repent. God was no one. I played divine house without a father. The more I tried to assign the role to some-one—say, First or the Dowager—the less sense the game made. It felt silly; after all, I was too old to play house.

Instead, I readied phantom hand for our debut. I rehearsed by pushing the Bible across the library floor, in small bursts at first. Even-tually, it slid from one end of the room to the other. It even rose off the floor an inch or two.

"Little! Speak to me, Little." In my deep concentration I hadn't no-ticed First quaking in the doorway. How the scene must have looked to her: a possessed Bible and me, trance-like, in the corner of the room. First ran in and scooped me up, knocking a potted daisy off the library desk as we fled.

She rushed from room to room, unable to locate a safe place for us to hide. She spat out clipped questions, unsure of what to ask. "What—evil? How are you?" She was losing her breath and her stride. Poor First, so used to having control, especially in her own home. She was painfully unequipped to deal with the unexplainable.

"It was me, First!" I had to kick and yell before she heard me. She held me at arm's length, shaking her puzzled head. "It's my magic," I told her. "I can touch things without really touching them. I can move things around."

"Your magic?"

"Yeah, I discovered my Glory magic."

First put me down and took a step back. "None of us have magic like that."

"Ling can attract stuff, like flowers. The Dowager has her wind."

"Ling, that's just parlour tricks. And the Dowager's wind isn't hers, it's a ghost," said First. "Royal's ghost." I explained that phantom hand was a kind of ghost too, one I could communicate with and command.

"How can your hand have a ghost if it's not dead?"

The question startled me. I cradled my left hand in my right, felt the warmth of my palms pressed together. First cringed a little each time my hands moved. "You scared of me, First?" I asked her.

"No. No, baby girl." Her lips stretched across her teeth in a forced smile. "I'd never be 'fraid of you. I just never seen a ghost hand, as you say, and I'm not sure that it's normal, is the thing. No one has this kind of magic."

Normal! I thought. Now we have to be concerned about being normal. "Trust me. Just for a minute," I told her as I placed phantom hand gently on her stomach. First slapped her own hand over top of it.

"Where did it go?" she asked, feeling around her tummy.

"Well, I'm not going to do it to you if you're scared," I said.

She told me to try again, stiffening her stance and closing her eyes. I swept a curl across her forehead.

"That's nothing to be 'fraid of, right?"

I tapped the tip of her nose and she nodded. I let phantom hand rest on her shoulder.

"Warm," she said. "I'd never suspect a ghost hand to be warm." She began to laugh, though I wasn't tickling her. "Arsen's gonna eat his words. He thinks you got no Glory specialty."

"Don't tell him!" First widened her eyes at me. She'd kept secrets from Arsen before—tucking away money or presents without his say-so. I could tell by the size of First's bugging eyes that she thought phantom hand was too big a secret to keep.

"He's making me debut as a healer tomorrow. We've been practising and practising. I was in the library all day today." I bleated the words to earn her pity. I probably sounded like Second when she whined, except

I had something of value to protect, while Second merely bellyached about freedom, whatever that means. Freedom to hang out at the Mayflower and act like a bitch, I suppose. Phantom hand was worth more than that. "He says that healers are 'it' in the city right now; eastern medicine and past lives recovery and energy healing and divine mystic therapy and all that stuff. That's the word he's spreading in the city about me. If we tell him now he'll want to postpone my party. I'll have to redo my entire debut theme. And besides—" I cupped my hands over my face, for effect.

"Besides what, little one?" First squatted down close to me.

"Phantom hand needs a lot of work still and … and maybe Arsen's not the best teacher? He doesn't train me like you do. So I can understand it."

"Well, I know he can be a bit hasty—"

"Yes, he is hasty," I said, cutting First off. "And he never listens to me. Not like you do. I'd rather just you and me train my magic, so it can be really good." First nibbled her lower lip as she mulled it over.

"Think of what we can do with it. We could be the most famous family on Sub Rosa. Suddenly we'll have the power to move things, just little things, but that's more magic than anyone else has got," I said. "If you'll help me learn to control it. Help me figure out the right way to use it. I know it can be put to better use than just pushing books around the library floor. What would you do with a phantom hand, First mommy?"

First closed her eyes and imagined the possibilities. "Touch me again." I lifted a whispered finger to her eyelid.

"Okay," she said, without laughing or flinching. "I can train you, in secret, just for a while."

XIV

A Sub Rosa debut, in theory, is the same as anywhere else. Its purpose is to introduce a newly trained Glory to the regular live ones and let them know she is available for companionship. It is important for the debut to be well-timed. The debutante must be mature enough to carry the crowd's attention. If she can't captivate the room, someone else surely will. After all, every Glory, not just the debutante, vies for the most attention—to be the one remembered at the end of the night. But if the debut is thrown too late, her House won't be able to cash in on the new Glory's freshness. "So much pressure, this whole virgin/whore thing," I complained to First.

We spent the better part of the afternoon primping. First reserved the entire Spa Rosa beauty shop. She hung the closed sign in the window herself to make sure we weren't disturbed. "Sleep," First ordered Second and me as we sat with hot roller sets under hair dryers. "Take a beauty nap any chance you get. This day is gonna be long."

Eartha and Astrid laboured over me with their polishes and sprays. They glued blue butterflies into my hair and pasted minuscule rhinestones on my eyelashes. Covering me in shimmering powder became a group affair during which I was made to strip naked while everyone tossed the powder at me like wedding rice. Second sprinkled some onto her hands and clapped, making a glittery cloud between her palms. When the dust settled I looked like I had a celestial sunburn. Even my armpits were sparkly.

After the longest six hours of my life, we were ready—too early. We hung around the Spa lobby killing time. "Stay clear of that window," said First. "Nobody suppose to see you yet." We awkwardly arranged ourselves on the waiting chairs so that our turquoise dresses wouldn't wrinkle in the back.

"You know what Arsen's going to present her as?" Second asked. First and I gave each other calculating looks. We had a big plan for phantom hand. I prayed she wouldn't give me away.

"A healer," said First.

"He's presenting Little as a healer! This I gotta see."

"I'm a healer," I snapped. "I could be if I wanted to."

"You can be a damn elephant, I don't give a fuck. It's Arsen I'm talking about," said Second. "Him and his jacked-up titles that don't say shit. If he heard it on one of those talk shows with women crying in the audience then he thinks it's cool."

"Be careful with that mouth of yours, Second, honey," warned First.

"Well, what'd he present you as, Candy?"

"Conquest."

"A conquest, like you're Mount Everest, or what?" Second made like she was scaling a rock face, yodeling as she climbed. First broke a smile before telling her to shut up. "I had it way worse," Second went on. "He called me an 'everywoman,' whatever that means."

"You forget Arsen growed up in a church family. Everyman, or woman, is a Christian story. It's after *Everyman*, the medieval morality play," said First. Second and I only blinked at her. "Mankind and God have a good chit-chat," First sighed. "There's a copy in our library."

"Is that why my live ones always cry out 'oh my god'?" Second snorted at her joke. First covered her laugh with her hand. I saw the toothy corners of her mouth peek out—what was left of the girl in her peeked out too. "You should get presented as something more unique, more you, is all I'm saying," Second said to me when the laughter subsided.

"Arsen is so stingy. Healers are so played out." First and I stared blankly; First's girlish smile dropped. Had Second given me a compliment? Second herself appeared to have tripped on her own words. Getting off her chair in a hurry, she started to glide around the red carpet. "We shouldn't have to leg it in these get-ups," she complained, changing the subject. "We should float there, like angels."

But First had us walk slowly and carefully, lifting our dresses a foot off the ground so that they wouldn't pick up what little dust or grime there was on the street. Not very glamorous, I thought, tiptoeing across the cobblestones. Mr Saragosa turned his key crank extra quickly as we passed the Pawnshop. The white steel doors unfurled with a noisy clatter. "Busy afternoon," he said. "You'll be getting some lovely gifts tonight, my dear." I wasn't expecting presents, but after Mr Saragosa mentioned them, I hoped someone got me diamond earrings. There was no Sub Rosa proverb that said I couldn't have diamond earrings.

There were cars parked up and down the street; I counted BMW and Mercedes hood ornaments along the way. Arsen's freshly washed and waxed Alfa Romeo sat right in front of the Mayflower's front door, parked directly under the ship's figurehead that resembled First. In sharp contrast to us, Arsen had decided on effortless panache. His butter-cream coloured linen suit was unbuttoned. An ostrich leather belt hung at his hips. He didn't baby step in his wingtip shoes the way we did in our heels.

"You ready?" he asked me. "You practised your lines?" I was ready, more ready than he could possibly have imagined. Second's comment, about being presented as original, rang in my mind, and phantom hand twitched with eagerness.

The Mayflower Ballroom was panelled in dark wood like the restaurant, but no ships in bottles and no booths. There was a small proscenium stage with velvet curtains where I'd be making my speech. The microphone drooped in its stand.

Shirley and Al had decorated the room in blues and greens. The ceiling was hung with floral garlands. First, who could reach them, touched a strand. "Dyed carnations. How beautiful!"

"We spent the day stringing them," Likka said. I turned to see red plunge neckline, red plunge neckline, red plunge neckline. The triplets had traded their pink marabou hairpins in for va-va-vixen dresses. It was the only time I'd seen them out of their booth, without the milkshakes and glitter-glue sticks. They were going to give House of Arsen a run for our money, I thought, hugging them with our customary squeal.

"Eddie Junior is here," Likka started in with the gossip. "I wonder if your Second will make out with him?" We responded to her question with a round of ewws, our grownup dresses doing nothing to mature our conversation.

Shirley had hired Eddie Junior and Senior as servers for the party. I don't know whose idea it was to make them turquoise cummerbunds and bow ties, but I watched them as they happily delivered trays of unidentifiable hors d'oeuvres shaped like tubes or puffs to incoming guests.

A man plucked Portia from our huddle and lifted her onto his right shoulder. She perched there as they wove through the room, lighting paper lanterns shaped like butterflies. I knew it had to be the elusive Klime, Daddy of House of Klime, by the way he cradled Portia's feet in his hands. Portia didn't mask her bliss; her face beamed amid the hanging flowers as her legs dangled from her Daddy's shoulder.

All of the Glories seemed happier to have their Daddies nearby. Ling intentionally brushed by Klime as she danced with a live one. She was a toy ballerina on a mechanical track, gliding and gliding across the dance floor. Men watched her like they were kids pressed up against the window of a toyshop at Christmas time. They unconsciously shuffled as they waited to be next on her dance card.

Fauxnique wore a tiara of blinking lights. She was feeding a live one a forkful of cake, smearing icing on his chin. Her Daddy, Emanuel, could have been Second Man's older brother: same side part and sculpted brows, but with a thin film of exhaustion. Worn down from living in the city, I guessed. He danced with Dearest balanced on top of his feet like a father dancing with his child.

Second and Ling's Second, two squared, as the triplets called them, sat in a corner together, drinking wine. Alcohol. Eddie Junior and Senior had traded their appetizer trays for bottles of red wine. They flitted behind the guests, pouring wine into glasses, unnoticed. Eddie Senior was particularly vigilant. I could almost hear him thinking, *top up, top up, this fellow needs to slow down already, top up, latent sloppy lush, splash, top up*. I felt sorry for him. Interpreting the nuances of drinkers from behind the scenes was a bummer job.

I suppose I hadn't gone all that long without a drink, myself. Booze seemed like it was from another universe, foreign and light-years away. First caught me, eyes trained on the wine bottles as they worked the room. "It's for the guests," she said.

It appeared that Second considered herself a guest. She clinked glasses with Ling's Second, their glasses probably kept full by Eddie Junior. Arsen headed for her, and seeing him come, Second tilted her glass back to finish her wine in a hurry.

"Leave her." First grabbed the cuff of his jacket. "Let her be with her friend. Let her have a little wine. It's a special night. Besides, you always tell us that if a live one offers a drink, we should at least taste it in appreciation." Second raised her glass in our direction. I returned the gesture out of habit, offering her an awkward salute with my empty hand.

Arsen busied himself shaking hands with live ones. There were at least fifty of them. As they arrived, I watched for incoming presents. The gift table by the door was growing crowded with tiny boxes. A couple of live ones passed Arsen envelopes, which he casually tucked in his jacket pocket. Once in a while, he'd bring someone over to meet me. "Little, this is Ted, this is Frank"—their names were so boring they must have been made up. I could barely keep track of their small talk, my focus darting around the room.

I bugged First to start the speeches. I knew I wouldn't be able to relax until they were over.

"Look around you," grumbled First. "Somebody's still missing." As soon as she said it, I noticed the Diamond Dowager's absence. If it was anyone else, we might have started without them. Diamond knew we would wait.

The wine began to take the room. There weren't enough Glories to go around. Ling had a whole crowd surrounding her. I heard her making jokes and the waves of well-timed laughter from the men. Second Man's dancing got a little bit wilder, taking up any empty floor space. A live one pawed his waist as if searching for a bit of body fat to squeeze. Men asked me to dance and somehow I held my own. They were too tipsy to notice my amateur steps. I made a note to myself to have Arsen teach me partners' dancing; there was still something useful I could learn from him.

"You're not bad at that cha-cha business," one told me as I was filling my punch glass. He was tucked behind the dessert table, holding a puff pastry with only a single bite taken. Cream filling oozed out, waiting for the man to take a second mouthful.

"You're being kind. I can barely keep time."

"You looked great, at least from this distance." He cleared his throat and I recognized his particular raspy breath as the Widower's.

What are you doing here? I almost said. I pressed my mouth shut, not knowing if I should speak to him at all. Every word, every sound I'd ever said to him had been well planned and timed. I wasn't about to spoil my mystique with an over-animated *Oh my god! I'm super happy you came to my party.*

The Widower laughed out of politeness. "I'm not one for parties. In fact, I was about to leave, but not before saying good night to you."

"Good night," I whispered. I gave him the sweetest embrace I could without overdoing it— no pelvic tilts, no rubbing the nape of his neck. He hugged me back in the same reserved manner.

This was the scene the Dowager walked in on: the Widower and me. A burst of wind rattled the garland along the ceiling. A couple candles blew out. The Diamond Dowager stood at the door with her orphan children behind her. The room grew silent. "Finally," I heard someone in the crowd say. I knew it was First, although she had disguised her voice. The Diamond Dowager glared at me, arm in arm with the Widower. He hadn't visited one of her orphans since he'd met me.

"Little, you look lovely." She glided over to me and kissed my cheek. Her lips were icy cold, and I swear she gnashed her teeth in my ear as she pulled away. She and her girls wore their usual black apparel to my party, but the orphans each had a spray of coloured ostrich feathers in their hair and matching ribbon chokers. They walked in their usually uniform line, except for one, on the end, who swayed slightly to the music. She should have been here a few minutes before when things had really been bumping, before the Dowager sobered everyone up. I saw this orphan's unfettered smile and, what was even better, the smear of lipstick on her teeth. *Don't these girls know anything about Glorying?* I laughed to myself. I said one last thank you to the Widower and ran after the orphan.

"I'm Little," I said.

"Yes. I read the invitation." Confused, she didn't say her name, just peered over my shoulder at the other orphans moving forward without her.

"What's your name?" Her face twisted as if I was speaking a foreign language.

"Isabella," she said finally.

"Sweet Isabella, between us girls, you have some lipstick on your teeth." Isabella froze as I slid my finger between her lips, the same way First always did with me, and wiped the smear of red away.

"Normally, we don't wear this bright lipstick," she explained.

"It looks very pretty. That gentleman right there even noticed," I pointed at the Widower as he exited out the door.

"The Widower? Noticed me?"

"That's right," I said, hoping she would tell the others. I wanted to put an end to this idea that I was purposefully trying to steal the orphans' regular. Isabella, at least, was happy. She skittered away with just a bit of bounce in her step.

I searched for First and Arsen to ask them, "Now?" Finally, they took me behind the black velvet curtain. Arsen hardly said a word of encouragement to me before he strutted across the stage. He clinked a spoon on a wine glass in front of the microphone to get the crowd's attention. "Good evening, friends," he sweetly repeated a few times. His overdone confidence told me he was nervous too. But the crowd only saw his strikingly upright posture as he sang a cappella loud enough to fill two ballrooms.

"He's singing Sub Rosa's official anthem," First told me. It was a French song, and so I didn't understand the words. I didn't need to understand to be completely taken. Arsen's voice sounded as if it tore free from his heart, gained momentum as it travelled up his throat, and leaped from his mouth, triumphant. First and I parted the curtains enough to see everyone falling into a trance, listening. Even the twirling breeze around the Diamond Dowager settled, and she took a seat, letting her layers of petticoats fan out around her. I was captivated as well, though not captivated enough not to worry if Arsen was too tough an act to follow. I had work to do on that stage.

"Make us proud," First whispered to me. And maybe it was the French song or the half glass of wine she had drank, but she kissed

She kissed me square on the lips, not for long, but long enough to show me exactly how soft her mouth was. It was neither motherly nor seductive. It was a kiss that, for a moment, balanced us. Made us equals. Partnered us in whatever was about to come. Then she turned me around and nudged me through the curtain. Arsen's song had ended and people were whistling enthusiastically. Their cheers grew louder as I came waving onstage, shyly at first, then, letting the applause sink in, I raised my hand high in the air for the crowd. First gave me a minute to soak it up before she stepped out after me.

Arsen told my story. It sounded not unlike the legend of Sub Rosa—prescriptive and fairytale-ish. I was a girl in terrible danger, a drifter, homeless. Drugs and drink and the worst type of city men infecting my purest heart. I was unrecognizable: underfed, sickly, and unloved. The audience made sounds of empathy, tsks and ahs. And through it all, I was a virgin. A Glory waiting to happen. I went from rags to pizzazz. From ill to thrill. "Not only did she save herself here on Sub Rosa, she can cure your ailments, too," Arsen declared in his best preacher voice. "That is her gift." He seemed satisfied with the audience's reaction and began to steer First and me away while people stood for an ovation. He subtly shook his head at me, signalling me not to make a speech. He thought I'd fumble my lines, that ass.

First skirted around him to the microphone. The audience leaned forward in unison as she spoke. "Hello, beautiful ones, let me just take a moment to look at you," First called out, shielding her eyes from the spotlight with her queenly hand. "As a matter of fact, have a look around you right now. Take a moment to notice your fair friends and neighbours in this room." As instructed, the crowd turned to each other with smiles and nods. Men shook hands. Cheeks were kissed. Little did they know First was simply buying me time to survey the room, to chart my plan of action. "Thank you, all of you for coming to this auspicious occasion. Little is a precious wonder, as some of you already have the pleasure of knowing. Now, she is a modest girl, though I bet you all could persuade her to come say a few words." She adjusted the mic to my height as the crowd broke into heavy applause. Arsen went to help her, a little too late, and I began my speech with First at my side.

The microphone hissed as I too eagerly snatched it up. Before I had even spoken a word, my lower lip grazed the mic head; I saw a smear of fuchsia pink lipstick on the metal mesh and took a deep breath.

"My Daddy, Arsen, has plainly retold my story. I am humbly without secrets in this room full of good people," I said, hoping I sounded sincere, hoping more so that Arsen would be taken aback by my crafted speech. He was about to be outdone. "I will only speak to these unhappy truths for a brief moment, if you'll hear me. There is no denying the link between indulging city ills and sorrow. I am most pleased to have reformed my ways and to be able to offer you my purest service. But there is something Arsen has left unsaid." Phantom hand drifted across the stage and slipped into the crowd. I needed a minute to blush and bat my eyelashes and stall while I got it under control.

"You see, all my life I've felt very alone. It seems odd that in a big city full of people I could feel this way. I suppose we all feel alone sometimes?" No one bit the bait; my question went unanswered. "I suppose we've all felt alone sometimes, alone and untouchable." For effect, my voice quavered on the word "untouchable," and to my relief, a few murmurs of affinity rose up. "No one should have to be alone, am I right?" I heard a few calls of agreement, a "hear, hear" and a "yes."

"It's because of all of you in this very room that I am finally a part of something. Something truly wonderful." Another "hear, hear" echoed at the back of the room. Encouraged, I spoke a little louder. "Perhaps it was because I came to Sub Rosa a virgin, unloved, untouched, that when I finally found my way here, to be sublimely touched by all of you, I found my Glory magic. The magic of shared touch. And if you'll only let me, I promise to touch you just like you've all touched me."

This is where my plan unfolded. I started touching people. I ran phantom hand along the curve of a live one's earlobe so that he shivered. Next, I traced a shirt collar, undid a top button with ease. "If you believe, reach out your hands and receive it." Hands shot out around the room. I rubbed a phantom finger in many wide-set palms. And bolder still, the inseam of finely pressed pants. "Praise be," someone shouted, "I feel you right now, Little."

"I feel it too. Glory be," someone else echoed. Soon I had the whole party squirming and gasping. I even chanced a quick feel up the Dowager's petticoats. She made a sound like a cat being squeezed. I could picture it all—how endless live ones would come for me to be touched by an unseen hand. "Touched by love itself," I shouted. In the corner of my eye I saw Arsen's chin-trembling false grin. Phantom hand tapped the bottom of his chin and his mouth clamped swiftly shut.

"Above all else, I'd like to thank my First, Della O'Kande," I said to rub Arsen's nose in it. "She has taught me so much, and also my Second …" I didn't know Second's Glory name. I almost called her Jill, but I caught myself. Birth names were never used on Sub Rosa. Besides, an ordinary name like Jill might have cheapened my speech. I scanned the room hoping to point her out in the absence of a name. It seemed too late to just cut the sentence off after Second. People smiled at me, seeming to urge me on. Others began to glance around them for Second.

"Where are they?" First held her hand across her forehead as a shield from the stage lights overhead as she searched the room. "I told Treasure Anne to make sure she was here for your speech."

Time can pass in a warped chronology on Sub Rosa; the actions of one live one can blend into the fleeting words of another and then blend again into Glory-talk gossip. Fine details are easily changed or forgotten. The night of my party, however, the details came together like the closely shouldered men in the crowded Mayflower Ballroom. I remembered the caller's voice over the pay phone desperate with need. *My Treasure. I'm taking you away. Saturday.* This was what the phone call in Advent Alley was all about. If I was right, the caller had planned to meet Ling's Second tonight.

The only thing to do then was cry some beauty pageant tears before rushing off the stage. Who can argue with a young woman in tears? I coughed up some parting sentiment: "I am so grateful to be here. Much love." First ran after me, catching me by the arm as soon as we were behind the curtain.

"Ling's Second is named Treasure?"

"Treasure Anne," First told me. "Why?"

"A man's come to get her."

"What?" First said. "How you know?"

"I just know a man's come for Treasure," I repeated.

That was all First needed to hear to take action. "Come on." We rushed, hand-in-hand, through the ballroom. Ling—her eyes bugging in panic—latched on to First's other side, and the three of us swept through the dim corners of the ballroom trying not to be seen by the crowd as we searched.

"You made her weep with happiness," I heard Arsen say before he started up another song. I hoped his choirboy voice was enough to cover up the mess.

We checked under the white table-clothed punch table. We checked backstage and both restrooms and every booth in the Mayflower Diner, and then we checked the ballroom again. Second and Treasure Anne were nowhere to be found. "Whoever came for them isn't here anymore," Ling cried. First guided her outside to calm her down. We stood out on Ling's track patch for only a split-second before we noticed a red Volvo stopped in Advent Alley. The old car did everything it could to be noticed, sputtering and smoking under the hood. It had to be the caller. Before I knew what I was doing, I ran. First and Ling followed with clomping strides.

"Damn, damn, damn," Ling repeated behind me. Our heels thundered against the pavement. I got close enough to see Treasure Anne in the passenger seat, just her—Second was still nowhere to be seen. And, as I'd anticipated, Treasure Anne wasn't struggling. The caller hadn't tied or gagged her. Second wasn't whispering over her shoulder, brainwashing her. Instead, she sat nervously twirling her curly red hair around her finger. I realized this was her get-away car. She was leaving voluntarily, or at least trying to. The wisps of smoke coming from under the Volvo's hood stank like burning oil. Treasure had been sort of nice to me, I recalled as I closed in on the car; she had put some effort into circulating my invitations, at least. Her head swung from me to the driver. I found myself slowing down, preparing what I would say when I caught up to her. The car wasn't going anywhere. Sub Rosa had denied its entry, as well as its speedy exit. I heard the motor coughing and stalling.

The driver was a junker, too: unkempt beard, knobby shoulders. A hint of embittered bohemian style was all he had going for him. A dud in rock star clothing. Was that the ex-boyfriend the triplets were whispering about? He truly was miserable looking. Why was Treasure Anne leaving Sub Rosa for that? She was a beauty; strawberry blonde and freckles so plump I could see their rosy colour through the grimy glass. It didn't seem right to conceal all that beauty behind a bug-splattered windshield. I mean, if she or any Glory really had to leave Sub Rosa, then they should ride away on a unicorn or something like that, with the rest of us tossing roses and waving white handkerchiefs. What kind of life would this ex-boyfriend give her? Even Nino was better than him. I reached the car; my hands slapped against the hood to stop myself from completely crashing into it. I screamed, "Don't do it! Don't do it. You're making a big mistake. This guy's a loser."

Treasure scrunched up her brow and looked over at the unfortunate-looking man beside her. This distracted her just enough not to notice Ling as she came up behind me, flung open the car door, and grabbed her. Treasure didn't even fight; she limply rolled out of the car and let herself be dragged to the Sub Rosa side of the alley.

The driver stepped out of the car. "I'm taking her. You have no right to keep her."

"You want her? Come get her." Ling held Treasure in front of her like a rag doll. I felt a swift churn of nausea in my gut watching Ling be so rough. What if I had made a mistake by telling Ling about any of this? Maybe I had sabotaged Treasure Anne's plans. But the driver was a coward. How could he possibly take care of her? He made no move, just beat on the hood of his crappy car. Several partygoers had caught up with us and stood gawking at the scene. Ling put her arm around Treasure Anne, shielding her face from the crowd.

"Do you want to go with him?" Ling asked. Her voice suddenly was kind, her breathing suddenly even. Treasure Anne's strawberry hair clung to Ling's cheek. "If you want to go with him, it's your choice," Ling said loud enough for the driver to hear. He called her name and Ling unwrapped her arms for Treasure Anne to go.

"Don't go," one of the onlookers pleaded.

"Come home with me instead," said another. He waved his wallet in the air.

Treasure Anne weighed both sides briefly. Her eyes took in the man's dirty sneakers, the smoke hovering above his car. "He was handsome once," she said. "Or, at least I remembered him that way." She curled back into Ling. The onlookers clapped and whistled.

"I'll call the cops. Or the fucking mob, or whoever it will take to get her back," the driver threatened while retreating back into his car, which turned over then without any trouble.

"Call the cops," Ling yelled at him. "I'll call them for you." She walked up to the place where all this started—the pay phone—ripped the receiver clean off and used it to smash the front window of the Volvo, the driver's shocked reaction masked by the web of cracks in the glass. The live ones cheered Ling and booed the retreating car. First put her arms around the two of them to lead them back to the party, bragging about me as they went. "It was our very own Little who saw the kidnapper coming. She's got a touch of intuitive abilities, wouldn't you say?" First chattered.

"We owe Treasure Anne's safely to you, Little," said Ling. Treasure Anne smiled at me, though the corners of her mouth trembled ever so slightly. She had a cut on her knee and had bled through her stockings. The stocking ran even more as she limped back to her track patch. Little rips of her pink skin showing through the black.

The words, "Jill's still in there. Hiding in the back seat," came from Treasure Anne's trembling mouth. It took me a moment to make sense of those words. A moment later Second's voice screeched like the Volvo's tires on the city side of the alley. "Fuck the Rosa," she yelled from the back seat of the get-away car. All of us—First, Ling, Treasure Anne, even the stray partygoers—swung around to see Second giving us the finger as the old car rattled away. No one yelled back. We were stunned silent.

Figures Second would ruin my party.

XV

It was a real charade having to smile and amuse guests for the rest of the party. It was worse to witness First's forced cheerfulness as live ones talked and grabbed at her. It was enough to make me want to slap them away with phantom hand. But, exhausted, I barely had the concentration to see phantom hand in front of my own face. My ring finger was numb. When I could, I buffered her from the men. I'd crawl into the lap of the live one sitting next to her. I cut in on her dances. I vied for the attention I knew she didn't want.

Meanwhile, the news of Second's departure spread from Treasure Anne to the triplets, from the triplets to the House of Klime, from Klime to the Daddies, the Daddies to the Glories, and lastly, I saw Ling slink over to the Diamond Dowager. I was embarrassed watching gossip telephone around the room. At least it brought the party to a quicker end. Glories cleared the room by dragging live ones back to their apartments for nightcaps. Diamond brought a half dozen men to her house, the group of them looking like death's wedding as they paired up with the orphans and marched away in their matching black dresses and dinner jackets.

Shirley and Al killed the music after they left and the Daddies escorted the remaining partygoers out, shaking hands and speaking in their business voices as they went. Finally, First and I had peace. The ballroom was spent: costume feathers floated in the air unsure of where to land; dyed carnations were stamped into the dark wood floor.

We helped Shirley and Al pull down the floral garlands. Old Maggie pushed a squeaky-wheeled cart around, collecting wine glasses. Although no one expected her to, First couldn't stop herself from tidying up. By the time we left, the expensive cars had all cleared out, except Arsen's.

"Stay," First asked him. And I knew what that meant. I told them that I'd take the sitting room sofa. I was too mad at Second to sleep in her bed. First kissed me goodnight at the front door; her forehead clunked against mine and her lips missed me entirely. They retreated to our room, and I stood, for a good while, a heap of tiny gift boxes collected in my arms. *I'll open them tomorrow*, I assured myself. *I'll wake up to a bounty.*

In the morning, a squad car was parked on the city side of the Smoke Shoppe. Ling had woken early to clean the stray cigarette butts and party favours from her track patch. She was just about to re-bless it with almond oil and rose petals when she noticed red and blue siren lights ricocheting against the alley wall for a few seconds, long enough to scare her into keeping watch for over an hour. The cop car's nose inched forward and blocked Advent Alley, and Ling ran straight to our window, screaming.

The bulky white bumper and a bit of royal blue trim on the hood were all that we could see from the Sub Rosa side of the alley. All the Glories got out of bed and huddled together in the street in our gauzy pyjamas and silk robes wondering what to do next.

"Don't worry none," First said. "They can't get in. Can't even see in here." Sub Rosa doesn't allow harm in, is what I'd been told again and again. Why then did everyone look so anxious?

"It's totally happened before. Who knows why they're here, but with nothing to see, they'll leave soon," said Fauxnique as she nervously chewed her candy-floss hair.

"How soon?" asked Second Man. "I have a breakfast date."

"Let's hope it's not too long." Arsen wouldn't quit tapping his foot. "This is what cops do. I've seen them park outside the girly bars in the city. It's as good as putting a black X on the door. No customers come when the cops are sitting out front. The strippers and hostesses lose business until the cops clear out."

"So no live ones until they go?" asked Second Man.

"I want my Daddy," Dearest cried. It made me cringe to hear her.

"No Daddy gonna come. No bodies gonna come, don't you listen?" First pointed at the squad car. Who would dare ask a cop to move his car so they could go visit a secret street of magical working girls? Dearest latched on to Arsen's pant leg as our situation fully dawned on her. All of the Glories seemed to be moving closer to him; their robes falling open slightly as they turned to him for help.

"What do you think I can do?" he asked. "Drive out of here, or walk, even? And where would it look like I came from? From out of a dead-end alley?" Arsen was stuck like the rest of us. Even if he could squeeze by the cops, the risk that they would stop him for questioning was too high. His only safe course of action was to call Klime or Emanuel for help. The pay phone receiver lay in the centre of the alley where Ling had thrown it. It was the only phone on Sub Rosa. Any other place in the world would have more than one phone, but not us. We didn't even get cell phone reception. What links us to the rest of the world are Daddies and live ones. Arsen picked up the severed phone and chucked it at the wall. His frustration made us all jump. Second's paranoia had come true: we were prisoners on Sub Rosa. I wouldn't have put it past her to have called the police herself.

"It all right." First attempted to pacify us, smoothing the air around her with her open palms. "Like Fauxnique says, the police can't keep watchin' an empty alley for long."

"How long?" Dearest asked. "I want my Daddy." Second Man picked her up and passed her to Fauxnique.

"We can survive perfectly well without your precious Daddies."
We turned to see the Diamond Dowager standing behind us. Dearest
wormed out of Fauxnique's arms and began to flap and stomp like a
hen trying to fly. I wanted to slap her; the other Glories tended to her
tantrum with gentle coos and shushes. "Come away from the alley,
child," said the Dowager. "You'll attract attention."

"Cops can't see us," First argued.

"The police don't see us because they don't think to see us. We are
outside their imagination. However, something—or someone, rather—tipped them off about our location. Without a doubt it was your
urchin of a Second Wife, Arsen. Haven't you put it together for yourself yet? Running off wasn't enough for that one—oh, no—she likely
called in an anonymous tip. And now all it would take is for them to
notice a single spark or overhear a single word, and the blind alley
might start to take shape. They might begin to see what is through
it." Diamond's speech caused the Glories to back away from Arsen a
little. Like me, Diamond suspected Second, though I saw no reason for
the entire House of Arsen to become suspect. Second Man narrowed
his eyes at us. The triplets began whispering in each other's ears. First
balled up the silky fabric of her nightie in her worried fists.

The Diamond Dowager led us to the Mayflower. I hate to admit
that the collective anxiety did subside as we followed the Dowager's
lead; she had been around longer than any of us, after all. She was the
mother of Sub Rosa. And she was the only one who had something
concrete to say.

"What if they're already on to us?" Ling wanted to know.

"There's no way of finding out until the squad car vacates. I should
be able to get to the bottom of it tonight or tomorrow," said Arsen.

"And what will you have figured out by tonight or tomorrow, all-
knowing Daddy?" the Dowager sang with sarcasm. "Remind me again
what it is you Daddies do to take care of these types of problems?"

Arsen resisted the question at first. I would have too if I were him. The Dowager was out to make him look like a fool. I was surprised First hadn't already jumped in. But she too stared at him, like the rest of us, waiting for him to answer. And when Arsen repeated that he'd take care of it, it was First who pressed him for details.

"We talk to certain city people, to start with," he said at last, "to figure out what information the police have. They've never had anything on us. Nothing but a rumour or two. But if the police or some local thugs or some social-worker types start sniffing around the Smoke Shoppe, then we create a distraction." He would have liked to end it at that. First leaned in to hear more. "So, last time we had a problem was back when Second Man was playing pinball at No's and he danced the line." A few Glories gave Second Man sideways glances; I bet Arsen was thankful to have some of the focus off him. "Remember, he tempted that redneck into the storage room with him," he continued. "If you recall, ladies, that redneck was so angry that he went into No's for a pack of Lucky Stripes and came out so vexed about his peculiar sexual flavours that he parked his Thunderbird outside with a loaded shotgun in hand. He caused a lot of headaches, yelling at live ones as they came and left Advent Alley. Scared off the business. So we took care of it," he said with a nod.

"Took care of it how?" the Dowager demanded.

"Well, in that case, we had to hire some skid hos to bait him. They kept him occupied for days. I guess it took days to convince him he was still a good ol' heterosexual boy." Arsen snickered at this a little, but First scolded him for having anything to do with skid hos.

"Well, I wasn't about to send you to tangle with him," said Arsen. First's disgust didn't soften much. "Skid hos can handle men like that. Sometimes the best thing you can do is let city sin be solved by city sin; like cures like."

"Seems like an okay solution to me," said Ling. "Skid hos deal with those types of city men all the time. They're good at it." She looked around the room and got nods of agreement from everyone, almost.

"If certain Glories would quit dancing the line, or constantly making trips to the city, or advertising Sub Rosa on their trips to the city, and if certain Daddies wouldn't recruit wayward city girls who run away bitter, then we wouldn't have these dilemmas. So then we'd have no need for you to create such cunning distractions. I suppose we'd have no use for you at all." The Diamond Dowager had eyed every single one of us as she ranted.

"My trips to the city are all dates. Very lucrative dates," Fauxnique defended herself. "It's no fault of mine that my regulars like nightlife. Besides, why should magic only be on Sub Rosa? City folks want a bit of Glory magic—like me—to walk their sad streets, too."

"You're right, Faux. There is no rule against trips to the city," said Ling. "I mean, me and my girls, we rarely leave. Why would we? But a Glory is a Glory no matter where she goes. Every new Glory has to make her dowry. I can't think of a better way than the Dark to filter out the girls who aren't worthy of Glorying. How was Arsen to know he'd marry a runaway? He believed in her and in our initiation customs. You won't catch me doubting my own House. Just like Candy and Arsen never doubted theirs."

"And fool-hearted faith in one another has done so much for Sub Rosa," sneered the Dowager.

"Why else are we here, then?" said Fauxnique. "To hate each other? You can find all types of hate elsewhere. Just walk to the end of Advent Alley, for starters. March your orphans on up to that cop car and see what an enemy actually looks like."

"The House of Royal has absolutely nothing to do with the police. It certainly isn't our House that has brought on this problem."

"Well then, why don't you take your dried-up bones back to your dried-up mansion?" First's comeback spat out from her like it had been bottled up with soda and shaken.

"Very spirited mama-bear routine," the Dowager said to Arsen. "How long did it take to train her, your dancing bear? Oh, my mistake, you didn't train her at all. She came to you loyal as the moon. Anyone else care to defend their Daddies, while we're on the subject?"

"My Daddy is king. I love him," said Dearest, totally ignorant of how idiotic she sounded. The Dowager patted her on the head.

No one else stepped in. I'm sure everyone was thinking the same thing, but only First had the courage to say it. "You forget what it's like to be with a man, you being without one for so long. And if the oh-so-good angel Royal was here, I reckon he'd tell you to quit your griping."

There was a pause, probably less than a second, long enough for us to brace ourselves for what was about to come. Wind shot through the place. Al and Shirley rushed out from the kitchen to see their collection of ships in bottles rattling against the wall. "Oh, Royal, how dare she, oh, Royal," the Dowager repeated like a prayer.

"Smoke and mirrors," First whispered to me, holding her ground. A jug freed itself from the wall and sailed toward First's head. First's scream was a deep one—a rock banging inside a steel drum. It would have hit her mouth, her row of girlish teeth, her soft lips. I knocked it off its course enough for it to miss her face. If phantom hand had been stronger I'd have turned the jug back on the Dowager, hit her square in the jaw. Shirley leapt for the bottle as it sailed past us. The ship inside collapsed as soon as she caught it.

Arsen and I rushed to First's side. Ling and Fauxnique packed around her too. And Shirley as well, but only to complain about her broken ship in a bottle. "It's ruined," she cried, phlegm gurgling in her throat.

"There's no need for your pathetic huddle," the Dowager stammered.

"My apologies for any trouble I've caused. We'll take our leave." I suspected she was only sorry to be outnumbered, not at all sorry that she ruined Shirley's ship or tried to take First's teeth out. She gathered her orphans up to go.

"Wait! Aren't we supposed to stick together, lay low?" Ling asked. "What do we do next?"

"You want my help," the Dowager laughed; it sounded strained, like tears in disguise. Arsen wasted no time after hearing that laugh.

"We *need* your help," he said. "You're Diamond." The Dowager backed away from him, although she was no longer headed for the door. Arsen approached like she was a wild cat to be tamed. His tone was the very same he took with me when we were having sex. "I may know all there is to know about cops and the city. But you've always led Sub Rosa through these situations."

The Dowager turned away from him. "Yes. However, these situations always have little to do with me. You got yourselves in, you can get yourselves out."

"We're all in this together, Diamond," Arsen said, touching her back. Her display of resistance was useless. I notice her back had lost its perfect, rigid posture. Her shoulders wrapped forward as if she was hugging herself, and I knew she'd fold. Arsen ran his hand down her and turned her around to face the room again. She fidgeted with the cloth-covered buttons on her dress; he had her.

It wasn't his hand on her elbow but his "I need you to stay with us" that stung me. I sank my face into First's side. I had little grounds to be angry with him. I'd touched live ones and said sweet things. Didn't I whisper "please" to the Widower, even when he asked me to say nothing? Didn't I let First kiss me behind the curtain? And besides, he was only manipulating the Dowager. Although knowing this made it smart the more. He'd used all the same lines on me; I'd fallen for them just as quickly.

Arsen whispered in the Dowager's ear. She took a deep breath and nodded. "This calls for a blackout," she announced. "We're going into hiding. We'll have to conceal any trace of our existence, especially charms. If you possess Glory magic, anything at all, including the power of persuasion, you must switch it off." She raised an authoritative eyebrow at Arsen as she said this. I regretted, more and more, the adolescent crush I had on him, all the promises I'd made him. My head swelled with flashbacks of his put-on longing.

"How do we switch our magic off?" asked Ling.

"Think un-Glory thoughts," commanded the Dowager. Everyone sat and focused on un-Glory thoughts, which I guessed, for them, would be things like doing the dishes or vomiting in a bar bathroom. First elbowed Fauxnique, who realized her own arms were wrapped backward around her. She uncoiled them, crossing them neatly in front of her with deliberation. The orphan children dropped out of their uniformity. One, perhaps Isabella, even scratched herself under the stiff lace dress she wore. I stuffed my hands into my pockets and pushed any thoughts of phantom hand from my head. Like everyone else, I knuckled down and concentrated on something terribly ordinary.

My un-Glory thoughts were city scenes, discarded take-out containers collected along the service roads, the cluster of pimples on the chin of one of Nino's friends. I could only capture these pictures for a few seconds at a time. When each dissolved, I was left with nothing. Literally nothing, just the blackness behind my eyelids. I felt I had to ransack my brain for the next pathetic image. The longer I concentrated the more I saw nothing.

"Everyone go home and change into your plainest clothes," the Dowager continued outlining the blackout procedure. "All Firsts turn off the lights in your apartments and wrap any good-luck charms in dark-coloured cloth. Then go outside and throw a bucket or two of water across your track patches. Not perfumed water, regular tap water."

"Triplets, go to the Smoke Shoppe. Knock loud enough for only Eddy Senior to hear. Get him to open up the power box behind the store and shut down the streetlights. Little, you and Dearest go around to all the businesses and tell them we're having a blackout. They'll know what to do."

"What are you going to do?" asked First.

"My children and I are going to communicate with Royal, to ask for his guidance and protection." More likely, I thought to myself, she was going to communicate with Arsen. He had his hand on her back like a puppeteer. First and I gave him identical warning glances, but she took my hand and stamped her feet so hard I swear the bottled ships in the Mayflower shook.

XVI

First and I tore apart the dressing room to find plain clothes. Not a single pair of her shoes were flats. "Suede boots?" she asked. I helped her switch the gold laces for black. I was grateful that the untroubled touch between us had not been disrupted. I leaned into her sturdy legs as I tied her laces, savouring the brief time we'd have together at home before returning to the Mayflower. I helped her into the nightdress she wore when she cleaned. It was plain enough, no lacy trim, no beads or embroidery. It was so sheer, however, that the outline of her panties showed through. She must have been very good at thinking un-Glory thoughts because her body had visibly shifted. Gravity claimed some of her levity. Her normally unmoving breasts swayed as she shut down the Wifey Wing.

Everything that hung inside my armoire was angel white. The black dress that Arsen had given me at his place was in there, somewhere. I had balled it up and tossed it to the back of the armoire the day I moved into the Wifey Wing. I crouched down, pushing my impressive row of shoes aside to find it. Above me, my Sub Rosa clothes fidgeted on their hangers. There was a black lump in the corner, barely noticeable against the black wood. It was my duffle bag. It smelled like stale cigarette smoke. The shoulder strap was frayed, and I had to force the cheap plastic zipper open. I found my old, ugly jeans and knew they'd be perfect. I pulled the unicorn belt out of the belt loops. It was cheap, but still too shiny to risk wearing. Sections of the glitter plastic had fallen out of the metal moulding; the unicorn was short a hoof, parts of its mane and tail were missing. I traced the empty holes with my finger. Another piece, the front leg, was coming loose. I began to pry it out with my fingernail.

"You put this on now." First plucked the unicorn from my hands and swapped it for a T-shirt. "It was Second's," she called as she rushed down the hallway. The shirt said it loved NY. I tied my hair in a sloppy ponytail, stuck flip-flops on my feet.

I regretted checking myself in the vanity mirror as soon as I saw my reflection. There was the girl I'd left behind. Alone. A waif. I pitied her. I pitied her, as if she were still there, in the city, while *I* was living the Rosa life. A curious idea came to me then: *If only I could bring her here, if only I could care for her and make her a Glory.* The mere thought of it made dark circles return to my eyes, and I swear I saw the colour of my skin grow dull. "You ready to go, First?" I shouted.

Outside, Dearest was splashing around in the shallow puddles left after Fauxnique doused their track patch. "I loved to play in the rain when I was a little kid," she told me.

"Come on," I said, disgruntled. To make things worse, she reached her tiny hand to me and curled it around mine. She played handsies as we walked. Holding her palm up to mine, she demonstrated how our hands were the same size. She showed me her ring, an oversized enamel ladybug, which didn't help her appear any older. She raised it to my nose and flipped the ring open like a locket. Inside was a very small picture of a man too blurry to identify. "Emanuel, my Daddy," she told me. "Sexy, hmm?"

We started at Babycakes Bakery. Maria, the baker, always had the exhaust fan positioned just so that the fragrance of sugar and butter would hit your nose as you passed. No one was immune to the smell-induced sugar cravings. "All these sweets will go stale," she said, holding a still-steaming tray of cinnamon buns. Her skin was oily like the caramelized glazes on her flans. She'd spent the morning baking, no doubt expecting post-party munchies. Maria clicked the fan off. "Wait," said Dearest before Maria could shut off the lights too. "I better stock up. I'll get a dozen Nanaimo bars, a dozen chocolate macaroons, four butter tarts, a box of snickerdoodles, and a bag of almond confetti. Oh, and chocolate truffles. They're not the same as fungus truffles," she told me. "I learned that when I was little." I stared at her incredulously as she pulled money from her pocket to pay for all of it.

"You want anything?" Maria asked me after she bagged up Dearest's loot. "I can start a tab for you." I declined. The moment I said "no," I regretted it. I deserved my own bag of sweets. "I'll leave the door unlocked. You just ring the bell if you run out." Maria tapped the silver bell next to the cash register.

"You get to carry your own money?" I asked as we left the bakery.

"Yes. Don't you?"

"I give all mine to First," I admitted. "She tucks it away for us."

Dearest screwed up her lips at this. Then, noticing my flabbergasted expression, she tried to backtrack. "Fauxnique doesn't spend the kind of time with me that Candy spends with you. I always see you two together. Like mommy and girly. Fauxnique's a socialite, always getting her regulars to take her and Second Man to grown-up places in the city. I'm too young to go with them, that's what they say. Besides, the city sucks. I don't even go to my Daddy's apartment. I make him come here. So I have to hold on to my money. How else would I be able to buy treats or give my Daddy his allowance or do anything? I bet I'm going to go through a lot of sweets without him." Dearest shook her bag of cookies. "You're so lucky to have Arsen around to keep you happy."

"I'm sure he'll be too busy with First or maybe even the Dowager to even notice me."

"What are you talking about? Don't you just tell him when you want him? That's what Daddies are there for, right? If we have to wait for them to come to us they may as well be live ones paying us." I couldn't believe what I was hearing, and from Dearest, no less.

"I've never actually asked Arsen for … you know."

Dearest shot me another pitiful look. Again, she covered it up with explanations. "You're stronger than me," she said. "You're a hero. You can go without. Me, I can barely go a day without asking for it. It's not my fault. Some of us are just weak-willed." She reached into the bag and popped a cookie in her mouth. Her effortless humility threw me even more. I was accustomed to First's constant bragging. First would never say she was weak.

When we called on Launderlove, June took the news much worse than Maria had. She fussed that her episode of *Cheers* wasn't finished. And the place was so big that once the overhead fluorescents were off, the outside sun barely lit half the room. "The dryers stay." She refused to be flexible on that. "Damp laundry will get moldy if it's left too long." We left her sitting on a wooden footstool, pointing a flashlight at the dryers as the clothes finished their cycle.

Mr Saragosa, at least, was familiar with the procedure. "It was ten years ago that we had our last blackout. A gang of pimps caught a whiff of Sub Rosa. Like dogs, they didn't know what exactly was under their noses, but they knew it smelled good. Rough bunch of boys. Bad for business. Let's hope this blackout passes more quickly." A thread of pink light burned in the dull neon tubing before the DIAMONDS sign went out.

At Spa Rosa, Eartha and Astrid had already turned off their rose-bulb marquee. Eartha was at the door before we knocked. "You want to know how long this will go on for?" she said, holding the door open for us. Inside there was a row of candles along the cosmetics counter. "Long enough for the Dark to settle on Sub Rosa like dust."

"Stop it, Eartha. You're scaring me," said Dearest, her mouth full of pastry. Eartha beckoned me over. From inside her white apron she drew a bottle of glowing green nail polish. She cupped it in her hand so that its strange light didn't attract Dearest's attention.

"Glow-in-the-dark top coat," she told me, grabbing my hand to run the brush across my nails. Astrid distracted Dearest with a free astrology reading. I listened in as Eartha finished my nails, impressed that Dearest remembered her own birthday. I wondered if mine was in August or if I was confusing it with the month that I came to Sub Rosa. The nail polish dried clear, undetectable. "Wait until night." She slid it back into her apron pocket.

While daylight lasted, the Mayflower was almost fun. Shirley and old Maggie gave us a round of root beer floats on the house. The triplets took turns reading aloud from a romance mystery, *The Hellion Bride*: "Ryder looked up at her then. She was standing there, silent as a stone, swathed in one of her voluminous white nightgowns, her hair loose down her back, her face as white as the Valenciennes lace at the collar of her gown."

"Only time a man know what kind of lace a lady's dress is made of is in books," First commented.

"Oh, I can tell you all about lace," said Second Man, spinning around in his seat to address the room. He started listing types of lace—and that became the next way we passed time. We made lists of spices and fragrances, cheeses, flowers, and movies we'd seen. Fauxnique suggested we make a list of places we'd been, and that pretty much killed the game. We played along for awhile, stumbling together through a list of city locales: shopping malls, movie theatres, bus stations. The triplets sneered throughout the game. The orphans fell silent; it was obvious they hadn't been outside of Sub Rosa for a while.

When dinner was served, the room-wide conversation ended and we divided up into our respective Houses. Shirley didn't bother taking orders. She just served us all from the same soup pot. I watched the way the orphan children delicately ripped their cracker packs open, trying not to make any noise with the cellophane wrappers. It must have been a challenge for them to be so nondescript all the time.

They occupied themselves with quiet activities after dinner, knitting and needlepoint and reading. The Dowager read an old hardcover book with gold-leaf-edged pages so thin that I kept imagining I saw a white moth fly up each time she turned the page.

Unfortunately, she and the orphans somehow set the tone, and everyone else found solitary things to do. The triplets rearranged their collage of heartthrob pictures on the window. They lent their back issues of *Vogue* to the House of Man, warning Dearest not to ruin them with her sugar-sticky fingerprints. Ling brushed Treasure Anne's hair, untwisting the tight red curls and wrapping them around her finger. The two had been inseparable since the blackout began. Ling had covered Treasure Anne's knee with pink bandages, and every hour or so checked her wounds. "You're healing so fast, Treasure," I heard Ling chirp. I wondered if Second had got out of the car, if she'd be receiving the same prodigal daughter treatment. So far no one had mentioned Second. No one questioned why she would have wanted to leave Sub Rosa. Instead, we acted as if she had never existed. The blackout had absorbed all our thoughts and actions.

Arsen checked Advent Alley every fifteen minutes to see if the cop car was still there, then every ten. Finally, he stayed outside on the curb, constantly watching. I put my head down on the table and imagined asking him to his car. The fantasy began dreamily enough, with kisses and a well-executed shedding of clothes. But fantasy soon gave way to revenge plots again. My favourite was lifting the safety brake on his car so it would roll down Sub Rosa into the Dark. Desire and vengeance locked horns for so long in my mind that I began to get lightheaded. I had too much emotion without a clear way to respond to it; I squeezed my eyes shut and blocked the sound of Glory chatter from my ears. When I jerked my head up, it was well past sunset. My fingernails were dimly green from Eartha's polish. I hid my hands under the table where it was darker, and they glowed. No one had noticed; they were all too occupied with their own restlessness.

Right about then, Sub Rosa should have been hopping with live ones. We all felt the absence. Al shoved some candles into empty soda pop bottles and brought one around to each table. "Thank you, Al, my love," Portia said as he offered her a book of matches. The triplets were the first to start pacing. During their initial laps around the room, they pretended they were interested in what each of us was doing, asking about books, squinting at the orphans' needlepoint. Eventually, their laps became unfettered from any niceties and they just shuffled drone-like, around and around.

First took up pacing next, and I understood just how long the night was going to be. Did she have to break so quickly? She masked her nervous laps better than the triplets though, taking a rag from the kitchen to polish Shirley's already polished surfaces. She dusted every bottle, except for the jug with the ruined ship that had nearly hit her, but each time she passed it she looked over at me and smiled, as if to say *thanks again*. We made our own game of it, seeing if we could make eye contact at the exact same time. I figured out how many steps it took her to loop around the room and get back to our jug—forty-two, give or take. This kept us relatively amused and able to ignore the other Glories' restlessness until Second Man stood up and announced, "I'm going to visit Mr Saragosa."

"You're not!" Dearest rushed over and clung to him. "We can play Crazy Eights! We can play Go Fish."

"You'll have to play cards with Fauxnique," Second Man told her as he pried her from his pant leg. He lit a candle, shielding the flame with his hand as he walked out. We all rushed to the window to watch his little flame sputter in the darkness then go pitch black. We wondered if he'd made it inside the Pawnshop before the candle went out. The night pressed hard against the glass as if parts of the Dark were getting closer, creeping in while the lights were out. I could feel the weight of it pushing back at us, as if warning us away from the window.

After that, everyone was climbing the walls. First grabbed a chair to dust the crown moulding. I crossed my fingers for luck as I watched her teeter on the thin-legged wooden chair. The last thing we needed was for First to fall. She threw the rag down dramatically when she was done, and I breathed a sigh of relief. But just as soon as I quit worrying, Arsen stormed through the front door to report that the squad car was still there. "They've got something on us for sure. They're trying to smoke us out of here." This was the kind of bad news that made First want consoling. She pawed at him until his smile returned. He kissed her in the doorway of the Mayflower, and every Glory watched with envy. The two of them retreated to the ballroom together. Arsen stole a candle from my table to light First's way into the empty room. I sat in near darkness, too stubborn to ask Al for another candle.

I waited to hear them through the long, wood-panelled wall. When I heard nothing I knew it was only because they were being polite. I pictured Arsen's hand cupped over First's mouth. Her sighs dampening his palm. I had the length of Arsen's wrist to the tip of his middle finger memorized. It was the same distance between my hip and bellybutton. I was even more than familiar with just how soft First's lips were. I knew both so well that I could have narrated their sex without even seeing or hearing it, so well their hands and mouths haunted me. I got the urge to pace, storm the room with the triplets. But I forced my body to be even more still.

Dearest pestered Fauxnique to play another, then another, then yet another game of cards. Her appetite for Go Fish could not be satiated. Fauxnique eventually threw down the deck. "This is why I taught you solitaire," she said sharply. Dearest collected her cards and retreated to an empty corner of the Mayflower, then started reciting each card aloud. "Seven of hearts," she whimpered, making sure we knew that she was offended.

The triplets—so weary for live ones—decided to proposition Shirley, Al, and Maggie. It was a welcome distraction to hear their little noises, the clanging of the silverware in the drawer, the bubbling of food left in the deep-fryer, forgotten. "We just got free burgers for everyone until this thing is over," they bragged as they came out of the kitchen.

It was around midnight when we ate a second dinner. The food tasted better after the triplets' romp in the kitchen. Al put garlic salt and chili pepper on the fries. Shirley added lime cordial to the water. "Eat," ordered Portia. "The triplets just worked to put this food on the table." First tsk-tsked at me for not touching my food. She and Arsen had returned from the ballroom with an appetite. Even though Arsen would have gladly eaten whatever I couldn't finish, I gave Dearest my leftovers. Her stomach was puffed out so far she looked like she was having a baby Dearest of her own.

The last person to cave into the blackout anxiety was the Diamond Dowager. She'd been too composed through all of this, practically motionless for the last nine hours, and so it only made sense that her fall would have to be something more than simply pacing the restaurant or bumping around in the kitchen.

She struck as old Maggie was clearing our plates away. I noticed her wandering in circles close to our table. I was proud to have outlasted her. For nine hours, I hadn't had as much as a book, much less sex, to distract me, and I was still handling the blackout better than everyone else. Unlike the older Glories, uneasiness was still somewhat fresh with me. I was still accustomed to sitting out a bad city situation. Arsen tugged at my arm from across the table, trying to get me to come sit beside him. I was sure my composure made him uncomfortable. His touch was warm and soft, but I sensed neediness at the way he grabbed at me, and I wouldn't go.

"It will make you feel better," First suggested, motioning me over to Arsen.

"Who says I need to feel better?" I crossed my arms in front of my chest so neither she nor Arsen could take up my hand. "I'm perfectly fine." They wore the same puzzled expression. First clapped her hand against her cheek.

"She doesn't care for you, does she, Arsen?" said the Dowager. "She's immune to you without your charm, then? I knew she was a smart one." This is the way the blackout finally got to the Dowager. She turned her frustration on Arsen. Confrontation, I thought, must be comforting to her. She went directly in for the kill, put her whole body into it. She faced Arsen, her arms outstretched to box us into our booth.

"It's none of your business," I told her, defending myself, not Arsen. My palms grew hot. This was the second time the Dowager had raised the question of Arsen's supposed charms, and this time it was more than a raised eyebrow, it was right from her mouth. Was it all just charms—right down to the powdered doughnuts? Were Arsen's affections as authentic as a caress from phantom hand?

"But your well-being *is* my business, Little. Once upon at time, I saw to the needs of all Glories on Sub Rosa, even Arsen. So if he is bothering you now, you can always sit with us."

"She's staying with her House." Arsen slammed his fist on the table. I jumped; the Dowager didn't.

"Yes, yes, you'd better hold her tightly. You've already lost two. That makes two for two, doesn't it? You've certainly proven yourself apt at running your House into the ground. Lucky for you that Candy darling is so loyal. Blindly loyal."

No Glory magic, I reminded myself as First got up to meet the Dowager. I put my left hand over my right to keep phantom hand contained. Everyone held their breath. Dearest even put down her bag of cookies. By the way the bag crumpled, I'd have said it was almost empty, anyway. We waited, but First had no poignant comebacks. She just locked her tired eyes with the Dowager's for an uncomfortable minute and walked past her out of the Mayflower. I couldn't tell for sure, but I thought I detected a twinge of sympathy from the Dowager, either that or she was disappointed to have missed the opportunity to fight. I rushed out after First, knowing that Arsen was left behind to bear the brunt of whatever condemnation the Dowager had yet to deliver.

I found First quickly in the darkness, running smack into her a foot outside the door. "Do you think Second told them police 'bout us?" she asked. "I shoulda never been so hard on her the way I was." I wrapped my arms around her. The fabric of her nightdress scratched my cheek; I never understood why she put up with such uncomfortable clothes. Before I could offer any kind words, she changed the subject, asking if I smelled the lingering sugars and florals, if I could see anything past the curb.

"I smell old roses, but I can't see a thing," I told her.

"If you're ever unhappy, please, please, Little, you tell me so I can make it good again." I just hugged her quietly. "Old witch is right, we oughta be the most powerful House on Sub Rosa. We got the most magic—what with your hand and my size. I don't get why we keep losin' family." She bent down to me and returned my hug, too tightly. The blackout was about to hit me. I felt it as sure as I could feel First's giant hands on my back. "Well, I'm not leaving you," I said. Our kiss was a contract. I delivered a row of kisses along her big bottom lip, assuring her that I intended to keep my part of the bargain.

"It's true, isn't it, that Arsen has Glory charms?" I asked First. "That's how come he could lure me to the Rosa so easily?" First rocked slightly, shifting her weight

"And what does 'two for two' mean, First?" I continued. Her body was too hot against me. I was certain that my question would make her uneasy, but maybe because I couldn't see her face, I had the courage to ask. "I saw a Glory in the Dark. Was it Jellyfish?" It was a relief just to say Jellyfish's name. As soon as I said it I realized how desperate I was to talk about her. I repeated her name several times, "Jellyfish, Jellyfish, Jellyfish …"

"What's gotten into you, Little?" First gave my shoulders a strong shake. "I been wantin' you to come out and ask me about her for a long time. But I knows Jellyfish is not somebody to be askin' after. This blackout got things stirred up that normally I put out of my head."

"Then tell me, First," I pleaded. I wrapped my arms around her tighter than I ever had before. I believe, for the first time, I hugged her as tightly as she hugged me.

"I always try to give you good advice, Little, plain and useful truths, not gossip. But what I'm tellin' you now, it's a story. A story that no longer gets told."

XVII

"By now, you caught on that the story of Sub Rosa is a story of love. Least, when Mr Saragosa is tellin' it, it is. He likes that story, jewels bein' love's business and all. He probably told it to you the very same way he told it to me many years ago. I suppose he thinks we're girls, and what we wanna hear is love stories, right? Royal and Diamond, oh my! Maybe you've caught on that I'm not much for storytellin'. I tried to spare you stories, Little, which isn't so easy on Sub Rosa. The ugly truth of it is, we all find ourselves here 'cause we got stories we wanted to forget."

First's story—as she told it to me that night—had no timeline. No places or dates to legitimatize it. How she and Arsen found one another, what her life was like before Sub Rosa, and other hows and whys were absent. When she came to Sub Rosa, she simply came.

"There are ways we can speak of Sub Rosa in the city, you know what I'm sayin'. Hints. Whispers. 'Oh yes, sir, I live right beside No's Smoke Shoppe,' like that. We never come out and ask, 'Do you know the way to Sub Rosa?' Same goes for wanna-be Glories—you can't tell 'em much 'til they done their Dark Days. But Arsen, Lord love him, told me less than nothin'. I'd say he brought me here with a deficit of knowledge. I had to earn my way into the black."

First, as much an ingénue then as I was when Arsen first brought me in, only knew that she had fallen completely in love with a man who promised her the good life, and for that love and that life she would do just about anything. The heated conversations she heard between Arsen and the Dowager made no sense to First. She just sat in Arsen's car, as he had instructed her to, and waited, taking in the strange sights of what seemed to be a ghost town from an old Western film. Storefront windows were all dark and CLOSED signs hung in every door. Street lamps were dim. Sidewalks vacant. And the great house in front of which Arsen had parked his car looked like it had survived a fire. First despairingly marvelled at the charred visage. Each brick and shingle, each windowpane and each fence picket was perfectly in place. But every inch of the property was uniformly grey. Like ash had rained on it for days. The lady who angrily gestured and raised her voice at Arsen didn't offer the scene any colour, either. When Arsen finally called Della O'Kande out of the car, she felt garish and stupid walking up the gloomy path in her pink leopard-print jump suit and gold running shoes.

First's Dark Days were set at $2,000. "All our dowries go to her. We all buy our way in to Sub Rosa," said First. "But Diamond made me pay the most. I bet she carries my dowry in her purse to this very day. I bet she still counts it." Hers was the highest Dark Days dowry to date because she really was the First, the first girl to be recruited from the city.

The Dowager refused to look at First when Arsen presented her. She kept her back turned as she spoke sternly, facing the Darkness in the distance. First was told that the only way Arsen would be allowed to keep her was if she went into the Dark and returned with the Dowager's fee. The Dowager's finger directed her to the vanishing point in the distance. A forceful wind pushed First's back as she walked. She wanted to look back and see the face of her banisher, but she didn't dare. When she had earned $2,000, then she would look, then she'd stare the Dowager down.

"Unending"—this was the stark description First offered of her Dark Days. The only other detail she knew or was willing to share was the precise bill count she brought back: twenty-seven twenty-dollar bills, thirty-six ten-dollar bills, and 220 five-dollar bills. The number of blue bills alone told me what an utterly grim time she had had out there. "This is why I now insist Arsen drive me to find new Glories when they go into the Dark. To break up their time there with some rest and encouragement. He never did them Dark Days, so he don't think up these things on his own."

After being so long in the darkness, First had severe duckling syndrome: The first person her eyes could focus on became mother, became home. This was Arsen. He met her at the twilight spot where the Dark and Sub Rosa overlapped. That evening the sun had set strangely. It hovered above the horizon line much longer than usual, oozing pink light for hours like it had sprung a leak. Arsen said the sun lingered because it knew she was on her way. When the sun was too weary to stay lit, he took over. He waited with a candle in a wax paper cup in his hand. His tiny flame was the whole world to her.

Arsen's world, however, was already occupied. Jellyfish was a living shaft of cold light; luminescence without a hot spark, like the unusual shimmer of meat left to rot. First could barely look at her. Jellyfish was difficult to pinpoint. She had obsidian skin: dark and hard and so beautiful that light constantly crowded her, trying to get inside her impermeable flesh, until she glowed with it. Her glow was brighter and more mysterious than a full moon, then she'd almost vanish altogether like a new moon on a foggy December night. First could make no sense of her. She watched Jellyfish wrap her arm around Arsen's and First's already strange world turned upside down.

"I thought a piece of the Dark had snuck ahead of me and stolen my man," said First. "She wasn't too keen on me, neither. I remember her asking Arsen, 'Is she broken?' as they helped me stumble to the living room sofa."

The more Arsen's House began to take shape, the more First realized what she was up against. Not only had she unknowingly become a second wife, she had joined a mutineer family. "Before I showed up, Glories were a few elite members of the Dowager's inner circle," said First. "And there weren't any Daddies."

The original Glories were Diamond, Ling, Jellyfish, Sadie orphan, and Arsen. They had all lived and worked together in the Diamond mansion. Live ones were scarce and diligently screened by Diamond before being permitted entrance. She insisted that the live ones' reasons for seeing the Glories were decent, or met her standards of decency; lonely widowers, closeted homosexuals, crippled veterans, and so on. Pleasure alone was not a good enough reason.

Arsen had set himself apart from the other Glories. Even in First's fresh eyes he was different. He had a car and would take himself on trips to the city. He and Jellyfish had moved out of the Mansion together to be independent, to start "their own life," as Arsen put it. But wanting independence didn't automatically give them independence. All the live ones were gate-kept by the Dowager. Jellyfish and Arsen needed their own regulars, their own money.

First caught on quickly that Arsen had brought her in for this reason. Even back then, she was a champion of silver linings, of pick-yourself-up-and-start-again, of when-life-gives-you-lemons—take any old adage, chances are First had to live by it. And Arsen knew it; he didn't hand pick her for her exaggerated hourglass figure. He knew that while most women would feel defeated by these very circumstances, First would hike up her skirt and go to work.

There was no model for training a new Glory. First began standing outside, on what was now the House of Arsen track patch, and attempting to intercept live ones as they drove toward Diamond's. The very best ones, wearing cashmere coats and secret passions behind their gentlemanly smiles, continued to go across the street to the Mansion. First took the odd and overzealous leftover up to the Wifey Wing.

"You ought to stand with me," First had persuaded Jellyfish. "They'll notice you." It was strategic, First's suggestion. Jellyfish did attract live ones. First had her stand in the threshold of Advent Alley after sunset and beam like a beacon. Live ones arrived convinced that they'd been called by the divine. Business aside, First preferred having Jellyfish outside with her, rather than upstairs and alone with Arsen. She was damned if she was going to hustle the track patch all night while Jellyfish and Arsen snuggled up together and waited for First to bring them live ones.

Apart from their nightly work, First stayed away from Jellyfish. But Jellyfish's story was a Sub Rosa favourite, one that First couldn't dodge. The local fable was that Arsen had burned the Jellyfish up with the truest love and that's how she got her colour. When the other Glories bothered to speak to First, it was only to ask about how Jellyfish and Arsen were doing.

Many of her days were spent by herself in the Wifey Wing library. It was the one room Arsen and Jellyfish didn't occupy. The Wifey Wing was stark then—before First filled it with her own objects and decorations. Every room acted as a bare stage for Arsen and Jellyfish to put on their ten shows a day of fucking and fighting. First's anguish filled her ears like cotton. She buried her head in books—geography, anatomy, geology. She avoided fiction altogether. Imagination had already gotten her into enough trouble.

First found a large, illustrated children's science book, *The ABCs of Nature*, and began the process of putting facts behind every tender, childlike question she could think of: *Why is the sky blue? What are clouds made of? How deep is the ocean?*

First kept stumbling upon passages that reminded her of Jellyfish, and facts that might answer the riddle of Jellyfish's glow—her bioluminescence—could be found in the pages of her books. But most marine creatures' light emissions, she read, are blue or green, and are used to attract prey. First thought Jellyfish's glow was more like a metallic silver, and she seldom used it to attract live ones. First eventually gave up on finding an explanation for Jellyfish; as long she and Jellyfish shared a house and a lover, not a heck of a lot would make sense.

Arsen encouraged First's sudden thirst for science. He brought her school textbooks from his trips to the city. "Same stuff they study at top schools," he'd tell her. Although the books were a consolation prize for his lack of time or affection, she read them anyway. But the most valuable thing First learned was not among the tables or figures or maps. It was only a few months into her stay at Wifey Wing when she heard something that lifted her head from her books.

"I got an apartment in the city," First had heard him tell Jellyfish. The vent was blocked up behind a pile of *Homemaker* magazines to cut the noise from the rest of the house, but when she heard him say it again, she toppled the stack of magazines and crouched to hear more. "I'm doing it to help us." He had been studying the city pimps, how they pushed their girls, selling them through tantalizing descriptions and offers, and had begun to copy them. Arsen whispered "Glory, Glory" all over the city.

"If you need to take the credit for our recent luck, then go ahead," said Jellyfish. "Spread your advertisement around the city all you wish. But I can't say I'm not surprised. You of all people should know it's not the uttering of dull words that leads live ones to Sub Rosa."

"You're thinking like her," said Arsen, referring to the Dowager. "To draw them in, we've got to be able to think like them—think like the live ones. I'm figuring them out. All their needs and desires. They're more interesting than you'd think, city people. And they'll spend big money on what interests them."

First felt sick as she listened to Arsen describe the street he would soon be living on. It was "wide" with "rows of sky-high condos," with hundreds of people living there. "There's enough live ones living on my street alone to keep us in business for years." What all of this meant for First is that she'd be left alone in the Wifey Wing with Jellyfish, a living arrangement far worse then tip-toeing around a tumultuous couple.

"I left the Dowager's house for you," Jellyfish pleaded. She was anxious too.

"You left the Dowager's house to go independent," Arsen argued. His decision had been made.

Arsen broke the news to First next, and First feigned surprise. She closed her heavy textbook and paddled meekly across the library floor to him. She bit her tongue purposely to make her eyes water a little. "That must be a hard choice to make, Arsen. You must really be devoted to this Sub Rosa of yours, of *ours*." First had her own charms, city charms that were unknown to Arsen. She knew how to delicately bend truths, how to play dumb. And she had a good hunch that Arsen wasn't going to the city solely for business. The city held some special attraction for him. She could tell by the way he fixated on her crocodile tears as she spoke that as a Glory, Arsen had never had a woman use her feminine wiles on him, he had never been conned or guilt-tripped. He was both enchanted and unprepared. "It takes a courageous man to make a big change. And change is comin', I feel it myself. Like you said, Sub Rosa is going to be big. Pretty soon we'll need some more girls 'round here. 'Course, you already thought of that. I'm only sayin' because maybe I could help you; me bein' a city girl, I know how to turn them out right. I know city men too, and from what I seen there are hundreds of 'em who would pay through the teeth to visit this place. It may not be much, but I'll tell you everythin' I know. Maybe with my city experience and your charms, we can go bigger than we ever dreamed?"

First's appearance had marked change on Sub Rosa. It was First who accompanied Arsen to the city for business. She was the one to bark and barter with the rush of new live ones passing her track patch. The floor-to-ceiling mirrors, the marbleized-glass wall lamps, the white sweetheart-shaped beds in the working room—all First's idea. "If the live ones want New Orleans bordello, they can go to the Mansion. Our workin' room will be as bright and pure as heaven," First advised Arsen. She started entertaining two or even three live ones at a time, and the mirrors helped her keep track of them all. Money was coming in, all of it smudged with First's chubby fingerprints.

Jellyfish didn't fare as well with the new regulars. There were the live ones she could enchant and those men left the Wifey Wing looking like they had seen God. Those men returned to the city whole and good. After Jellyfish, they probably kissed their elderly mothers, donated an entire pantry of canned goods to their company's food drive, and finally quit smoking.

Then there were the men so distanced from the idea of pure goodness that even a Glory couldn't convince them of it. These men came and left with scraps of shame clinging to their hearts. But they paid. Oh, how they paid to be distracted from the city and themselves. Jellyfish began to turn bitter toward these live ones. They dug too deeply at her seemingly endless dimensions. First had heard her hiss at some. First had heard her snarl.

"If I'd only tried to turn her out right back then, maybe Jellyfish would still be our First. But she woulda refused to learn anythin' from me," First told me. "And I was still vexed, and besides, I didn't have the skills with turning other girls like I got now."

Instead, First took herself out for lunches, or to No's for a game or two of pinball. It was a great time to be on Sub Rosa; it was First's time. Shop owners came out of their shops to wave; they knew First was making money. It was then that the Mayflower Diner hung the ship's figurehead carved in First's likeness over the door—an extravagant welcome sign made specifically for First and her new breed of live ones.

Ling was the first to seek First's advice. It started with a series of hellos. Next came the courtesy questions: "And how are you today?" First was so grateful just to be spoken to by another Glory that she stumbled through elaborate details about the meal she'd just eaten or the book she'd just read, hoping to prolong the conversation. So when Ling began to ask about what it would take to run a successful track patch, she had First gushing with tips and hints.

But when she returned to the Wifey Wing, there was nothing to say. Jellyfish had become a living sculpture posed beside the window. First would leave her in a thinker's pose as she left for lunch, then come home to find her imitating a marble Saint Cecilia in her Roman tomb. At sunset, First picked out a dress from Jellyfish's closet and timidly laid it out for her. "Maybe just a few tonight? Only what you can manage." On nights when Arsen didn't show up to share a bed with Jellyfish, she'd weep and speak nonsense until morning. First slept in the working room, often opting to service the graveyard shift regulars rather than trying to sleep anywhere near Jellyfish.

One night Arsen didn't come at all. For twenty-four hours he stayed in the city. Jellyfish stripped down to an iridescent-beaded fishnet dress and stormed the track patch. First had to look in the opposite direction to keep herself from staring at Jellyfish's ostentatiously reddish nipples bleeding out through her flimsy outfit. "Trouble-free rapture. Instant elation. On special tonight," Jellyfish barked at passing cars. First stopped counting Jellyfish's live ones after she ran out of fingers and toes to count them on. Men fell back down the Wifey Wing stairs shaken, with twisted trousers and sweat-soaked hair.

"I shoulda known." First whispered her confession in the dark. Her hair tickled my forehead as she paused telling her story, and I guessed she was turning her head to see if anyone was nearby. "I shoulda kept my eye on the shifty two she took up with her. They patted each other's shoulders as they followed Jellyfish to the workin' room, and they chuckled like drunks. But I was spineless when it came to Jellyfish. Too afraid to nose up on her business."

First heard shouting from inside the working room and did what she always did when Jellyfish threw a tantrum—tuned it out. The shouting was joined by banging. It was the silence afterward that First couldn't ignore. She pressed her ear to the other side of the working room door and heard men whispering. When she tried the door, it refused to move. There was, and never has been, a lock on the working room door. Something was barricading it. First, accustomed to being able to push her weight through any kind of blockade, knew something was very wrong. "Open this goddamn door," she threatened but got no response. The only thing she could think of to do was run straight across the street to the Dowager's house. "Help!" she called out as she stormed inside.

First could still picture the Dowager's stone face as she attempted to describe what she had seen and heard at the Wifey Wing. When she finished, the Dowager poured First a cup of tea and patted her on the cheek. She gathered the other Glories in the house, Ling and Sadie, and led them toward the Wifey Wing. "Stay put," she ordered First. First was too anxious to do anything but sip the Dowager's brew. She told herself it wasn't as bad as it sounded. Arsen had promised First that Sub Rosa was safe. What was the worst that could happen?

First remained alone in the Dowager's armchair for a long while, a half-cup of cold tea in her hand. Then the Dowager returned with the Glories, their eyes bloodshot. First had forgotten what distress looked like as their long faces crowded around her.

The Dowager spoke slowly and flatly as she explained that Jellyfish was gone when the Glories had got there. The Wifey Wing was deserted. The Dowager dryly listed off the places they had searched: "Under the bed, between the mattress and the box spring, behind the drapes." After a few minutes, First heard only monosyllabic nonsense. Her vision blurred. "Those men took her?" slurred First. No one answered.

When Arsen arrived later that night he was given a similar report, except that the Dowager's voice had a heavy tone of blame when she spoke to him.

Rumours of what happened went around the Rosa for several months afterward. First kept her ears perked to them, just as she had to the library vent. She heard a version that claimed Jellyfish and one of the men were secret lovers—the banging was Jellyfish packing before they ran away together. She heard that the Dowager banished the bad men to the Dark, and Jellyfish, in a state of rage, stalked after them, never to be seen again. The reigning story, the one retold again and again, was that Jellyfish staged the whole thing so that she could leave Sub Rosa and go live with Arsen in the city.

One final story didn't hold much weight on Sub Rosa, but it was the one that bothered First the most. She heard that she herself had lied about the entire incident. It was First who attacked Jellyfish and ran her from her home. After hearing this rendition, First lost all taste for gossip and storytelling.

What was worse than the gossip was what never got said about Jellyfish. First had witnessed things the other Glories had not. It was First who had returned to the Wifey Wing after Jellyfish's disappearance. She was the one who had seen how the end tables and lamps and pillows had been put back in the wrong places, like the room had been cleaned up in a hurry. She was left alone with truths like the dent in the doorframe and the clump of shimmering black hair caught under the leg of a work bed. And all alone, First practised the Glory art of forgetting.

"We've based our lives on forgettin' about her. Most new Glories don't even know who she was. Only one to mention her is Diamond, and she does it to just to smart Arsen. Jellyfish's story don't get told because it isn't a love story."

"So this means Sub Rosa is as fucked up as any other place?"

"Little, don't say such a thing," First said.

But I had already said it, and by saying it, I plainly understood that Sub Rosa wasn't merely the land of soda pop and ponytails. It was the last stop for girls like me. If I fell on Sub Rosa, there would be no getting up. I heard the Dark groan unnervingly in the distance. Growing pains? It was getting bigger. Who knew how far away it really was without the lamps to mark the border? The Dark was unfolding its catch-all arms. Its voice grew louder, calling a name that seemed to beg me to claim it as my own. I wondered what else was lost in there.

"She is missing ... and everyone goes about their merry way. Sorry to sound like a city girl, but that is fucked up. I mean, aside from all the gossip, did anyone even bother to feel sad that she was gone? What if it was me, First? If I was lost tomorrow, you'd forget about me?"

"Don't worry, Little," said First, distressed. She rubbed my back to soothe both of us. "Nothin' even close to that is gonna happen."

"How can you be sure?"

"Because I love you, Little." Her hands found my shoulders and gave me the slightest shake, as if she could shake her love into me. "You're the only one I love."

"Arsen loved Jellyfish, didn't he? You know what he did when I told him she was out there? He drove as fast as he could in the opposite direction."

"If she was in the Dark, she'd come back by now. Even the girls that give up and don't make it through their Dark Days come back."

"What if she was killed or something?"

"There's no killing on Sub Rosa," First sighed, as if I had asked a truly stupid question. "Little, this is all startin' to get to me, this non-sense talk. It's this damn darkness, seems like the longest night God could make, and it's makin' everyone crazy. Why are we standing out-side in this blackout? Let's get ourselves back in." She hug-dragged me back into the Mayflower.

XVIII

Arsen's lullaby buzzed like mosquitoes over stagnant water. Each hook looped incessantly before it gave over to the next, the tune never progressing to the end of a song. "Are ya sure you're not usin' Glory magic?" First whispered in his ear. Arsen only shook his head so as not to interrupt his melody. "'Cause I'm sure gettin' sleepy from hearin' it." She lay her cheek down on the table. Her mouth fell open in a sleepy smile, her breath steamy on the shiny lacquered wood tabletop.

I watched the orphans doze off in narcotic trances while still sitting. I wanted to topple them, press their pale heads against the floor. Why couldn't they just lie down to sleep like everyone else? Every so often a word or broken phrase punctuated Arsen's melody, revealing that his bedtime songs once had lyrics that he had either forgotten or didn't care to perform. But whenever a stray "love" or "moonlight" or "dreaming of you" sprang from his lips, the orphans' eyes would collectively pop open like the eyes of porcelain dolls, and they'd stare straight ahead, at who knows what, until their heavy eyelids lowered again.

First's stomach growled. The sound was nonsense to me; I thought it was some sort of warped reverberation from Arsen's hum before I realized it came from First's belly. Dearest shook herself out of drowsiness and yelled, "I'm hungry!" into the kitchen. She climbed atop a barstool and spun and spun, until the seat was about ready to pop off, shouting, "Maggie, make me a cream pie!"

"You just ate," came the reply from the kitchen.

"That was a long time ago," Dearest protested. "Fauxnique, when did we last eat? Not since yesterday, right?" Fauxnique shrugged and looked to Ling for the answer. A bloodshot-eyed Ling twisted Treasure Anne's hair around her finger as she thought about it. Since the blackout began, she had been braiding and unbraiding, vigorously twisting and unfurling pin curls, and even raking Treasure Anne's scalp for imaginary nits. For Treasure Anne, this type of sisterly affection between a First and a Second was long overdue. She tilted her head toward Ling's busy fingers the same way I often leaned into First. But after a few hours, I noticed Treasure wince as Ling yanked out hair elastics to start another hairdo. A noticeable collection of strawberry-blonde hair stuck to Ling's black dress. "I'm not quite sure how long we've been here," Ling said.

"If Arsen would quit that time-warped tune of his, perhaps we'd know how long it's been," grumbled the Dowager. A pair of wire-framed glasses had appeared at the end of her nose. She was nearing the end of her weighty old book with the tissue-thin pages.

"Breakfast, dinner, a snack, something," Dearest persisted. She hopped over to another barstool, one that squeaked as she spun. Shirley briefly appeared from the kitchen in a flannel housecoat to slam down a jar of honey and a spoon on the bar. "This won't tide me over for long," Dearest called out to her after swallowing a spoonful of honey.

"You better share," Portia warned her. Dearest hesitated for a moment, holding the already-dripping jar close to her chest, but when all three triplets motioned for her to bring the jar to them, Dearest slid down from her barstool perch and padded over to them, beads of spilled honey trailing behind her. That's when I saw it—the horrible blood-sucker—a tiny spreader of parasites that flew down from who knows what god-forsaken place and landed on a fallen honey splat.

"Black fly!" I stood up and screamed.

First's heavy head shot up with a start. "Little, you must be dreamin'. No flies ever come here," she said before she and the rest of the Glories saw what I was pointing at. The fly stood firmly on its newfound sweet spot while gasps of "impossible" and "kill it" filled the room.

"No killing on Sub Rosa," First recited our golden rule. The others stopped to consider this for a second before someone shouted, "What do we kill it with?"

"A flyswatter," said Arsen. Unsure of what exactly a flyswatter was, the Glories looked around, confused. Dearest let out an impish battle cry and swung her spoon in the air, sending more honey droplets to the floor. The fly, unperturbed, moved to a newer drop of honey. Portia stared down at the fashion magazine in her hands for a few determined seconds before rolling it up and going after the fly. The ugly insect took off, spinning circles in the air above Portia's head. Likka took up a magazine, too, and tore after the fly, but she tripped on the sticky floor and fell with a distressing thud onto her back. Her magazine landed beside her, its page opened to "101 Anti-Aging Tips," and a photograph of a woman swathed in white gauze, fuchsia-pink letters dissecting her body that read, "Shield your skin from sun, pollution, and other environmental damage." I wondered what the hell was going to happen next.

First, ignoring her aforementioned rule, began waving a dust rag in the air. She could reach the ceiling beams when she jumped from a chair. The fly kept buzzing. Ling shot hair elastics at it. The fly kept buzzing. The Dowager held her huge hardcover book over her head, then threw it down with a karate cry of *kiai*. The insect flew into the closed window, probably wanting to get away from this pitiful display as badly as I did. Its delicate opalescent wings fluttered on high speed as it beat itself against the glass.

"Is this for fucking real?" I yelled. It got the room's attention. From the corner of my eye, I could see First about to tell me not to cuss, but she kept it to herself. "We're going to let a fly beat us?"

"It's not something we're used to, Little. I mean, I for one am glad we don't know how to deal with flies, or any other bug," said Ling, slightly out of breath. The Glories around her nodded in agreement.

"We're not used to being hungry, either, or being so tired that we fall asleep sitting up. Diamond is wearing glasses, for fuck's sake," I said.

"Oh, they're not any different from any of my other antique collectables," said the Dowager. "They just make reading a bit easier. Normally I wouldn't read an entire book in one sitting."

"Yeah, well, Treasure's hair is falling out," I huffed. "And Arsen can't even get a children's song right." Treasure Anne clapped her hands over her head, and Arsen's low hum finally fell silent. "And I'll tell you where that fly came from. Not from the city. Like Ling said, we don't get city flies here. That fly is from the Dark. I remember seeing them—that same size, that same colour—in the Dark. They'd cooked themselves on the one frigging light out there. Now this one's going to die trying to get out the window." It was true, the black fly moved feebly along the windowsill until its buzz was staccato, then slowed, until finally it lay unmoving.

"I wonder what else the Dark will bring to our door?" This was my way of breaking, I suppose. Since the blackout began, I had avoided pacing and muttering and fidgeting. But when I started unravelling, I wanted to unravel over everyone. I wanted to kick shit up. A brawl—the streak-free windows kicked in; the gleaming tables overturned. My city clothes twitched on my body. I felt hot. Why couldn't I just walk out of here? I flung open the Mayflower door. The room held its breath. Something blew in as I stood there. It swirled in on the floor in a tender whirlwind. Blue money. "Shut the door," the triplets screeched. The five-dollar bill breezed over toward their table. Likka stood up on the booth bench as if a mouse was scurrying below. "You let it in, you get it," she ordered me.

The Glories glared at me as I scooped it up and into my jeans pocket. "She knows something," Fauxnique hissed. "I knew it all along. She knows something about the Dark that the rest of us don't."

"What's that supposed to mean?" First asked, stepping between me and Fauxnique.

"Little," Likka called, still perched on top of the bench. "Fauxnique told us that Second Man told her that you found something in the Dark. Something that helped you make all that money. She thinks you found another Advent Alley."

"This is hardly the time for yesterday's gossip," First scolded.

"Now, now, Candy," said Fauxnique. "It's not the girl's title that is in question. It's just that maybe she knows a way out of here. A passage through the Dark? I'll go there myself if I have to. Anything to end this blackout."

Portia patted the bench beside her and, despite First tugging at the back of my T-shirt, I sat down on her cue. "Think," Portia commanded. "Remember. Did you see an Advent Alley in the Dark?"

"You can't see anything in the Dark, that's the whole problem," said one of the orphans, not loudly, though orphans' voices are so rarely heard that everyone turned to the Dowager's booth. The Dowager herself turned her head to see which one of her orphans had spoke.

"Please, Sadie, you've never been to the Dark," said Arsen. "You've barely seen anything outside of the Mansion."

"It wasn't me who said that, idiot," snapped Sadie orphan. Isabella (at least I thought it was Isabella) sunk down in her seat. Arsen looked as if he had a comeback, and Diamond and Sadie were poised to fight again, but then he shrugged and turned away.

Portia tried me again. "Did you see or hear anything, *anything* that could have been an Advent Alley?"

"Or anything that might have come through an Advent Alley? A live one, with money?" Fauxnique said from the booth beside us.

"You made $500 in two days," said Myra. "Couldn't all be from zombie men."

"Picture the money, Little. It's in your hands now. What do you see?" The counterfeit hypnotist, Portia, drawled her words. The only thing I could see was her flickering eyes as she rolled them back in a mock trance. It must have taken a fair bit of willpower on her part not to use any of her Glory charms.

"Oh, for the love of fuck," Fauxnique said, running her hands through her bubblegum hair. "Arsen, what kind of dowry did the kid bring back? Crumpled small bills or warmer?"

Arsen slid further into his booth, shaking his head. "I won't get tangled up in this."

"Too late." The Dowager sauntered across the Mayflower to Arsen's booth, her wooden-heeled boots punching the over-lacquered floorboards. "You're already tangled. We all are, sorry to say. And Little, as you are well aware, earned more than her dowry, including three one-hundred dollar bills. Crisp bills."

"That's city money!" Dearest shouted, standing on top of the bar.

"Second Man was right all along," said Fauxnique. The triplets leaned in to me looking for answers. The throng of orphan black lace stirred. I looked at First, hoping I remembered right—that there were no rules in the Dark. I didn't want to say something that could get me in trouble.

"I'm pretty sure there was a truck."

Portia's hands landed on my cheeks. "A real truck!"

"A real truck," I said again, even more sure as I repeated it. "With a real radio that was tuned into a city station."

First cupped her hand over her mouth. "Radio? Little, are you sure?" she asked. "The city must have been very close to get radio."

Dearest began chiming, "Little can save us, Little can save us."

"Why Little?" First asked. "What should she have to go?" But it was too late, the Glories clapped and cheered my name. Dearest jumped up and down, kicking flatware off the tabletop.

"Go with her, Arsen," First pleaded. "Little can show you the way out of here so you can call for help." The Glories clapped again. The triplets started fixing their lip gloss as if the blackout was about to end in mere moments.

"No cars," the Dowager protested. "Especially Arsen's bellowing, over-revved engine. Whoever goes there has to go on foot."

This quieted the Glories for a moment, even First, who was the only Glory who had actually journeyed by foot into the Dark and back out again. Dearest leaned her elbows on the table beside Arsen. "Will you go with Little?" she asked him.

"Yeah," added Likka. "It only makes sense for Arsen to go. When he reaches the city he can call the other Daddies."

"What are you still sitting there for?" Myra asked him. The triplets slid out of their booth, chanting, "Go, Arsen, go," like crazed cheerleaders. They crowded around him.

Arsen fumbled with a cloth napkin on the table. The gold and ebony ring he wore on his finger was loose and turned backward. His hand must have shrunk ever so slightly during the blackout. There was dirt, *dirt*, under his fingernails as he pressed his palms against the table. He was going to push himself up. Stand and face what he was being called to do.

I beat him to it. "I go alone," I repeated until everyone else was quiet and seated. Arsen slumped back into his seat. Al, Shirley, and Maggie reappeared from the kitchen. Al helped Maggie perch herself on a barstool. She held his hand as she looked at me with hope in her old eyes. Dearest pulled her shirt collar up halfway over her young face as she waited for me to speak. The simplest and most honest thing I could have said is that I really knew nothing about a second Advent Alley. It was Jellyfish who discovered the men in the truck. Maybe she had lured them somehow with her glow. But I didn't dare say her name. Besides, who was I to deny their hope? I was their hero. I opened my mouth and every Glory leaned forward in anticipation.

"I don't need Arsen. There is a guide in the Dark who has helped me before, and if I'm lucky she'll help me again. I haven't forgotten how to use a phone. If I find my way to the city I will call the Daddies. Arsen, I want you to stay here. If I get lost, you're the only person with a car who knows how to find me." Arsen exhaled in relief. He nodded in hasty agreement at my request. I didn't want him with me, anyway. Whatever I found in the Dark, an alley to the city or Jellyfish or anything, would be mine and mine alone. I wasn't about to share my glory with him.

"I'll need supplies," I announced, and the Glories eagerly sprang up to help me gather whatever I needed. Matches. A thermos of Maggie's coffee. A box of pushpins. Dearest offered me the last of her stash of almond confetti, wrapped in silver and gold foil. I asked Shirley for a pen. She hated loaning them out, but she called me "an angel" and gave up her nicest felt-tip. From Ling I borrowed a couple of hair elastics, which she pulled directly from Treasure Anne's hair. I emptied my purse, then repacked it with only the supplies I needed.

I had a plan: with the elastic bands I'd fasten the pen to the end of my hair so I wouldn't lose it. Once I was in the Dark, I could use phantom hand to draw on my T-shirt. I'd make a map of the path I'd travelled on my back. I knew I'd worn white cotton for a reason. Paper would be too easy to lose; one gust of wind and I could kiss my map goodbye. This was too valuable, it would be the very first map of the Dark. I imagined we'd name it after me, something like "Little's path."

The pushpins I'd use like Hansel and Gretel's breadcrumbs. Whenever I felt a telephone pole or a wooden door soft enough, I'd mark it with a tack. I figured if I charted my way in then I would be able to find my way back.

My last task was to say goodbye to First. As she walked me to the door I wondered if she'd kiss me again or if she'd be too upset with me for going and send me off brusquely. I made a game out of it—a gamble. Like pulling petals off a daisy. If she kissed me, my journey would be lucky, if she didn't …

"I love you," I said the second we were out the door. I suppose I wanted my dramatic farewell scene. Her kiss was the softest and warmest a kiss could be, like it was behind the curtain, but too quick.

"You don't have to go," she said. "I never meant for you to have to go."

"I choose this," I said. I walked away with my lips tucked in-between my teeth so I didn't change my mind. A solid minute, maybe two, passed before I heard the swish of the Mayflower door open and close. *Let me be. I'm sick with worry for my Little,* I imagined her saying to the other Glories.

It was my fingernails that alerted me to the Dark. Their faint green glow began to beam neon bright, and I was in. The polish had been saving itself for the real Dark. It still wasn't enough to light my way. All I could really see were my own hands and anything within one inch of them, which looked to be pretty much empty air. I found an elastic hair band and Shirley's pen inside my purse. Reaching behind me, I fastened the pen to my ponytail and guided phantom hand to it. Phantom hand took its position at my back, and the felt-tip skipped against my T-shirt for a few strides before it fell into perfect pace behind me. I drew a short line for each ten steps I took. When I stopped, phantom hand would push me onward. I thought I was making it up, but each time I slowed my pace it pressed harder against me. "Don't," I whined, and it quit its poking. *It's as scared as you are,* I told myself. *It doesn't want to fall behind.*

There was every reason to be scared. The chronic hum. The chilly air. The slippery concrete beneath my feet. The fact that I had no idea where to look. I figured since I had only just entered that I was on the outskirts of the Dark. I decided to walk left. I would circle the entire perimeter. Map from the outside in.

Jellyfish had come to me before, and I hoped she'd find me again. She probably wouldn't be able to resist some of my company, her being Glory kin and all. "Let's save Sub Rosa," I'd say. "We'll be famous Glories. No one will every forget us." Soda pop ... sweet tea ... embroidered silk ... streetlamps ... sparklers on top of cakes. I made a list of all the reasons for her to return. The inventory of Sub Rosa favourites was so appealing I lost count of my steps. My map was already flawed and I had hardly begun. It should have been easy to count from one to ten, then draw a short line on my back. Carrying out these two actions demanded all my focus. No more daydreaming, I told myself. I made myself count out loud, one through ten, and deliberately made my mark on the map, not caring who or what might hear me.

After about forty paces, I hit my first building—oddly placed in the middle of my path. I determined it was brick by the way the wall scraped my fingertips as I felt my way along it. I was grateful to have a hold of something concrete. I circled the building twice. It was a predictable square with windows that were taller than me. I reached up to press a couple of pushpins into the worn wood sill to mark my path. Reluctant to leave, I stretched my hands up several times to touch my markers. The building offered no clues or reason to stick around, so I drew it as a square on my back and continued my blind journey. My footsteps began to sound like numbers: left, right, left, one, two, three. My map sprawled across my back, fragment by fragment.

I found my way to what might have been an old town square. The ground was the same smoothly polished cobblestone as the sidewalks of Sub Rosa. I recognized it as soon as I stepped onto it. I couldn't have done that during my first trip, when I ran dumbly in the Dark with only fear to steer me. I slid my foot from my flip-flop and dragged my toes along the cracks, searching for little plants growing between the stones, but, of course, it was too dark there for anything to grow. I did find water. I traced my foot along a rounded stone lip and almost-warm water splashed under my toes. The basin was perfectly round, and I guessed it must have been a fountain. I placed both feet into the warm pool. Memory soaked into my skin the longer I stood there. I remembered city parks; people posing for photos or taking their lunches on a nearby bench. I remembered happy gangs of dogs wrestling over Frisbees. It made me wonder, just as First did, what else had been lost in the Dark. I searched my pockets and found a coin to make a wish with. I touched copper and she was there.

"I knew I'd find you. You've got to save us," I said. "Sub Rosa is in big trouble. I've been sent out here to find a second Advent Ally, you know, a way out. Back to the city. Do you know the way out?" I spouted. She lit up like a lunar ring.

"Yes, lost one, I know a way," she said. I caught hold of her cool dark wrist. I saw her shimmering fingers lace into mine. Both of us pulled; she was stronger.

The earth dropped out below me and I fell. There wasn't even time to wonder what had happened, much less why. If my various encounters in the Dark had at all unnerved me, this was far worse. I was ten times more helpless, lost times ten. At least the Dark had filled my ears with a little white noise and given my feet an occasional pothole to trip over. There was nothing in this new Dark. I flailed my arms in wide arcs then stopped, not wanting to propel myself any deeper, if that was even possible. I fell for so long that I exhausted my fear of hitting bottom and began hoping for it. I tried to curl into a ball to fall faster. I couldn't bring my knees to my chest. I couldn't wrap my arms around my head and brace for oncoming impact. My body was gone. The word "help" passed me to my left. Another to my right. More cries of "help" percolated below me, where my feet should have been. Without eyes I looked down and there was light. I'm no Christian, like Arsen, but praise be, I was ready for this light to be heaven. Heaven had a red lampshade. Heaven had a burgundy-red lampshade made of velvet nap paper. Heaven had dust on the bulb. Heaven was honeyed-pine side table; there was a tooled-leather cigarette case and a shamrock-shaped ashtray, too. Gauzy threads of smoke ascending. A slim brown cigarette steadily spun out more smoke as it burned. A woman was there. She was nothing like the angels in paintings. Her knuckles were bunched together like the sheets of an unmade bed. For a split second I experienced a sense of ease. As if she was someone I had known forever. But a moment later her presence made no more sense than the lamp or the ashtray. "Am I dead?" I asked, supposing she was a ghost, like Jellyfish. She lifted her head, so I repeated the question.

"Is someone there?" Her face tilted into the lamplight was wrinkled and confused.

"My name is Little," I said in my nicest Glory voice. "I'm not sure why I'm here, but I'd like to go back to Sub Rosa now." I thought about telling her more about Sub Rosa for she had the heavy tread of sadness stamped on her like her whole life had been a boot fight. Sub Rosa might have lifted her spirits, but before I breathed a word of it I was back in the Dark, my bare feet against the cobble, my wrist again in the Jellyfish's manacle grip.

"Who was that woman?" I asked her.

"You must use your real name," she said, shaking me hard. "You can't use your Glory name or speak of Sub Rosa. To leave Sub Rosa, you must speak your birth name."

"What name?" I mumbled. As I stood in Jellyfish's beautiful phosphorescent glow, I was suddenly giddy. It had been too long since I'd been around Glory charms. "That's some magic. You're a Glory," I practically shouted at her, remembering my mission. "Sub Rosa is in trouble."

"You want to return to the Rosa?" Her hands clamped down on me too hard and I held my breath. She was handling me with too much force for me to hazard a wrong answer. "You look elsewhere for your Glory, stupid child." Jellyfish dropped my wrist. My hand throbbed as she faded from view. I called her name many times, though I knew she wouldn't answer.

If I could tell this story differently, I would. I'd like to say I was transformed then and there. That Jellyfish had wakened something deeply buried: myself. That I had some sort of mortal homecoming. But everything about me was still Glory. Same phantom hand. Same notions of heroism. Even the penny I intended to throw in the fountain was still in my grasp. I wished for the blackout to be over, for the shops to unlock their doors, for the live ones to broadside us with admiration and gifts and money.

The instant the coin hit the water, a terrible buzzing rose from the fountain. The air shifted around me, giving me a swift warning before I was attacked by flying bugs. They clicked and nipped as they hit me. Waving these flying beetles away was useless; I wore my arms out, and they didn't slow for a second. I screamed, only once, and was immediately choking on a mouthful of beetles. So I ran with my eyes closed to keep them from blinding me. Dozens, maybe hundreds, pelted my back as hard as stones. I crashed into something and fell down on top of dozens more, their bodies crushed under my weight. Dabs of warm ooze were smeared on both my knees where they must have split open. My hands were soon covered in the same goo as I crawled, unable to stand up again as they pressed collectively down on my back. Saliva leaked from my firmly shut lips, but I didn't dare cry out.

Something other than beetles tapped persistently at my hand. Phantom hand, thinking for itself, though I was in no position to fret over its developing autonomy. It pushed the pack of matches into my palm, and clumsily, desperately, lit one.

The flying beetles leapt toward the flame, blood-veined wings fluttering out from their twisted black bodies. I set the whole matchbook on fire and crawled away, leaving the swarm around the flame. I had less than a minute to find shelter before the matches expired. The something I had crashed into was an empty trashcan. An overturned city-park trashcan. It was sticky as I scrambled inside and pulled it overtop of me.

For a while, I sat with the sound of the beetles hailing down. The clanging was enough to make me want to do a suicide run. The glow from my nail polish revealed sticky red blood on my palms and kneecaps, some of it bug blood, some of it my own. The sight and smell of it kept me from leaving my trashcan shelter. I searched my purse for the second and last matchbook. It had only three matches in it. Three matches and a phone number written beside the name Bob. I took a moment to hate this unknown Bob, wishing it was him out there instead of me. Pieces of Dearest's almond confetti were strewn inside my purse. I unwrapped one and sucked, letting chocolate coat the bug taste in my mouth. The foil wrapper flashed in my hand. It was the best gift Dearest could have given me.

I proceeded to unwrap and then stuffed all of the confetti in my mouth. As the chocolate dissolved, I peeled back the gauze-thin paper from the foil wrappers. When lit, the paper should separate from the foil, lift off, and burn into the sky. This trick was one I'd done before with the foil from packs of cigarettes. I must be a genius, I thought, lighting the first match. But the flame quit before it caught the candy wrappers. The air inside the trashcan was too thin. I tried again. Propping the trashcan up, I managed to make a good flame with my last two matches. Bugs scuttled for the opening. It was dumb luck that the wrappers were lit before my shelter filled with bugs. One of the burning wrappers took off for the sky and the swarm followed. I edged away from the fire, carrying the garbage can over me as I picked up the pace.

I couldn't see how well my plan worked, but the sound of beetles splitting underfoot lessened until all I heard was buzzing behind me. I tossed the trashcan off and ran full tilt. Ahead of me there was a sliver-thin beam: a crack beneath a door. I drew close enough to see the painted wood. I was almost there when the first beetle struck my back. Then another. And the horrible sound of the swarm. The door—my great escape—was locked and handle-less, like the one at the Smoke Shoppe. I pounded, though there was next to no chance that someone, someone normal, was inside. Soon the bugs were pounding at the door too, and at me. The blows to my legs made me buckle to the ground. But it was the blows to my head that did me in. I suppose this was when everything would have gone black if it wasn't already Dark. I wished I would have used my coin differently; in my pain, I wished that I was still with the burgundy-lamp lady somewhere down inside Jellyfish, but these wishes, or any other last wishes I may have had, were buried in bugs. I saw the crack of light warp and disappear.

When I came to, I was still surrounded by buzzing. I must have spent hours like that, dizzy, aching, until I noticed I'd been laid in a bed. A shabby bed with wool blankets that smelled of gasoline and man. Hours more passed before I could turn over to see where I was.

XIX

The garage was littered with car skeletons. Chrome femurs and rusted spines, disconnected parts that had been dead for so long they were unrecognizable. Other cars lay gutted in corners, their hoods open in a rigor mortis scream. Old models I was familiar with only from period films—Studebakers, Ford Galaxie 500s with fins and running boards. The walls and floor and ceiling were the same stained concrete pasted over with weathered posters. Pin-up girls looking just as dated as the car parts. Drawings, not photos, of curvy models in marching-band uniforms, polka-dotted dresses twirling up in the breeze. All of them held a prop—a garden hose, a trumpet, a picnic basket—and all wore surprised expressions on their faces as if taken aback by their own sex appeal. So very different from the girls in the glossy mags at No's. Those lingerie models stare you down; even their exposed nipples stare. One of the old-fashioned pin-up dames hung right above my head. Her pale thighs were smudged with fingerprints. A lonely man belongs to this bed, I guessed.

"Hello," I whispered. "Anybody?" All I could hear were bugs raining against the garage roof. They weren't getting in, there wasn't a single window to break, and both doors were made of steel. Beside the door, the one I must have come in through, several of them were stamped into red and brown smears on the floor. A man sat sleeping in a bucket car seat leaned up against the garage wall. The thermos of Maggie's coffee was open by his feet; I guess Maggie made a weak brew judging by his deep-slumbering snores. He was a grease monkey version of Rip Van Winkle, with unkempt grey hair grown over most of his face and neck—even his hands were mittened in hair. The soles of his work boots were coated in bug blood, and a rifle rested on his lap. I wondered whether he was guarding the door so that the swarm didn't get in or whether he was guarding the door so that I didn't get out. Either way, it was a bad idea to startle a man sleeping with a rifle in his hands. I slipped out of bed slowly so the bedsprings would stay quiet.

"I'd say it's a bit soon to be up and around after a stone bug attack, missy," he said. Two denim-blue eyes checked me out, dark like his unwashed coveralls. "Let's see how you're mending, then." He motioned for me to turn around. I waited for him to put the gun well out of reach before I'd turn my back to him. "Fast healer, eh," he said. "Must be a Glory."

He introduced himself only as the Night Watchman. I didn't press him for a first or family name. He was not a question-and-answer man. He was unable to tell me how long he'd been in his garage, scrunching up his hairy face for several minutes trying to recall. Finally he explained, with great pride, that he wasn't actually a watchman at all.

"I'm a mechanic by trade. One of the best. There wasn't an engine that I couldn't get to purr. American. European. Four-cylinder, six-cylinder, you name it. I do body work. I do brakes. I do transmissions. Or I did, until I got this arthritis. You could say it spoiled my touch. So I wound up living in this garage in exchange for keeping watch on the place at night. Luck is a real bitch sometimes, excuse my language. It could always be worse, though.

"Besides, there's all sorts of desperate types out there who'd rob the garage just for the scrap metal. Damn fools that can't tell the difference between a fender skirt and a wing, but they'd steal if they had the chance. Someone's got to keep lookout while the sun is down; it may as well be me."

It occurred to me that the sun had gone down for the Night Watchman a long, long time ago. I did the math in my head. Most of the cars must have been forty years old or more.

He showed me his hands—"arthritic" came nowhere close to describing them. They ought to have been soaking in formaldehyde in a glass jar at the freak show: *Step right up and see a set of genuine werewolf paws.* Tightly packed hairballs, they were. He held a gun with those hands?

He puttered across the room to a row of lockers. "You a Glory?" he asked again.

"Yes. I'm on a quest out here. Or I was until those bugs got me."

"Stone bugs don't let up, neither. I expect they'll buzz around for a good while yet." I was curious exactly how long a good while was to this man who never saw sunrise. His overgrown eyebrows hooded his eyes as he drew a metal lock box from a locker. I pictured the humble amount of money in there. His wrecked fingers counting out tattered bills. The Glory in me, though still bruised and tired, sensed his simple need. What little effort it would take to make him happy.

"You got something for me in that box?" My flirty question sweetened my tongue. I realized the blackout had had me parched.

"If you want it," he said, looking a little less sunken. He showed me the old bills, money I hadn't seen in print before. For a brief moment I worried that money might be counterfeit. But when I held the hundred-dollar bills in my hands, I felt the familiar rush of handling live money. It was as warm as any live one's payment. Eyeballing the metal box, I'd say there was enough to get several girls out of the Dark Days, paying their dowries. This man was a living trust fund. I took only what I thought was a humble amount. I didn't want to deplete the resource.

"Take more than that, miss," he said.

"I didn't come to the Dark for money," I said. The Night Watchman screwed up his fur face. The poor man probably wasn't even aware of the Dark. Maybe that was why he hadn't turned evil like the zombie men; he was oblivious to his surroundings. "I mean, I wasn't planning on working tonight. But how can I resist a swell fellow like you?" When I tried to find his cheek for a kiss, my lips were blocked by a thicket of wiry whiskers. His beard smelled dank.

"You could use a haircut and a shave," I told him.

"I got some scissors, and a barber set in the washroom." He got up to retrieve the objects. His posture had changed. It was upright as any young man who knows he was about to get some loving.

"Oh, let me," I said. I wanted an excuse to visit the washroom myself. Too much time had passed without looking in a mirror. For all I knew, I had bug wings caught in my teeth. I passed a fridge humming in the narrow galley kitchen and paused. The handle looked like it had fallen off and been welded back on. Inside there was nothing but glass bottles of Coca-Cola. The cupboards were filled with cans of pork and beans and chicken noodle soup. Rows of cans lined up so neatly they gave me an eerie chill. As if they were organized, poised for attack. But what they guarded was too tempting to prevent me from snooping. The base of each cupboard shelf was lined in newspaper, dog-eared and fraying. I held my breath as I scrambled on top of the counter to get a better look. The print was unreadable, save for one swatch of newsprint, which was cut in a long column and fixed with old, brittle tape to the inside of the cupboard door. The article had yellowed. The grimy fluorescent tube above me barely cast enough light to read. "You find it?" the Watchman shouted from around the corner. I could hear him getting up out of his bucket chair again.

"I just need to freshen up. Make myself pretty for you," I shouted back to keep him away. I hadn't seen a newspaper in so long, I wanted time alone with it. *Nun Worried about Girls' Safety* was the headline.

Sister Mary Mackenzie, a Catholic nun from the Sisters of Hope of Nazareth, is worried about the safety of local teenage girls, worried they may face the possibility of being kidnapped and transported elsewhere for illicit purposes.

Sister Mary has been highly concerned since the disappearance of 15-year-old Brianna Mills. Mills lived at the Our Lady of Hope orphanage, where the nun works. Mills disappeared after she left school at the nearby Lady of Hope High School the night of March 19. Sister Mary suspects Mills was kidnapped.

Sister Mary also believes there may be a connection between the disappearances of Mills and that of Maria Murray, a 16-year-old girl from the nearby Cranfield township. Murray disappeared the night of February 9 after an alleged dispute with her foster-care parents.

"My own theory," said Sister Mary, "is there may be a market for these girls in the Inner City area. I have some indication of it."

Local police investigators haven't ruled out a connection, although federal police investigators have officially told the media they don't believe there is any case for child prostitution.

"The police have their ways of going about things. So does our congregation," said Sister Mary. She has organized hundreds of members from her own church and other Roman Catholic churches across the city to search for Mills. Each day the nun leads a prayer group at Our Lady of Hope, asking 'God to lead her [Mills] home again.'"

The article ended with a Crime Tips number for anyone with information on the disappearance of Brianna Mills, who, I was almost certain, was Isabella from the House of Diamond. The poorly feigned smile tagged the photo as a class portrait. Brianna Mills with two great tiles for front teeth, the same teeth that had been smudged with lipstick at my debut party. But the girl in the photo had hairspray-teased bangs and dangle earrings. The damn orphan children all wore the same braided and bunned hair, and no jewellery apart from their identical cameo rings. The orphan children only resembled each other. They didn't look like high school students or teenagers or real people from the city at all.

"You're not sick, are you?" the Night Watchman called out again. "Maybe you're not well enough yet? We could wait." He was being as patient as a man who hasn't seen a woman in who knows how long could be. I peeked around the corner to see him raking his curled fingers through his beard—a feeble and touching attempt at pre-date grooming—and I left the news clipping alone.

In the medicine cabinet was a bar of shaving soap and a brush with a heavy ceramic handle, a hand-held mirror, and scissors too small and impossible for his big gnarled hands. I noticed the fading bruises on my shoulders and the blood on my T-shirt and decided not to spend any time in front of the mirror.

The Watchman bumped into me, twice, as he followed me to the large, trough-like sink. He leaned his head far into the basin with enthusiasm. The faucet coughed up greyish water. I splashed as much of it over him as I could with my tiny cupped hands, but instead of washing him clean, the water beaded on top of his oily hair. Whiskers stuck to my fingers in clumps as I cut them away. The floor was quickly covered in locks of his hair. "A Glory won't cut me," he said as I took up the razor. I thought he was giving me an order, but as he tightened his lips nervously, I saw he only meant to reassure himself.

"I won't cut you," I said, dragging the straight blade across his face. His skin moved with the razor, then dropped back into its slack place again. After a few strokes he relaxed and I could get at the underside of his chin, his throat, and the nape of his neck. Tiny sighs leaked from my lips as I uncovered clean, bare skin. Beneath the layer of wiry hair was pink flesh, much younger than I would have guessed. I held up the hand mirror and, after a stunned pause, he chuckled loudly at his reflection. I'd uncovered his lost years, at least a decade's worth. I never would have expected the dimple on his chin.

The garage sink clogged with his hair. I unbuttoned the left clasp of his coveralls and the left side of his mouth curled in a crooked grin. I removed his shirt and started on his woolly chest. When enough hair was cleared away, I pulled my T-shirt over my head and pressed my breasts to newly shaved skin. His moans came out garbled as if his throat, too, were a clogged drain. There was a flower-shaped birthmark on his shoulder.

My final task was his hands. Fortunately for him, I'd learned a thing or two watching Eartha give manicures. I sat on his lap and got to work scrubbing the dirt that outlined his thick nails. I thought of First, scrubbing the Wifey Wing floor, a chore that she always took pride in. "Sparklin' clean," I said, just as First would. With a fair bit of coaxing, I had his fingers loose and nimble enough to undo the stiff metal button on my jeans. This man, whose hands hadn't touched a woman in eons, said to me, "I want to make you purr." And my very best purr rose up to meet him.

Those hands didn't stop when he was finished with me. "I'm going to get this Ford running again." He clicked on a light that hung over the hood of the car he intended to fix. I bet before I came along, he couldn't even have turned that light switch, much less wielded his array of screwdrivers and wrenches. "You ever drive before, Little?" he asked me.

"Sort of," I said blankly. With a bit more thought I almost recalled stealing a car, not getting any further than a couple of blocks away before I lost my nerve and rolled into a ditch. I wondered if I had made that up.

The Night Watchman reached up and, under the right tire well, his arm disappeared into the Ford's mint-green body. Occasionally he craned his head to look at the job he was doing. Mostly, he just whistled a tune and waited as if his hand were a beagle he'd sent down a foxhole. Inside the body of the car there was grinding and clinking and, I imagined, some wonderful struggle between his hand and whatever the brakes looked like. When he was finished, he claimed a tire from the row along the wall and gave the car back its missing leg.

"And then there's the brake pedal," he said, brushing some grease across his brow before opening the driver's side door. I'd have to clean him all over again. I hopped into the passenger seat and watched him ease himself under the steering wheel. A small woman, like me, could have fit under there. He had to contort his back, his feet dangling outside the car, the top half of him curled under the steering wheel. Still shirtless, sweat broke on his skin like groundwater rising up through dry land.

"Let's go for dinner. I haven't eaten a meal in a restaurant for—" he said, leaving the sentence unfinished. "This place will be okay without me for a while." He stood proud in front of his newly repaired automobile. I hadn't mapped very much. I hadn't saved Sub Rosa or found an Advent Alley. And I had only angered Jellyfish when I tried to talk to her. I accepted Night Watchman's offer anyway. I wasn't going back out there alone. I'd have better luck driving around with him than in blind wandering. For all I knew, the blackout was over already. At the very least, I'd be bringing the Glories a fresh live one with money. The Watchman was far better than a live one. He was a kind and decent Dark dweller. He was something none of us thought existed. I discovered new life. My eureka (as I'd begun to think of him) combed pomade through his hair and put on the cleanest shirt he could find. "Is this okay? It's the best I got around here."

"It's very handsome," I told him and he smiled like he believed me.

He sat me in the driver's seat, talked me through turning the key in the ignition, introduced me to the brake pedal. "Nowadays, it's perfectly normal for a woman to drive a car," he informed me. "What's more, someone's got to open that garage door, and I bet you already had enough of those stone bugs, so I'll do it." The engine roared then spit, then its comeback roared even louder. I shifted into first gear, eased up the safety brake, and waited for him to open the garage door. On the seat beside me was his tin box of money and a pair of old shoes. He gave me a brave smile before pushing the door up and letting the stone bugs in. Just like he told me, I let go of the brake and eased my foot on the gas. I thought I knew what I was doing, but I lurched forward, almost hitting him as I pulled out. I stopped outside the garage with a screech. The Watchman hurled himself into the car with a dozen bugs on his tail, and the two of us swatted at them with the old shoes until we were out of breath and the interior was covered in bug splats. They surrounded the car, dimming the headlights completely. The Watchman instructed me to press hard on the gas and the brakes at the same time. "We'll smoke them out!" The Ford wheezed. Smoke began to seep out from under the hood. The car rattled hard and I wished that he was in the driver's seat. He seemed perfectly calm as he flipped on the heat to prevent the engine from overheating. "Heat from the engine's got to go somewhere." He tapped the heat gauge—the needle turned from the red line to the blue. We hot-boxed the car until I was woozy and covered in sweat, but at last the stone bugs had fled.

"You done well," he said, calm as could be. "How'd you like to drive us into town?" I kept driving only because I didn't want to reject his offer. I ground the gears and stalled when I turned, taking the corner so wide the back tires skidded against the curb. The headlights did the best they could to pierce the darkness, though there was not much to see. To my disappointment, the Dark, even when lit by car headlights, was unlike any city streets. There were no yellow dotted lines on the road, the street signs were mangled and useless. I should have given Arsen more credit for driving through the Dark to find me.

I was somewhat reassured by the idea that I had just done this trip, and all I needed to do was retrace my route. Phantom hand rose up on the dashboard, pointing like a compass. I felt a bit uneasy that it seemed to remember the way while I was lost. But I needed any help I could get.

"Gosh, the garage really is out in the middle of nowhere," said the Watchman. His calmness was ebbing. He thrummed his fingers anxiously against the dashboard. There was no music, no singing divas like in Arsen's car, only silence and the moneybox between us. I kept waiting for him to complain about the circles I was sure we were driving in. He switched on the radio and flipped from static to more static to find a station. We don't get radio on Sub Rosa. I didn't bother telling him that. I would have rather listened to static than nothing. He tuned into some warped melody and ran the dial over it again and again trying to find clear song. He ended up whistling along to distortion.

Jellyfish must have been close, close enough to watch our weaving and backtracking. I thought I spotted her lunar glow in my peripheral vision, a blink of light in the driver's side mirror, then the sound of something being dragged, metal scraping concrete. Disregarding the disordered street, I headed straight for the sound, driving the wide car over curb corners. The Watchman latched onto the handle above the passenger side door. "The 'oh shit' handle," I blurted out, suddenly remembering the name of that handle. "That's what it's called."

"Spoken like a truck driver, missy." He forced out a faint chuckle, followed by a barking scream. "Whoa!"

A construction zone sign sat in the centre of the street. Mud clouded the orange and black checkers, but clearly tacked in the centre was a single white glove—the index finger signalled left. I recognized my glove, still as white as the day First bought it for me. "Now that's odd," said the Watchman, scratching his absent whiskers at the pointing white hand.

"Someone wants to show me the way," I told him. And I turned the car in the direction Jellyfish's finger pointed.

XX

Phantom hand squeezed my shoulder as soon as we were on the right road. Its ghostly fingers had gotten stronger during the journey, its independent will made firm. It massaged my neck, which only made me involuntarily stiffen at first, but when I gave in I gave in entirely, surprised at how much tension I'd been holding.

Phantom hand had established itself as a friend, not just a party trick; after all, it had come with me to the Dark, it fought the stone bugs by my side, and now it was giving me a much-needed massage. It understood, too, that I couldn't return to Sub Rosa rigid as a live one. I leaned back into its invisible fingers. Some tight spot popped near the base of my skull and I peeked over at the Watchman, hoping he didn't hear. How embarrassing.

"Are we going to the land of lost girls?" he asked.

"Where?"

"The place where the Glories, like yourself, have all gone. Is that where you're taking me?"

"That's right. I'm taking you to Sub Rosa, and you're going to love it."

"I always wanted to meet one. One of the ones that I read about, that is."

"The newspaper ..." I said, feeling uneasy. Phantom hand went to work on my neck again.

"You saw one of my clippings, did you? I kept all the news I came across in case I ever met one."

"Met one what?" My hands gripped the wheel. I was nervous that we were going to crash.

"One of you lost children turned Glory. I guess I have something of a school-boy crush on you girls." He touched my side so gently, not sure where to put his hand. When he retracted it, it clanged clumsily against the metal lock box. "I wish I had something about you. I'm sure you were in all the papers. I bet they even talked about you on the television."

No one is searching for me, I thought matter-of-factly. Why hadn't I been in the newspaper? I ought to have been. I didn't even know exactly how long I'd been away from the city. Hell, I didn't even know how long I'd spent in the Watchman's garage. But certainly it was long enough for someone to notice? I tried harder to consider who might possibly be looking, and again I came up blank.

My body nagged me. Clenching jaw, sour belly. I tasted salt before I realized I was crying. I hadn't cried since First threatened me in Arsen's apartment. I turned my head toward the driver's side window for a moment so the Night Watchman wouldn't see. He turned his face away, too, as if sensing my sudden need for privacy. I pictured the sad lamp lady. Her coarse, grey roller-set curls, her cracked lips poorly painted cerise pink—she took shape the longer I gazed into the Dark. And although I hadn't been able to see her clearly before, this time I knew the polyester knit of her white trousers, the depressed weave of her slippers. She was my grandmother. The connection made me swerve the car. Maybe my grandmother was looking for me? She must have liked me, right?

I had long lists of strange things that I trusted more than memory: I trusted phantom hand and my cursed ring; I trusted the enormous arms of Della O'Kande, my First; I trusted that the sun would rise at the very same time each day on Sub Rosa. But memory—untrustworthy. Maybe I was just jealous of the girl in the newspaper, and I was making the whole thing up. I mean, how dare a mere orphan have a brigade of nuns searching for her when I had nothing? It wasn't fair. Or maybe it was the Night Watchman's influence; I wanted to be the lost girl in his fantasies.

But I'd seen my grandmother before I saw the newspaper. The memory, or whatever it was, came to me out in the Dark. With Jellyfish. "Use your birth name," she had commanded so urgently. It sounded like gibberish.

I did know for certain that the Glories wouldn't think the Night Watchman was much of a find if he started going on about newspapers and city folk, and lost girls. This information was dangerous. It was forbidden; First had warned me again and again. This was the type of information that might make a Glory … it might make a Glory want to leave Sub Rosa.

Outside the passenger-side window, the Night Watchman gasped at the bit of light: the crescent moon, the strip of stars that had shaken off the blanket of city smog to shine especially over Sub Rosa. I hoped the blackout was over and that we were about to drive up to an enchanting Sub Rosa night. But we found the streetlamps and shop lights out. The blackout was still on. I must have left the night before, maybe two nights, and spent at least a day passed out in the Watchman's bed. Forty-eight hours was a long time to be gone without returning with a solution. The Watchman rolled down his window to drape his arm in the warm, sweet air. His enthusiasm for the Sub Rosa climate was contagious, and I grinned along with him as we drove the last length. "You can't say anything about the lost girls," I told him, a touch of Glory persuasion with my words. "It's bad manners on Sub Rosa. Understand?" He nodded without hesitation. I bet he would have agreed to just about anything in that moment. The metal lockbox of money rattled in his eager hands. I pushed down on the gas, getting us there a little faster.

I cut the headlights as we passed the Dowager's Mansion. There were no other cars on this side of the street to manoeuvre around, and I managed to park perfectly in front of the Mayflower. The Watchman got out of the car and ran to open my door for me. "You sure this place is open?" he asked, peering in at the candlelight.

"It never closes," I told him.

So much for our dramatic entrance. The Mayflower had turned into a crash pad. I assumed the place would be empty until I saw First's feet jutting out from a booth. The needlepoint and magazines and hair-braiding had all been abandoned for sleep. One Glory to each booth, twisted into uncomfortable positions, sleeping like the dead. The Watchman took up a candle to look them over. "This one has pink hair, look at that," he called to me. "This girl here is as big as my mattress." He waved the candle over the Diamond Dowager, then blew it out, retreating away from her. "Best not to disturb them," he whispered.

I did disturb them. And they would have wanted to be disturbed. It was a sad day when a Glory sleeps through the sound of a live one's voice. He may not have been much, but I hadn't brought this freshly shaven beast-turned-man all the way from the Dark to be received by the sleeping. I rapped my knuckles on the kitchen door. Shirley emerged with wild strands of hair loose from her bun. "Customers," I snapped.

"I just fed you a few hours ago," she complained, then saw it was me. When she saw the Watchman's happy grin she tied the gingham apron around her waist in a hurry.

First sat up sleepily in her booth, her arms stretching out for a hug. "Baby girl," she yawned. "I've been dreaming about you. Horrible dreams. But you're really here now, right?" She was warm with sleep as she hugged me.

"How long was I gone?" I whispered.

"Hard to say. The sun never came up proper. It was like a sunrise in the Dark, kind of purple and weak. We got to get some city money through here soon or else. Everyone got so nervous I guess we all passed out. I can barely feel my body anymore." First massaged her limbs. "What are we going to do, Little?"

"How do you do, ma'am." The Night Watchman had been standing a foot behind me. He thrust his hand forward to introduce himself to First.

"How am I?" First sputtered, taken aback by the stranger suddenly before her. "Well, good sir, I'm afraid you caught me, well, all of us girls, in a bit of a dilemma. Forgive my poor manners."

"I'd be happy to help out, any way I can," offered the Watchman. I started to tug him away. I could almost hear the wheels of First's thoughts being put into motion, and I wanted the Watchman to at least have a decent meal before the Glories made their claims on him.

I woke the triplets and shooed them out of their sleeping spots. Their booth was the best in the house, and I could count on them to wake the others and start the well-earned gossip. The Watchman swaggered when he came up to our table, trying to impress the ladies. The triplets giggled, hastily fixing their hair and clothes as he said hello.

I shouldered up to Myra for a quick report. "Cops searched the Smoke Shoppe yesterday. I think it was yesterday. They claimed it was a routine inspection—Cuban cigars and all that. Mr Eddie looked scared to death as he told us. He barely poked his head out the back door." Myra spoke in a sleepy monotone "Who's the live one?" she asked, her voice perking up a little.

"I found him in the Dark," I told her, and took my seat across from him. Shirley attempted to give us menus. I'd never seen a menu at the

Mayflower before. Everyone who ate there was a regular. I waved the menus away before she got a chance to put them down on the table. "Fish and chips," I ordered, which was my favourite. "And the gentleman will have anything that isn't chicken soup or beans." I winked at the Watchman. He'd never had a lady order for him, I was sure. I bet he liked it, especially when within minutes he was brought the best pepper steak with mashed potatoes and peas. He nearly wept at the sight of his dinner plate. "Good food. Pretty girl, prettiest girl, I mean that," he said and took my hand from across the table. "It must be a miracle that you ended up at my garage."

He ate in rounds; a bite of peas, of mashed potatoes, steak, then a sip of water before going back to the peas again. I was quietly tickled by this, by the way he swished each sip of water in his cheeks to clear his palate. I could barely imagine his face before I'd shaved and cut his hair, before his greasy skin came clean. The dimple in the centre of his chin deepened as he chewed his food.

Arsen flicked and fumbled with a dead lighter on the other side of the room. First had their candle in her hand, ready for the flame. I could feel her giving me the eye. They were whispering. I wondered what kind of plan was coming together between them.

Next to her the triplets chattered at full volume and not-so-discreetly pointed in our direction. Glories started circling like buzzards. Their actions were ridiculously contrived: polishing the spotless windows around us; coyly dropping coins so that they would roll toward our table—anything so they might get closer. They restrained themselves until the Watchman finished his dinner. When he started on his apple pie and coffee, First slid into the booth beside me, clicking coffee cups with him as she re-introduced herself. Fauxnique slipped in beside him. She had her hand on his thigh under the table; I could tell by his suddenly embarrassed expression.

"It's okay," I said. "I'm not the jealous type." Fauxnique took this as her cue to shimmy onto his lap, making room for Ling to sit down on the bench beside him. First and Ling tag-teamed the flattery: "That shirt makes you look so handsome," "What a healthy appetite you have," "That chin dimple is *soooo* old Hollywood," and on and on.

Outside, the sunrise previewed its purples and pinks. First leaned into me like a plant growing toward a sunny window. "Today's sunrise is brighter already, my little angel," she cooed in my ear. The Watchman craned his neck to see the oncoming daylight, nearly tipping Fauxnique off his lap. His once dog-like face achieved a new level of humanness as he watched the Sub Rosa sun spill colours over the rooftops. "What a sunrise," the Dowager said as she strode up. "I bet it will be a beautiful day in the city. The sun sparkling off tall buildings, ladies in their summer dresses." Fauxnique and Ling grimaced at the Dowager as Fauxnique re-rooted herself in the Watchman's lap.

"Well, I really should be getting back," the Watchman said with barely an acknowledgement of the Dowager. "Can't leave the garage unprotected for too long." He shifted under Fauxnique, trying politely to get up.

"My dear man," said the Dowager. "You've only just got here. There's no reason why we can't enjoy a second slice of pie together, hmm?" The Dowager urged Ling and Fauxnique out of their seats and sat herself beside him. He flinched when she looped her arm around his.

"I was just myself thinkin' that today is the perfect day to visit the city," said First. I couldn't believe what I was hearing. First hated the city.

"You're too right, Candy," I said. "After a long, very long, work week, you deserve a little painting of the town. Why not take in the sights?"

"I can't imagine the city has any sights more beautiful than you girls," said the Watchman.

"Yeah," barked Fauxnique. "Why bother with the city when you can stay here with us?"

"It's true, Sub Rosa is the nicest place on earth. But sometimes I miss those lemon gelati cones you can get in Little Italy. You ever have those?" asked the Dowager. The Watchman nodded in recognition.

"Or hot smokies," said First. She closed her eyes as she described the smell of beef smokies cooking in the street stalls, the sound of the buskers' flute music floating around the subway station, the coo of pigeons gathered on the art gallery lawn. I doubted she really remembered the taste of a smokie. I didn't. She was just reciting stories that Arsen had told us about the habits of live ones. Still, her depiction of the city got to me until I was authentically and vividly imagining everything she described. She was using Glory magic, I was sure.

"Candy apples," I said. "Granny Smiths dipped in caramel and sprinkled with chocolate shavings. And the city centre pool in the summer. They have a water slide there."

"A water slide?" First puzzled.

"It's just like it sounds, Candy," Fauxnique said. "You slide, you land in water."

"Oh, oh," I piped in again. "At the city zoo you can buy a bag of feed for a dollar, and they let you feed it to the deer yourself. They must have forty deer, or more." And then I told the Watchman about kids playing skip rope in the street and jazz bands on a summer night. To my surprise, I had a whole arsenal of these images; I fired them off one after another, getting more and more astonished and excited as I did. The other Glories crowded around the table, urging me for more. I had no idea if the places or people were real or regurgitated tales I'd heard from Arsen or just stuff I was making up on the spot.

"You see?" said the Dowager. "You really should go. You could be downtown before noon and make a whole day of it." The Watchman agreed in shy nods.

"You could go to the horse-race track. I bet *you'd* be lucky if I gave you a kiss," First suggested. I noticed her beckoning Arsen, her hand held low so only he would see.

"And if Little kissed you, I bet you'd come up lucky at the casino," Arsen said in what sounded like his bedroom voice. I began to grow suspicious as he edged toward us. "Think of all the people gathered around you to applaud as your cards came up winners."

"The thing is, I'm not sure how to find my way," the Watchman managed to say. How he would find his way back was what most concerned me.

"That's easy," said the Dowager. "Your car is already parked in the entrance to the city. Ready to go." I turned to the window and saw that the Watchman's mint-green Ford was missing. I spotted its tailfins sticking out of Advent Alley. I looked back at the Watchman, panicked. Diamond's arm was around him as he gawked at his mysteriously transported car. The Dowager blew me a little kiss, one that I actually felt hit my cheek. Phantom hand was itching to slap her. "You car's been sitting there, ready, for ages. All you have to do is drive toward the tallest building and you're downtown," Diamond continued. "And when you want to find your way back, look for the 24 Hour Coffee Hut at the end of Trench Street." I opened my mouth to correct her and she kicked me under the table. "All of us pretty working girls can be found just behind the Coffee Hut. This man here can draw you a map."

First shifted over to make room in the booth for Arsen. I was squished tight against the window as Arsen scrawled out his map leading from downtown to the skids on a paper placemat. *Girls*, he wrote beside a heavy-inked 'x.'

The Dowager tapped the 'x' with her slender finger. "All the girls are right here, behind the Coffee Hut," she repeated softly. "Right, girls?"

"Yes, that's right," Ling joined her. "All the girls are behind the Coffee Hut." Soon all of the Glories were saying it as if the words were a prayer or a song sung in rounds. By this point all of us had caught on: the Dowager was fixing to send the Night Watchman through Advent Alley, past the police car. It was a fine plan, seeing as none of us could risk going through the alley. The Night Watchman, in his old-model car and his tin box full of dated money, was soon to be the only action the police had seen in days.

The Dowager turned to me. "Little, where are the girls, again?" she asked. I didn't want to take part in their lies. But when she kicked me again under the table, I told the Watchman I would be there, waiting at the Coffee Hut, along with all the beautiful lost children turned Glories. We would all be there. His eyes lit up and he studied Arsen's map, bewitched.

"I'm off to the city," the Watchman said. "To get back, I go to the Coffee Hut on Trench Street, it's where the girls are." There was no discussion of the squad car, which had moved away from Advent Alley a little, but still sat in front of the Smoke Shoppe.

"I wish I could come with you, Watchman," I lied again, leaning into his car to give him a big kiss. I doubted this would be fair payment for whatever might happen to him on the city side.

As he pulled through the alley we gathered behind to watch him leave. A moment later, the squad car started its engine, the quietest I'd ever heard, and followed him. I knew it wouldn't be long before they saw his expired driver's licence and the "girls" map. I worried how he'd explain where he'd just come from if asked. Any explanation he could give would sound as if he were mentally ill. They wouldn't know what to make of him. If he was detained for any amount of time, I worried that his hair would start to grow back and his arthritis would return. I pictured him a stubbly, gnarled shadow of himself, pacing a holding cell. After all the work I'd done to uncover him, the thought of him in yet another prison sickened me.

"He won't turn us in?" Ling asked.

"Turn who in? The skid hos who hustle behind the Coffee Hut?" said Arsen. "That man is under such a spell, he won't even remember Sub Rosa. We'll get old No to say they thought his car was abandoned. Been there forever. Once we're out of here, Klime and I will start making some anonymous calls about gunfire and junkie prostitutes and other disturbances in that same area, and the heat will be off us." Although his usual confidence had returned to his voice, we all stood slightly crouched and still, not yet sure that it was over.

"He will be let down when he sees the city," Myra said. Likka and Portia nodded and hung their heads. "All your wild stories, Little. I guess you had to say something good to get him to go."

The Diamond Dowager was not the least bit sorry for him. "That shabby Dark dweller is a small sacrifice, Little," she said. She turned and thanked me, "for protecting Sub Rosa." Hearing her, the Glories cheered for me, quietly though, as they were still concerned about being heard. I braced against their gratitude, as if their cheers were stones.

"You'll forget him," First assured me. "The Dark will wear off like it always does."

We turned Sub Rosa back on slowly, starting with the brown glass lamps at the Mayflower. Al counted to three before he flicked the switch. The lights tinkled like little bells as they lit up.

Arsen drove in and out of Advent Alley a few times just to make sure he wasn't being watched or followed. He headed back to his apartment without saying goodbye to anyone. I heard his tires screech as he accelerated away from us.

The Dowager, in her final moments of authority, instructed us to re-do our blackout jobs, but backward. The Firsts went home to brighten the apartments and take the charms out of hiding. The triplets visited the Smoke Shoppe. And I was back with Dearest, making the rounds. Her lips were cracked from all the sugar, and each time she smiled at me I winced at the thin red splits in the corners of her mouth. "My hero," she said and took my arm, tracing her sticky fingers along my side, as if I were a live one. I shook her off.

The beauty shop had beat us to it. Its rose-bulb marquee was already on before we arrived. It read: DARK CIRCLE EYE TREATMENTS AND SKIN BRIGHTENING. Eartha poked her head out the door. "I've had many visions," she told me. "And you?"

"The Night Watchman?" I asked and handed her half of what he paid me. She tucked the red bills in her apron pocket.

"He has already done his Dark time in this life. The worst is already over for him," she said. "There is no need for worry." She had a point; anywhere was better than the garage, I assured myself.

Mr Saragosa was also quick to get back to business, turning his neon back on as soon as we knocked on his door. Second Man came, bleary-eyed, out of the Pawnshop and crept back to the House of Man. Maria in Babycakes and June at Launderlove had not weathered the blackout as well. Maria had eaten herself sick. June had fallen into a deep slumber, from which we had to awaken her. When she did, she was angry. We hurried out of the laundromat as she launched mini-bottles of laundry soap at our backs.

It didn't take long before the first car entered Sub Rosa. Then another and another, as if the first car had broken the dam for all the others to rush in. Too excited to wait on our track patches to be chosen, we charged at the cars before their drivers had even parked. Alluring poses and sly comments were put aside. We were all raring to go to work. I tucked a wad of bills in my back pocket without counting it. I was not the only one. Glories wrapped their arms and legs around the live ones without naming a price. It was Dearest who started taking live ones outdoors, the last of her sugar buzz burned up as she flung herself around the back seat of a station wagon like damp clothes in Launderlove's dryers. Bumper to bumper, the cars lined the curb on either side. Not one window was closed for modesty. Car stereos and squeaking vinyl and sex noises combined into a single ringing note. It rang louder than the Dark's hum or the hailstorm of stone bugs or the vacuum silence when I fell down Jellyfish's hole. It stayed in my ears after the last live one was gone and First carried me up the narrow stairs to our apartment.

Exhausted, we didn't bother to do much more than wash our hands and throw our clothes in a pile on the floor. "What's that you've got on the back of your T-shirt, Little?" she asked. "Did a live one draw that on you?"

I had forgotten about the map I had drawn to chart the Dark. My exploration seemed long ago. I retrieved the T-shirt to see what was left of it after the busy night. The lines were crooked and disconnected where I must have stumbled. I could see where I hit dead ends and had to retrace my steps. Looping circles represented the cobblestone square and strange fountain. In its sloppy entirety, the map appeared roughly to spell "go home." First and I stared at it for a while before she plucked it from my hand.

"I should keep it," I said.

"It's filthy," First argued. "Besides, you've come home. No need for it now." She tossed it into the wastebasket. A moment later, phantom hand dragged it out again.

XXI

Mr Saragosa's pawnshop had a new sign in the window. QUALITY WATCHES it read in neon-yellow letters, wrapped around a glowing clock face.

"First!" I hollered from the bottom of the Wifey Wing stairs. What idiot needed a watch? The low-slung sun already made it clear that it was time for breakfast. The aroma of sugary dough wafting from Baby-cakes put the time at roughly half past eight. I didn't need to be told by some cartoon-like clock. The sign was too close to the Wifey Wing door. Mr Saragosa could hardly expect us to walk past that thing every day. I sprinted back up the stairs.

"Did you see the clock in the Pawnshop window?"

"Don't worry none," said First. "I already spoke with Mr Saragosa about it. It's only gonna be on in the daytime. He promised to switch it off at dusk. Last thing we wants the live ones thinkin' of is time."

"Yeah," I said. "Live ones don't want that."

"Mr Saragosa swears that watches will be the next big thing on Sub Rosa," First sighed. "Seems everyone got a bright idea about somethin' lately."

Recent changes had First on the defence. Mostly the changes were small, small and gratifying, I thought. At the triplets' request, Eddie Senior bought a soft-serve ice cream machine for No's, complete with a mini-bar stocked with crushed nuts and coloured sprinkles.

Second Man got himself a cherry-red motorcycle, and every day he took turns parading us Glories up and down the street. "Sub Rosa was forced too fast, and now it's time to feast," is how First explained it. She still wasn't so open, however, to the possibility of adding a new darling to the House of Arsen. Ever since Arsen suggested it, a few days after the blackout ended, First had retreated back into nonfiction. She started hitting the library daily, pulling whole stacks of books off the shelves at a time and piling them around the living room sofa where she sat for hours. She woke earlier and earlier each morning to read. I suspected she got up early to avoid me. We never spoke again about Jellyfish. I'd lie awake and alone in our bed with Jellyfish loose in my head, but the few times I tried to mention her First just urged me back to bed and encouraged me to get more rest. "Sleep in, you deserve it," she had said several times. I took it as a sign that the entire topic of Jellyfish was also put to bed.

I peered over her shoulder at the heavy textbook that she was almost finished reading. It was about atmospheric science, whatever that means, and there were illustrations of different types of clouds scattered alongside the tiny text. I looked at the two-dimensional storm clouds wistfully.

"Breakfast?" I asked her.

"Had it," she said, pointing at the muffin wrapper and empty teacup on the coffee table. "I bought a dozen—apple cinnamon—if you're hungry."

"Well, I was on my way to the Mayflower, before I ran into that awful clock. If you don't mind?" First waved goodbye with a smile, her eyes focused on her book.

I avoided the neon clock on my way out. It was late enough in the morning that the triplets would be well caffeinated and ready to gossip, this I knew. Their table was covered in beads and felt and smears of glue when I arrived. Collaging menu covers was their latest project. "But we never use the menus," I said. Magazine clippings crumpled under my arms as I took a spot at their table. As I slid over, a pair of cut-out eyes stuck to my elbow.

"These are daily special menus," Portia explained, holding one up. "There are seven different menus, one for each day of the week."

"Maggie and Al are testing out new recipes," said Likka. "It's because of our influence, don't you think? We've been very encouraging." The triplets nodded and giggled in agreement. A second later they were arguing about how long it had been since a new dish had been added to the menu.

I had a more serious topic in mind for discussion. "So, I hear that all Diamond's children were once real orphans," I said.

Likka dropped her glitter glue. "Where did you hear that?"

"We always thought that was a rumour so that the live ones would feel sorry for them," said Myra.

"It's no rumour," snapped Likka. "You know all the zombie men? It was the Dowager who banished them to the Dark in the first place, right? Well, the orphan children are all their girlfriends and sisters that got left behind when the zombies were exiled."

"The zombie's sisters. That's rich!" Portia snorted. "The Dowager's girls, for your information, are all the darlings who never made their dowries. Some girls just don't have what it takes. The city leaves them too broken, like, say, *orphans*. Orphans are particularly broken. It's these girls who don't do so good on their Dark Days. That's how Diamond's children got their name."

"That's right, isn't it?" said Myra. "I remember, because when Arsen opened the bets on you, a lot of Glories bet you'd end up with the Dowager. You had that look, you know, that a-little-too-far-gone look about you. Were you an orphan, Little?"

Either Portia or Likka kicked Myra from under the table. Myra let out a short yelp, then pressed her lips together and resumed gluing sparkles onto Mayflower menus. "Don't ask stupid questions," Likka scolded. "I was just curious. Is that so wrong?" Myra said sternly as she pushed the clippings around the table, searching for a head to fit on top of a collage body.

Portia ripped into a baggie of plastic googly eyes, which spilled across the table. "Shit," she blurted out. "I never thought you looked too far gone," she said a second later. "It must be hard for the Daddies. They have to pick just the right girl. One that wants desperately to leave the city, but not so desperate that she can't succeed as a Glory. You'd think if anyone was going to be good at picking darlings, it would be Arsen. But the way I heard it is he's lost girls to the Dowager. At least two, as far as I know. That's why most Glories thought you'd wind up an orphan child. That's the only reason."

Shirley sprang up with cups of their new seafood chowder for us to sample. She laid the placemats on top of the triplet's art supplies and offered us the steaming ceramic mugs. The chowder had roasted yellow peppers and whitefish that dissolved on my tongue. It was just what was needed to quell the tension after what Portia said. The triplets examined their collages between bites. Hearts and lady legs and marabou feathers. Portia put her soup aside to craft four-leaf clovers with a green bingo dabber.

"My grandmother used to have an ashtray shaped like a four-leaf clover," I said, half-consciously. A moment later the words sunk in and as they did, I nearly leaped out of my seat. I wasn't an orphan—I had a grandmother.

"You mean a candy dish?" asked Myra.

"No, an ashtray! She smoked her lungs out!" I grinned at the thought of it.

"It's not funny, poor woman. And she put out her nasty cigarettes in a four-leaf clover, no less. City people—they just don't know any better, do they?"

City people visited us every day. In a few hours they'd begin their routine visits that we depended on. We call them live ones simply because they've passed through the invisible border to Sub Rosa. They stop being city people and become cherished, valuable. Most city people would never make it to Sub Rosa. Did that make them useless? Invisible? It was Thursday—the day the Widower had chosen for his regular appointment. This time I planned to look, hard, out his car window. And hopefully, I wouldn't be the only one.

The Dowager and her orphan children wore soiled garden gloves and were armed with little metal claws and hoes. As I approached, I could hear very faint girlish grunts as they laboured away at the cracked earth, pushing black soil around from tiny pile to hole and back again. There were, undeniably, more blooms on her wisteria vine, more buds on her roses than before.

"They're really starting to bloom," I said, standing on the edge of her property.

The Diamond Dowager stood, and her orphan children all scrambled to their feet after her. "Come smell one, if you like," she offered. "They are quite fragrant." As I stood on my tiptoes to reach her roses, I spotted Isabella. She looked like a dishevelled soldier, mud-stained knees, her ivory slip showing beneath her black lace dress. Soil smeared across both cheeks. Had she been lying in the dirt?

"I have tea inside," the Dowager said, beckoning me from behind the roses and thorns. The orphan children moved drone-like toward the house; Diamond stopped them with a single upturned finger. We left them tending the nearly lifeless earth.

The inside of the Dowager's house was the same as the outside: gloomy. Dark wood that looked to be polished with ash. I feared that if I touched the walls, they would stain my skin. Cut-crystal chandeliers hung side by side from the ceiling, thousands of sparkling arrows pointed at my head. They chimed precariously in the cool draft that pushed the front door shut behind us. I wondered what kind of live one found himself in this house.

Yet there were objects inside the house that, like the Dowager's roses, were full of colour and hope. A tiny brass bell hung by a red ribbon above her doorway. A melancholic rendition of "Moon River" played on a gramophone in the corner. The sugar cubes for our tea were contained in a ceramic rabbit-shaped bowl, its little face desperately cute in the drab surroundings. I began to understand what kind of live one would visit. The Wifey Wing overwhelms one with gratification. What could possibly be yearned for that we don't already have? The House of Diamond was full of wanting. She needed an entire mansion to hold all that want. I imagined live ones ascending to the upstairs rooms, each as sad as the sitting room, maybe containing a painting of a summer garden or an old portrait to interrupt the emptiness. I imagined undressing an orphan child, unwrapping the layers of black crepe to find her skin, pale and pure. As if she were the only precious thing that survived fire or flood. As if she were the last untouched thing left on this spoiled earth.

"If you're finished scrutinizing my home, you can tell me why you've come." The Dowager narrowed her eyes at me. I figured I should get right to the point.

"The Widower has requested a duo," I lied. "I'd like to take one of the orphans with me to his house."

"My girls don't do duos with Glories from other houses."

I had anticipated this answer. "Believe me," I said carefully, "I prefer to bring someone more … complementary to my working style. More flexible. Your children are too obedient to you to serve me personally, in any way. I'd take First, but she can be a bit overwhelming at times. I don't want to jeopardize the relationship I have with the Widower. He's head shy."

"I know all about him. As do my girls, if you recall." Diamond poured me more tea. I took this as a sign she was still willing to hear my proposition.

"He knows your girls, all right. He was asking after Isabella at my debut party. Maybe she mentioned it?"

"Of course she did," said the Dowager. "But I already knew Isabella was a favourite of his." I didn't care whether she was telling the truth or boasting. My only aim was to arrange some time alone with Isabella. "I'll consider it," said the Dowager.

"Well if you decided to send her, have her be ready and waiting curbside at seven sharp," I said, doing my best to come off indifferent. I gulped back the remainder of my tea. The sugar had sunk to the bottom of the cup, leaving my mouth sweet.

"A duo will be a healing experience for you," I explained to the Widower as I opened his car door and let Isabella in. He held back his reservations as we drove to his waterfront home the same way he later held back his gratitude as I led a naked Isabella to the blanket laid out before him.

The Widower sat on his firm leather sofa, watching. Isabella squirmed under me and, I must admit, put on a very good show. Her heightened breathing whistled through the gap in her front teeth. How I wanted to pry her mouth open to free her sounds. I gripped her throat tightly for seconds at a time, pressing my fingernails into the soft flesh beneath her earlobe, hoping for a scream. She curled her toes, pressed her palms flat into the blanket. Nothing was escaping her. I handed her over to the Widower, flush and dizzy, and took a turn at watching. And I might have enjoyed the spectacle if I hadn't been so preoccupied with what I would say to her during the cab ride home.

I could hardly wait to tell Isabella about the newspaper clipping taped to the Watchman's cupboard door. Glories liked fame, after all. They enjoyed being sought out, even dullards like the orphans. But more than this, if I told Isabella, I wouldn't be alone with memory any more. If I told First, she would just scold me for reading a newspaper and that would be the end of our conversation. But I wasn't nervous about confessing my discovery to an orphan—not when she was the topic of the newspaper article herself.

In the taxi, Isabella fanned herself with the Widower's envelope. "I have never felt so good. Did you have fun?"

"Duos are more fun than being alone with a live one," I explained. "Glories are better than everyone else—except maybe Daddies."

"I wouldn't know."

"Oh, sorry."

"Don't be sorry. Royal generously gives his love to me."

"Yeah? But you can't … you know … with a ghost," I said. Isabella raised a suggestive eyebrow at me. "Sex?" I asked.

"Well, not sex. But my feelings aren't based solely upon physical, tangible things." She looked out the window. The sky was the colour of dirty mop-bucket water. Isabella scrunched her nose at the rain drops that splattered against the window. "I try not to let people or things dictate what I feel. We orphans keep our emotion deep within ourselves. I don't need a Daddy to feel loved."

"Daddies aren't about love," I corrected her. Who was she to be spouting off words of so-called wisdom? She was a brainwashed orphan, as far as I was concerned, staring back at me with big round empty eyes. "The Daddies help us stay connected to that 'emotion deep within ourselves.' It's called 'roots,' Isabella. Once upon a time we came from the city, and that's what the Daddies give us, a little bit of the city, in a good way, get it? It can't be all Sub Rosa all the time. We'd all be exactly the same if it was like that."

As soon I said this, I understood that it was utterly true. The Daddies provide what we are unable to get for ourselves. When I was a runaway, Arsen tempted me with a home. He made me beautiful when I was pathetic and ugly. He removed me from harm's way and put me on Sub Rosa. Now that I was a Glory, he offered me snippets of the city. That was my favourite thing about him, his retelling of city stories. Which restaurants city people liked and how long they were willing to wait in line to eat at them, what kind of toy dog was becoming the most popular pet, and if royal or navy was the fashionable blue for the season. He told these stories so that First and I might better understand our live ones. Based on Arsen's reports, First would decide whether to serve chai or green tea to live ones or use light lavender- or vanilla-scented candles in the working room. But aside from their practical function, these stories kept us from feeling like we'd lost ourselves by coming to Sub Rosa. Arsen's city stories were personal; that's why we liked them. The realization made me momentarily proud of myself.

"Is that your way of insulting me?" Isabella snapped "'We'd all be exactly the same'? What do you know about me?" The suddenly bitchy tone of her voice irked me. She was so clueless compared to me.

"I know you never had a dad or a mom," I said. "I heard that orphan business was a Glory gimmick. But you're no fake, are you? You're the read deal, little orphan Annie Brianna Isabella, or whoever." At last Isabella's stiff lips fell wide open. Her face went slack and she sank into the cheap taxi upholstery with the sudden weight of it all. I gave her a few moments to take it all in. She was so still she didn't seem to be breathing. This wasn't how I had imagined her reacting. My delivery was too rough. I was beating her with her own past. I may as well have seized her hand and slapped her face with it.

"I know about the Sisters of Hope of Nazareth. Sister Mary," I tried again, gentle-like. "Do you remember? Brianna—that's your real name?"

"How do you know that?" she asked. "How could you know that when I barely know that? Your magic? You can touch people without touching them *and* you can see the past? True Glory magic like the old legends?"

"I get glimpses," I said, liking the credit she was giving me. I inched closer, ready to bait her with more prophecies when a bellowing sob exploded out of her, her spittle hitting my cheek. I hugged her close, just to shut her up. "Listen quietly, this cab ride won't last forever." I lowered my own voice so that the cabbie wouldn't hear. "The truth is, I've been thinking lots about the city since my second trip to the Dark. My own memories, they're all mashed up together in my head. But you, I found something of yours out there. It was a newspaper clipping in the Night Watchman's garage, and it was all about you. There was a picture of you and everything. Sister Mary is worried about you. She put out a missing person's. She started a prayer group. She went to the newspapers, the police. It was all right there in the paper I saw."

"When was it written?" Isabella stammered.

It had never occurred to me to look at the date. I shrugged my shoulders. "A long time ago. The ink was old and faded."

"What did it say, exactly?" I had stopped hugging her, but she continued to cling to me.

"Just like I said." Isabella held me closer, shaking me slightly for more. I racked my brain for the fine details. "Sister Mary, she thought the police weren't doing enough to find you. So she gathered a whole bunch of church people together to do their own search. And in your picture, you had big rocker hair, and you were wearing a school cardigan. Our Lady of Hope High School, was that it?"

"Lady of Hope," she said, and fell back into the seat, repeating it again to herself every few seconds. Each time she said it her voice varied in tone, and the words seemed to take on a new meaning. Except Isabella spoke only to herself. I grew nervous that I had dislodged too much emotion for her orphan mind to handle.

"You have no idea how lucky you are to have a newspaper story, from an actual newspaper. Newspapers don't lie. I don't even have proof of when my own birthday is," I told her, and she fell silent. We didn't speak for the rest of the cab ride. When we stopped outside the Dowager's Mansion, Isabella turned to me and asked, "When can you arrange another duo?"

"Give me a week," I told her. "The Widower comes every week at the same time." She walked up her garden path without a word. "Or sooner," I called out. She didn't turn back, though her steps sprang up a little as I said it. She was gone before she even made it inside—lost in the dull shade of the yard, the sunless veranda of the Mansion.

Our conversation, however, did not disappear with her. I would add this cab ride to my growing collection of "unforgettables." I had never forgotten the map scrawled on the back of my T-shirt, the handcuff strength of Jellyfish's grasp, or my grandmother's lolling, cigarette-stained hand. I still itched from the mess of the Night Watchman's hair trimmings. Not to mention the pile-up of hazy memories that I wasn't even certain were real. They were beginning to weigh on me, yet I wanted more. I wanted to be smothered in memory the same way live ones paid First to be smothered. If memory was going to press itself on me, then I wanted real, measurable weight. Pound for pound. Hold it in my hands. See it. Feel it. Name it. Declare its existence. But for what? What can you do with memory on Sub Rosa? You can't eat memory. You can't wear it on your ring finger or charge it by the hour. It didn't help me be a Glory in any way.

More than ever, I looked like a Glory. Each strand of my hair was a fine brush stroke from a calligraphy pen, my skin silk-charmeuse smooth; light trailed behind me like a firefly when I moved. I was still as desirable as any Glory could hope to be. I belonged to a house of legends. I myself had been a heroine at least twice. Stories about me would be told for lifetimes. I doubted any storybook heroine had ever asked, "Isn't there something else, something more?" Was any Glory unnerved by memory like me?

There was.

That night I discovered there was wondering besides mine. Portia approached me as I lingered on my track patch. It was rare that we both had a lull at the same time. Rarer still to see her alone. I stumbled out an awkward greeting as she wandered over. I noticed she was a little long in the torso, a little short in the legs. She walked like a Slinky, a wide sway in her hips with each step.

"I made this for you," she said. "If it reminds you of your grandmother, then you should have it." She held out a hand-folded greeting card with a sparkly four-leaf clover stamped on the front. Her fingertips were stained inky green. She didn't let go as I took the card in my hand and both of us stood there.

"Ling is calling you," I said, looking over her shoulder. Ling was waving her long arm in the air. I could hear her snapping her fingers. Portia finally let go of the card and ran back to the Mayflower.

Her card read: *My father had a shamrock tattoo on his arm and a fighting leprechaun and an Irish harp. When he flexed his bicep the leprechaun would dance. It always made me laugh. Your friend forever, P.*

XXII

"How am I supposed to get away?" Isabella grumbled as we rode home. I shushed her. The orphan had become terrible at keeping her voice down. The cabbie glanced in his rear-view mirror; I was convinced he had overheard us. If he leaked this to Treasure Anne, our secret would be out. So I got closer to Isabella, rested my chin on her shoulder, and continued the hushed conversation.

"You are away," I said, gesturing at the boulevard stretched behind us. "It's not that hard."

"Only because I'm working." In this hopeless mood, Isabella could bury herself in the back seat of a cab. Upholstery turned to grains of sand beneath her. Her body was a sieve. The scenery kept its distance from the car window. The sky, the passing cars, the city lights—none wanted anything to do with our dilemma. I swear the branches of trees twitched each time I looked out at them, losing leaves as we passed.

During the seven days between our visits to the Widower's house, I had founded a club. The Cherished Memory Club—a darn good name, I thought. There were three members already: Isabella, Portia, and me. We had agreed on one rule: secrecy. No one but members could know about the club, except on one condition. If we had not just a suspicion but proof that another Glory was actively and fondly remembering her pre-Glory past, then, and only then, could we break the vow of secrecy and divulge information about the club. In private, I wished First would somehow fit this description. She knew every last secret about me, or at least all the secrets I remembered.

First had no idea I was planting notes for Isabella under rocks in the Dowager's garden. She paid little attention when Portia and I took up pin-ball at No's. I almost wanted her to catch me.

Isabella had the opposite problem. We stood in the middle of Sub Rosa after the cabbie ejected us from our temporary meeting place. "There isn't anywhere Diamond won't come looking for me," Isabella said.

I might have tried to seduce Eddie Junior into hiding us out at the Smoke Shoppe, except, thanks to Second, Eddie was hesitant to let any of us in through the back door. What a waste of an impressionable heart he had turned out to be. "I'm not allowed to play pinball, anyway," sighed Isabella.

Even if Isabella had the freedom to roam Sub Rosa, there wasn't a single spot where we could meet without stirring up gossip. *An orphan hanging out with a triplet!* What would we tell the others we were doing together?

"There is a place where we'd be completely hidden," I said, turning to the Dark horizon. It wasn't the clubhouse I'd dreamed of. There'd be no scrapbook making or family portraits painting or show-and-tell in the Dark. But if the Cherished Memory Club could claim a birthplace, the Dark was it. "Your newspaper is out there," I reminded her. If that blind wasteland held Isabella's newspaper, it must be holding other artefacts from the past. I had an insistent suspicion that the Dark was as likely to give a girl memory as it was to give her amnesia. So much of the city—my city—had returned to me since my last visit to the Dark, memories that I craved proof of.

Isabella took my hand. "It does somewhat beckon, doesn't it?"

"It hums. If you listen, you can hear it all the way from here." The Dark's hum was a thousand voices scrambled into hypnotic white noise. A ribbon loosened itself from Isabella's hair and blew down the centre of the street. Isabella only ran a few steps to catch it before giving up. The red velvet ribbon rose higher and higher, twirling mad circles in a breeze that carried it to the Dark.

"You're not going back out there, are you?" Dearest stood beside us, pink watering can in one hand.

"Don't creep up on us like that," I snapped.

"I wanted to show you my flowers," She motioned to her track patch. "Come see the row of violets I've trained to grow between the cobble stones." Isabella, too polite to ignore Dearest's request, followed her toward the House of Man. Dearest took the opportunity to natter away at her. "Every day I wished, so hard, for violets," she chirped. "Just like in my front yard when I was I kid." Isabella looked over her shoulder at me, wide-eyed.

"Dearest," I said. "Do you want to know a secret?"

XXIII

The first Cherished Memory Club meeting took place at the House of Man early on a Saturday morning. Saturday, because every Friday night Fauxnique and Second Man stayed in the city at decadent live one parties or weekend getaways, and Dearest had the run of the house. It was a cinch to convince her to host. She was alone too much for her own liking and was starved for company. And she had nothing to lose. Hers was the newest House on Sub Rosa, and also the least strict. No one minded what Dearest did. Not like with Isabella, and not like with me.

First was spread out on the sofa reading an encyclopaedia all about insects. "I hear the Mayflower is making black cherry and chocolate pancakes now," she said. "I'll get up and take you right after I finish this section on centipedes." I had counted on her being housebound until noon, as she had the past several mornings. There was no way to slip past her.

"Dearest invited me over to her house for breakfast," I told her. "I don't think all this alone time is so good for her. Makes her needy and strange. I know! Why don't we invite her to come with us? I bet the company of a First is just what she needs."

"Oh," said First, closing her eyes for a moment, weighing whether or not she could put up with Dearest first thing in the morning. "Go on ahead to your friend's house. Have your girly times." First smiled and blew me a kiss. Dearest wasn't a threat—that was one good thing about her. Even the Dowager was allowing Isabella over to Dearest's house. Of course, I had a different, and more elaborate lie to make that arrangement. "Now hold on a second," First called after me before I was out the door. "What do you think you are doing?" I nearly bolted down the stairs, pretending I didn't hear her question. "You gonna put some clothes on?" she asked, to my relief.

My cropped cardigan barely covered the baby-doll nightgown I was wearing. It did, however, conceal the money I had folded between my breasts. "I can't wear my good clothes. Dearest is always latching on to me with her sticky fingers. And the triplets say Fauxnique never cleans." First folded her arms in front of her chest and cocked her head at me. "Do you really think Dearest will care?" I asked.

"I suppose not," First said reluctantly. "But unless you wanna be insultin', don't you go there in p.j.s when Fauxnique's around."

Outside, the Dowager was waiting at the end of her garden path with Isabella. They managed to make holding hands a scene completely devoid of affection. Isabella trembled ever so slightly, like a toy poodle at the end of its leash. Her pyjamas were all frills and embroidered flowers, at least three layers worth, and came down past her knees. I told the Dowager that this live one didn't like the colour black, just so I could see Isabella dressed in something different.

"Where is this live one?" the Dowager demanded, searching the street for parked cars.

"On his way," I said. "He requested that we all be tucked into our sleeping bags, sleeping, so he can pretend he's Dearest's older brother crashing her slumber party."

"Juvenile role play," Diamond scoffed. "My girls rarely entertain such tastes."

"Isabella will be perfect. She's small, impish even. Virginal. Selfless.

Effortless to work with." I felt sleazy rating Isabella's Glory qualities while she stood right beside me. But it did the trick; Diamond released her into my care.

"Mind the time, Isabella," the Dowager called after us as we walked arm and arm. There was a watch on Isabella's wrist.

"She told me I have no internal clock," Isabella whispered. "And that our trips to see the Widower are too long. Now I have to wear this." She held up her wrist, and the two of us looked at the watch in mild disgust. What did it matter if our dates with the live ones lasted too long? Since when was anyone on Sub Rosa preoccupied with time?

When Isabella rang the doorbell at Dearest's, I caught her checking her watch. I pushed through the door and began to climb the stairs. I didn't see the need for formalities with Dearest. Their stairwell smelled so strongly of the bakery below that I began salivating. No wonder Dearest had a sweet tooth. I stopped Isabella half way up and unbuttoned my cardigan. She stared at the floor, embarrassed.

I had had to beg her to go along with the plan: to pretend the Cherished Memory Club meeting was a date with a live one. I promised to give her the payment from my own money. I took a deep breath; my chest swelled as I pulled the bills from my nightie. It was easy to talk about giving it to her. As I did, however, I felt a pang of regret. First so rarely let me keep my money. An unimaginable sum of cash was tucked away in hiding spots, but my own purse was rather meagre. I looked again at Isabella's watch and wondered if the Dowager forced her to buy it with her own money. A watch and a warning, that's what her Glory work got her. I towered two steps and a pair of high-heeled pompom slippers above her. She touched my bare leg, traced a tiny circle behind my knee. *You don't have to*, was what she was about to say. I gave her the money before she had a chance to.

Isabella's kiss was finite. Not like First's—First's mouth was a wide-open entrance to an inexhaustible world of delight. But, reminiscent of my kiss with First, ours was the kiss of complete choice. I had nothing to gain from it. I wasn't sure if that gave it more or less value, only that it had been so long since I had done the choosing. I curled my tongue around Isabella's upper lip and held on for a final second. Our lips made a popping sound as we separated.

She sneezed as we reached Dearest's door. "Bless you," I said instinctively; we were both puzzled. "Who sneezes on Sub Rosa?" I asked.

The entire House of Man apartment was covered in flowers. Moss met our feet as Dearest greeted us. Whole stretches of floor were covered in rock and dirt and moss and flowers. Hollyhocks and honeysuckle, snapdragons and daffodils. Flowers with no regard for season—crocuses and Queen Anne's lace grew side by side. Sweet peas vined up the walls. Spanish moss hung from the ceiling. Isabella sneezed again.

Portia was stretched out on a green velvet sofa. I don't know how long she had been there, but her mouth and eyes were still gaping at her surroundings. "This is worth sneaking around for," she said. "Likka is totally on to us, by the way."

"What did you tell them?"

"That I was going to clean the spray paint from Advent Alley. I said I thought red-lettered messages might attract unwanted attention. Al's out there right now doing it for me, dirty old goat."

"And the car?"

"Don't worry, my new best friends. I've arranged for Ling's regular to park outside of House of Man. He'll be here in … wait for it …" Portia lifted an authoritative finger in the air and sure enough, we heard a car pull up outside. Our alibi was sound.

"Our garden," Isabella sneezed again, "is—"

"Completely pathetic. Yeah, we know."

"Gardening is what I do in my spare time," said Dearest, showing Isabella to a toadstool-shaped ottoman. "Aren't flowers great? If I wasn't a Glory, I would definitely want to be a flower. I've been gardening since

I was born." I took a deep breath, we all did, knowing Dearest was about to launch into a drawn-out childhood memory. I figured she deserved her due time; she had provided us with a clubhouse, after all.

"It all starts with dirt," Dearest told us, her eyes squeezed shut as if she was about to be presented with a surprise gift. "Soil. Peat moss. Manure. Mulch. Coconut hulls. Sand. Black and crawling with earthworms, red and packed tight like clay." She counted these gardening ingredients on her fingers.

"Mother was a gardener. She wasn't pretty, like me. She smelled like grass clippings. She whistled snippets of tunes as she scrubbed her hands with honey oatmeal soap at the end of the day. She never had manicures. Honey oatmeal soap, that's all.

"I got to ride in wheelbarrows when I went to work with her. I'd sit in the biggest gardens, watching Mother trim branches and pull weeds. The ladies who employed her brought me lemonade or, if I was lucky, freezer bags filled with bridge mixture. 'Are you helping Mummy today?' they'd ask. They couldn't resist my cute pigtails and smile. I'd go home with candy in my pockets. Mother never kept sweets in the house. She made me eat yogurt for dessert. So I had to hide my candy in my room.

"On Sundays, me and Mother would drive right to the city centre. We had a stand at the farmer's market. You see, that was Mother's real job—she was a mushroom farmer. She loved mushrooms, isn't that silly? What I liked about the market was I got to be the very first one to buy the morning's pies and tarts. We were there so early, before the sun came up. We'd load up mother's van when it was still dark, and by sunrise city people would be forming a line to buy our mushrooms. We were the only mushroom farmers at the market. 'Are they wild?' someone always asked. I waited for that question. Mother always had the same answer. 'We try to train them, but, alas, they can't be house broken.' I must have heard her say that a thousand times."

Dearest shared her home, on sixteen acres as she remembers, with mushrooms. Her mother spent long hours in the barn mixing corn-cobs and horse manure and straw with a pitchfork, then mixing spores into the compost with a fine-pronged rake. Long sacks of oyster mush-rooms hung from the beams like body bags. The barn was steaming and warm and put Dearest to sleep if she spent too long in there.

Not too far from her mother's house there were craggy rock faces that sweated cool water for Dearest to climb. There were ferns and snapdragons and Douglas firs shouldered up to one another. There were scrawny maples that vied for room but never reached the canopy. But mushrooms reigned. "Shelf fungus stuck to the side of our house," Dearest exclaimed. "Slippery Jacks took over any sick or fallen tree. Morels arrived in the spring. Pine mushrooms in the fall. Mother was always hunting our land for mushrooms. I didn't really like going with her. The soil was so damp it could swallow up my legs, pulling the gumboots off my feet." Dearest was convinced that if she stayed still for too long, mushrooms would have taken her too, grow along her spine, suck her bones hollow.

"Bridget Grace Catherine McCrudden," Portia said suddenly, leap-ing off the end of Dearest's last sentence. Any fungal odour I'd con-jured quickly dissipated with Portia's words and turned to jealousy. How was it she could so surely state her name? Four names, no less! "Everything about me is in my name," she said. McCrudden was Irish. McCruddens claimed to come from the coast of the Irish Sea, though there'd been no ocean anywhere near her kin for generations. The only brackishness Portia's McCruddens knew was drinking Bloody Marys from salt-rimmed glasses.

She picked the name Catherine when she confirmed her devotion to the Catholic Church. "Confirmation is the last of four steps," she explained. "Baptism, first communion, first confession, and confirma-tion." She was one of four girls in her eighth-grade class who picked

Saint Catherine of Siena as their confirmation name. The week before the confirmation ceremony their social studies class put the Great Depression on hold so they could study the lives of saints. "Saint Catherine walked barefoot in the Vatican. It was a really big deal. She was a total bad ass. She taught herself how to read. She had her own gang of ladies that helped the poor and the sick! Like outlaw, sexy nurses for God!" Portia liked Saint Catherine because she referred to God as being *pazzo d'amore*, crazy with love. Portia was crazy with love for Matt Knocksworth, who wore rock concert T-shirts under his school uniform, goats' heads and guitars subtly showing through his monogrammed Oxford shirts. For Matt, Portia stole cigarettes from her father's nightstand and sips of whiskey from the bottle on top of the fridge. She let Matt finger bang her three times. Each time she swelled up so much she worried she'd stretch her white cotton underpants. "Now, if any of us Glories had a sore pussy, there would be something wrong with us. But trust me, with Matt, it was exciting!" she told us.

She wore a white robe at the confirmation ceremony with a red banner that spelled out "Catherine" in felt letters. Her class walked down the aisle past relatives and teachers taking pictures. She'd already genuflected before the altar and took her seat in the front pew before she noticed her father wasn't there.

Grace was her dad's mum. It had taken Portia years to realize this, because she always called her Nan. "Christmas/Easter Catholics" was what Nan called Portia and her dad because they only went to mass twice a year, on those two holidays, then once for her mother's funeral. Bridget had also been her mother's name. "My dad stopped calling me anything at all after she died," said Portia.

"I didn't join this club to talk about the bad stuff," Dearest interrupted her. "I vote we have a happy-memory-only rule."

Portia let out a deep sigh. I couldn't tell if she was annoyed with

Dearest or relieved to be cut off before her memory got any darker. "I inherited my mother's vanity set," she said.

"Wow, a hand mirror and hairbrush?" asked Dearest.

"Mirror, hairbrush, perfume bottle, and powder pot. All pewter."

"Were they engraved with flowers?" asked Dearest.

I looked over at Isabella; she was checking her awful watch. "You can't leave until you've had a turn," I told her, and we all looked toward her. There was an uncomfortable pause before Isabella spoke. I offered what prompting I could, gently mentioning the orphanage, the nuns. I called her Brianna.

"I threw a good punch," Isabella said finally, dead serious. Dearest gasped. The same nuns that ran the orphanage had enrolled Isabella in Catholic school, even though her hair was far curlier and her skin, back then, was noticeably darker than all the other students. She had never thought of them—not a one—until Portia mentioned confirmation, the procession of robed pre-teens walking up the church aisle to kneel at the altar. Then she remembered Jenny Lynn, the other girl who sat in the back of the church, who also sat at the back of the classroom. Jenny arrived at school with a knee-length kilt like the rest of the girls. Then, throughout the day, Jenny's kilt got shorter and shorter. Isabella saw her rolling it up at the waistband under her desk. When the recess bell rang, Isabella would pass by Jenny's empty chair and sometimes there would be two sweaty thigh prints left behind, glistening slightly. One day, Jenny passed Isabella a note: *Are you looking at my legs?*

The gymnasium storage room was their kissing spot. Isabella had previously used the room to hide from the other students during lunch hour. She'd made a fort out of dusty hockey nets and school banners. She stabbed holes in basketballs, cut weak spots in the climbing ropes. Only a few minutes after bringing Jenny to her hide-away, the pair were kissing. Isabella's very first kiss. Jenny tasted like pot smoke and

watermelon bubblegum and a better heaven than their religious studies teacher could ever describe.

When one of the popular boys called Jenny fat, Isabella punched
him square in the nose. Like a red finch through an open cage door, his
blood took flight. It sprayed his white uniform shirt; Isabella's cheek
was splashed with red. "No one mess with Brianna," she remembers
someone shouting as the boy crumpled to the ground. A grin crept
across her face as she described the scene for us. "I wish I had that
blood-stained shirt as a souvenir. Is that sick? I shouldn't even think
that sort of thing."

"Anything goes, here. It's *our* club," I said.

"Except sad memories," Dearest slipped in. I gave her the stink-eye
and, for once, she caught on. "You punching that boy isn't sad," she
backtracked. "It's pretty funny, right?"

"I'd do anything to see Jenny Lynn again." She was giddy—each of
us was.

"I can't even remember what a morel tastes like anymore," said
Dearest.

"I'll have Al order some for the Mayflower," offered Portia, but
Dearest shrugged, saying they wouldn't be fresh. "I'm not sure how big
my father's nose is. Or the shape of his mouth." Portia traced her own
mouth with her finger. "I wonder if he loved me. I'd like that. I'd like
him to say, *You're the apple of my eye*, just like fathers are supposed to
tell their daughters. It makes me tingly just thinking about it. How
strange."

"I'm tingly too. And hot." Isabella fanned herself with the skirting
of her nightie. "These memories make me more flush than sex with the
live ones."

"They're better than when the seamstress gets a new dress catalogue," said Portia.

"It's almost as good as when Maria puts out the fresh baked goods in the morning," added Dearest. "Maybe better."

In that moment the members of the Cherished Memory Club were friends, close and true, although after the meeting we knew that each of us would return to our separate Glory routines. Dearest plucked a violet from her potted garden and tucked it into a buttonhole on Isabella's nightie. "These grow in … April, I think." I hated to think of Isabella marching back to the grey-washed mansion. Dearest didn't want her to leave either. She had forgotten the flower's name, and begged us to stay until she remembered. "As soon as I'm by myself again, I'm afraid my mind will go blank. Just a few more minutes. Please. I've just got to know the name of this purple flower. If I think about it hard enough …" Isabella checked her watch again and Portia politely got up to leave. Dearest's voice regained its usual whine, knowing she couldn't delay us any longer. I wondered how long it had been since anyone actually listened to her.

"We're doing this again? We have to," said Dearest.

"Even if we wanted to, I doubt we could stop," said Isabella.

"Unless we run out of memories," said Portia. It struck us then that getting caught wasn't the club's biggest threat—it was failing to remember. "Can that happen, Little? What if I only remember my dad's tattoos, but I never have that memory of him telling me he loves me?" Portia unconsciously plucked a leaf from a nearby plant, tearing it up into tiny green shreds as she spoke. "How long did it take you to come up with all those visions of the city, Little? The ones you told the Night Watchman? And are you still having memories? You didn't share any memories at this meeting. It's not because you've run out, right?" asked Portia. The others leaned forward for my response.

"I haven't run out," I said. "Some of those city places I've seen with Arsen, and the others, they kind of appear in my head like stray pictures. They're there all the time, in fact, ever since I came back from my trip to the Dark. There is this one I see again and again."

"What is it?" Isabella asked.

"It's a set of weathered concrete steps, painted red. Except the red paint is all chipping away. At the top of the steps, there's a lawn chair made out of orange and brown nylon woven over a rusted aluminum frame."

"And?" asked Isabella. Dearest was about to tuck a second purple flower behind Isabella's ear.

"And nothing," I said. "That's it."

"You've been seeing the same steps since you've come back from the Dark? Doesn't that strike you as totally weird?" asked Portia.

"Well, who do the steps belong to? Is it your childhood house?" asked Dearest.

"Can you see anything else? A number on the house? A name on a mailbox, maybe?" asked Isabella.

"I can't say," I interrupted before they asked more questions. "It's like all my city memories. I see them so clearly. So clearly they actually bug me sometimes. Like I can't get them to stop. But I don't know what they have to do with me. I don't personally remember being at any of these places."

"How do you know they really exist, then?"

"I guess I don't," I said. Isabella looked disappointed. She and Portia exchanged sceptical glances.

"Great," cried Portia. "So, pretty much, we can't predict how long these memories will last and we don't even know if they're real or not. You may as well call all of us unmemorable."

"Oh, mine are real," said Dearest, now holding a collection of tiny purple flowers in her hands. "This violet is real," she said, remembering the flower's name. "We're not going to run out of memories. I remember stuff all the time." No one was terribly reassured by Dearest's conviction.

"Unmemorable means we, ourselves, aren't worth remembering," Isabella corrected Portia.

Portia threw her arms up in a frustrated shrug. "Is there a difference?"

Isabella pulled me to her outside Dearest's door. "My memories are real, too, right?" she questioned. "Little, you saw my newspaper with your own eyes."

"Believe me," I assured her. "Your newspaper is out there in the Dark."

XXIV

Underneath the living room sofa sat a wooden cigar box filled with money. It was one of First's many secret deposit spots. I hastily counted out $6,000 while First toasted us bagels for breakfast.

She bounced up to me carrying two new Royal Doulton Bunnykins china plates, each stacked with bagels with cream cheese and lox and sliced fresh fruit and a melting scoop of crème fraîche that nearly slid off the plate as she placed it on my lap. It was the first time she'd served me breakfast in weeks, maybe months.

The day before, we had dropped a small fortune at the Pawnshop. First spent the morning putting her books back on the shelves in the library, humming and whistling as she did. "We ought to spruce up the Wifey Wing. What do ya say, Little?" she had asked, though it wasn't really a question. She already had her splashy pink crocodile bag in hand, ready to lead me down the front steps. She had bought everything I looked at; the Bunnykins china set, the Chinese war horse in a shadowbox wall-hanging, the Depression glass decanter, a pair of gold hoop earrings for each of us, and a Hawaiian quilt so that we could finally re-do Second's old bed. "We'll send the whole lot of stuffed animals away with a live one to give them to poor city children, or something nice like that," she'd said. She must have been on to me. I was getting too spoiled for a regular weekday afternoon.

Why, all of a sudden, would three Third wives—the babies of each family—start spending so much time together? All of the Firsts must have suspected. Our excuses got more complicated and implausible. The Cherished Memory Club meetings continued as planned, no matter how sloppy our alibis were. I was going bankrupt paying Isabella phoney live-one money. Even as First and I finished our morning bagels and set down our new Bunnykins plates, I was calculating how many club meetings I could buy Isabella with six grand. Numbers bounced around in my head as First babbled to me about our weekend plans, her feet planted just inches away from the hidden cash. I wondered how much I could pinch without her noticing. Missing money would only be one crumb in the trail the Cherished Memory Club was leaving along Sub Rosa.

Portia had started a journal. Not an account of day-to-day life on Sub Rosa, but a Cherished Memory journal. *Dear Journal*, the first page read. *Today we had a stupid Geography quiz. Mr Debeau expected us to memorize all major rivers and lakes in North America. I'm pretty sure I did good, except for I spent too long on the Mississippi. I started daydreaming about thunderstorms. When I was a little girl, my father taught me that whenever I saw lightning to spell Mississippi. If I only got to m-i-s before the thunder struck, that meant the storm was coming closer. If I could spell the whole word, then the storm was moving away. It's probably bull crap. But whenever I hear Mississippi I get that song in my head—m-i-s-s-i-s-s-i-p-p-i. And I can almost hear the rain coming down.*

"It's a memory inside a memory," Isabella marvelled when Portia read it at the club meeting.

But when she started writing in her journal at the Mayflower, while sitting in her booth with Likka and Myra, I grew nervous. Portia claimed she was writing a fantasy romance novel, the kind that often littered the triplet's table. If she cracked a smile while remembering she'd say, "I'm writing a love scene."

"Read it!" Likka and Myra requested.

"Not until I'm finished."

I doubted it would be very long before Likka and Myra's patience ran out and they snatched the journal away. Portia was smart, though. She kept her sisters busy by commissioning them to illustrate the novel. Gradually the collage of pop stars was torn down from the Mayflower window and was replaced by pen-and-ink drawings of bare-chested men holding swords and women warriors riding on the backs of sabre-toothed tigers.

The evidence of Dearest's memories wasn't contained in a book. Hers exploded over half a Sub Rosa block. She remembered a new flower, the morning glory. A harmless enough name for a flower. Within twenty-four hours, Dearest's underground garden supplier had the seed pods in her hand, and an overexcited Dearest planted them in the offering tar along their track patch. Thin green shoots rose up almost instantly. They danced with life like charmed snakes, twisting and twirling, until they found the brick wall to cling to. Glories gathered outside the House of Man to marvel. Beside the multitude of cut flowers brought by live ones or the struggling roses at the Mansion, flora was a bit of a novelty on Sub Rosa. There was chatter in the Mayflower the day the morning glory vine produced a string of bell-shaped white flowers. Days later, the vine climbed half way up the House of Man, and began to blanket the Babycakes wall mural. Later still, Dearest's track patch was turned into a tangle of morning glory. Fauxnique and Second Man tripped on it. Maria, the baker, got her feet caught in it. Its heart-shaped leaves vibrated in the sun as if laughing at us. Dearest would yank up one vine and three more sprang up in its place. Soon the entire building was choking in white flowers.

As usual, Dearest's explanation was naïveté—a cover easily bought by everyone. "How could I know?" Dearest whined to the crowd of disapproving Glories. "The live one said he had magic Glory beans, so I offered them to our track patch."

Second Man was given a pair of hedge clippers and a ladder and was put in charge of terminating the vine. He begrudgingly accepted a pair of filthy gardening gloves from the Dowager and got to work. The Firsts pulled up patio chairs and watched. Shirley brought out lemonade for them. Dearest watched too, humming a spirited tune under her breath. Sometimes she was a bit smarter and more wicked than she seemed. "You should give him your magic touch while he's up that ladder," she giggled at me. "Come on, just a little poke."

Only sweet Isabella's hands remained clean. She hadn't lied to her sisters. She hadn't contemplated stealing from her house. But anyone with eyes could see that she was different. She was still a black smudge in the Sub Rosa panorama, but side-by-side with the other orphans, her ability to be a perfect carbon copy was failing. Her elegant Gothic Lolita uniform weighed heavily on her. Isabella's hemline seemed higher, her stockings sheerer. She sashayed while the others marched.

When she could, she'd slip in secret moments together with me. Pouncing on me as I picked up our laundry at Launderlove, the two of us tripping as we kissed. She was acting out her former self, the schoolgirl, I believed, because her kisses weren't orphan sips anymore. They were full mouthfuls.

"When can we go to the Widower's again?" she said loudly. I had to shush her before sending her back the Mansion. She lifted up the back of her skirt as she walked away. Her stiff black girdle was gone, swapped for girlish cotton panties, pink and white and patterned. "Daisies," I gasped. There were daisies on her underwear. The sight of them made me dizzy.

Daisies followed me throughout my day—floating daisy-shaped spots in my eyesight whenever I blinked. Daisies appeared in my dreams at night. They sang songs like drunk men do, making messes of words, slurring, bearing fire and grit. I had arrived at Sub Rosa wearing daisy-print panties and bra. The set still lived in the bottom of my wardrobe drawer, crumpled beneath the layers of silk knickers and nightgowns trimmed in tulle. They had survived the city. The pilled cotton-blend fabric and warped underwire had out-survived memory, out-survived the story of my life.

My happiness for her was cut with longing. Her memories of Jenny were so vivid that she felt them on her skin. I could almost feel Jenny on my own skin when Isabella held me close. I wanted Isabella to be touching me constantly. It thrilled me, but I had no memories of my own like those. There were barely any people in my memories. The more I tried to hear Nino's voice or see Eli's face, the cloudier the memory became. The one tangible memory of an actual person was the lampshade lady, my grandmother. She spoke to me. Her voice was a smoker's rasp, thin yet kind. I'd travel back into the Dark to hear that voice again, I thought. The horrors of that place felt powerless in comparison to my longing for memory.

I wandered outside the Dowager's Mansion at sunrise. Then again before lunch. After dinner. Between live ones throughout the night. Isabella wasn't on her track patch. The morning after, she was missing from the orphans' morning chores. I thought I spotted her by the tool shed behind the Mansion, but it was only a black rain slicker hanging from a nail. I started determinedly across Diamond's property. Why be afraid to ask after her? And I wasn't about to dumb it down either. "Can Isabella come out and play?" No, Diamond wouldn't be hearing that from me, I told myself for courage.

The orphans were hunched in a row along the garden path, an assembly line of weeding. One lifted her head from her work to warn me, "Go back." She blankly lowered her head again and returned to her weeds. It may as well have been the voice of the wind, a stone gargoyle, or lifeless tree speaking to me. My black pearl ring felt hot on my finger. The sky suddenly seemed supernaturally dark. I ran, like I had run from the Dowager's front veranda so long ago, frantic and ungainly on my feet. Any other Glory would have giggled at the site. Not the orphans. I left a wake of eerie silence behind me.

"What in heavens has got into you?" asked First as I tore past her in the living room.

"Nothing," I said. And for once she left it at that.

"Nothing" is what I told her again as we stood out on our track patch at night. I was squirming in my spot, fixed on the Dowager's property.

"Don't tell me *nothing*," she scolded, holding her authoritative carnelian red fingernail inches away from my nose. "You are up to something."

"Please, First," I pleaded. She was breaking my concentration. Phantom hand was perched at the bottom of the Mansion drainpipe, ready to climb. In its grip was a note I had written: *Are you ok?* It had made it across the street and past the line of orphans. My fingers tickled as it crept through the brittle grass on Diamond's front lawn. I had never sent it so far before. A dull headache spread between my eyes as I sent it up and up, to the second-floor window. It hesitated on the windowsill for several moments, rapping its ghostly hand on the glass. I saw the window open, just a crack, the person who opened it unseen behind the heavy velvet curtains. But who else could it have been besides Isabella? Phantom hand entered the Mansion. My own hand went numb.

It wasn't until First squawked in alarm that I noticed my hand turning black. Inky spots spread from between my fingers over my palm. I was scooped up like a fallen bird. "Listen to me, First," I whispered. "Phantom hand is inside the Dowager mansion. You have to stay calm and act normal." First jerked her gaze across the street, wildly searching Diamond's property with her eyes. "You have to act normal," I told her again, and she corrected herself as best as she could.

"Say, Little," she said in an affected voice. "We really should change our outfits. Why don't we go upstairs?" Robot-like, she turned and carried me up to the Wifey Wing.

"I got to get my hand back," I protested.

"You think I don't know that?" First plopped me down on our bed. "Concentrate now," she said, switching off the bedroom light. "Look out into the night and think, Little, really think. Don't look at the stars or the live ones in their cars. Just concentrate."

I reached my arm out the bedroom window and pointed a blackened finger at the Mansion. My heart raced and then I composed myself again about a dozen times or more. In the fretful moments I begged, *Please don't let another thing go missing.* In my level-headed moments, all I did was breathe.

And phantom hand did appear. I imagined drawing it closer with each inhalation. It still held a tiny slip of paper, my note to Isabella. First and I watched it float across the sky like the last batch of confetti in a ticker tape parade. Soon I held the note in my own hand. The black on my fingers faded as quickly as it had spread.

"Why would ya do that?" First's moment of cool collectedness had passed. She plucked the note from my tingling fingers. Reading it, she scrunched up her nose. *Help*, I read as First held it up for me. *Help* written in saliva and lipstick smears. As if Isabella had licked the word onto the paper.

"Do you love her?" First asked. I held my breath. The question felt like a trick. "I don't own your love, Little. You get to love her if you want to." I still said nothing. Neither yes nor no felt like the real answer. First sighed. "Do you want to help her?"

"Yes, I want to help her," I said. That I knew.

First folded me into her large arms. "If you want to help her, then you'd better talk to Arsen."

XXV

I had my nails painted carnelian red—the colour First wore. Red was a First Wife colour. One hundred small bottles of red polish perpetually revolved inside a glass and mirrored carousel display. The queens' one hundred, they were called. One hundred shades, always in stock, reserved for the Firsts.

I loitered by the display, watching "my" shade spin past, and pass again. "If you only wore it for one night—" Astrid said, as she intuitively plucked the carnelian shade I wanted and banged it down on the counter. I laid down all the money I had in my purse beside it. As she tried to claim it, I pressed my hand over hers. "I also need to know how serious Isabella's absence is."

"Not serious ... yet," she said. "She has made a vow of silence. This silence will protect her, for now."

"If you want to grow up a bit, to look like a boss lady," said Eartha, sliding between us with a pair of scissors, "try a Cleopatra cut." She showed me to her salon chair, and turned me away from the mirror. "Trust me," she said as I watched a long chunk of black hair fall to the marble floor.

"Severe beauty is a good plan," Eartha remarked. "It will work."

"What will work?" I asked, teased by her alluded prediction.

"Whatever it is you have planned." The two turned me around to see their finished work. Red nails, red lips, blunt bangs; I certainly looked like I meant business.

Astrid thrust a small gift bag into my hand and turned me toward the lobby. "Fragrance samples," she said as I peeked in the bag. "And your new lipstick."

After the Wifey Wing's doors closed to live ones at the end of the night, I shut myself in the bathroom with my perfumes. The fragrance samples came in tiny glass tubes, like specimen containers. I chose to wear one that smelled like the burnt sugar on top of crème caramel. In the other room, I heard Arsen's teacup clink against his saucer, and the sure-handed swish of money being counted. I dragged the blood red lipstick across my mouth and conjured Dearest's words, *Don't you just tell him when you want him? That's what Daddies are there for.* "I'll spend the night with you, Arsen," I said, cracking the bathroom door open.

I couldn't even look at First as he held my coat for me. Apart from the night Second ran away, I had always slept next to her; I'd been like a shellfish on her rock. "You want gloves?" she asked. "I think it's gettin' to be cold season in the city." I squeezed her hands as she put them on me, a touch code that I hoped she understood to mean *I love you, forever and ever.*

"When did we get snow?" I asked, carelessly speaking like I was still a part of the "we," the scores of city people.

"A month, or so." I was taken aback to think that much time had passed. It didn't make sense to me; my last trip to the Widower's was only a week ago. There was a thunderstorm then. I remember because I spelled out "Mississippi" under my breath between thunderclaps, just like Portia had taught us at the Cherished Memory Club. Lightning flashes pierced through the car, and the Widower and I flinched in unison. After our date, I remember walking alone down the gasoline-stained driveway, turned technicolour in the rain, and wishing so badly that I could have shown Isabella the greasy purples and greens in the puddles.

Arsen was alert at the wheel, as if he was new to driving in the winter weather, and I questioned how long the snow had really been around. His car fishtailed as we pulled out of Advent Alley. A snowplow had recently been up the street out front of No's; both the curb and the entrance to the Alley were banked in dirty snow. Yesterday's faded bouquets and discarded candy wrappers were crushed in the frozen sludge. Any tire tracks the live ones left during their visits were covered over. Eddie Junior stood outside, wearing orange ski gloves, salting the front steps. He held the salt bag tight to his chest and pretended not to notice Arsen's car. Arsen didn't slow to wave at him, either. Gusts of icy wind rolled off the hood of the car. The air hissed at us. I almost asked to turn around and go back to Sub Rosa.

"Toro loves snow," Arsen said, and I realized how much I missed his apartment, with his photos and dog hair and static on the stereo. As we drove closer and began passing places I knew—street signs I recognized, familiar buildings hooded in winter white—the more my confidence grew. I curled my toes inside my boots. I pressed my lips together and tasted the velvety layer of lipstick. I even wished I could stain his bed sheets all over again. I bit my lip; I was as giddy as the Glories at our Club meetings.

Arsen fidgeted with the thermostat on his bedroom wall before coming to bed. The sound of dry heat rushing out the vents was peculiar to me. I was surprised to find Arsen's fingers and toes cold. Even his ass was cold under his jeans. I wished he hadn't warmed so quickly under my hands; I enjoyed touching his goose-bumped skin. He tossed me around his bed, pinning me with one arm until I wriggled free, and then he wrestled me down again. I screamed. I laughed until I coughed. I wanted to feel worn out, I wanted to wear him out. I was pleased when he pressed his chest against mine and I felt sweat. Phantom hand guided his cock inside me and I jokingly mimicked the stunned expression on his face as I began to grind against him. I wrapped my arms around his shoulders, looped my ankles around his waist, kept phantom hand pressed against his back. He smothered me. I liked it.

"I don't blame you for leaving Sub Rosa," I said, as we lay on opposite sides of his king-size bed.

"Why's that?"

"Because you have family. Aunties and cousins. You have those places in the photographs. How long did it take you to find them?"

"They're not my family," he said. The afterglow drained from his face. He was suddenly grave. "They're make-believe."

"What?"

"I made them up. Those photos I found in second-hand stores. You can never tell Candy. Never tell anyone." His hand around my slender arm felt so different than it had when we were having sex. I pulled away from him.

"Why stay in the city then? Why even come here in the first place?"

"Because that's life." Arsen reached for me again. I was too far away for him to touch me and he didn't move any closer. "And I want it ... life. Everyone else has a real life. So, why not me?" I was dumbfounded, but I promised him that I'd keep his secret. How could I refuse, with his needy, chiselled limbs stretching across the bed for me? He hooked his toes around mine, gingerly pinched the bed sheets an inch from my body. His eyes were distant and glassy.

"I had a real life once," I mumbled.

"Little, don't think twice about the runaway's life you left behind."

"Look who's talking. You leave the city and move back to Sub Rosa, then."

"You've got the itch, don't you?" he asked. "First gets it a lot. She wants life too, as much as she's afraid of it. Each time she has me bring her a fresh girl from the city. Maybe it's time for a new family member?"

"You read my mind, Daddy," I said, as sweetly as I could. I rolled across the bed until my chin rested on his shoulder. I noticed a blot of burgundy lipstick on his neck, and I told him about Isabella. About how her creamy skin and pink-tongued kisses and her earning potential were wasting away at the Dowager's Mansion. "It is my understanding that the orphans' service was indebted to the Dowager because they never made their Dark Day dowries. If that's true, then why can't they just try again? Go back to the Dark and try again? And if they do try, and they made their dowry, could they then return to their intended House? Or any House?" Arsen puzzled over my question. "Can we take her?" I asked, exasperated.

"I want you to know," Arsen said, slow and cautious, "that I was one-hundred percent certain that you'd make it through your Dark Days. No matter what you may have heard ..."

"I'm not talking about me," I interrupted. "You're way too late for that conversation. I'm over it." I sat up, leaning across him so he was forced to look into my eyes.

"I'm not sure if Isabella was one of my recruits," he said, turning away. "Two of the Dowager's orphans were supposed to be Wifeys of mine. You understand, Little? Only two of mine didn't make their dowry; I make sure to choose girls who can handle the Dark. So, really, there is only a thirty-percent chance that Isabella was originally one of mine."

"But there is a chance? Like, that's how it works, right? Anyone can go back to the Dark and try for their dowry again?"

"That's the idea. Except no one does that. Only you are mad enough to go twice." He pinched a strand of my hair. "How do you know she'll go back? And if she does, how can you be sure she'll make it out again? I won't be the one to drive her out there. I won't call out her name searching for her. Worrying."

"No one asked you to." I pulled away, collecting my hair and tucking it behind my ear. I already had all I needed from him; he'd made the rules clear. I could take Isabella into the Dark myself. I was already planning a journey to the Dark. Maybe the whole Club would go. Like a pilgrimage. Maybe we'd see Jellyfish, and she'd show all of us our forgotten grandmothers.

"Don't go back there, Little," he said, clueing in to my plan. "You've been lucky. Lucky—that's all." I slid to the end of his bed and sat there, my feet inches above the carpet. Phantom hand retrieved my dress from the floor and brought it to me. "First will worry herself sick," he said. "You don't return, and she'll fall apart. Besides, wouldn't you rather have a nice new city girl? Someone you could teach and take care of in your own way? I bet you'd be good at that."

I quickly pulled my dress on over my head and stood up. "Isabella was a city girl once. We all were. With city friends and family and stuff. Except maybe you."

"That is not the way to get on my good side." I turned to face him as he was inching the silk sheets over his body. I felt defiant, stronger in my red dress, while he tried coyly to cover his nakedness. Arsen always underestimated me. The only time he cheered me on was when he profited from my actions—when he opened bets on my Dark Days. I would have liked to rip the sheet from his hand then, but he was worth more as an ally than an enemy.

"Gamble on it," I said. "There's been nothing to gamble on for ages. I'll make it worth your while. Under forty-eight hours return, I guarantee. Before we go, I'll act like I've gone soft. That I'm bent on a kamikaze mission. No one will believe a fallen hero and an orphan will make dowry in less than two days. You'll make a fortune."

Arsen turned down his silk sheets and patted the bed beside him. He pretended to be neutral. "I'll sleep on it."

In the morning, at the breakfast table, he said, "Isabella benefits from already knowing the Rosa, and so her dowry will be set high.

Diamond will want to see that she, and anyone accompanying her, enters the Dark empty-handed; no lighters, no rations, and nothing of value. So you will want to spend a week or so preparing. *Pre-par-ing.* Fine-tune any magic you might have." He gave me a clumsy kiss before clearing our plates and teacups.

Throughout the apartment, Arsen's collection of false family photographs crowded the shelves. I wondered how he'd decided on a name for each bogus auntie, each sham of a cousin. How many made-up histories did he have—only the anecdotes he'd told me, or dozens, maybe hundreds more he'd told himself? I worried about the Cherished Memory Club becoming nothing more than a bunch of memory fabricators. Would we even be able to distinguish the real memories from the made-up ones? It's not as if anyone could even prove we, ourselves, were real. Sub Rosa had made me so fantastic and clandestine even I didn't understand myself half the time.

Arsen shook his car keys in the air, breaking the spell. "Thanks for last night," I said as I stood to leave.

XXVI

A place for everything and everything in its place! It's beyond that with First and her treasured apartment. Looting the Wifey Wing—even the delicate looting I was doing—was like molesting a coma patient, or a sheep while it slept, or worse. I knew the house couldn't feel anything, but somehow I was abusing it. Each time I overturned a photograph or flipped through the pages of a book, I was doing something very wrong. I ransacked as tidily as a ransacker could, although part of me wanted First to burst in, demand to know what I was doing, and wring a full confession out of me. Forgiveness is really what I was after, to fast forward to the part where I am wrapped in First's forgiving arms and she tells me, in her motherly way, how she's going make it all right and good again.

But this was my plan, my time to act alone. After all, all my famous Sub Rosa moments starred me and only me. Me in the Dark.

The Wifey Wing was peppered with money. Even with First's shopping sprees and the payments we gave Arsen, we never spent all our earnings. *I'll just tuck this away,* I'd heard First say many times.

The trick was to make it look like no money had gone missing. I took only three bills from the wooden cigar box under the sofa, hoping that First wouldn't notice. There were fifties stuck in the French flaps of several books and hundred-dollar bills taped to the back of several photo frames. But which books or photo frames were the right ones to pinch money from? Did First have a system? She didn't check the money daily, that much I was sure of.

After an hour of searching I'd only come up with $550, total. I kicked off my shoes and crept into our bedroom; no one else was home, but I tiptoed anyway.

Intimacy in our bedroom had become paradoxical since Second's absence. At first, the room felt marked, as though there was a massive red stain on Second's old bed that First and I had to ignore. But soon enough First and I filled the room with our easy closeness, our companionship now uninterrupted by Second's jealousy and bitterness. Her bed had been stripped and remade with new linens, then covered with the gorgeous maroon and white pineapple pattern Hawaiian quilt we'd bought at the Pawn Shop. I hoped Isabella would like the quilt as much as I did. If everything worked as planned, the bed would soon be hers.

A black plastic garbage bag filled with Second's stuffed animals still leaned against the bed—the last of her possessions that we needed to get rid of. I removed the twist-tie, and dozens of round plastic eyes stared up at me from inside the bag. I sent phantom hand in before reaching into the bag with my actual hand. I snatched up one of her old stuffed toys. A teddy bear in corduroy coveralls. Pink elephants and sock monkeys toppled out after it. I handled it like crime scene evidence. But when I discovered $200 tucked in the bear's tiny coveralls, I loosened up a bit. "I hope to hell this is Second's earnings," I said, dropping the bear to the ground. More money was hidden in a hippo's ballerina tutu and in the top hat of a stuffed frog. After manhandling all the toys, my count was up to $900. But I suspected it would take much more than that to free Isabella from the Dowager's house.

Whatever money I found, I planned to hide near the Dark, right at the boundary, the twilight spot, ready for our journey. Plotting it out thrilled me. I could see it now; we'd simply step into the Dark, and moments later I'd have Isabella's dowry in hand. A new Dark Days record. I'd use phantom hand to secure a hiding spot close to the Dark's threshold, where no one would even think to go looking. I just needed to get the money first.

Pushing the quilt aside, I slid my arm between the bed's mattress and box spring. I had to convince myself that the money I was collecting was owed to me, that I was doing something good, that First and Isabella would love each other. Our family fame would be on the rise. We'd be a House run completely by city girls turned Glories, aside from Arsen. He was an original, but he didn't count. We could tell our city stories, our memories, while living Sub Rosa lives. We'd have it all.

However convincing my justifications were, I was stealing from our House. No stealing was the very first rule First taught me. I wasn't about to put the money back, as hot as it felt in my hands. I sunk my arm deeper between the mattress and the box spring. What I found hidden there wasn't money.

"Do you love me, First?" That's how I greeted her when she pulled back the lace curtain to find me waiting in the bedroom.

"'Course I do," she said without pause.

"Because you never tell me you do."

"Little, I loved you before you was even a Glory, when you was still sickly from the city," she said. She stepped into our room. I had remade the bed, not as perfectly as she had, and I caught her noticing something, a lopsided hospital corner, a wrinkle in the spread. I pressed her to talk on about love. "Think 'bout how I didn't want you to do your Dark Days? Well, that was me lovin' you. All the times I spend a bit extra on you, a bit more than Arsen likes me to. That's me lovin' you. And keepin' phantom hand a secret—that's love."

I cuddled into her. Her body was always a sanctuary.

"I can tell you anything, right?"

"You done somethin', Little?"

"I found something." I unlocked myself from her hug and slid my hand under her pillow, where I had temporarily hidden the photograph: a twin to the only family portrait in the Wifey Wing. The one that hung lower than my eye level in our sitting room, below the portraits of wild birds and Saint Theresa and other people we'd never met. The headless woman portrait.

The mother in this photo, however, had a face. Venus of Urbino. Desdemona. Salome. I'd never seen anyone (who wasn't a Glory) as beautiful. Not even the famous actresses in the triplets' magazines. It was her eyes—they stared at me as if daring me to love and ache and hope as vehemently as she. That woman's eyes gave me the courage to reveal the photo then, in which baby First nestled in her strong arms, looking up at her mother, learning.

First looked frozen with anger. "You should never poke around through my things," she said. She plunked herself down on Second's bed. The stuffed bear I had robbed toppled to the floor. I caught myself glimpsing at him for more money. "Does anyone else know?" First asked.

"Like I'd rat on you. We keep each other's secrets, in the vault."

"What you goin' to do with it?"

"The way I see it, memories are a gift," I said, beginning the speech I'd prepared for our next meeting. It was pretty motivational, I thought. "Not everyone is lucky enough to have memory. And those who do shouldn't waste it. We wouldn't throw away a gift from a live one. If we don't really like silver earrings or the smell of lilies, we still keep them. Well, memories are gifts, too. Even if we didn't expect to receive them. Even if we might think they are not that valuable at first, they are valuable, because they are gifts that come from inside us. One-of-a-kind and custom-made just for us. We should be able to flaunt them like any other gift. Not hide them under our mattresses like we're ashamed."

I told her about the Cherished Memory Club, about our visions and our games and the frenzied full-body recollections we'd often experience. The club would be the next best thing, I promised her, better than makeover day at the Spa Rosa or the Mayflower's pancake brunch. Best of all, we could be together. "The club is where people like us—rememberers—go so they don't have to be alone anymore."

First flopped back on Second's bed, reclining in what I hoped was relief. "Tell me exactly what you do at these meetin's," she said, gazing up at the ceiling.

"Mostly talk, about our pre-Sub Rosa memories. They're not always so clear, but we go ahead with the remembering anyway. Sometimes we like to fill in the missing parts for each other. Just make it up like a game. Last time we invented a whole family tree for … someone." It sounded foolish and trite as I said it. I wished I had the right words, but the more I spoke the more I came across like a juvenile bimbo describing a sale at the mall. I expected First to balk. She closed her eyes and folded her hands across her chest. I considered crawling onto the little bed beside her.

"Do they make you feel good? These meetin's?" I couldn't tell if it was one of those moments where First asks me if I liked something as a way of declaring that she didn't. I stalled on answering her question. The Cherished Memory Club wasn't just about feeling good or not; it wasn't as simple as that. "Because this photo—" First sat up and reached for the photo. I passed it to her, hesitantly, slightly fearful that she'd do something rash like rip it up. "This photo makes me feel good. That stuff you was sayin' 'bout playin' games. I do that. I make up all the things the woman in this photo might say to me. She always says nice things, comforting things. It's not always easy for us Firsts, you know. Being the mommy. Who mothers me? That why I saved it for all these years. It's a little something for me, you know what I'm sayin'?"

"You should bring it to our next meeting," I told her, encouragingly. Again, First paused for what seemed far too long for it to be good. If the woman in the photograph could speak, I was sure she would have told First to go for it.

"Too bad you didn't start your club sooner," First said, finally. "That is why I think Second didn't last so long here. She had nothing from the past. Deep down inside I believe we need it. Arsen, of all the people, shoulda understood. Nope, he brought her here with only the clothes on her back. And even them got lost in the Dark. I bet she would have joined your club."

"You miss Second?" I asked, steering the conversation toward Isabella. I needed to bring her up sooner than later.

First stared at the pile of stuffed animals on the floor around us, noticing the mess I'd made of them. "I worry 'bout her in the city. And I don't want the others thinkin' we're an unhappy family," First sighed. "Sometimes I think she's asleep right here. I guess that's my way of missin' her."

"Maybe this bed was made for somebody else," I said.

"What you up to, Little?"

"Maybe there is some other girl that should have been in our House all along. I know a way that we can show them," I told her. "We can show them all that we're the best house in Sub Rosa. Let me tell you my plan."

As I spoke at length, First's mount fell open and stayed open. But I needed to spill it all out. My body felt effervescent with each disclosure: Isabella's newspaper clipping at the Night Watchman's garage, my second meeting with Jellyfish, the cab rides home from the Widower's house, Portia's cherished memory journal, the dreaded morning glory vine … the stolen money. That's when my tongue got tied, when I admitted to stealing money from the Wifey Wing. The stash I had collected for Isabella's dowry was tucked in my wardrobe drawer. I considered lying, telling First that I had already deposited it in the Dark. I couldn't cough up a lie after all the truths I'd told. But when my lengthy speech was through, it wasn't the money that First was concerned about.

"You never told me you seen Jellyfish again!"

"I ended that blackout, didn't I," I said. "That's all the Glories cared about, even you." First looked as if she was going to argue with me. "It's not like you asked me, First," I told her. "Think back to the blackout— did you really want to know?"

"S'pose not," she said. "But I'll hear 'bout her now, please."

"Well, it's just like I described it," I said, taking a deep breath. "She met me at the water fountain. When I first saw her I got really happy, or something, like everything would be all right with her there. But then she grabbed onto me, so tight it hurt my wrist. And the next thing I knew I was falling through space. Then, my grandma, right? That's the part I always think about. The crepe-like skin on her hands, her perfect roller-set hair, and her voice. 'Hello,' she said. I'm sure she said 'hello.'"

"Sounds like she knew you were there, Little."

"Yes, I guess so," I said quietly, as it seemed like too much to admit. "First, it really felt like I was there, in grandma's house, and that she somehow felt me there, too."

"I was on to you, Little. Same time you started goin' with that orphan girl, I couldn't help but notice your purse was emptied out. Now that you've pieced it all together for me, I can't say I blame you. I would trade every dollar in this house for a hello," First said, suddenly standing. She showed me her photo again, proudly. Pointed to her mother's lovely, bold face. "I'd clean the Wifey Wing out to hear this woman say a single word to me."

XXVII

Della O'Kande left her shoes at Dearest's door. They sat like black patent leather guard dogs, keeping watch so no one snuck up behind us. One tipped over as Dearest passed by, and it squashed a cluster of goldenrod. I expected Dearest to squeal over her trampled plant, but the flowers sprung upright again, like they'd never been bent. Dearest froze with First's shoe in her hand, realizing that she held one of Goddesszilla's eight-inch platform heels. She nervously placed it down again as if laying down a live bomb.

"Them orange flowers are very pretty," First commented. "Pretty and hardy. Just the way beauty should be." First sat on the floor, cross-legged. I'd only seen her sit like that when she was still in her bathrobe and had a book in her lap. She propped her elbow on the lip of a large terra cotta urn, trying to look casual. I appreciated her effort. However, the jasmine plant inside the urn moved over for her. So did Portia, Dearest, and Isabella. They leaned way back in their seats, posed between formal and intimidated—a First had come to join our club.

First held the photo of her mother: her passport in. She didn't offer up any memories. Instead, she let the photo be passed around the room. Each of us made comments about what we saw. Isabella had the photo first. She was a bit shy and only smiled down at it and whispered, "How lovely."

"Those eyes!" Portia said. "It's like she's reading my mind with her eyes. She's more beautiful than any of us." First nodded at each of us as we spoke, as if we were her students answering questions correctly.

"I hid this photograph for so long that I stopped thinkin' anything 'bout it, 'cept that it was a secret, you know. That is was somethin' I really wasn't s'posed to have," was all she said about it. But as the photo was passed back to her, I saw her eyes gloss over. She looked away for a moment, and Portia, Isabella, and Dearest shot quick glances at each other. Was First going to cry? No one had cried at the Cherished Memory Club yet. Then First drew in such a deep breath that her face pointed toward the ceiling. When she finally exhaled, her body relaxed so much that her back was curled forward, slouching. She reached her arms behind her and rubbed her own shoulders, shifting somewhat uncomfortably. I wondered how memory would affect her towering form.

Colour dabbled Isabella's once bone-white skin now; her cheeks were brushed in bronze. At the meeting she unbuttoned her stiff black lace blouse; sun freckles spotted her chest and neck, even though she'd been kept inside the Mansion and out of the sun for days. If she had loosened her tortuously tight bun, her hair would surely have been curly. She was becoming the Brianna she told us about: tan-skinned and moppy-maned and vibrant. But there were circles under her eyes. She was tired. We all were. That Saturday morning we met at five a.m. Sub Rosa slept while we remembered. "I couldn't miss a meeting," said Isabella. "Diamond locked me in my room, and I just about gave up. But then I remembered how I used to sneak out of the orphanage. I left a bundle under my bedroll to look like I was still in bed. I even stuffed my slippers and let them peep out the end of the quilt, like my feet were sticking out. Then I snuck out the window."

"How'd you get down from your window?" asked Dearest.

"Little arranged a rope," First exclaimed. "She has her ways, you know. She's got big plans for Isabella, don't you, Little?"

I moved closer to Isabella. "What is this look you're giving me?" she asked as I sat down beside her.

"First and I talked a lot about it, and we want to bring you over to the House of Arsen. You deserve better than being an orphan. And, really, the only thing keeping you there is your dowry."

"A stingy bit of money," said First. The topic of dowries was still a sore spot for her.

Dearest cupped her hands over her ears before we managed to say too much. "I don't wanna know. I don't wanna know."

Portia gave her a warning nudge. "This is important, Dearest." Dearest pressed her hands to her ears harder and started humming frantically. Portia wrestled with her, half-playful, half-forceful. I readied myself to break it up. "What if it was you, Dearest?" Portia shouted. "What if all your pretty pink clothes were gone and all you had to wear was stiff black lace, hmm? What if you had to give up your plants and go work in the Dowager's crappy garden? Wouldn't you want someone to rescue you?" Dearest stopped struggling and Portia let go of her arms. "I say, right on, Little. You show that Dowager what family is all about."

"Thanks, Portia," I said, a little taken aback by her call to arms.

"I'd do it for my sisters," said Portia.

"Likka and Myra?" asked Dearest.

"Well, yes, them. But I meant my real sisters. Did you know I had sisters? As soon as I can remember their names, I'm going to ask Klime to find them and bring them to the Rosa." Portia pressed her thumb to her forehead as though she might jimmy her sisters' names out of her brain. The rest of us watched her, silent and anxious. No Glory had ever thought to recruit someone from the city before, not someone they knew.

"That's not what the Club is for," Dearest said. "It's called the Cherished Memory Club for a reason. I'm here to have happy, cherished memories, not to change Sub Rosa. Not cause a mutiny. "

"Mutiny," said First. "That's quite the grownup word you're using. You really have been playin' with the big girls." Dearest blinked at her. "Say, now that we're talkin' grownup, let me ask you where you got them seeds for your garden, Dearest? There's no greenhouse on Sub Rosa. The Smoke Shoppe only carries fresh roses. Your seeds come from the city. You do such a good job pretendin' they all sprung up by accident. Or like some one-time live one gave them to you, claimin' they were magic beans. However, you get them from Mr Anderson, who owns Anderson's Nursery. I know this for certain because he also visits the Wifey Wing. Seems strange that your regular would also have a fondness for me, us being such opposites. But don't worry none, you're his favourite. He talks all about you and that green thumb of yours. You must grow every kind of plant you can buy in that city nursery. How do you know these city plants won't cause some kinda reaction on Sub Rosa? There is always a reaction when you introduce a new species to a place. Some kinda mu-tin-y?"

Isabella sneezed. I plucked a tiny white flower from the jasmine plant, rolled it between my forefinger and thumb and brought my fingertips to my nostrils, smiling. Dearest was scared; she shuffled around the room as if trying to hide the landscape of plants behind her back. "She's not going to tell on you, Dearest," I assured her.

"No, I'm not gonna tell," First confirmed. "I'm just sayin' look around you. Look at the five of us meetin' before sunup on a Saturday. Change is happenin', as sure as the city seed you planted in Sub Rosa soil is growin'."

"Besides, if an orphan pays her dowry off, she's then entitled to leave the Mansion and go back to her rightful House," I said. Isabella began sinking into Dearest's sofa like a stone.

"Oh, you're buying Isabella? It's that easy?" asked Dearest, her voiced still a panicked whine.

Portia shook her head. "I hate to break it to you, but you can't just buy an orphan. She'll have to go back to the Dark for her dowry."

"I'll never be able to," Isabella said from her fetal position. "I'm not like you, Little."

"That's why we're going with you." I patted her hunched shoulder. "There's no rules about us coming with you."

"The Dowager probably never made that rule 'cause it don't occur to her that us Glories will band together. She thinks we're out for nothin' but ourselves," said First.

"Because she's a fucking bitch," Isabella said. Everyone in the room gasped in unison. "Well, she is," Isabella added.

"We're going to get you out of there," First told her.

"Hold on," Portia blurted. "What do you mean 'we'? What is all this 'we' talk?"

"We're going as a family," said First. "Isabella, Little, and me." It was First's idea. Once she got the notion that Jellyfish might show her her mother the same way she showed me my grandmother, she made up her mind about the Dark. I let First hope for what she wanted to hope for. She seemed so determined. I watched her inch up to Isabella to pat her knee. Their first touch. Isabella kicked involuntarily, like she had been tapped with a doctor's mallet.

"I was the very first Glory to make the trip, back when I made my dowry, and I survived just fine," First told her. "And Little's got her magic touch to help feel her way around, and she's been to the Dark twice now. Both times she came back with more smarts and strength than when she went in. All her city memories started in the Dark. She reckons that's where the memories are kept. So we're happy to go with you. We'll make it an adventure."

"Thank you," Isabella managed. "No one has ever done anything …" She trailed off—maybe to reflect on Jenny or the nun who had spent years searching for her.

"I'm going, too, then," said Portia, clearing her throat. She wiped her nose with her sleeve. "I never do anything. Seriously, if I bead one more necklace or glitter-glue one more gift box, I am going to puke. I want to be famous. And Little, what if you're right about the second trip to the Dark bringing the memories back? You've already got more than me, and better ones. After these meetings you all leave here laughing and kissing, and I end up with my dead mother stuck in my head for hours, days even." Dearest groaned at the mention of death. "You should go too, Dearest, maybe you'd grow up a little."

"Have you all gone bonkers? We could get hurt out there." Dearest yanked at her pigtails fretfully.

"But we'll be together," said Portia. "Right? Can I come?"

"Ling is gonna kill me," said First. "I can handle the Dowager being cross, but I don't want to upset anyone else's House."

"Treasure Anne tried to run away with some gross, ugly, bearded guy, and Ling loves her more than ever now," argued Portia. First tapped her big bare foot. "I'll take the blame, Candy. I'll say I just followed you, or something. I'm going—that is that."

"Strength in numbers, I s'pose," said First.

"You ought to come, Dearest." Portia nudged Dearest with her elbow. "You don't want to be left behind, do you? That's the whole point of the Club. So we don't have to be alone anymore. We stick together."

"Maybe we can get my news clipping," Isabella wondered. Portia and Dearest cooed in response.

"I want to find something about me. Hey, what if I find out my sister's names in the Dark?" squealed Portia.

Dearest kicked a rose quartz pebble out of her garden bed. I'm sure she was weighing the danger against the feeling of being left out. "Do you get to choose your memory when you go to back to the Dark?" she asked.

"No," I said. I was beginning to wish I could take back my words.

The Dark guaranteed nothing. "No, the memory sort of came at me; I didn't get to decide. I didn't even know it was coming."

"Sometimes the best gifts are the ones we don't choose," said First, borrowing a line from the speech I made to her in our bedroom. Again, she held up her mother's portrait, as if it were a cue card, with our answer clearly written across it in capital letters.

XXVIII

We made the announcement on a Wednesday at 12:30 p.m. I knew the day of the week because the Mayflower was serving Oysters Rockefeller, their new Wednesday lunch special. I knew the time because someone had strapped a watch to Shirley's wrist. "It's so handy," she said, waving it in front of the First and me. "It tells me exactly when to get the side dishes started before you girls get here."

"But we're never in a hurry, Shirley," I told her. "We'll always wait for macaroni salad." She walked away annoyed, scribbling our orders with her favourite orange feather-topped pen.

Each time a Glory came in through the front door, First's arm shot up so they'd notice her. "You're not getting lunch to go, are ya? We got some news." The mere mention of First having news incited great interest. First never had news—she didn't care for it. Ling and Treasure Anne grabbed the booth closest to us so that they might be the first to hear whatever it was First had to say. The triplets were sent into a state of high-pitched chatter in their booth. Portia widened her eyes in our direction, mouthing the word *now*. But First wanted to wait until all the Glories were there.

Two orphans, neither of them Isabella, arrived to pick up a large order. "Shepherd's pie for the Dowager," they said in unison. They stared at the kitchen door placidly, waiting for their food.

First pushed a fifty-dollar bill at me. "Little, go into the kitchen and tell Al to delay their order, at least ten minutes."

The orphans didn't blink as I passed them and snuck into the kitchen. It was an oily sauna in there. Al wore a funny white handkerchief tied around his head and aimed his wooden spoon at me as I entered. I thrust the fifty at him before he shooed me out. "Only ten minutes," he said. "I run a timely kitchen." Shirley was checking her watch as I exited. Has the Mayflower gone crazy or what, I wondered as I left the kitchen. This watch business gave me the creeps. It was as if the whole street was anticipating something that they themselves didn't even know. Maybe they were anticipating the rise of the Cherished Memory Club? I certainly was eager to announce us.

Fortunately, the House of Man had arrived while I was busy bribing Al. "It's too early for eating," Second Man said as he dramatically threw his menu down on the table. He and Fauxnique both donned sunglasses. Dearest probably had to drag them out of bed.

I expected First to stand up once everyone was together. She checked her makeup in her compact mirror enough times. "You tell them, Little. You're better with the speeches," she said.

It wasn't hard to get everyone's attention. As soon as I mentioned the Dark there was a communal groan, then silence. Second Man took off his sunglasses. The orphans turned away from the kitchen door to listen. I mentioned Isabella and they rushed down the aisle and out the front door, their black pixie-girl shoes clapping the floorboards as they went. It was the closest thing to applause my speech about returning Isabella to her rightful home at the House of Arsen got. I didn't bother mentioning the Cherished Memory Club.

"You can't do this, First," Fauxnique shouted, as Dearest slid out of her booth to stand beside me. For once, I didn't mind Dearest taking my hand in solidarity.

"I am not forcing anyone," First said. "Dearest made up her own mind."

"Oh please," Second Man sneered. "Dearest doesn't have her own mind. No offence, Dearest girl. You have many assets, but the mind isn't one of them."

"How can you say that?" First rose to stand behind Dearest. "She has mind enough to run your whole House and all her gardens, all on her own."

"You've been to our House?" asked Fauxnique.

"Covered in flowers!" I heard Portia say to the triplets.

Fauxnique heard her too. "You've all been to our House? Is that where you cooked up your demented scheme? Dearest, I told you breathing in too much pollen would warp your mind."

"My mind isn't warped." Portia was the last to stand up and join our small huddle in the centre of the Mayflower. "I'm more than just some outrageously pretty girl who sits in a diner booth all day. I'm not afraid of the Dark." Likka and Myra gawked at her. For once they had nothing to say. No one did. We stood like display mannequins until the six sets of eyes on us began to burn.

"I suppose we ought to finish our lunch," First sighed. We wordlessly slid back into our places. We quietly chewed the remainder of our meal and set out the money to pay our bills. The only sound that followed was Al slamming the unclaimed pan of Shepherd's pie on the counter.

The silence continued all day and into the evening. Conversations halted as I entered Babycakes and Launderlove. Glories and shopkeepers alike quietly shot me sideways glances wherever I went. First brought supper home in a huff. "Everyone else got their order before me. All I was trying to do was pick up a couple soups and sandwiches."

We were happier than ever to greet the live ones that night. First practically pushed them up the stairs two at a time. Before it got too busy, I had scanned the Dowager's property for Isabella. She was still absent from her track patch. The orphans positioned themselves in their abridged line until, one-by-one, live ones picked them off like dolls off a toy-store shelf.

Dearest wasn't sticking around at the House of Man, either. "Let's go to your place for a change," I overheard her saying as she leapt into a navy Volvo. Her little pink watering can was left abandoned on the curb. Fauxnique didn't bother reaching down to retrieve it. She just nudged it with her foot; it tipped over, spilling water across their track patch.

I tried to spy on how Portia's night was going. Ling was leading live ones into the Mayflower in rapid succession. Her hair was pulled into a severe bun and, for some reason, she carried a riding switch. She directed live ones with it, waving whoever was next in line until there were too many to keep track.

It was one of Sub Rosa's whirlwind nights—dizzy with work. Arsen organized the other Daddies to announce a "last call for your Sub Rosa favourites" throughout the city. "Is it true?" the live ones asked First and me. "You may never return from your quest?" It never occurred to us that we might not return. Or course we would return. We let the live ones think there was about to be a famine, anyway.

"Oh, yes," said First, baiting them like only First could, convincing them to spend more and more. "It's very dangerous, our journey. I imagine when we return, we'll all need a holiday to recover. At least a week." They were greedy for us. They outbid each other to get ahead in the line-up. They paid extra to extend their visits. Even after their bodies were spent and soft, they still thrust money at me so that they could linger in the working room for a little longer.

Then they got the idea to pool their money together to visit in groups. "Little," a man shouted from the back of the line. "We got the $1,600 between the four of us. Can we be next, please?" As I led them up the Wifey Wing stairs, live ones in line shouted and waved their cash in the air. I saw other gangs promptly forming—men piling their bills together with maddened expressions.

At one point I simply closed my eyes and let myself float, or be floated, around the working room. There was a constant hammock of hands to hold me up, a rotation of flesh and want to kept me from crashing down. I rose until I left a sticky handprint on the ceiling. I rose until everyone and everything lay on the floor in a used-up heap.

Arsen turned up with the other Daddies to clear out the delirious, left-over live ones, and then to take us out for an early breakfast. "I'm gettin' pancakes and corned beef hash," said First. "It will be a good sleep for me." We hadn't all gathered at the Mayflower—both Daddies and Glories—since my debut party. We were a very different look-ing bunch then. No more formal attire, no more glitz. We wore our hair wild and loose, our clothes were misbuttoned and stretched and soiled. I could tell by the Glories' appearance and the large plates of food being ordered that it had been a goldmine night for all.

But despite the inflow of dollars, we were as quiet as we had been right after our announcement to return to the Dark was made. Por-tia waved hello to me from under her table before Myra crowded into the bench beside her, forcing her next to the window. Dearest lay half asleep in her Daddy's lap; Emanuel hushed a low lullaby in her ear to keep her quiet. I didn't even dare to look at Isabella. The Dowager sat with her orphans on the far side of the diner; their forks and knives chimed rhythmically against their plates.

I might have worried then that Sub Rosa could never change. That being a Glory was about being a Glory, nothing less, nothing more. And Glorydom excluded reflection. But I was so exhausted that all I could do was chew and swallow the considerable meal before me. And—as always—it was very good food.

When I woke the next day, the silence had broken. The sound of persistent knocking travelled up from the front door to our bedroom. "What is that racket?" First said, sliding the lace-trimmed sleep mask from her eyes.

The two orphans at our door declined our yawning invitation to come inside. But when First told them she wasn't about to have a conversation at the front door while wearing nothing but her robe and a head full of pin-curls, the orphans reluctantly came in. The blonde orphan (who would have had beautiful flowing hair if it hadn't been slicked back and braided), quickly scanned our living room before planting herself squarely beside the brunette. I offered them tea. They both said no.

"Isabella's dowry is set at $2,000," the brunette said. "Which day do you intend to leave?"

"Isabella was unable to provide the details," said the blonde.

First and I looked at each other. "Two days?" First asked me. Saturday, the same day as our Club meetings.

"Two days," I confirmed. At this statement, the orphans showed themselves out.

The Dowager must have wanted to take a stab at First when she set the price. It was the exact same amount as First's dowry had been. First sprang up after the orphans left and seized her ostrich feather duster. She dusted the doorframe, the railing along the stairs, and anything the orphans may have passed.

"Are you upset, First?" I asked.

"Two Gs is a lot of money," she said, then tossed her head back, laughing. "If you're alone in the Dark, that is. But that witch has no idea we already got that two grand in the bag. I put aside triple that, just in case."

But the price of Isabella's dowry wasn't the only dig Diamond had made. It seemed that while First and I were sleeping, the Dowager had been busy spreading sensational stories. The minute I stepped out my front door, Second Man rushed at me, saying, "A couple of orphans came around here this morning. They told me that Royal spoke from the dead; he says you're not going to make it." Fauxnique and Dearest stood behind him; Fauxnique fidgeted with Dearest's pigtails anxiously. I could have reassured them then, told them how certain I was of Dearest's safe return. But I had made a deal with Arsen to pretend to be soft until the bets were in. I needed to act like a gamble.

"Well, our journey to certain doom requires a bit of planning," I said, peering around Second Man at Dearest. "Planning meeting at our house in two hours," I told her.

Ling cut me off as I approached the Mayflower, shaking her head and waving me away. "The triplets are worked up into a frenzy," she said. "And you're not the person to calm them down."

"It's all right," I said in a low, deadpan voice. "It will all be over soon." I walked a few steps past her and stopped. I hated playing with Ling. She was a good First, like my own, and was surely worried. I backtracked to meet her eyes again. "I didn't rescue Treasure Anne from being kidnapped just to lose Portia. I won't split up the triplets, Ling." There was a look of immediate relief, but less than a second later she seemed worried again. I darted past her before she could ask for further reassurance.

As Ling had warned, the triplets were yelling over each other. Their rants met my ear as soon as I pushed the Mayflower door open. I was also fond of them, all three of them, and the sound of them fighting made me wince. I stood beside their table watching them point and throw their hands up and pound the tabletop. Their voices blended together into one loud, high-pitched siren. It took me awhile to realize Likka was talking to me. "Do you know that Diamond has Isabella sleeping in the garden shed thanks to you?"

"She's being fed only rice and water," Myra added. "One bowl of rice a day—did you know?"

Too quickly I was sucked into their tantrum. "You're blaming me because Diamond is a shitty First?"

"When are you going to call this whole thing off?" Myra demanded. "What happens if you all die out there?"

I grabbed one of their coloured markers from the table and wrote Portia a note. *Our House. Two hours. Planning meeting.* More angry questions ricocheted off my back as I fled the diner.

I marched past Ling, past Dearest and Second Man eating Danishes outside of Babycakes, past Launderlove where Fauxnique was being fitted for a new dress (black and formal, like a funeral dress), past the Dowager's Mansion, and down the street to where the broken street lamps stood. I didn't stop until I reached the last lamppost, the twilight place right before the Dark. This is where First and I planned to deposit the money that we put aside for Isabella's Dowry. I understood very well that I couldn't risk being witnessed planting an envelope of cash anywhere, but especially near the Dark. If I so much as crouched suspiciously near the road's shoulder or seemed to be fixing something to the lamppost, someone surely would see me and get suspicious. They had to be watching.

I stared head on at the Darkness. Like a mad woman I raised my hands into the air, waving and screaming at the black curtain before me. I felt clever; not only did I look crazy, but my hands were in plain sight. Phantom hand removed the hidden envelope tucked inside my shirt. I watched the manila paper float forward and disappear. I heard phantom hand scratching around in the dirt, scouting out a secure burial spot. Our plan was sure-fire—phantom hand would be able to uncover the dowry on our way into the Dark, and all we would have to do was simply step in and stay safe for an hour at most before returning to Sub Rosa with our pockets full of money. If we were lucky, Jellyfish would show herself and grant each of us a memory.

I planned to go there three more times for effect. Each time I'd stare into the Dark, arms flailing, talking gibberish. I imagined the Glories; "There she goes again, to the Dark," they'd say. "Poor girl."

By 2:10 p.m., First had transformed the Wifey Wing library into a strategy room. This time there were no jinxes or rules to quiet her. She was ready to discuss everything we knew about the Dark. Portia, Dearest, Isabella, and I brainstormed all possible details. First filled scrolls of paper with notes and hung them from the bookshelves. "What else?" she kept asking. I had told her about the blue light, the scrap yard, the tractor tires, the fountain, the Night Watchman's garage, and any other lane or corner I could squeeze from my mind. Portia mostly remembered monsters: zombie men and wild dogs and bugs. Isabella was blank and Dearest started to cry at the thought of it all. Her dowry had been only one hundred dollars, and it still took her a week. First shushed her and rocked her in her arms while I poorly attempted to recreate my map, phantom hand scribbling indecisively.

We bought glow-in-the-dark nail polish from the beauty shop. We had the seamstress make us dresses with reflective-tape piping and long sashes for us to tie ourselves together. Dearest stocked up on sweets. "Sweet Georgia Browns help us now," she said, hugging her brown bakery bag.

On my last trip to the twilight spot, I leaned forward into the Dark and said, "Get ready for us." The Dark sent a cool breeze to my cheek; it rang in my ear. I accidentally took a step too far forward and everything went black. I panicked and turned straight around and ran. What should have been a simple step backward took immeasurable time. There were dozens of voices, all calling my name. Not villainous or creepy voices, but familiar ones, though I couldn't identify a single one. "I'm here," I cried, but just once, for I knew it was a bad idea to engage in the tricks the Dark played. When I got back to Sub Rosa. the day was almost over. Phantom hand waved at me from beside the lamppost. At least it had remained on track. I saw the neon clock in the Pawnshop window just as it switched off for the evening. I knew what time it was—just past eight o'clock—but I couldn't figure out how much time had passed.

That night I dreamed of falling. Even my dream self understood that a falling dream was not normal for Sub Rosa sleep. I fell toward the brown-shingled roof of a house I thought I should know. Each shingle flapped as I got closer, saying my name in a hundred different voices. This time I heard it clearly. I believed the name was mine. And I answered back.

I woke up with sweat on my brow and First's hands nowhere near me.

XXIX

On Saturday morning Sub Rosa gathered outside the House of Diamond. The Dowager marched to the end of her garden path, dragging Isabella by the ruffled collar behind her. I was grateful that Diamond opted for a cruel goodbye; it didn't earn her any sympathy from the crowd. No one disputed Isabella's choice to leave, though onlookers had other reasons for protest. Likka and Myra wore T-shirts with BRING BACK OUR SISTER hand-painted on the front. A sandwich-board sign of the same design was hung over Treasure Anne's shoulders; in glitter paint, the back of the sign read WE LOVE YOU, PORTIA. Except Treasure Anne wasn't giving Portia any love. She just shuffled around awkwardly with her signage while the triplets and Ling hugged goodbye.

Second Man and Fauxnique clung to Dearest as they never had before.

Arsen did his bit by showing up with a farewell kiss for each of us. "Come back," he breathed in my ear. He had already exhausted all my promises. When he kissed Isabella's forehead, he froze, seizing her suddenly by the shoulders. "It is you," he cried loud enough to get the entire crowd's attention. "Do you remember tobogganing in Sugar Bowl Park? You lost a blue mitten." Sweet lies, I thought, rolling my eyes. He had starting taking bets the night before.

Isabella crinkled her nose. "Maybe," she said, excusing herself from his stare by lowering her head. Arsen held her a second or two longer, waiting for her to play along, to please the onlookers in some way.

"I've kept that mitten all these years," he loudly declared and took out of his jacket pocket a girl's baby blue wool mitten. The Glories whooped in dazed wonder. Normally, a ratty old mitten from the city would be tossed immediately in the trash, but as Arsen put this mitten—this proof of the past—on Isabella's hand, everyone gathered closer to see it. The thumb was frayed and Isabella's pale pink thumbnail poked through. Isabella put her mittened hand to her own cheek and a chorus of "ahs" simultaneously slipped from the Glories' lips. The Dowager kept her arms firmly folded behind her back and her lips pressed into an unwavering frown.

"Lost lamb!" First squealed and rushed to scoop Isabella off her feet. First, unlike Arsen, was sincere; she couldn't be anything but sincere. "If I'd a-known, I would never have let you fail your Dark Days," she told Isabella. The crowd was moved by her sincerity. More "ahs" punctuated the perfect morning air.

"Well, now we know we can correct the past," said Arsen. "But ... !" His voice deepened, embellished. "It will be dangerous. We're taking many risks to reunite our family."

"I'd do the same if it was you girls," I heard Ling tell the triplets.

"I'd do it for you, Second Man," said Fauxnique.

"Then do it," the Dowager shouted over our scene. "Enough of these lip-service sentiments. Go to the Dark." And with that she called her orphan children from her shaded veranda. Diamond ordered us to surrender any money, light sources or comfort items, then set the orphans on us. Like a nest of black rabbits, they dug through our purses and pockets. Dearest's sweets were confiscated; a couple pieces of Sweet Georgia Browns fell out of her purse as it was handed over to the Dowager.

"But it's not my dowry," Dearest protested. "I'm going to the Dark voluntarily. Why can't I bring them?"

"How do I know you won't sell them to help pay Isabella's dowry?"

"Sell them to who?" First asked. "To zombies?"

Behind me the triplets began to debate whether zombie men eat or not. "They can have sex, so they can probably eat too," Myra said.

"They can vomit," I said, joining their debate. "If they can vomit, they must have something in their stomachs."

"They vomit!" Dearest exclaimed. Her eyes moved from the Dark ahead of us to her discarded sweets. She shook her head at me. "I can't go," she said. She retreated back into Fauxnique and Second Man's arms. Second Man seemed slightly disappointed, slackly draping an arm around her for consolation.

I expected Portia to quit then, too, but she took the first step. "Let's do this," she said. The crowd tagged along behind us until we got to the end of the Dowager's property. They waved from the safety of her thirsty lawn. Cheers followed us to the twilight place.

As we approached the last lamppost I released phantom hand to fetch our envelope of money. *As soon as we're in, drag the envelope along the ground*, I mentally ordered phantom hand, *and tuck it in my boot*. I was concentrating so hard my head began to ache. It didn't make it any easier that Isabella and Portia were nervously chattering.

"How far in do I have to go before I start remembering things?" Portia asked. Isabella was chanting Jenny Lynn's name, for luck. "Maybe we can retrieve my newspaper article?" she asked. "You know where to find it, don't you, Little?"

Our collective hopes and fears were cumbersome. "How about I get hold of the damn dowry before we start asking a million questions," I said through clenched teeth.

"There it is," Portia shrieked. "Little, your magic touch has got it!" First and I shushed her to lower her voice. The manila envelope appeared from the Dark, dirty and crumpled. Phantom hand pushed it along the dusty road to meet us. I fidgeted as it tucked the money into my left boot. Isabella made happy little warbling noises, Portia joined her. I nearly joined them, my steps bouncing along, exhilarated. But nothing that's been to the Dark ever returned exactly the same. My only hope at that moment was that the envelope was still full of money. I wanted to check. I scratched my thigh and First slapped my hand.

"The Dowager is trained on us, Little," she hissed, looking over her shoulder. "Don't jinx it. Just wait."

First had us stand in a line; Portia beside me, then First, and Isabella on the end. We tied the reflective sashes of our custom-made dresses together. "I don't have one," Isabella complained. She was dressed in the Dowager's dullest orphan wear. First reached for Isabella's dress. The old threads snapping sounded abnormally loud as First tore off a yard of ribbon. She tied the frayed lace to her own dress and said, "There now. I fixed us together just fine."

We linked arms and stepped forward, but the Dark, unpredictable as it was, only admitted Portia. First, Isabella, and I, still locked together, heard her screaming from the other side. I was half shadowed; I felt Portia scratching and jerking at the end of my darkened arm. Her glow-in-the-dark nails streaked fireflies that faded from view.

"Pull!" I shouted, and we began a hysterical tug-of-war. The Dark held on, letting Portia go in small increments as if purposely teasing us. A blackened arm was birthed from the dark. Then Portia's screaming head. Her yelps set off our own alarmed voices. First's face turned beet red before the Dark released Portia's feet and we all collapsed backwards onto the hard pavement.

Portia was raked in black. Dark handprints streaked her entire body. Portia had a Dark slap mark across her crying face. "My hair, my eyes, my mouth, my throat—" she called the names of her body parts as she ran her hands over them.

"It's okay," First told her. "You're in one piece." Portia continued her manic checklist. Each of us took turns trying to calm her down, growing more anxious ourselves as we watched her poke and grab at herself, convinced parts of her were missing.

"I have the mark." Portia stopped listing body parts only to parrot, "The mark! The mark! The mark!"

"It will wash off," I told her.

"This black is a warning. It's the mark of death, isn't it? Isn't it? Likka and Myra would know." She narrowed her eyes at me, as if I were withholding the answer. I had had the mark, but I was never sure what it was. I felt a chill when I thought of it.

"You gonna survive the Dark mark all right," First told Portia. "Little herself had it."

"Maybe she'll die, too, then," Portia sobbed.

"No one is dyin'," First shouted. The Dark thunderclapped in response.

"There is no way I'm going back in there," Portia said, trembling as she stood up. With a hasty apology, she announced that she was going home. We watched in dismay as she limped back toward her house.

"If I don't make it, I'll have nowhere to drag myself back too," said Isabella. "I'll have to live in the Dark."

"Little knows a nice vacant garage we can live in," First laughed, terrified. She was not usually one to make jokes, and she swallowed hard to compose herself. "We go in as a family," she said.

I suggested we run at it, full speed. "On the count of three." As we ran, First's cherry hair swept across my face, and for a moment all I saw was red, then nothing.

"We all here?" First gripped my arm so tightly my reply came out in a squeak. Isabella squawked; her voice echoed, more distressed each time it repeated in the distance. We were together. We had achieved that much.

"Where do we go?" Isabella asked.

"Can't we stand right here?" asked First. "Just lettin' a little time pass before going back."

"We have to go left," I said. "We're in the Dark now. We might as well find memories for the Club." We headed in the direction of the Night Watchman's garage, and toward the last place I saw Jellyfish. "Let's count our steps," I suggested, just as I had done before. It should have been only fifty paces or so until we reached the square brick building. It was the one place in the Dark where nothing bad happened to me, and I was sure I could get us that far. We walked in unison, and for a few moments I was proud of how well we counted together. Our numbers ascended in order effortlessly. At twenty-seven, Isabella sounded the distress signal.

"Something's pulling me," she screamed. "Pulling my legs."

"Don't let go of me, child." First spun around, sweeping me off my feet. I latched on to her, to her dress, her hair, anything I could hold. "I can't feel her, Little, she gone."

"How can she be gone?"

"Her arm was wrigglin' on the ground for a second. Then gone," First said. Her large body trembled beside me. "Her ribbon is still tied to me, but no Isabella."

"What do we do?" I asked.

"You're the one who comes here. You tell me what to do," First said.

She was right. If it was anyone's job to lead us, it would have been mine. "Let's stay calm and keep looking," I said. Hand clutching hand, First and I lowered ourselves to the ground, feeling for Isabella like she was a dropped earring on a dance floor. I ran my hand over shards of glass and oily smears, but nothing human. Not even a shoe.

"I forgot how bad this place really is," First said. Her hand was practically fused to mine by her palm sweat.

"We'll find her." I called Isabella's name at the top of my voice. Her reply came from below us. I pressed my ear to the ground and heard her voice again. She was definitely underneath us. First and I scrambled along on our hands and knees, calling and calling again. Isabella called back from below.

"Oh my god, she's buried alive!" cried First, and she scurried up ahead of me wailing Isabella's name. The sash on my dress tugged suddenly, jerking me forward a few feet. I heard the sound of fabric ripping.

"First," I said. "First, please still be here."

"My leg! I lost my leg," First replied. The tips of her fingers grazed my head. She got hold of my hair and yanked me over to her. "Find it!" she screamed. "Find my leg!" I traced my hands along her torso, her hips. Her right leg was twisted awkwardly behind her, her enormous stiletto heel still secured to her foot. But her left leg was cut off by the cold concrete as if the ground had swallowed it up. I imagined the Dark earth making a mean mouthful of First's leg, digesting a bite before taking a second out of her. Suddenly, the miserable outcome of all this exploded in my mind. I would return without Isabella and First would be missing her beautiful leg. I wasn't helping Sub Rosa; I was ruining it.

"Maybe it's stuck down some hole," First said, panting and struggling.

Around First's trunk-like thigh I felt a metal rim with my finger, a perfect circle. "I think … you are stuck in a man hole," I said, laughing a little, delirious. I hooked my arms around her waist and tried to pull her out. I had never borne First's weight before. It was always the opposite, and I hadn't half the strength she did. She had no choice but to heave herself up with her own arms while I guided her soft fleshy thigh so it might not be too badly cut or bruised on the way out.

When the manhole let her go, we heard Isabella again. "Get me out of here!" her voice rose up.

"I already proved I don't fit," First said. She held my legs and lowered me, head first, into the hole. Isabella jumped up toward me. Water splashed under her feet; a dank smell slapped my senses. Her voice reverberated, pleaded. "Lower," I said to First. At least I could be sure she wouldn't drop me. She let me sink deeper until Isabella held my hand.

She was soaked with the foulest sewage when we pulled her up. First and I wrapped ourselves around her like a blanket. She sat down silently for a while, her teeth chattering, until finally she spoke. "I'd rather die than stay here any longer."

"No need to speak of death," First shushed her. "Little has your dowry, don't you, Little?"

The envelope was in my boot. I didn't want to let go of First's hand to retrieve it. I truly didn't want to reach inside the envelope, but instead stay in that split second where everything was going right First's breath looped in my ear. She was too antsy to be kept waiting. *Please, phantom hand, please*, I said to myself as I slipped my hand inside and found a stack of paper bills. "Don't jostle me," I told First and Isabella. There were exactly twenty bills. My head whooshed with denominations. "Remind me, First, what kind of money did we put in here?"

"One five-hundred-dollar bill. Eleven one-hundred dollar bills. And eight fifty-dollar bills." I loved her for her ability to memorize figures.

"Congratulations, ladies, we just bought ourselves a new House of Arsen member."

"And they say you can't choose your family," First said, hugging us close.

"Who says that First?" I asked.

"Oh, I don't know. City folks, I guess."

A strange feeling came over me then, a nagging. Out of the corner of my eye I saw something flash. The Dark was charring in the distance, a cool white radiance hypnotized me. My name was being called. I smiled at how pretty it sounded, and how I knew it was mine. It was as simple as a bird chirp or a pebble dropping into quiet water. I barely noticed Isabella and First were leading me back. "Wait," I said. "We're so close to the Night Watchman's garage. Don't you want your newspaper article? Shouldn't we try to bring more memories for our Club?" But Isabella couldn't move quickly enough. She counted her steps as she marched us along.

"It's not worth my life," she said.

"It *is* your life," I told her. This slowed First's steps.

"Isabella, slow down or you'll wind up in another hole," First advised. She was trying to buy us time. "Slow and steady makes for safe passage."

"There. Our safe passage is right there," Isabella said firmly. She must have been pointing, but since we couldn't see, she snapped her fingers in the air until we were all facing the right direction. A Sub Rosa street lamp shone up ahead. It was distant, but as we looked toward it, it kaleidoscoped into patterns and shades of glowing yellow and green, as only a Sub Rosa lamp could. First and Isabella cooed together. "We're so close to home," said Isabella.

Behind me a different kind of light toiled in the darkness. Jellyfish waved her shimmering thread of an arm at me.

"You go," I told them and released First's hand. "I have to stay."

"The Cherished Memory Club isn't everything, Little," Isabella grumbled. "We've been remembering stuff just fine on our own."

"There are things that Sub Rosa will keep forgotten forever," I said. "There are things that the Rosa will never let us have. And I want those things."

"Well, I'm not giving up my Glory for a bunch of daydreams. Who even knows if they are real or not? Who even knows if I was that girl the nuns prayed for? I have my dowry now. I'll be truly famous."

First drew me into her with both arms, letting Isabella go. "I'm not leaving you," she said. Her lips knocked against my head until they found my ear. "I said I wouldn't forget you, and I won't," she whispered.

But Isabella had other ideas. She unhooked from both of us. "The lamp is close. All I have to do is walk toward it, and I'll be a real Glory, not an orphan anymore. I can almost hear the fanfare now." We listened to her heavy steps leaving.

"See you on Sub Rosa," First called to her, desperate.

"See you on Sub Rosa," Isabella's voice replied. First shook my arm with enthusiasm. The two continued calling and echoing until Isabella's voice was too far to hear. First repeated the call to herself anyway. The words rumbled out from her mouth, tripping her as we walked. "I hate not knowing where it is I'm headin'."

"You can go back," I told her.

She responded the way I expected: "Not without you." The Dark wheezed one of its haunting breaths; a chilly wind swirled around our feet. I heard First's teeth clack.

"You should be there when Isabella hands her dowry to the Dowager. Don't you want to lead the family into its new fame?"

"I'd like to see the Dowager's face," First said. "Little, maybe I shoulda followed the light."

"You could still catch up with her, First. I wouldn't blame you if you did." I wasn't sure if I was having a selfish moment, or a selfless one. I did want First to have her moment of fame, not wander the threatening Dark with me. But there was this other yearning, the urge to meet Jellyfish alone. Somehow I understood that what Jellyfish had to show me could only be seen if I was alone.

"You think I can catch up? My legs are good and longer than hers," she laughed, nervous. "I'm not like you, Little. I don't have enough faith to turn my back to the light."

It wasn't faith that drove me. It wasn't anything I could name. Or if

I did name it, I would name it after myself. The name had called from some far-off place since I arrived on Sub Rosa. The right way wasn't toward the beautiful light, it was toward my name. First nearly encased me with her body as I told her this. If I had held on, she would have carried me like that. But realizing I wasn't going to change my mind, First's hug was swift. She was eager to get back to Sub Rosa. I savoured the ache of her embrace for the last time.

I gave her phantom hand to hold. "Phantom hand will lead you back if you get lost," I said. "It's magic. It knows the way."

"Yes, give me phantom hand. That way I know you'll be coming back for it soon," said First.

"That's right," I played along.

"I'll tell everyone to expect you."

"Don't tell them anything," I said. "Keep them guessing. The suspense will stir up wild gossip." It was the closest I could get to saying goodbye.

She hurried off after Isabella. It took only a moment for my skin to grow cold without her touch and the Dark to grow dead quiet without her voice.

XXX

A row of greeting cards sits along a windowsill; each has the words *birthday* and *girl* written in pink curly cursive.

The yellow tulip-pattern kitchen curtains smell like cigarettes and fried onions.

A hole in the screen door has been patched with silver gift-wrapping ribbon.

A red plastic mailbox leans back, askew, on a wooden stake at the end of the driveway.

Maple keys are sprouting in the un-mowed grass.

There is a tire swing hanging in the backyard, even though no children live there anymore.

Again, there are the red-painted steps of my grandmother's stucco bungalow. Why is it that I now ache for red peeling paint more than the perfumed rooms of the Wifey Wing? I would sooner sit on those steps until chips of that paint stick to the back of my jeans. Maybe I already have. Maybe I've spent hours on those steps, watching sunsets or passing cars or neighbour kids playing street hockey.

"The first thing you forget on Sub Rosa is yourself," her voice whispers, close by.

I know that as soon as I turn around, I will see Jellyfish. "I'm here," I say, preparing to face her. She is misplaced moonlight standing beside me. I gaze at her in awe. The world is reborn in the wondrous halo above her head.

"I'm here," she echoes, even though she is in plain sight. Her woman's voice is gentle. She brightens so that I can see my arms and hands in the Dark. I step toward her.

"You are ready?"

"Am I'm going to the place in my memories? To my grandmother's?"

"I only know my own memories. I can't see yours."

"Can't you tell me anything about what's going to happen?" I ask. "This is big. I thought I'd stay on Sub Rosa forever. And now, how do I trust that all these memories are real? I mean, I'm missing from every single memory I've seen. I'm not even in the picture."

"You are missing yourself?"

"Yes, I'm missing myself," I say. Jellyfish's light suddenly dies out, leaving me to stand alone in utter darkness. "Oh," I sigh after a minute of silence. "That's the whole point, isn't it? I'm missing myself."

Jellyfish exhales. Her breath lights up the Dark just like breath mists the winter air. There's another memory, I think to myself—walking to school during the first cold snap of November. I reach for her, ready. "The only memory you need for this journey is your name," she says.

"I have my name. It's Leila. I'll say it. I promise," I tell her. And I will say it. I will say it even if I don't yet understand what meaning it has attached to it or if this name was passed to me from other women or from a motherland, from a tradition or a legend. I don't know, but I will say it. It's meaning I can learn in time, I hope. And I hope it will only take my name to connect me back to all the city scenes I've imagined. Now, now all there is to do is say it.

There are stars in Jellyfish's belly. And space enough for bigger worlds than Sub Rosa. I wonder where I'll say I've been all this time and who will listen. I wonder if I'll find Second, or the Night Watchman, or even the Widower—someone who knows me as Little. Or maybe they won't exist in this new world. Maybe I'll never find another place where I'm known as Little.

Jellyfish doesn't need to use force to bring my hand to her belly. Her skin is cold and melts at my touch. I feel air. I get the urge to stick my head inside her—and so I do. It is too late after that. There isn't a second left to reconsider. When my feet lift off the ground I already know my high heels are gone. When I reach instinctively for something solid, I know my ring is also gone. I fall and I fall and wait for what will come.

AMBER DAWN is a writer, film-maker and performance artist. *Sub Rosa* is her first novel, and won the Lambda Literary Award for lesbian debut fiction. She is also author of the memoir *How Poetry Saved My Life* (winner of the Vancouver Book Award), editor of *Fist of the Spider Woman: Tales of Fear and Queer Desire,* and co-editor of *With a Rough Tongue: Femmes Write Porn.* She has an MFA in Creative Writing (UBC), and her award-winning docuporn *Girl on Girl* has been screened in eight countries. Until 2012, she was director of programming for the Vancouver Queer Film Festival. Amber Dawn was the 2012 winner of the Writers' Trust of Canada Dayne Ogilvie Prize for LGBT writers. *amberdawnwrites.com*